The Seven or Eight Deaths
of Stella Fortuna

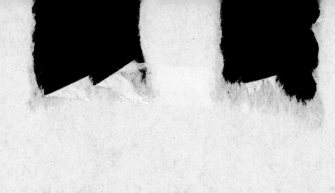

The Seven or Eight Deaths
of Stella Fortuna

Juliet Grames

HODDER

First published in Great Britain in 2019 by Hodder & Stoughton
An Hachette UK company

This paperback edition published in 2020

1

A CIP catalogue record for this title is available from the British Library

Paperback ISBN 978 1 473 68629 8
eBook ISBN 978 1 473 68630 4

Typeset in Sabon MT by Hewer Text UK Ltd, Edinburgh
Printed and bound in Great Britain by Clays Ltd, Elcograf S.p.A.

Hodder & Stoughton policy is to use papers that are natural, renewable
and recyclable products and made from wood grown in sustainable
forests. The logging and manufacturing processes are expected to
conform to the environmental regulations of the country of origin.

Hodder & Stoughton Ltd
Carmelite House
50 Victoria Embankment
London EC4Y 0DZ

www.hodder.co.uk

To my immigrant grandparents,
Antonette Rotundo and Serafino Pasquale Cusano,
and especially the nonbiological one,
Concetta Rotundo Sanelli

CONTENTS

Preface

This is the story of Mariastella Fortuna the Second, called Stella, formerly of Ievoli, a mountain village in Calabria, Italy, and lately of Connecticut, in the United States of America. Her life stretched over more than a century, and during that life she endured much bad luck and hardship. This is the story of how she never died.

Over the course of her hundred years, the second Stella Fortuna (I will tell you about the first in a little bit) would survive eight near-death experiences—or seven, depending on how you count them. She would be bludgeoned and concussed, she would asphyxiate, she would hemorrhage, and she would be lobotomized. She would be partially submerged in boiling oil, be split from belly to bowel on two unrelated occasions, and on a different day have her life saved only by a typo. Once she would almost accidentally commit suicide.

Was it fantastically bad luck that the second Stella encountered such danger or fantastically good luck she survived it? I can't decide. In either case, it is rather a lot of adventure to pack into a single life story, but the Calabrese are a tough people. It is what we are known for, being stubborn beyond any reason and without any care for self or well-being. For so many centuries of our history we had so little we were able to fight for that this instinct is irrepressible: when we have set our mind on something, the force of our will is greater than the threat of disorder, disgrace, or death. What Stella Fortuna fought for so stubbornly was her life, seven (or eight) different times. I wish I could say no one ever faulted her for that.

*　　*　　*

Most of what I know about Stella's extraordinary life story I learned from her little sister, Concettina, who is also still alive. She is in her late nineties now and goes by the name Tina Caramanico, "Tina" because "Concettina" was too old-fashioned for America, and "Caramanico" because here in the United States, she was told, a woman takes her husband's surname instead of keeping her father's.

Auntie Tina lives alone in the marshy lowlands of Dorchester, Connecticut, in a house her husband built for her in 1954. Her husband is dead, of course, so the only person she has to cook for is you when you come to her house. You probably don't come to visit as often as you should, and when you do come to visit, it is offensive to Auntie Tina how little you'll eat. All this seems like an Italian grandmother joke, but I assure you Tina Caramanico is quite serious. There are two ways to handle this overfeeding situation. You can yell at her to stop putting food on your plate, then feel guilty about yelling at an old woman. Or you can avoid the conflict, eat quietly, and suffer only physically afterward. The first time I brought my husband to meet her, Auntie Tina told me admiringly, "He eats so nicely." This is a thing Italian grandmothers say about men who don't yell at them during dinner.

It is hard to remember that Auntie Tina is in her upper nineties; she seems as pink and sweaty and vigorous as she was at sixty-five. Her brown eyes are milky but bright; her knuckles bulge with strength and the tendons of her hands stand out angry against the carpals, yearning for something to grip—a wooden spoon, a meat tenderizer, a great-nephew's cheek. She shines with the perspiration of frantic activity at all times; she wears a mustache of sweat beads. She has shrunken with age— she is five two now, although she was once five seven, a tall woman in her day—but her arms are thick and muscular. She famously came over to "help clean" my cousin Lyndsay's house when Lyndsay was pregnant and beat the braided kitchen rug so energetically that the rug uncoiled itself all over the back porch. At least, in the end, it was truly clean.

Family memory is a tricky thing; we repeat some stories to ourselves until we are bored of them, while others inexplicably fall away. Or maybe not inexplicably; maybe some stories, if remembered, would fit too uncomfortably into the present family narrative. One generation resists them, and then the generation that follows never knew them, and then they are gone, overwritten by the gentler sound bites.

I think this is why I was already grown up before I first heard the story of Stella Fortuna's seven (or eight) almost-deaths. I was sitting at Auntie Tina's table eating zucchini bread one afternoon when she first counted them out for me.

"Everyone knows about the Accident," I remember her saying, "but do you know about the eggplant?"

"What eggplant?" I said, suspicious.

"The time Stella was almost killed by an eggplant."

"By an eggplant?" I glanced out the window at the four-foot-long Sicilian zucchini hanging from the trellis in Auntie Tina's backyard. I hadn't heard of anyone's life being imperiled by a vegetable before, but it didn't seem out of the realm of possibility.

"Where you think she got those scars on her arms?"

And then there were six other times she almost died, too—six or maybe five. Auntie Tina ticked them off on her knobby beige fingers: the pigs; the schoolhouse; the boat, which was controversial; the rapist; the stupid doctor; the choking.

As Tina rattled through the litany of traumas, I was overcome by a warm nausea. How many times Stella had come so close—what surreal violence her body had endured. How statistically improbable that she should have survived. I listened to Tina's list while the saliva dried from my mouth; the zucchini bread, which was quite dense to begin with, became difficult to swallow. I had that same helpless, dreadful feeling you have when you are sitting next to a coughing person on a bus and you know, you just know, you've caught whatever they've got. I had been infected by Tina's story, the story of the life and deaths of Stella Fortuna.

"Auntie Tina," I said when the list was concluded, "will you tell me again? So I can write it down?" I was already rummaging in her pencil-and-coupon drawer for an old phone bill envelope to take notes on.

She hesitated, looking at my poised pen. Later, when I knew the whole story, I would wonder what went through her head during that long moment. But the hesitation ended and she said, decisively, "I tell you again, and you write it down."

"Yes, please," I said. She was watching me out of her watery pink-rimmed eyes. I couldn't tell if her expression was excited or doleful. "Tell me everything you remember."

"Some parts of the story, they no nice," she warned me, in all fairness.

But who ever understands or believes a warning like that?

Among my many sources, Tina Caramanico is the most important. I think finally, after all these years, she wanted to set the record straight. She knew better than anyone else, alive or dead, all of the details, because she had been there at Stella's side the whole time. She has the most at stake—the most compelling reason to tell me the whole truth, but also the most compelling reason to hide it.

She is still there at Stella's side now, although the sisters have not spoken to each other in thirty years.

Across the street from Tina's little white ranch house, not forty yards away, Stella sits in an armchair by the picture window in her own little white ranch house. The arrangement is ideal for the estranged sisters to spy on each other, watching each other's driveways to tally up which relative is coming to visit whom.

Stella will sit in this window for most of the day, crocheting then taking apart the beginnings of blankets she'll never finish. She is trapped in the prison of her mind, and so is the rest of her family, although no one but Stella knows exactly what the inside of that prison looks like.

Around 11 a.m., Stella will disappear from the picture window to go lie down for a while. At this time, Tina will fetch whatever food she has prepared for Stella's lunch—a vegetable *minestra* or a plate of pork cutlets—hustle across the street, and let herself in through the back door. Tina will deposit the food on the stove and leave as quickly as she possibly can, what with being almost one hundred years old. Stella will only eat her sister's cooking if they can all pretend she doesn't know who made it. Later, Tina's nephew Tommy will wash the pot or plate and walk it back across the street.

Stella Fortuna's eighth almost-death, the one referred to as the Accident, occurred in December 1988, and resulted in a cerebral hemorrhage and a lifesaving lobotomy. This particular procedure was experimental at that time, and the surgeon said it was unlikely Stella would live; if she did, she would spend the rest of her life in a wheelchair with a feeding tube. The surgeon, as we know, was proven wrong; Stella, the survivor, survived yet again. But with thirty years of retrospective wisdom we can see that the Accident ruined lives—is still ruining them.

The hardest break—the most enigmatic—was between Stella and Tina. For sixty-seven years they'd been best friends, constant companions, but when Stella woke from her coma she refused to speak to her sister ever again, for reasons she hasn't been able to explain. Or maybe it's that no one has been willing to listen when she's tried.

From the time they were children, Stella's and Tina's lives were stitched together, the warp and weft of the same fabric. For twenty-four years the sisters slept in the same bed, until marriage split them apart. After that, they lived in neighboring houses that overlooked the same swampy backyard, sharing meals and gossip every day for another forty years. What in Stella's tampered-with mind made her turn on her sister? Tina, the sweet old woman who has cooked for Stella, cleaned up her messes, cried her tears for her for the ten long decades of their lives?

What could it be?

Auntie Tina's lonely story—the selfless spurned sister, invisibly taking care of her lost best friend—has always drawn me to her. A human tragedy, I thought. As I have gotten older, though, I have realized there's another tragedy, one in plain sight: Stella's. The people who remember Stella Fortuna will remember the person she was for this last third of her life, demented and resented. I have seen how this thirty-year chore of looking after Stella has eroded her own family's affections; when they tell stories about her, they remember the worst ones, although I don't think they realize they are doing it. And I don't blame them—it has not been an easy thirty years. Stella is not even dead—may never die at the rate she is going—but all the good she did in this world has already been forgotten and buried.

This is the reason I had to set my life aside to write this book. I hope the fruits of my obsession will be the disinterment of Stella Fortuna, an explication of her too-strange life and a restoration of her besmirched good name. I have tried to reconstruct here the pieces of her legacy that are missing from what is remembered by the living. What follows is my best effort, an effort that has relied heavily upon anecdotal recollections as well as my own research. To the family, friends, enemies, well-wishers, victims, neighbors, and other *conoscenti* of Mariastella Fortuna who have been so generous to me with their time and contributions, my most sincere gratitude. Any error in fact or judgment is entirely on the part of the author.

Brooklyn, New York, 2019

Part I

CHILDHOOD

I ligna cumu su fhanu e vrasce,
e l'agianti cumu su fhanu e cose.
A fire is as good as the wood being burned;
work is as good as the people who do it.
—CALABRESE PROVERB

Quandu u gattu un c'è i surici abbalanu.
When the cat's not around the mice dance.
—CALABRESE PROVERB

DEATH I
Burns (Cognitive Development)

The village of Ievoli, wedged into the cliff face on the highest plateau of a moderately sized mountain in central Calabria, was never very large. When Stella Fortuna was a little girl, in the days when Ievoli was at its most robust, there were only six hundred inhabitants crowded into the abutting stone cottages. But when I tell you Stella Fortuna was a special girl, I hope you aren't thinking small-town special. Other people would underestimate Stella Fortuna during her long life, and not one of them didn't end up regretting it.

First, there was her name, which no lesser woman could have stood up to. She'd been named after her grandmother, which was proper, but still; "Stella" and "Fortuna"—"star luck" or maybe even "lucky star"—what a terrifying thing to call a little girl. There's no better way to bring down the Evil Eye than to brag about your good fortune; a name like Stella Fortuna was just asking for trouble. And whether or not you believe in the Evil Eye, you have to admit Stella had plenty of trouble.

"I've gotten out of plenty of trouble, too," Stella would often remind her mother, Assunta. Assunta was a great worrywart, if not a great disciplinarian.

Yes, Stella Fortuna stuck out, and not only for her name. There were also her looks. At sixteen, when she left Ievoli to go to America, Stella Fortuna was the most beautiful girl in the village. She had grand breasts that trembled when she laughed and jounced hypnotically when she tramped down the steep mountain road that cut through the village center. Stella had inherited these breasts from her mother; her younger sister,

9

Cettina, had been less successful in the heredity department and acquired only her mother's derriere, which, it should be said, was nothing to sneeze at. Stella had clear, tanned cheeks as smooth as olives, and her pursed lips looked as pink and yielding as the fleshy insides of a ripe fig—essentially Stella was a fruit salad of Ievolitan male desires. She had her scars, it's true, the crescent cut into her brow and the stitch marks up her arms, but scars become alluring when you know where they came from, and in a village the size of Ievoli everyone knows everything. Stella was effortlessly provocative and categorically unaccommodating. When she stepped into the street for the evening stroll, the *chiazza* fell silent, breathtaken, but Stella Fortuna didn't notice or care. The soft curves of her figure distracted ambitious men and boys from the ruthlessness of her dark eyes, and she cut down and made fools out of the unwise.

Stella's desirability mattered little to Stella herself. She'd already decided she would never marry and didn't care to use her looks to attract suitors. She scandalized good, obedient Cettina with her rough treatment of the hopefuls. Later the sisters would spend thirty years locked in a blood feud, it's true, but no one in the world saw that coming, and when they were girls they were the best of friends. Prospective suitors approached them together, because they were always together.

"You have to be nicer, Stella!" Cettina would tell her sister fearfully. She was the younger of the Fortuna girls, but she worried about Stella almost as much as Assunta did. What with Stella's bad luck, it was no wonder. "They call you a bitch!"

"Whose problem is that?" Stella would reply. "Not mine."

Stella wasn't exactly vain about her appearance—she had never even seen her reflection in a mirror—but it did give her great satisfaction to know she was the prettiest. Stella liked power, and her charisma was one of the greatest powers available to her, one of the few powers a young woman in a southern

Italian village could possibly wield in these years between the wars.

Third, she had natural smarts. Stella liked to be the best, and she was the best at most things. She was the best needlewoman in the village; her silkworms produced the most silk and she could shuck the most chestnuts during a harvest day's piecework at Don Mancuso's orchards. She was quick with numbers and could make combinations in her mind; her memory was keen and she never lost an argument because she could always quote back what her opponent said better than they could themselves. She was gentle with animals and even the damn hens laid more eggs when she was the one to feed them in the morning. She was not the best cook, so she did not cook at all—it was important to know your limitations and not waste time attempting to do poorly what you could have someone else do for you. Stella was quick-witted and self-sufficient, not to be trifled with or taken advantage of. She had inherited her mother's discipline and her father's pervasive distrust, which made her hardworking but wily. Stella Fortuna got things done. You hoped she was working with you, not against you.

Fourth—and this is what her Calabrese village respected most about her and the thing that got her in the most trouble when she left—Stella Fortuna was tough. Life had tried to take her down, and Stella Fortuna had resisted. Each bad thing that happened to her only made her more stubborn, more retaliatory, less compromising. Stella allowed for no weakness in herself and she had no tolerance for weakness in others. Except, of course, in her mother, who required special dispensations.

By the time she was sixteen, when she left Ievoli, Stella Fortuna had already almost died three times—hence all those great scars. I will tell you about the Ievolitan deaths now. They have been referred to affectionately by her family as "the eggplant attack," "that time with the pigs," and "the haunted door." They're the weirdest of Stella's death stories, in my opinion, but of course they would be; everything was a little weirder in a remote mountain village a hundred years ago. Modernity has stripped some of the magic out of the ways we live and die.

Ievoli was a secret that had kept itself for two hundred years. Like most other Calabrian villages, Ievoli was poor and deliberately inaccessible, with no roads to connect it to any other village, only donkey paths cut into the mountains' discreetly bushy mimosa and mistletoe. The Ievolitani didn't have much, but they were safe from the barbarians, the invaders, the outside world—from everyone but one another. Well, and the brigands who lived in the forests, stole the occasional goat, and accosted travelers. Another reason not to leave the village.

The men of Ievoli were *contadini,* day laborers who followed the sun to whatever field was in harvest, whichever rich landowner was paying. They had no land of their own. The men earned just about enough to keep their families alive, as long as their wives provided all the food from their terraced mountain gardens and as long as their children went to work in the fields as soon as they were smart enough.

Calabria is a land of improbable mountaintop towns like Ievoli, their streets so steep that to walk up them is nearly to crawl on one's hands and knees. The Calabresi built these inaccessible villages defensively. For two thousand years, Calabria was besieged—by Romans, who stripped away all her timber; Byzantines, who made the whole region Orthodox; North African Saracens, who made it Muslim; castle-building Normans, who made it Catholic; Bourbons, Angevins, Habsburgs; and, finally, Italians. Each wave of conquerors slaved, pillaged, feasted, and despoiled, thrashing their way through the lush olive and citrus groves with their swords out, splashing blood and DNA over the fertile hillsides. Our people fled the pirates and the rapists and the feudalists, taking refuge in the mountains. Now nesting in these absurdly steep villages is a way of life, although the threats of malaria and Saracens have abated somewhat these days, depending on whom you ask.

There is evidence of the conquerors' passing in the faces of the Calabresi, a many-colored people, in their languages and their cuisine. The landscape is studded with Norman castles as well as the ruins of Greek temples built three centuries before the birth of Christ. The Calabresi carry on, unmoved, among these remnants of past conquerors, for they have never been masters of their own homeland.

Stella Fortuna is like most women in that you can't understand her life story if you don't understand her mother's. Stella loved her mother more than anything in the world, tough Stella with her cold stony heart. But everyone loved Assunta. She was a saint, as every person who remembers her will tell you—and there are people who remember her still. In Italian mountain villages, hearts are strong, and those who survive life's surprises live a very long time.

Assunta was born in Ievoli on the feast of the Assumption of the Most Blessed Virgin, Santissima Maria, Madre di Dio, August 15, 1899—hence her name, Assunta, from the word *Assunzione*. She was a devoutly religious woman, the kind who prayed extra to make up for the fact that her husband did not. There were lots of such women in Ievoli; I suspect there still are. Assunta was raised by her mother, Maria, to have pure, all-sustaining faith in Jesus Christ and in God's heaven, where she would someday ascend after death if she did exactly what the priest told her to. Assunta was no casually obedient churchgoer; she *believed*. At mass, especially when she was in her early teens, in those hormonally violent years of incipient womanhood, she was often overcome with emotion when she contemplated the suffering heart of the Most Blessed Virgin and would begin to sob in her pew. Assunta had voluminous, spectacular emotions that only grew more impressive as she got older. Her weeping displays were one of two reasons her daughter Stella would vow never, ever to cry, and kept her vow for forty-eight years.

Now the reason Assunta married Antonio Fortuna when she was only fourteen years old—on the young side even back then—was because her father died suddenly, leaving his women in a tight spot. No matter how hard a *contadino* works the *padrone*'s land his whole life, he owns only his labor; when he dies he most likely has nothing to leave behind for his wife. Assunta had very little dowry, and the longer she lived with her widowed mother, the less they would both have. It would be better if Assunta were the responsibility of another household.

But it also seemed that she was ready for marriage. She had a matronly aspect about her, not least because of the aforementioned bosoms Stella would inherit from her. Assunta had a nurturing presence and an assuredness of carriage. She had a memorable face, with large dark eyes shaped like upside-down crescent moons that cupped her round cheeks. She was a striking womanly girl. When neighbor ladies came to visit they started thinking about which of the young men in the village she might marry, or maybe a young man from Galli or Polverini or Marcantoni, where so-and-so had an eligible cousin.

In the end Assunta married a young man from Tracci, an hour's walk south. Antonio Fortuna was seventeen years old, a stone layer who came to Ievoli to build the new schoolhouse. Assunta saw him often, lunching with the men under the single fat, ancient tree in the church *chiazza*. Antonio followed Assunta with his lascivious eye when she came to the well to get water. She liked the look of him, broad-shouldered and strong, a meaty young man with a crazed cap of shiny black curls, and she liked that he expressed interest in her. She never gave him her handkerchief, however. Assunta was shy of boys and had been successfully trained to channel that groin-tightening teenage energy into concentrating on Mother Mary's virginity while reciting the rosary. She was the kind of girl who liked love songs but never thought of herself when she sang them.

Assunta didn't say anything about the handsome young stone layer to her mother, because what was there to say? But it all came out in the way things do: one of the Ievoli stone layers mentioned to his wife that Antonio Fortuna, son of Giuseppe Fortuna from Tracci, had been giving the eye to Assunta, poor dead Francescu Mascaro's youngest daughter. Then the wife went over to pay a visit to Assunta's mother, and mentioned the boy from Tracci—and then, well. When you talk about something enough, pretty soon it comes about. Even though Assunta and Antonio had never spoken to each other, everyone else had spoken to each of them about the other so much it seemed like they had already decided everything without saying anything at all.

That was the whole of the courtship. It doesn't sound like much, but it was very exciting for Assunta, who spent that winter sewing her nervous energy into her rather rushed trousseau, warming up to her mental picture of herself standing in her own kitchen surrounded by babies, enduring the premature and stomach-curdling mourning of her soon-to-be-lost virginity. There wasn't a long formal engagement because the young men had started to be called up for obligatory military service. It didn't suit anyone for the couple to wait until whenever Antonio might be allowed to come home, so Assunta and Antonio were married in February 1914, three months after first speaking to each other.

On the day they were married, a rare snow came down from the Sila mountains. As Assunta climbed up the hill to the church for the ceremony, her sister Rosina used one of the table runners Assunta had embroidered for her trousseau to protect the bride's black dress. Hailstones collected like salt in the baskets of *mustazzoli* cookies the flower girl, Assunta's nine-year-old sister-in-law Mariangela, handed out to the mass-goers.

The couple's wedding night was spent in their new home, a basement apartment of a stone house terraced into the mountainside on the third alley off via Fontana. The basement apartment faced the olive valley, and wooden boards had been jammed into the hillside to form a steep stair leading down from the street. Antonio had arranged to rent the basement from the owner, a widow named Marianina Fazio, for terms that included Assunta's help with the cleaning and the garden. The apartment was difficult to fumigate because there was no chimney, only the wide windows, which, when thrown open, looked out directly onto the widow's hens and two spotted goats.

The newlyweds' first night in the basement apartment, the wet air was thick with the smell of chicken feathers. The exposed stone walls were damp to the touch, and Assunta lay awake for a long time, picking at the mortar with her fingernail and thinking about the strangeness of being so close to a snoring man, the strangeness of the night shadows in the unfamiliar corners, the strangeness of what hurt.

In the middle of the night, there was a screaming outside their window, a human but inhuman shriek that woke Antonio and Assunta from their awkward first shared sleep. Antonio pulled on his trousers and scrambled to light the lamp.

The awful scream sounded again before they had reached the door. It took Assunta precious heartbeats to understand what she saw through the gauze of falling snow: standing over the still-heaving carcass of one of the widow's white goats, two gray, long-faced wolves. They must have come down from the Sila forest because of the snow—they were driven to these parts only when they were starving. Their mouths were red and their eyes small and black in their pointed faces. A gelatinous white fog filled the courtyard between them like a cloudy aspic and snowflakes caught in the wolves' ruffs as the four of them stood looking at one another.

Antonio, man of the house, was frozen in fear or perhaps disorientation. Assunta, who was, rightly or wrongly, not afraid of wolves, grabbed the iron fire poker from the floor, ducked under Antonio's arm, and ran outside barefoot. "Go away!" she cried, lunging at the closest beast, who crouched and growled but gave ground before she did. "Away!" It was just as well she didn't stand by, because for the rest of their fifty-five-year marriage her husband would almost never be around to drive the wolves away.

Luckily for the newlyweds, the screams of the dying goat had woken the neighbors, and men rushed to the Fortunas' aid with their own shovels and axes. By the time they had driven the wolves off, plenty of witnesses could tell the story: Assunta in her matrimonial nightgown and Antonio bare-chested in the snow, fighting off the wedding-night wolves. There might be other beasts about, so while Gino Fragale from two houses down helped Antonio gut and skin the goat carcass for the dismayed widow Marianina, Assunta brought the chickens inside and shut them in her kitchen. Then she tried to scrub away as much of the goat's blood as she could with only snow and her broom; she didn't want the scent luring the wolves back. Assunta and Antonio spent the rest of their wedding night listening to the flustered chickens scratching at the stone floor.

Eight months after the Fortunas married, Antonio left to join the army regiment in Catanzaro. An army enrollment officer had come through Ievoli in the summer to make sure all the eligible men had been registered for the draft. The young nation of Italy was building an army to reassume its rightful place as a world power—you remember, that rightful place it had relinquished sixteen hundred years earlier, back when those Visigoths sacked the great imperial city of Rome. Not that Assunta had any notion of Roman history or the cataclysm that was already tearing Europe apart.

When he left for the army, Antonio didn't promise to send his wife letters. He could read and write but didn't like to; Assunta could not read or write at all. She assumed he would come back to her if he lived, but only *il Signore*, God the Father, knew how long he'd be gone.

Assunta, who was six months pregnant, walked with Antonio down the mountain to the railroad station, which was in Feroleto, the largest town in their cluster of villages. Maria led the donkey with Antonio's pack tied to its back. It was not a very romantic good-bye; when the train came, Antonio kissed his wife's cheeks, hoisted his pack, and disappeared into one of the carriages. Assunta had learned during her young marriage that Antonio was not a romantic man, although he was certainly a sexual one.

The women stood on the platform until the train rumbled down the mountain toward far-off Catanzaro. Assunta cried silently, open-eyed, her tears sliding off her cheeks and landing on the protrusion of her belly. She was crying because a part of her was relieved at Antonio's going away, at not having to cater to his insatiable alimentary and sexual appetites, which had become very trying when she was tired from the pregnancy. She felt guilty for feeling this way. As, the priest told her at confession, she should.

The baby came on the afternoon of January 11, 1915. Assunta woke up with some cramping and then her water broke as she was cleaning out the fireplace. She mopped up the mess nervously, wondering if she should waddle down the mountain to tell her mother, or if then she wouldn't be able to climb back up via Fontana to her own house to give birth. Her anxiety over this decision paralyzed her, but luckily Maria and Rosina dropped in for a visit of their own accord. That's what life in a village is like; if you haven't seen someone all day, you go and check on them.

The older women heated water and hung mint over the bed to ward off the Evil Eye. They gripped Assunta by the elbows and made her walk in circles. They helped her use her chamber pot and fed her a chamomile infusion to relax her muscles and her mind. In the late afternoon, when the contractions were starting to come closer, Ros went up to the church to fetch the nun, Suora Letizia. The *suora* was very holy and knew women's medicine, even though she had never had any children herself. She had attended many births over her sixty-five years and had seen all kinds of things, babies born feetfirst and babies tangled in their cords and babies that turned out to be twins. Her lilting northern accent soothed laboring mothers. Everyone felt better with her there.

Assunta was nervous and did not want to die, which was a possibility. Maria and Ros were not nervous, though, because they had total faith in God and His will. Assunta knew she should have had this faith, too, and as she worried about dying she also worried about worrying about dying. But the baby was born absolutely without incident, with only as much pain and misery as every mother experiences in a healthy birth. It was a pink, fat little girl with a patch of black hair that covered the whole top of her head. Her eyes were light brown, like her father's.

Antonio had left instructions for how his child was to be named: Giuseppe if it was a boy, after Antonio's father, and Mariastella if it was a girl, after Antonio's mother. The child was not an hour old before her mother had shortened Mariastella to Stella. "My little star," Assunta said, because it was too easy to say, because the baby was too beautiful.

Maria and Ros blessed the baby and performed the *cruce* incantation to banish the Evil Eye. They were, as mentioned, women of total faith who trusted wholly in the saving grace of Jesus, but from a practical standpoint it never hurt to back up His good efforts with a little mountain witchcraft.

In May 1915, when Assunta's meticulously cultivated bean garden was in full purple and yellow flower, the news arrived that

Italy had gone to war against Austria. Infant Stella was four months old and splendidly fat; she had the kind of heavy-cheeked dangling baby face that sat smiling directly on her own chest. This was, needless to say, very popular with all the neighbor ladies, who came over to affectionately press those cheeks with their lips and fingers. Stella's mother had no way of guessing how short these golden days of baby fat would be or of the privation that was coming.

"How long does a war take?" Assunta asked her brother, Nicola, when he brought her the news.

Nicola didn't have an answer for this. He had avoided the draft by virtue of his age—he was thirty-five, separated from Assunta by the four babies their mother had lost at birth—but Ievoli had sent seventeen *ragazzi*, a generation, and no family in the village was unaffected.

In June, the same day little Stella sat up all by herself without any help from her exuberant mother, Assunta received a letter from Antonio, which Nicola read out for her. Antonio's division was being sent north, to the Austrian border. The letter was at least a month old.

During the war, there were two years of famine. The winter of 1916–17 was the harshest on record, with documented snowfall of eight meters in the Isonzo River valley, where the boys were fighting. Spring simply never broke, and winter extended into 1918, when some of the contested peaks in the Alps thawed for the first time and revealed brigades of corpses that had been buried in snowdrifts for eighteen months.

At home in Ievoli, the abortive growing season yielded only half the usual wheat; after the war tariff was collected, Assunta cried. She wished she could believe this wheat being taken away from her would somehow make its way to Antonio on the Austrian front, but as the taxman's donkey pulled his cart down the road toward Pianopoli, she couldn't suppress the notion that he was just another mountain brigand, extorting with a wax-sealed order from the king instead of a rifle.

Assunta's *orto* struggled in the unseasonably cold summer; potatoes were small and tomatoes refused to ripen and wrinkled on the vine. As summer withered into fall, there was almost nothing to eat. There were stories of housewives scraping the powdery stucco off their walls to replace the flour they didn't have. But Assunta's walls weren't stuccoed, and they weren't her walls, anyway.

In her seventeen years Assunta had never known this kind of hunger. She had no money, no father or husband to provide for her, and no way to earn money herself; she could not control the weather or make the garden fruit. She felt as helpless as a child, but now she had a child. Every day seemed like it must be the worst it could get, but then sometimes it got even worse.

Little Stella had grown into a bashful, gentle-tempered toddler who rarely cried. She took without complaint the strange and increasingly desperate things Assunta fed her: mashed fava beans one day, then a *minestra* cooked from their leftover pods the next. Onions fried in olive oil but no bread to eat them on. Broths made from pine bark or bitter mountain herbs. Unripe oranges she stole from the gullies off the side of the road to Tracci and which she stewed until the rinds were soft enough to swallow. Assunta boiled the last of her supply of chestnuts from the fall harvest, drinking off the thinly flavored water and feeding the nuts to little Stella only when they had turned to mush. On many days Assunta did without, relishing the growling in her stomach as proof that there was no sacrifice she had not made on the *bambina*'s behalf.

Assunta did her best. She got by; her baby grew. When Stella got too big for her infant dress, there was no cloth to make her a bigger one. Instead Assunta stitched together old kitchen linens, and Stella learned to walk in a dress that had once wiped the table. Around them, the whole village grew thinner. The farm animals dwindled and disappeared, even the ones that wouldn't normally be eaten—the donkeys, for example; Calabresi love their donkeys more than they love their wives, as the old song goes. Even Maria's old *ciucciu* did not survive the war. I'm not sure what happened to her—I can't imagine Maria or sentimental Ros killing and cooking her, but I've also never gone hungry.

The dark years passed, and Ievoli prayed. One by one, the new widows and grieving mothers replaced their red *pacchiana* skirts with black mourning ones.

The war against Austria ended on November 3, 1918. A messenger on horseback rode to all the parishes along the road from Nicastro with the news. At sundown the bells rang in the *campanile* of each church so the countryside echoed with the thanks of the living and the prayers for the dead. Ievoli had lost eleven young men—a terrible price for a tiny hamlet to absorb. One family, Angelo and Franceschina who lived off the road to Pianopoli, lost all three of their sons as well as two nephews, one on his side, one on hers.

Assunta and Ros took little Stella to Feroleto to meet the train that was carrying home the soldiers. Assunta wasn't sure what time it would arrive and was afraid of being late, so the women headed out at dawn. There was no donkey to help with Antonio's bag this time. Stella walked half the journey on her own stubby legs and let Assunta carry her for the remainder.

Assunta was quietly panicked about seeing her husband. She wasn't sure if she remembered what he looked like. She sang to Stella, bouncing the little girl on one hip to quell her own nerves. The station was crowded with women and old men, almost everyone clothed entirely in black. While they waited for the train, Assunta walked with Stella up and down the cobblestoned *chiazza,* which curved around the mountain like a barbican keeping a strategic eye on the valley below. Assunta and Stella peered in the artisans' shops. The *bambina* greeted the shopkeepers politely, *buon jurno,* like she'd been taught, and the artisans laughed and said how smart the little girl was, *benedic',* God bless.

The train arrived shortly after the bells of Santa Maria had rung ten o'clock. It had been traveling all through the night and the night before that, a grueling slow journey from Trieste to Rome and then to Napoli, stopping in each village to unload veterans and caskets. Finally the train had made it to Calabria, the farthest part of the peninsula from where the war had been, to deposit the last of the survivors. The returning soldiers from Feroleto, Pianopoli, and all the smaller surrounding towns filed off the train. Assunta searched their faces, wondering with a fresh lurch of terror which was Antonio. They all looked like they might have been him, and yet none of them looked exactly right.

Assunta stood dumbly, but clever Rosina called out Antonio's nickname, "Tonnon!," and a man was striding toward them. This Antonio looked like the older, leaner brother of the Antonio Assunta had married. His face was taut and his silhouette reduced. He was no longer the strapping, meaty young man who had gone to war. But he exhibited no visible scars except, if you looked closely, the perpetually flaking patches of skin on the tops of his ears from an old frostbite.

"Antonio," Assunta said. She tried to smile, but she hiccupped with tears. She hadn't remembered him as handsome but here he was, so handsome, strong though thinned, darkness sparkling in his amber eyes. She had her man back when so many women would never see theirs again. God forgive her for enjoying his absence.

He kissed her cheeks, left then right. He had many days' stubble on his face. "Is this my daughter?" he said. He kissed Stella's cheek. "Mariastella, my daughter."

Stella turned away and buried her face in Assunta's chest. Ros laughed and grasped Antonio's arm so he would bend over to kiss her cheeks. "She's shy," Ros told him. "But she's very happy you're home. Aren't you, Stella, my little star?" Stella peeked at her aunt Ros, but wouldn't look at her father. "She's been talking about you all morning, saying, 'I'm going to see Papa soon, where's Papa,' haven't you, Stella?" It was the kind of lie that aunts tell.

The three Fortunas lived together as a family for five days.

The day Antonio came home, they all ate lunch together in Maria's house, all the Mascaro women and Nicola and his family. Antonio was quiet and drank copiously through the meal, then leaned heavily on Assunta's arm on the way back up the hillside. As soon as they were inside their basement, Antonio locked the door and pushed Assunta onto the bed. He lifted her skirts and entered her without even removing his trousers. His wife, surprised, was unready and dry, and the act itself took longer than she remembered it had in the first year of their marriage, which suddenly felt like a very long time ago, a forgotten world and lifestyle.

Assunta endured in silence, her mind tortured by the thought that little Stella was watching them, that she should stop her husband, but that she couldn't stop her husband, not when he had been gone for more than three years, when he'd waited this long, when this was her duty to him. Assunta had become so used to her chastity that it hadn't even crossed her mind that she would have to give herself to her husband in the same room where her daughter slept. Would it be like this from now on? She turned her face to the wall, trying not to see Stella's wide, inquiring eyes.

When it was over, Antonio fell so heavily asleep that Assunta struggled against the dead weight of his legs to pull off his boots. She spent the afternoon cleaning the apartment and urging Stella to play quietly. Assunta needn't have hushed the baby; nothing would have woken her husband.

His second day home, Antonio slept. Well-wishers came over, wanting to kiss his cheeks and bless him and cry and ask questions about their boys who hadn't come back or other boys they had heard about—Assunta thought this through and understood how terrible that kind of affection might be for Antonio. She closed and bolted the windows and the door to discourage visitors. Some people, of course, still knocked. She would open the top half of the door and shoo them away. "Tomorrow," she would whisper, "or the day after." Meanwhile she cooked so that when her husband woke up hungry he could be served immediately. She had no bread to offer him—no flour, still, this winter—and fretted over how to make a *minestra* from the withered potatoes and dried fruits in her stockpile. Little Stella watched her somberly. She understood the gravity of the task.

His third day in Ievoli, Antonio was ready to leave again. "We are going to Nicastro," he told his wife. He had a small but meaningful amount of money, active duty severance, and he had already decided how he wanted to spend it.

It was a Thursday, and not so cold for early December. Assunta did not see why they had to go to Nicastro right then, but now that she had a husband again it was her sacred duty as a Christian woman to do as he told her. "I will bring the baby to my mother," she said.

"No, Mariastella must come with us," Antonio said. That was part of the errand. "Get her dressed."

"She can't walk all that way," Assunta protested. It was at least two hours on foot; Assunta herself had only been to Nicastro twice in her life. She thought of the broad palm-lined boulevards and the strange men who would be sitting in the bars lining the *corso*. A terrifying place for a child.

"I'll carry her," Antonio said.

The thing he had in mind was a family portrait. It had become an obsession of his during the snowy days in the Alps. Some men had brought photographs with them, and by the end of the war Antonio remembered what other men's wives looked like, but not his own. He had decided that when you have a family you should have something to show for them.

The Nicastro portraitist fit in a sitting for the Fortuna family even though they didn't have an appointment, which wasn't something Antonio had thought of. The photographer was used to people like Antonio, bumpkins from the mountain villages who showed up at his shop with only word-of-mouth notions about what would happen there. Between all the boys going off to war and all the emigrants sailing for the Americas, people needed tokens to remember one another by, and he had been doing a lot of business even through the privation of the last few years.

Many of the people who came to be photographed were poor and even their best clothing looked shabby, so the portraitist kept a chest of clothes, four women's dresses in different colors and sizes, two full men's suits, and lots of children's outfits, since sometimes men brought their whole large family. He didn't charge extra for use of his costumes; he didn't want people complaining that the photograph he'd taken looked bad, even if the reason was the appearance of the subject rather than the quality of the photo. The portraitist showed the Fortunas how they might pose and suggested they do their best to keep the baby still; they would only have one shot.

The photograph wouldn't be ready for a week. Antonio could pay half the fee now and the other half when he came to pick up the photo. Or he could pay the full cost plus an extra fee and have the photograph delivered, but the portraitist warned this might take longer, since it depended on when he had enough delivery orders to justify a trip up to the mountain villages.

Antonio chose the former; he was not one to waste money when there was another option, however inconvenient.

The next day, the fourth day Antonio was home in Ievoli, the Fortunas set out after lunch for Tracci to visit Antonio's family. Antonio had Assunta pack the present they had bought in Nicastro—a pickling jar, the famous white ceramic from the town of Squillace, painted with flowers and leaves in ochre, yellow, and green—as well as anything she might want to spend the night. Tracci was an hour's walk from Ievoli, and Assunta wished they could return after dinner rather than stay overnight. But there had been trouble with brigands lately, and Assunta hardly wanted to expose her daughter to the evil night winds that carried diseases like cholera. Only the malicious walked about after sunset, breathing the poisonous night air so that they could in turn infect others. Assunta was not malicious.

As they walked, Assunta rehearsed things she could say to Antonio's mother, whom she barely knew. Mariastella Callipo had come to visit Assunta and Stella in Ievoli only once during the war. The visit had been awkward; Assunta found the older woman harsh and difficult to communicate with. Antonio's mother was the type who always wore black, although she wasn't widowed, and even on feast days. It was a dour form of Christian modesty Assunta knew she should have admired but which nonetheless struck her as backward. Mariastella Callipo made her daughters do the same—when Assunta thought of Antonio's family she always pictured the mother and sisters lined up in the identical black dresses and veils they had worn to Assunta's wedding, even little Mariangela, who had been Assunta's flower girl.

Three years later, on this December afternoon in 1918, Assunta, Antonio, and little Stella arrived in Tracci in the middle of the postlunch siesta, when the streets were empty, silent except for muted kitchen noises, the sloshing and pounding and scraping of wifely cleanup, that filtered through the wooden-shuttered windows.

It took a long time for Assunta's mother-in-law to answer the door. The elder Mariastella was a tall woman of about forty with a deeply trenched brow and a squinting expression. All her hair had turned white since Assunta had last seen her.

"Oh, you're back," Antonio's mother said. She proffered her cheek for a kiss, then she gestured them into the house, where without further comment she sat down at the table and picked up an in-progress sewing project. Assunta was disconcerted by this unemotional reunion. After her son, flesh of her flesh, had been away at war for years? Had she not feared for his life, prayed for him every day, the way Assunta had?

The Fortunas' house was old, the kind of house they didn't build anymore for fear of bad ventilation, with a ceiling so low Assunta could reach up and touch it. There was only one window, facing the street. On the bed that filled half the interior sat a girl jiggling a baby sibling in her lap. Assunta recognized the girl as Mariangela, Antonio's sister, who must be thirteen by now. Antonio kissed Mariangela's cheeks and touched the baby's head, then left to find his father in the garden a little ways down the mountain.

Assunta unwrapped the Squillace ceramic and showed it to the elder Mariastella, who set aside her sewing long enough to place it on a shelf. Then, feeling clumsy in the silence, Assunta said, "Did you see how big my Mariastella is?"

It was the baby's cue to show off a little, but she was shy. Stella clutched her skirt in both hands and twisted from side to side, staring at the floor.

"Stella, go salute your *nonna*," Assunta said. "Can you go give her a kiss?"

Stella crossed the room obediently and her grandmother Mariastella stooped to receive the baby's shining wet lips on her cheek. "Did you know," Assunta told Stella as the little girl rushed back toward the safety of her mother, "you are named after your Nonna Mariastella, this *nonna* right here?"

Stella put a finger in her mouth to cover her bashfulness. The elder Mariastella waved jerkily to the little girl; Assunta felt a pang of compassion for this age-toughened woman who was so awkward, even with her grandchildren.

"And this is your Aunt Mariangela, Stella," Assunta said, turning Stella by her shoulders to face her adolescent aunt and the infant she was rocking. "Can you say hello to your *zia*?"

"*Ciao,* Zia," Stella said.

Mariangela smiled. Her hair was greasy and there was a red splatter of pimples over her forehead and chin, but her large, dark eyes were beautiful, Assunta thought.

"What's this one's name?" Assunta asked, pointing to the baby, who she guessed to be three or four months old.

"Angela," Mariangela said.

"Oh, almost like you," Assunta said, wondering why the sisters had been given such similar names. "Stella, see the little baby? That's your Aunt Angela. Isn't that funny, that you have a little auntie who is even littler than you?"

Stella laughed and then hid her face in her mother's skirt. Assunta cupped her daughter's round head, feeling the heat radiating from Stella's scalp. "Don't be shy," she said. "Someday your Auntie Angela will be bigger and you can play together."

"Not Angela like me," Mariangela corrected Assunta. She lowered the sleeping baby so Stella could see her. "She's named Angela for my mother who died."

Assunta hesitated, looking at her mother-in-law for clarification, but the older woman was busy with her piece of linen and didn't make eye contact. "Your mother who died?" Assunta repeated.

"Yes, she died when I was little." Mariangela watched Assunta intently. "I was only three. But I can remember her. Only a little bit, but I can remember."

Assunta's mother-in-law stood suddenly, dropped her sewing on the bed, and walked outside, letting the bottom half of the split door bang heavily behind her. She did not like this conversation.

"I didn't know," Assunta said. "I'm so sorry." The girl said nothing further, so Assunta asked tentatively, "How did she die?"

Mariangela looked down at her baby sister in her lap. "Giving birth to a baby, who also died."

"I'm sorry," Assunta said again. "What a shame." Was Mariangela saying that the elder Mariastella was not actually her mother? Did that make her Antonio's stepmother, too? Was that why she seemed so cold with him?

Assunta thought of one of her mother's proverbs: *I guai da pignata i sapa sulu a cucchjiara cchi c'è vota,* the problems inside the pot are known only by the spoon who stirs it. In other words, only a family can know all its own secrets. Assunta should mind her own business, her mother would have scolded her. But her husband's family was also her daughter's family; didn't that make it Assunta's business?

"Where are your brothers?" Assunta asked Mariangela carefully.

"They must be playing in the *chiazza,* I think."

"What about the big ones?" There were two teenage boys, Assunta knew; she wished she could remember their names— now it seemed to her strange that Antonio never spoke of them. "Are they working?"

"They went to l'America last year," the girl said after a long hesitation. "Mamma didn't want them to get called to war like Tonnon."

Now Mariangela had called Mariastella "Mamma" despite having just said the woman wasn't her mother. Was it possible the girl was crazy, or confused?

Assunta let the matter drop.

The visit passed slowly. It was the feast of San Nicola, and they all went to evening mass at the tiny Tracci chapel, a relief for Assunta because it was a way to make the tedious hours with her in-laws pass. After, they returned to the Fortuna house and Mariastella boiled water for pasta, a holiday treat for which she used the last of a precious sack of flour. The woman was finally warming up to the idea that this was a special occasion. Nevertheless, as the sun set and Mariastella Callipo cut dough into strips to twist into *gemelli,* Assunta regretted that it was too late for her and Antonio to take the baby home to Ievoli.

That night was the worst, long hours of boredom and anxiety during which Assunta was unable to keep her eyes closed. They all lay together in the one wide bed: Mariangela against the wall, then infant Angela with Mariastella the elder, then Assunta's father-in-law, then Antonio, and finally Assunta, rigid so as not to fall off the mattress. Stella lay on her mother's chest and was restless all night. The little boys, Luigi and Egidio, made room for the guests by sleeping on the floor.

Assunta was not used to so many people sleeping in the same place. The bed had the dank, clotted smell of many years' worth of unlaundered sleep. Assunta had found a flea on her leg while they were eating dinner and now couldn't escape the thought that the dirty bed was crawling with vermin. But she had no choice but to lie there and offer up her body to them until it was light enough to take her daughter home.

In the murky twilight that comes an hour before dawn, Assunta heard the infant Angela start to fuss. There was maternal murmuring from the far side of the bed, and then fabric sliding against skin as her mother sat up to soothe her. Assunta heard the familiar wet sounds of a baby suckling, barely audible over the steady, damp snoring of Mariastella the elder, who Assunta was certain was not awake. The baby Angela wasn't thirteen-year-old Mariangela's sister; she was her daughter.

The next morning, Antonio and Assunta set off for Ievoli as soon as it was light enough to see the road. Assunta was desperate to be home. She wanted to strip off all their clothes and check the baby for lice and fleas.

As they followed the donkey path through the gully between the villages, Assunta got up the courage to say to Antonio, "I didn't know your mother died when you were little."

"What the hell are you talking about?" Antonio turned away from her, glaring into the olive valley. "My mother didn't die. My mother cooked you dinner last night."

Stella was heavy in Assunta's arms, dozing on her chest as they walked. She, like Assunta, must not have gotten any sleep in the stinky crowded bed. Assunta shifted her daughter's weight and tried again. "But yesterday Mariangela told me that . . . that the, the new baby is named after her dead mother."

Assunta waited nervously until finally her husband said, "Mariangela had a different mother than I did, but my mother is the one you know."

That made even less sense. Unless—had Antonio's father had a mistress? Was Mariangela a bastard? But Antonio was not going to say anything else on the topic. "Here, give me the baby, we'll get home faster." He took Stella in his arms and picked up the pace so that Assunta had to trot to keep up.

Assunta took off Stella's contaminated dress and put the little girl straight to bed when they got home. She would have liked to lie down herself, but Antonio had gone out to replenish their firewood and he would want a hot lunch when he came home.

Her day was haunted by the revelation of the night before— her unmarried adolescent sister-in-law suckling an unexplained infant. The ungodliness was shocking—Mariangela, who had been such a sweet little flower girl only five years earlier, had let some man do the job to her. Assunta was frightened by the very notion of sex before marriage, a mortal sin, a soul-killing betrayal of a girl's grace before God—she was frightened even though she could never commit the sin herself. And a girl of

Mariangela's age, too? Assunta had been almost fifteen when she'd married; she couldn't imagine enduring that milestone any younger. At twelve she had been a child, without even her monthly bleeding. How had little Mariangela gone so far astray?

Assunta was sick to her stomach by what she now knew, and didn't know, about her husband's family, wary of their morals and their seedy habits. She kept herself moving, shedding her Tracci dress and putting on the nicer dress she usually saved for mass. Leaving the baby sleeping, she hiked up to the cistern at the top of via Fontana, where she scrubbed all their dirty clothes on the rocky bottom of the laundry trough. The cold mountain water numbed her fingers. She didn't have any soap this year, because there hadn't been spare olive oil to make any. But now that Antonio was home things would be better. To shatter her own black thoughts, she said out loud several times, "The war is over. It's a new life. The worst is behind us."

When Assunta got home, Stella was still sleeping, poor thing. Assunta hung the laundry on the line that stretched over the widow Marianina's chickens. She went back up to the fountain to fill her cooking pot with water, then stoked the fire. She peeled a handful of roasted chestnuts and dropped them in the water, added chopped potatoes, dried pear, and a sprinkle of salt. She filled a bowl with persimmons from the tree in the yard—the fruits were just in season—then sat at her table, feeling anxious. Antonio would come home for lunch and they would learn how to live a life together. They had done it before, albeit not for long. She felt like she was getting used to a completely new husband, as if there were no history or existing affection between them.

She thought about this as the church bells of Santa Maria Addolorata sounded the quarter hours. It was not only Antonio, she decided. She was a different person than when he had left. She was a mother now, and understood the thing that mothers understand, that nothing in the world is more important than the tiny breaths of your child—not obeying your husband, not romance or desire or even one's own physical self. To be a good Christian wife she would have to remind herself to prioritize the needs of her husband the way she had done naturally before, when there had been nothing more important than he was.

When the church bells sounded one o'clock, Assunta checked on Stella. Should she wake the little girl up to eat lunch? Assunta felt her daughter's forehead, which might have been a little bit warm. She thought of the heavy air of the poorly lit hut in Tracci and her anxiety increased. She decided to let Stella sleep.

Antonio came home with more wood than Assunta would have guessed one man could carry. He stacked it in the yard, then sat and ate the food Assunta presented to him. He didn't compliment her cooking, but he didn't complain, either. Then he went out again—perhaps to catch up with the men at the bar.

Assunta cleaned up her kitchen and tried to wake her daughter. "Aren't you hungry, little star?" Stella finally opened her eyes, looking as disoriented as any unhappily wakened baby. "Let's have some soup," Assunta said. She collected Stella in her arms with a blanket wrapped around her naked torso—the *bambina*'s linen dress was still drying outside—and brought her to the table. Stella fussed and only took a few mouthfuls of potato. Assunta helped her daughter use the chamber pot, although there wasn't much, and then put Stella back in bed, wondering if she felt warmer than she had before.

It looked like rain, so Assunta pulled the laundry in to finish drying by the fire. Her anxiety had taken over her mind now, so she worked her way through the rosary, chanting as slowly as she could make herself, concentrating on the Virgin and her grace. She was about two-thirds of the way through when her sister, Rosina, came over, and they finished the recitation together.

Ros felt the baby's head. "I don't think she's well, Assunta." She performed a *cruce* under her breath and took some of the mint from the bundle on her neck to crush against Stella's forehead to drive away the Evil Eye.

"What should I do?"

Ros studied the baby. "Babies have fevers all the time, poor things, you know that. It might just go away. Get her to drink some *gagumil'* and wait two hours. If she gets warmer, though, you will want to get the doctor."

Assunta was unsure. "If I have to go to Feroleto, maybe it would be better to go now." There were two more hours of daylight; Assunta could take Stella to Feroleto, where the closest doctor was, before dark, although being outdoors in the wet December air might be the worst thing for her. Assunta could go to Feroleto alone and fetch the doctor to come back to Ievoli, but she couldn't even imagine how much a house call would cost. She didn't have any money; she would need Antonio to come home so she could ask him for some to make that plan work.

"Listen, Assù. You try the first thing first, and then if you still need to go to Feroleto, you go." Diminutive Ros reached up to put her child-size hand on her younger sister's shoulder, and Assunta could feel her calming warm palm through the fabric of her dress. "Don't worry about things ahead of time or you'll make bad decisions. If you need to go, you'll know. And then you go."

Rosina went back to collect her herbs and returned with Maria in tow. They brewed a tincture of chamomile, dried lemon peel, and anise to dispel whatever badness might have collected in little Stella's blood. Stella sat up with her grandmother and aunt for a while, docilely sipping and smiling at them as they sang some of her favorite songs, holding her little hands and pinching her feet. But Stella looked listless, her eyes sunken and sad, so Assunta clothed her in her now-dry dress and put her back in bed. Maria and Ros sat with Assunta, crocheting and listening to the rain, until Antonio came home, when they filed out.

For dinner Assunta served the leftover *minestra,* which she had expanded with some carrots and an onion. They ate in silence, Assunta tortured by her nerves. Antonio gave off the sour smell that came from hours of drinking, which under normal circumstances would have made Assunta unhappy. Tonight she was too anxious about her daughter to worry about her husband.

After she'd cleaned the plates up, Assunta checked again on Stella, whose forehead was shockingly hot to the touch. The change was so drastic that Assunta gasped out loud. "Antonio," she said when she found her voice. "We need to go to Feroleto. We need to get the doctor for Stella."

Antonio came over to the bed and tested Stella's temperature with his rough hand. Assunta swallowed at seeing his big, indelicate fingers on her daughter, but Stella didn't stir.

"It's just a fever," Antonio said. "It will pass. If she's not better tomorrow I will go to Feroleto to get the doctor after mass."

Assunta remembered what Ros had said to her—that if she needed to go, she would know. She knew—she knew. She needed to go to Feroleto. She said so.

"That's ridiculous," Antonio said. "Listen to the rain. Do you know what time it is? It's not safe to go out this late at night."

"Antonio, please." Assunta was sobbing. She realized her husband would not respect her for crying, but she couldn't stop herself. "She needs the doctor. I will go, I'm not afraid."

"The doctor might not even come at this hour!" Antonio shouted. "You think I am so rich that we can have the doctor make a nighttime house call whenever the baby gets a fever? Are you crazy?"

Assunta swallowed a mouthful of air and wiped her tears and snot from her face with her sleeve. "You don't understand," she said, fighting to keep her manner unhysterical. "You're not her mother. I *know.* I *know* she needs a doctor."

"I'm her father," he countered, "and I *know* that this can wait until the morning."

"I—"

Antonio's fist was in the air. He didn't strike Assunta, it was only a gesture, but the conversation was over. He turned away from her and went back to the fire.

"Sit down," he said to her. "Relax. You'll see, it will pass. If it doesn't, I'll get the doctor in the morning."

Assunta didn't know what to do. She crawled into bed with Stella, pulling off her dress so that she could press her daughter's hot flesh to her own, hoping she could draw the fever into herself instead. Stella lay against her, fiery with baby heat, for a little while, but then moaned and pushed herself away. Assunta cried, stuffing back her hyperventilation so as not to upset the baby or aggravate her husband's pique. Her tears sounded loud to her as they dropped onto the mattress, hissing as they were absorbed into the linen fibers of the bedsheet.

The same thoughts ran again and again through her terror: the brigands, the rain, the long dark road to Feroleto, the fact that Antonio thought of himself as a parent although he had never lived with his daughter, so his faith in his own authority was false. Should she have fought him harder? She felt that every word she had said had been poorly chosen, every decision she had allowed to be made had been wrong, but she couldn't think of what she could have said or done instead.

Assunta remembered watching the soft orange of dawn appear in the cracks of the windows, so she must not have fallen asleep until after day had broken. But fallen asleep she had—how?— deeply asleep, after two nights of sleepless exhaustion and panic. When Antonio shook her awake, the bells of the church were ringing the loud call to mass. It must be almost ten o'clock; she would have missed the rosary recitation. Before she had even opened her eyes her hand stretched, per habit, out toward Stella and met the cold flesh of her daughter's arm.

Assunta jolted upright, wide awake and livid with fear. Antonio was gripping her shoulder—his fingers bruised her.

"Assunta. The baby is dead."

This is not the Stella Fortuna who would survive seven (or eight) deaths. This was the first Stella, her older sister and namesake. This was the Stella who died.

There is a theory—a controversial one, depending on your religious sensibilities—about why the second Stella nearly died so many times in her life. Some people wonder if she was haunted by the ghost of her dead sister, the first baby whom she replaced in body and in name. It isn't a very Catholic thing to believe in ghosts, and those of purest faith would never consider the idea— or so Assunta told herself, and prayed harder.

The second Stella would live out the first's aborted narrative and play out all of the ugly scenarios her sister demurred by dying so tragically young. It is easier to remember the first Stella as the perfect little girl she was than to imagine the real person she never had a chance to be, a real person like the second Stella. A woman who grows to adulthood is often a damaged thing; the first Stella might have grown up to be beaten by her husband, or might have been caught stepping out on him; she might have turned out to be unchristian or unattractive, petulant or flatulent, embittered or stupid; she might have died early of something else, anyway. Lived-life stories end in decrepitude, resentments, and squandered opportunities; in crumbling faculties, unrecoupable disappointments, in loneliness. This—the ugliness of reality—is the gap in the story of the two Stellas, the first, who died at age three and a half, and the second, who wouldn't die at all.

The baby's funeral was held on Monday afternoon. The entire village came to the mass. Every pew was full and the foyer was packed with those who had arrived too late to find seats. Everyone loved Assunta, and their hearts were broken for her, as well as for her young husband who had only just returned from the hardships of war to this fresh grief.

Afterward Assunta remembered nothing of the service, only that when the church doors were thrown open and the mourners spilled out, filling the *chiazza* to its iron balconies, the sun was beginning its wintry descent into the Tyrrhenian Sea. A black and gray storm was moving in over the mountains and a spatter of cold rain followed the mourners on the slow procession down to the cemetery, but to the west the sky was clear, and the water in the marina was a vibrant aquamarine.

The pallbearers were Assunta's brother, Nicola, who had been little Stella's godfather, and Father Giacomo himself, whose priestly robe trailed through the muddied dust. Normally there would have been six pallbearers, but Stella's little casket was so small only two were required. The casket was tied around the middle with a rope so that if one of the pallbearers were to trip on the steep path the body wouldn't go flying out. Assunta walked behind the casket, her mother and sister gripping her arms. Maria and Rosina were both sobbing, but for once Assunta was not. She held off her grief by the force of her will because she knew that when it finally came she would die.

A hundred mourners followed the coffin all the way to the aboveground cemetery, a walled city of marble mausoleums that stood like miniature houses on uniform narrow streets. Family members were stacked in pairs, a nameplate announcing their respective dates. There had never been a Fortuna buried in Ievoli before, and so little Stella's remains would slide into the first shelf of an empty death house, where she would wait for her family to follow.

Assunta and Antonio stood in front of the stone portico and received the mourners. There were many wet faces, but they pressed hands and kissed cheeks quickly so that the next in line could step through. No one wanted to be out after dark, lest they encounter the same ill air that had killed the baby.

Two days before Christmas, in the midafternoon, there was a knock on the door. Assunta answered in her bare feet and the dress she had been wearing for four days. On the other side of the door, with his fine leather boots standing in the mud of the widow Marianina's chicken yard, was a man Assunta knew, but she couldn't remember how.

"Good afternoon, *signora*," the man said, which was no help to her in placing him. He had a leather satchel that struck her as particular.

"*Ciao*," she replied. She labored to concentrate in her stupor.

"You never came," the man said. "I was in the area—I had to come to Marcantoni for a delivery—so I thought I would stop by to save you the journey."

She couldn't pretend anymore; she didn't have the energy. "Never came where?"

"To pick up the photograph you ordered, what do you think?"

Ah yes, now she recognized him—the Nicastro portraitist. "We don't need the photo anymore," was the first thing she thought to say.

The portraitist's Adam's apple bobbed as he swallowed. She had made him angry. "There is the matter of the other half of the fee," he said. "Your husband only paid half up front. The other half was to be paid on receipt."

"*Signore*," Assunta said. She could have been exhorting the portraitist or God Himself. "We have just spent the last of our money burying our daughter. That's the little girl in the picture you made for us. *Capito?*" She wanted nothing more than to end this conversation and get back in bed.

The portraitist was both a human being with a heart and also a businessman who saw when there was nothing more to be gained. "I'm so sorry, *signora*," he said. "Listen, I will make you a present of the photo as my condolence to you. Forget the other half of the fee." He was pulling a brown paper packet out of his satchel. "No, it is nothing. You should have this photo of your daughter to remember her by." He handed her the packet, tipped his hat, and left.

Somewhere, I think, a copy of the portrait might still exist, if the second Stella didn't destroy it during the purge. It's ingrained in my memory, although I admit it's been many years since I've seen it.

In the portrait, nineteen-year-old Assunta casts the impression of a much older woman, with her full bosom and weathered face. She wears a long-sleeved black dress and the kind of hang-dog expression one sees in so many photos of her immigrant contemporaries. She'd felt nervous during the sitting, disoriented by the photographer's instructions. Antonio, meanwhile, is a vaudeville patriarch with his square-buttoned vest and handlebar mustache. The first Stella, the lost *bambina,* is strung between them like a rosary, her Christ-like pigeon toes propped over a small standing table. The photo is an eerie one: the first Stella's face in the black-and-gray is melancholy and unbabyish, with deep shadows under her dark, unfocused eyes. She has the look of one who has passed through the vale of frivolous youth and is relieved she will not have to tire herself with it again.

Assunta and Antonio never again took formal portraits of their young children. It was expensive, for one thing, but more importantly they had learned their lesson: not to commemorate something that hadn't yet committed itself to the flesh. Assunta couldn't escape the idea that, by taking the first Stella's picture, by which they would remember her, she and Antonio had doomed their daughter to die.

Assunta was a woman of great faith. But at the death of her daughter she was challenged. She had lost the love and light of her life, the precious little girl into whom she had poured herself, the most beloved baby in all of Ievoli, who had delighted Assunta with her cleverness and affection, whom she had gone hungry for, who had cuddled her in their lonely basement and been her companion for the long seasons she hadn't known if her husband would return. Assunta could not conquer her grief, and so at this darkest hour of her life she lost not only her daughter but also, for a time, her God.

She was to believe that for baptized Christians, the paradise that awaited was vastly better than life here on this squalid earth. If she were truly faithful she'd have nothing to grieve, because her departed daughter must be endlessly happy now. She was to believe that God did as God willed in taking Stella, and God made no mistakes.

But she struggled with this, she struggled. She couldn't stop herself; she missed her daughter bitterly, she could not shake the thought that Stella was gone forever, and no amount of praying gave her spirit any comfort. As a result Assunta feared her own faith, and that in turn made her fear the faith she had given her daughter, and *that* made her question whether either she or her baby would ever be allowed into paradise. Yet even with this urgent pressure to correct herself so she did not shut them both out of God's heaven, Assunta could not make herself stop crying.

News had reached Ievoli of the influenza, which had appeared in the battlefields and spread all over Europe as soldiers trickled home, one last war-born misery to shred already suffering families. Suora Letizia explained the influenza to Assunta when she came to the Fortuna house to pray with the grieving mother. Two other Ievolitani succumbed to flu-like symptoms; the diagnosis made sense, considering Antonio might have carried the disease home with him.

"You must stop blaming yourself," the *suora* said. "It would have not made any difference at all if you had gone to Feroleto to get the doctor. Not even the smallest difference," she repeated, because we Italians say things many times and with many words. "You might have caused yourself great harm, running around in the dark in the rain, with all the brigands in the woods who might have taken advantage of you or killed you or both."

In an ungodly passage of soul-searching, Assunta wondered how, if her baby had died from influenza Antonio had brought back from the war, she would ever forgive her husband for surviving to come home. Why could he not have been one of the eleven Ievoli boys to fall on Asiago Plateau? If he had died, her Stella would still be alive.

Assunta lulled herself to sleep playacting in her head a negotiation with God, where she traded Him her husband in exchange for her daughter. She would have to explain this unwifely fantasy at confession someday, and would do grim penance, but until then she imagined and reimagined the scenario, just in case her mental fervency could somehow effect this kind of reconciliation in real life.

Starting again afterward—it's impossible, if you think about it.

"Don't think about it," Maria told her daughter. Maria had lost many children of her own—four beautiful full-term babies, every one lost during labor because before Suora Letizia came to Ievoli there was only the stupid doctor who didn't know how to deliver breech babies. "Just do it. It's the only way."

Assunta did it. It was maybe the best way to get through, because it was the smallest change she could make—she didn't even need to get out of bed, or change into clean clothes. Antonio took what he could get. Her body was sore with her sadness and she pressed her face into the pillow because she couldn't look at her husband, who quickly learned it was easiest for everyone if he took her from behind, so they could each think about their own things. It was the most distasteful act Assunta could imagine, this loveless, angry offering of her body to her husband

43

while her heart ached in her chest, but it was the only way that she could make another baby.

Like this, a year passed for the Fortuna household. Neither wife nor husband was the person they had been when they got married, because they had each been through their own version of hell. But they got by. Assunta worked hard in her garden and her house and she prayed to the Most Blessed Virgin, who had also lost her child and who understood Assunta's heart's pain. Her sadness never went away, but she eased, without even noticing when the transition happened, into thinking also about the new baby growing inside her.

Antonio had come home from war a changed man. He was only twenty-one, but he was grizzled-looking, with lines in his forehead from squinting into the dry, cold Alpine air. He came home with a penchant for drink. A distaste for drunkenness is culturally typical in a place like Ievoli, where a man drinks wine in moderation all day long but would be humiliated to appear inebriated in public. War had banished this distaste; Antonio had learned to drink to blind himself.

Assunta was mortified by and afraid of this behavior. She asked him, "But what will people say?"

"I don't give a goddamn what people say!" he roared. When she criticized him, Antonio enjoyed reducing his wife to tears, which was not difficult since she had an involuntary weeping response to raised voices. "You want to know something? Never once in history has anyone asked a rich man what people will say. No one tells a rich man to be ashamed of himself. So why should I!"

That was another change the war had brought about in her husband: a fresh and boiling hatred for the gentry. The officers he'd fought under had been rich, weak young gentlemen with no respect for the peasants they were sending to slaughter. They spat on men like Antonio, and Antonio spat right back.

"I'm fed up with this country and the *stronzi* who run it. There is nothing for us here."

Antonio had his mind set on emigrating. Men from the Nicastro area were going to a place called Pennsylvania to build railroads. He arranged his passport paperwork so he could leave first thing in the spring, right after his son was born.

Assunta didn't say so, but she was glad Antonio had decided to emigrate. She'd sworn to love him before God, and she wasn't a woman to break an oath, but it would be much easier to love him if he didn't live in her house. She wished he wouldn't wait until the baby was born to leave. On top of her other bad feelings, she found his presence irritating. Antonio shattered the harmony of her home with his bodily desires, his entitled voice, his farts, his mustache that shed short black hairs on the kitchen table.

Assunta's second baby was born in widow Marianina's basement on the bitterly cold night of January 11, 1920. It was five years to the day after the first Stella Fortuna had been born.

Antonio was disappointed yet again; the baby was a girl. "Well, there you go," he said to Assunta. "At least you have a new Mariastella now."

Her heart pounding with that new-mother desperation, Assunta looked into the infant's face for similarities. But even though she was just a baby, she looked very different from the last baby. "Are you my Stella, my *piccirijl*'?" she asked, but she felt stupid as she said it. This wasn't her Stella; this was a different person. This was a different Stella.

Assunta thought of all the love she hadn't had a chance to give to the first Mariastella. This baby was her second chance. No more casual love—no more mistakes.

Antonio left for l'America three weeks after the second Mariastella was born, in early February 1920. He had signed a *padrone* contract to work on the railroad and stayed through the fall. In l'America, there was snow in the winter—snow as tall as a man some days—so the railroad work stopped until spring. He came home for this snowy time, when the second Stella was ten months old, but now that he had seen America, he couldn't stand the idea of Ievoli, and stayed only through the winter. It was long enough to plant another baby in Assunta's womb.

Concettina, poor thing, was a disappointment from the beginning.

First of all, she was an in utero trial to her mother. Unlike either of the Stellas, this baby had Assunta vomiting four times a day. Village ladies told Assù the vomiting would stop before she was halfway to term, and they were wrong about that. The second Stella, who was not even two years old but a precocious baby, learned to say tricky words like *"Mamma malata"*— Mommy's sick—and to stroke her mother's tummy to calm the wrath of the invisible sibling.

Assunta spent August bedridden in the sopping sweat of the afternoon, on her knees in the garden in the earliest hours of the morning in an attempt to weed while it was cool enough, leaning over to fertilize the potatoes periodically with another dribble of vomit. She sobbed to her mother that she hated Antonio, who had left her alone to die of his seed, that she would never survive this pregnancy. Maria rubbed Assunta's back and reiterated her thesis that this was a strong, tough boy.

Antonio came back from l'America again in October 1921 to witness the birth of his first son. He'd been home for a week when Assunta went into labor. The cramping started as she was brewing Antonio his morning coffee, the contractions lasted through the afternoon, and the pushing started around midnight. Suora Letizia, Rosina, and Maria were in attendance, of course, and so was Antonio, because there was nowhere for him to go at that hour to get out of the women's way. He sat impatiently through the last hours of labor, his rifle loaded so that he could fire the traditional two shots to let the village know an heir had been born.

"*Mannaggia!*" Antonio swore when the baby issued forth sporting a tiny pink vagina. He seized his gun and stomped outside. Rosina and Suora Letizia, who was wiping the baby clean, exchanged looks as the too-close sound of rifle shots— two of them—reverberated through the house.

"Guess he didn't care that she wasn't a boy after all," Suora Letizia said placidly.

The girl baby was completely bald. "She looks like a bug," her father said when he came back in.

"Antonio," Rosina chided.

"She's my little bug, Tonnon," said Assunta. "*Muscarella mia.*" She was very tired; the baby was big and she was torn from the delivery.

The infant was supposed to have been named Giuseppe, after Antonio's father. Since that name wasn't going to work, Assunta said hopefully, "We could name her Maria, after my mamma."

"No!" Antonio would have said no to anything at this moment, even something he didn't have a stake in. "She'll be Concettina, after my mother's mother."

Assunta was too tired to argue.

Stella was a year and nine months older than Cettina. When they were babies, this meant that Cettina always seemed to be many steps behind.

At first, this was difficult for Stella, the way it is always difficult for an older sibling to be saddled with a younger, stupider one who can't transport itself or communicate, and whom everyone is paying attention to because it is so helpless. Sibling jealousy, the oldest human interaction after that of husband and wife—just read the book of Genesis.

Jealousy is, though, the most harmful human emotion—the thing that must be safeguarded against at all costs. Assunta knew the destructive power of the Evil Eye and did her best to discourage any jealousy she spotted among her children.

"You have to watch out for Cettina," Assunta told Stella. "She's just little. She's not smart like you. She needs you to protect and help her."

"Concettina *muscarella*," Stella replied.

"That's right. Our little bug." Assunta helped Stella stroke the baby's soft dark head. "Our little bug."

"My little bug," Stella said.

Assunta laughed. "*Certo,* she is your little bug. But you have to look out for her always."

In February of 1922, Antonio left for l'America again, again leaving a baby in his wife's belly. This one did turn out to be a boy who could finally take his grandfather Giuseppe's name, but Antonio was no longer charmed by the idea of fatherhood and hadn't bothered to come home for this one. In fact, he didn't bother to send money to his wife, either, or even to write and let her know he hadn't fallen into a ditch and died. Assunta, who was twenty-three and had three infants under three years old, learned as many new lessons about resourcefulness as she had during the war.

This was how the years passed. Assunta tended her three living children and prayed for the deceased one. She stitched their clothes and scrubbed them, washed out their diapers and kept them fed with bread she baked from flour she ground from wheat she grew in the garden she tended. She preserved and pickled and salted and stored so they would never go hungry, even when there was nothing. To keep them warm through the winter she gathered firewood on the mountain and carried it home tied up in a linen cloth she balanced on her head, with Giuseppe strapped to her chest, Stella holding her left hand, Cettina her right. Assunta dug her own stones out and turned her own soil and pruned her own trees and drew her own water from the well five, ten times a day to cook and clean.

This was the trouble with emigration—it dismantled the patriarchy. Because really, what did Assunta, or any woman, need a husband for, when she did every goddamn thing herself?

Stella Fortuna the Second's earliest memory is of the day she almost died for the first time, the episode with the eggplant. Most of us have memories from when we are three or four years old—often foggy, impressionistic, colors or words instead of whole, solid moments. Stella had none of these. Her first memory was vivid, complete, and late: she was four and a half, and she was waking up in a shadowy brown room redolent with the sweet-rot smell of mint. She was in intense pain.

Later in life Stella would think that it was proof of a benevolent God that He had excused her from any recollection of the eggplant incident itself. It was somewhat regrettable that He hadn't seen fit to excuse her from its aftermath. But what kind of Heavenly Father would He be if He didn't help us learn from our own mistakes?

In the segment Stella doesn't remember, Assunta was frying slices of eggplant in her cast-iron trencher—her finest possession—over her open hearth. Little Stella, just tall enough to see over the lip of the frying pot, must have reached out and pressed her fingertips into the sizzling top skin of breadcrumbs, then drawn back her hand in shock at the heat. In this jolting movement, the pan tipped toward her, splashing boiling olive oil onto Stella's right arm, oil that rushed through her dress sleeve and wrapped her from knuckle to chest. Stella might have cried out, but it is also possible she was silent, as later in life she was quietest during the worst times. Her baby sister, Concettina, was the opposite, and seeing Stella collapse by the fireplace she began to shriek for her mother.

Assunta rushed over to find the damage already done, red florets blossoming on her daughter's arm. Assunta tried to pull off the oil-soaked sleeve, but it had fused into Stella's skin. When she tugged at Stella's dress, the material resisted only slightly in her hands before springing upward, the flesh releasing, choosing fabric over arm, and blood spilled out so suddenly that neither of them, mother or daughter, even screamed.

Stella was unconscious during Assunta's dash down the mountain to Feroleto. Deep in her physical memory Stella knew the waddle-jog, waddle-jog of her mother in a hurry, her wounded daughter clutched to her chest; imagined Assunta's asthmatic breath freckling her face with spittle. The gallop was an aerobic one, three-quarters of an hour over the uneven weather-soft ground of the donkey path through the mistletoe-laced jungle of alder and ash. Later everyone told Assunta she had been crazy to take the child down the mountain, that she should have gone to fetch the doctor instead. But she worried it would be too late if she waited for the doctor to gather his things, that he wouldn't take her seriously if he couldn't see Stella himself. And who can say she wasn't right?

Assunta ran down the mountain the day of the eggplant for another reason, too—because she had not run that December day five years earlier. Because last time, she'd hesitated through the danger. Last time, she had let someone else—her husband—talk sense into her, and so she had woken the next morning to find there was no longer any reason to worry about whether the doctor was worth the expense. If this second Stella died, at least it would not be because her mother had not run.

So—and this was a story often retold in Ievoli, because everyone likes stories about feats of heroism by distressed mothers—Assunta picked her daughter up and ran.

Stella remembered nothing of the eighteen hours she spent in the doctor's surgery, where twice during the night she was nearly lost. Skin graft science was new and risky—it took the doctor more than an hour to explain to the frantic mother why she should let him cut into her daughter, that if he did not she might never heal and faced a dangerous chance of infection from the open wounds.

Stella would remember nothing of the blankets they used to soak up her blood—so much from a small body! How could there be any left inside?—or her skin lifting away from her arm in tidy packets, as unresisting as late-July squash blossoms prized from their whorls. Stella would recall nothing of the graft, when the doctor sliced his knife into the good, pure flesh of her left arm and then, when he needed more, of her buttocks. Later, Assunta couldn't quite describe the procedure the doctor had performed, as she had not been allowed in the surgery—she had been incoherent, slapping her own face and ululating with preemptive grief.

It was just as well Assunta didn't know more about the execution of the skin graft. The whole precarious operation was performed in that candlelit back room by that squirrelly bachelor doctor in a mountain village without running water where the canon of conventional medical wisdom included no concept of antiseptic beyond a squeeze of lemon juice. Assunta could have no idea how fortunate she was that the doctor, with his small hairy hands and his odor of chicken skin, had left his village to be educated far away in Sicily, despite everything his father had told him was generally unsavory about Sicily, but where a medical program had been flourishing for almost five hundred years, and where skin grafting science had been pioneered.

During her nightlong vigil outside the surgery door, on which she pounded periodically, Assunta convinced herself that her daughter was dead and that the doctor was hiding from a mother's wrath. Delirious with her own failure—first one Stella, and now the second—she clutched her own torso, feeling the stiffened death-cold first Stella in her arms. Her hands vibrated with the memory of that morning; she felt the ringing of the church bells in the skin of her palms, which would never caress either of her Stellas again.

When the doctor finally emerged he found Assunta lying in front of the door, half her face pressed into the unswept floor, asleep with her flaming eyes open. Each hand was a slick-knuckled fist containing a skein of her own uprooted black hair, oily from clutching. From that day on Assunta wore a kerchief over her head to cover these bald patches, and also the gray hair that grew back in, even though she was only twenty-five.

Fifteen, twenty years later, when Stella rolled up her sleeves before washing dishes, she would pause to mull over the scars. She never remembered her arms without them, but they were still interesting to her. Her right forearm was swathed in wrinkled brown skin, white around the edges of the skin graft, like an independent island country on an antique map. On the left arm, the scar was less obvious: the meaty outside was pinched into a scientifically precise line, straight as if it had been made with a ruler until you looked very closely to see the bric-a-brac of handstitching. The suture marks became more visible in the summer, when her skin tanned around them.

She often wondered: What had made her—almost five years old, old enough to know better—put her hand into the pan for a piece of eggplant? Greed? Hunger? Curiosity? As an adult, she knew those were the three things that motivated her most often. She just couldn't believe she would have made a mistake like that, even as a child.

Even stranger, where had her mother been? Assunta was skittish, overloving, like many mothers who have lost children in the past. Stella had almost no memories of her childhood in which Assunta was not standing by, or over, or behind. There was no explanation for why Assunta had left her daughters unsupervised by an open fire and a vat of boiling oil—except, perhaps, bewitchment.

Minty brownness, heat. Stella's arms were beginning to wake, throbbing where they lay on the coverlet. Even as the brownness settled over her, her newly won consciousness was already compromising itself, sparkles rising in her vision as the terror of her pain set in. It was a frustratingly imbalanced pain, the right arm burning with imaginary heat, radiating a halo of raw untouchability, the left arm rippling with the acute pinching sensation of surgically sliced skin.

The smell of mint was the most familiar point of orientation: spicy near-rot, at once fetid and antiseptic. The second Stella had broached the world in a cloud of mint just like this one, mint her grandmother, her first human contact on the other side of the womb, had tied in a bundle around her neck. There was nothing better than the stench of mint to ward off the Evil Eye. The smell would always call up Stella's most ineffable memories, sunset-dim walls, the oppression of sweat-tangled blankets, blood pounding in and around her—a foggy, green-brown arc of connected traumas.

There in that double pain was Assunta, leaning over her, marking the cross on Stella's forehead with her thumb. Assunta's breathy whisper dipped into Stella's consciousness, binding her into the present, to the pain that roiled and bulged as her nerves came back to life. Assunta inhaled deeply, sucking air through fluted lips so the whistle of her breath was audible, deliberate. On each exhale, she chanted voicelessly, fast, slurred lines of an eerie poem whose meaning Stella couldn't quite grasp. It was the unfascination, the incantation to banish the Evil Eye curse that must have been fixed on her forehead.

Around Stella's sickbed sat Nonna Maria, Stella's miniature godmother Za Rosina, and her Uncle Nicola's wife, Za Violetta, who held the unhappy two-year-old Cettina on her lap. Stella, groggy with pain, listened as her mother told her side of the story. "I don't remember looking away for even a moment," Assunta insisted. "It's such a strange thing. You know I would never leave the girls alone."

Za Ros placed her warm palm on Stella's head like a benediction. "Who has fixed the Eye on you, my *piccirijl'*?" she asked.

Stella was still learning to identify rhetorical questions. "Cettina," she replied, glancing at her grimacing sister. The answer came out with no forethought, but seemed like it might be correct as soon as Stella said it.

All four women laughed quickly, saying "No, no" to shake away that bad idea.

"Listen, *piccirijl'*," Za Ros said, her voice gentle. "Saying someone cast the Eye on you means you are saying they intended you great evil, so we don't name names, all right? Instead we ask *il Signore* and the saints to protect you and turn the Eye away."

Stella studied her aunts' faces, trying to figure out what she had said wrong.

"Ah, but maybe she knows, Ros," Za Violetta countered. She was a hard, round woman with clear, mean brown eyes. "Why shouldn't she say if she knows? Why shouldn't she protect herself if she knows who to protect against?"

"Violèt!" Tiny Ros's voice rose, which was unusual. "You have to protect yourself from the whole world! *Invidia* is everywhere." She lifted her hands, and all the women thought they could see the miasma hanging over them in the dust-filtered late-afternoon light. "Jealousy can come from anyone, even someone who loves you. But for you to point a finger at someone and say that they have cursed you is as bad as for you to curse them yourself. *Capit'*?"

"You remember that, *piccirijl'*," Nonna Maria said to Stella. "You can only name someone else's sins if you know those sins yourself." This was a proverb; Stella would hear her grandmother say it often. "You make sure you are good, but you don't worry whether other people are good or not because they must make their own peace with God."

The *mal'oicch'*, as it's called in Calabrese, the Evil Eye, is the bad atmosphere generated by suppressed resentments, jealousy with the power to wound, ruin, craze, or even kill. The *mal'oicch'* is particularly dangerous for blessed or beautiful or wealthy people, who often seem to have the best and worst luck because of all the accumulated jealousy, *invidia,* around them. The truly good among us may experience no distress at the good fortune of our loved ones, but for the rest of us jealousy is shameful, secret, and poisonous. The Mediterranean is home to diverse ancient religions and ethnic cultures, but the Evil Eye is one thing Maghrebian Berbers, Andalucian Sephardim, Greek Orthodox, Turkish Muslims, Palestinian Arabs, and Catholics of the Italian Mezzogiorno comfortably agreed upon. In Ievoli, the *mal'oicch'* was simple, sinister, and sometimes eradicable with some quasi-Christian witchcraft.

Assunta wondered if it was true, what Rosina said, if it really was impossible to guess who might be behind an *invidia* without being the source of it yourself. She did not know how to protect her children against her own misjudgments, but the Evil Eye, at least, she knew how to keep away. The curse she worked, mint in hand, was a string of magical words she had learned from her mother, sacred words that could never be written down, not even here, a century later. The voiceless, sucking rhyme to which Stella opened her eyes that horrible brown morning would become so familiar that Stella would hear its rhythm in the dark when she was drifting off to sleep. Even as an adult, especially on off-tempo nights when it stormed or was too hot or she felt that itch of unrest, she would hear her mother's breathy chant.

Stella never learned the charm herself; she didn't have Assunta's gift of open spirit, and never really believed. Without faith there are no miracles, just coincidences.

Assunta performed the rites, but privately she wondered if it was not the Evil Eye that had hexed her daughter. Perhaps defensively, she had convinced herself she never would have left the girls alone with the boiling oil if she had been in her right mind. Every moment of every day she felt the phantom of her dead daughter dragging on her conscience, her limbs heavy under the weight of her guilt and grief. She knew this phantom existed in her head and heart only; Assunta did not believe in ghosts, because she had restored her perfect faith in *il Signore* and knew that He was caring for the first Stella in heaven.

Well, she had almost restored her perfect faith.

This episode with the eggplant—this was a moment when it seemed an awful lot like she had been haunted.

What if Assunta had brought on the eggplant attack through her own neglect—by loosening her grief for her lost Stella once she was distracted by her other, living children?

She took out the photograph the portraitist had brought and she hung it on her wall in the corner where the sun wouldn't fade it. She made an altar on her kitchen counter, where she kept a candle burning whenever she had money for candles.

If there was, in fact, a ghost Assunta was trying to appease, though, this altar did not do the trick. After all, the boiling oil wasn't the worst of the second Stella's cursed bad luck; it was only the beginning.

DEATH 2
Evisceration (Growing Pains)

The second Stella Fortuna's second death was probably the most dramatic—eviscerations generally are. It all came about because poor Assunta, who had been abandoned by her husband and without a *lira* to her name, had suddenly come into just a tiny bit of relative prosperity and tried to use it to make life richer for her children. Poverty is dangerous, but prosperity, too, can be deadly, especially when a person blinds themselves to its pitfalls.

Prosperity was what Antonio had hoped to find in America, and Assunta didn't begrudge him that goal, although he could have sent money home, as other emigrant men did. Just a little bit of money would have made such a difference.

How much time has to pass before it's safe to say a husband has forgotten his family? It's hard to know where to draw that line.

Za Ros was Assunta's stand-in husband. As luck would have it—or as God would will it—widowed Rosina no longer had anyone but Assunta's family to devote herself to. Ros was seventeen years older than her sister. She was a tiny woman, not much bigger than her nieces and nephew, the perfect size for them to adore. She was stern but gentle, a much more organized disciplinarian than Assunta, and gave patient instructions on how to do things like squash lice or gently collect an egg from a chicken without getting pecked. Stella loved to impress her aunt and hated to disappoint her.

In 1924, Ros's two grown boys, Franco and Lorenzo, had left to seek their fortunes in southern France. Rosina was all alone in her marital home at the top of the mountain by the church *chiazza*. After one last summer silkworm harvest, Ros decided to move in with her mother and to give her struggling sister the house and the plot of land adjacent to it.

Assunta had protested, of course. "Where will your sons live when they come back? Where will they put their wives?"

Ros shrugged. She had a feeling they would never come back to Ievoli. That was not the way the world was turning lately. She helped Assunta tie up her belongings in linen bundles they balanced on their heads to carry up steep via Fontana.

Ros's late husband had built the house for her just before the war in the more modern style, with a ten-foot ceiling to let good air circulate and to keep the interior cool in the summer. Its walls were made of mortar and river rocks that had been hauled up from Pianopoli on the backs of donkeys. The walls of the house were five inches thick, built to withstand earthquakes like the one that had leveled much of Calabria in 1905. There was a shuttered window on every wall, nails on which Assunta could hang pots, and a double bed that would do until the children were larger.

The new house was the break Assunta needed. Since her marriage she had grown food for her family in her late father's small *orto* down below the cemetery. Now she had room to grow enough wheat that her family would have bread all the time; it wouldn't matter if she could afford to buy flour. Wealth would beget itself; it's that initial purchase that is the hardest for women like Assunta, with armfuls of babies to nurse and no spare moment to earn a *lira* more than they need to keep their families alive.

Now she could have a whole chicken roost of her own. She could have a pigsty.

In 1925, when the pig peddler came around just after Easter, Assunta bought two piglets. They were the size of her hand, snuffly as puppies, with wagging rumps and bright, black eyes in their patchwork faces. But in nine months they would each be six hundred pounds of cured pork—*prosciutto* and fat-streaked *capicolo*, spicy *suppressata* sausages she would encase in the pigs' own intestines and slice up for her children for lunch. Assunta had eaten meat twice a year—a chicken at Christmas and goat at Easter—for her whole life, but her children would have meat every day.

Pigs, Assunta learned, made you work for the treasures of their haunches. They ate like, well, pigs. They grunted with pleasure when they were fed and with annoyance when they weren't. And they were disgusting. They were as smart as dogs, with intelligent human eyes, but they did their business wherever they were standing, rolled in it, and ate out of it if Assunta didn't watch out. She cleaned the pen every morning, which required extra trips up the mountain to the cistern above the church. If she missed cleaning the pen, even for only a day or two, it started to reek, a sour unholy smell, the air so thick and putrid that walking through their enclosure made Assunta think of swimming in a vat of the urine of a sick old man. The smell sank into clothes fibers and couldn't be scrubbed out; it gamboled across the alley and into her kitchen, ruining her own taste for her cooking. This was the year Assunta became vigorous about rubbing down her household surfaces with lemon—the lemon helped disguise the smell of the pigs.

By summer, the pigs were too big to feed with leftovers alone, and she had to ration out potatoes for them. In December, on her sister-in-law Violetta's advice, Assunta went to the trough and morosely scattered all the precious chestnuts she'd harvested that fall, sweet crunchy pearls before the swine. Violetta promised the chestnut meat would make the pigs' flesh white and tender with fat.

Stella and Cettina loved the pigs, as they loved all animals—the cats who milled in Ievoli's alleys, the sweet-tempered stray dogs who wandered around the town accepting scraps. Stella spent hours playing with the creatures, and the pigs nuzzled her like a sister. The girls would run between them, patting their rumps, climbing over and tumbling off their good-natured backs.

Assunta hoped the upcoming slaughter wasn't going to be too painful a lesson for her daughters.

The winter of 1925 into 1926, Ievoli was giddy in precipitation. On four separate occasions, the snow fell tall enough for Stella and Cettina to throw and kick at each other. In the mornings, before it could melt, they rolled in the shallow banks, tossing handfuls at the other children who tilted and shrieked up and down the steep, icy mountain road. Assunta was convinced they would expire of ague. Cettina's red nose would run, but Stella never got sick, never even seemed to feel cold. Since the oil had fallen on her in the previous summer, the skin of her boiled arm and torso was constantly feverish; she loved to feel the snow soaking into her clothes. This behavior did nothing for Assunta's nerves.

The day of the trouble with the pigs, in January 1926, a nighttime snowfall melted into dawn slush. Assunta had forgotten the laundry on the line the evening before and spent a good portion of the foggy morning taking down the clothes and rearranging them to dry in the house by the fire. Now the sun had come out, and she was hanging them back up again on the line that stretched from her roof to the pigs' hut. The alley between them was churned into cold mud.

Stella and Cettina were standing in the doorway watching their mother hang the clothes. Stella straddled the doorframe, blocking it with her feet so baby Giuseppe couldn't run outside. Stella had become tall over the summer, her baby fat vanishing from her taut child-thighs and her hair darkening into black curls like her father's. She stood head and shoulders over four-year-old Cettina, her arm around her little sister's shoulder, as it often was. Assunta realized they were staring down the alley. She turned to see her sister-in-law Violetta huffing up the hill for her daily visit, which was usually full of uncompassionate gossip and sanctimonious observations about child-rearing. Assunta felt no enthusiasm, but called across the laundry, "Stella, invite your Za Violèt inside while I finish this."

Violetta, who was on the heavy side, paused in their lane to catch her breath. She had a tied-linen bundle clutched in one hand.

"Stella," Assunta prompted again.

Stella pursed her lips as she watched her fat aunt gasp for air. She did not like Za Violetta, and the feeling was mutual. They had recently had a fight, which had started with Violetta telling Stella she needed to be more respectful of her elders; Stella had replied that she didn't respect Violetta because she didn't like her. This had resulted in Violetta's dealing Stella a smack across the face. Stella, who did not, as a rule, cry, had said to her aunt, "That's why I don't like you. You're not nice." And she had walked out the door and hadn't come home again until Violetta was gone.

Assunta had never seen anything like it. The girl wasn't even six. Ros, who was also visiting that day, laughed herself to tears watching.

"It's not funny, Ros," Violetta said. "Someone has to teach that girl respect, Assunta, or you're going to have a real problem on your hands."

"Ooo, she's a tough one!" Ros said, wiping her eyes.

Now as Violetta stood in the alley, head cocked, hoping Stella would give her another excuse for a confrontation, Stella met her gaze and scowled back.

Assunta tried again. "Say, please come inside, Zia."

"Please come inside, Zia," four-year-old Cettina echoed, always eager to please. Stella stepped back from the doorframe to let her aunt pass.

By the time Assunta joined her sister-in-law in the kitchen, Violetta had spread the contents of her bundle on the table. Four loaves of bread, which Violetta was cutting into quarters with Assunta's knife.

"Old loaves from last week," Violetta explained. "I thought they would be good for the pigs."

Assunta scooped up baby Giuseppe, who was not wearing any pants at this moment. She wrapped her elbow under his cold naked bum. "That's very kind of you, Violèt."

Violetta shrugged. "It's no trouble to me. I am happy to go without for you." Ah, there it was, the bitterness. The poor woman couldn't even let a gift feel like a nice thing.

"Well, thank you." Assunta brought Giuseppe over to her sister-in-law. "Give your auntie a kiss, Giuseppe." He complied, then smiled. "There's a good boy." He didn't talk much yet, but he was already the most outgoing of her children. Assunta put him down on the floor again. "Now go put on your pants."

Violetta wiped the crumbs from her hands on her skirt. "You want to take some out to the pigs now?" she asked the girls. She handed them each two crusts.

"Should we feed the pigs, Mamma?" Stella asked, her voice meaningful—*I'll only do it if you tell me, Mamma.*

Assunta tried not to laugh. What a sharp little thing she was, with her sharp little face! Like an adult, and with the wickedness of an adult. "Yes, yes, go feed them," she said. "Then come back in and we'll fix some lunch."

There was absolutely no reason to worry about her daughters as they stepped out into the wintry sunshine.

The two girls entered the pigpen without trepidation; the pigs, as anticipated, approached for fondling. Cettina offered up her ends of bread, and they snouted it, making piggy noises. They bumped their rib cages, which would soon yield delicious *pancetta,* into the girls' torsos, the roiling force of their body weight inexorable. When one had finished with Cettina's bread, it turned to Stella, black-ringed eyes level with her collarbone. For some reason, at the wet snuffling of the pig's nose against her wrist, Stella recoiled. In an inexplicable spasm, she clenched her hand and pulled back her right arm.

The second pig caught on that there was bread being withheld, and it rounded on her. The two pig heads pushed into her chest as they fought for the elusive crust. Stella felt herself pushing back, the forward pressure becoming less playful and more defensive.

"Pigs, Stella," Cettina said. Her spit-wet hands were bunched in her skirt, her eyes wide. "The pigs."

Stella realized that she had only to release her bread, and the pigs would take it and leave her alone. So she let go. Or at least, her brain made the decision to let go. But her hand stayed clenched. In that initial moment of betrayal, as Stella wondered what was wrong with her body, one pig or the other pushed her to the muddy ground, where she landed on her back, her spine reverberating with the fall. The pigs began to step on her, clamor over each other in a gnawing, snorting ruckus. Stella stared in shock at her hand. It was as though—and she would remember this exact sensation for the rest of her life—another hand was wrapped around hers, squeezing, so the bread was trapped tightly within the binding of her little fingers.

There was silence in the courtyard as Cettina, stiff with confusion, watched, as Stella fought her own hand and the pigs fought each other. It was Stella's scream that ripped through the damp post-rain air and brought Assunta and Violetta running, a piercing, full-bodied child scream as the pigs chewed and stepped one then the other over Stella's abdomen, which split and poured forth its contents, just like the pigs' own abdomens were destined to be split to make and fill sausage casings.

Thence came Assunta's second run down the mountain to the doctor's. This trip was so much more hopeless than the first—her daughter's stomach had cracked up the middle like a boiled chestnut, and the pigs had done some heavy mixing of intestines and mud.

On this tromp down the mountain—her daughter's torso swaddled tightly in once-white kitchen linens, now a frightening vibrant red—it seemed obvious that these were Assunta's last moments with her second Stella, and over the stupidity of a crust of bread from her noxious sister-in-law. She gasped for breath, tasting blood in the raw back of her throat, fought for balance on the steep, muddy donkey path. "Hail Mary, full of grace, the Lord is with thee," she rasped into the wet winter air, over and then over again—the rest of the rosary eluded her. She was certain her daughter had been cursed.

That afternoon and night, during the washing and stitching, and the next day while they waited to see if infection had set in, Stella lingered at a point of acute danger. The intestines—the doctor identified them for the sober Assunta, who had never butchered a mammal and wasn't sure of the frothy substance that had come out of her daughter—had survived the trampling somehow intact. The doctor, with his now-familiar smell of chicken skin, washed the innards to remove dirt, pushed them back in with his bare fingers, and stitched up the bloody mass of tissue with a needle and thread, just as Assunta would have darned her blouse. Stella's eyes were open, dry and staring, throughout the procedure. No one, including Stella, knew whether she was conscious or not. A number of ribs had been broken, but neither lung had been punctured, as the child was evincing no blood from her respiratory tract. The doctor credited the suppleness of the childish bone structure, which had apparently accommodated the crushing weight of the pigs instead of snapping in fatal places like the neck or spine. He explained that the real test, now, would be to see whether any poisons had already infested her cavity. If she should survive the week, it would remain to be seen whether her female nest had been ruined, whether as an adult she would be able to conceive or give birth.

Assunta, weeping her silent tears, considered this last statement as she held her daughter's hand in the doctor's lying-in room. How interesting that this thought had occurred to the doctor now, at this moment, Stella's blood still tucked into the creases in his hands. In the same breath, he had told Assunta *she may not survive the week,* and also *if she does, she may not be able to have children.* Was it an off-the-cuff medical observation? Or was it something he'd learned to address for other village mothers, because other mothers would ask? Was the doctor's narrative just a progression of statements, or was its implication true? Was a life without children a life at all, for a woman? Assunta would never know, as she had had children since she was a child herself. Assunta ran her mind over these questions with philosophical disinterest. Nothing mattered except that the doctor's miracle needle might somehow, somehow have stitched her Stella back into this world.

When the bachelor doctor had left her alone with her daughter, Assunta stood over the bed and laid her hands against the sides of Stella's abdomen, away from the stitching. Stella's belly burned like a pot on the stove. When all the cool had gone from her palms, Assunta flipped them, the same way she had done that night in 1918 when her first Stella had fought the fever, and when Assunta had tried to suck the heat out of her daughter's skin with her own hands.

Stella awoke to the hush of her grandmother's voice, but she didn't open her eyes. She felt an intense nausea and a bursting sensation in her gut. As she lay unmoving in the buttoned-up darkness, thinking about whether she ever wanted to open her eyes again, the room began to creep up on her, the nostalgic odor of unnumbered strangers' body liquids and mint, sharp and sweet.

"Mint," Stella said, her voice raspy. "The mint."

The doctor, who hadn't been sanguine about his patient's surviving the operation, found this unnerving. Maria, however, did not.

"Yes, little mouse, the mint," Maria said. Her granddaughter was asking for a spell to fight the Eye. Before the doctor could see what he must not, Maria wrested his candle from his hands and used it to drive him from his own operating room.

As Assunta worked the unfascination, she tried to stop herself from thinking about whose jealousy could have cursed her little daughter. This was the second time her Stella had been brought to death's door by bizarre bad luck. Was the Eye fixed on her? Some affectionate-looking villager who was secretly jealous of Assunta's beautiful, clever child? Or jealous of Assunta for having her?

Or was it the jealousy of a ghost, who every year was a little further forgotten by her loved ones, while her replacement shone like a star in their hearts?

The doctor didn't dare move Stella for at least a week, lest the barely reinstalled intestines shake loose. She would have to stay in Feroleto; Assunta could sleep on the floor. He tactfully did not mention the added expense when he delivered the news.

Antonio hadn't sent Assunta any money in three years. While she sat by the bed, Assunta sucked her teeth and tried not to think about the cost, remembering that it was thinking about the cost that had killed her first Stella.

They butchered one of the doctor's chickens and boiled it in a pot. The chicken would be added to Assunta's bill. They tried to feed Stella the chicken broth, but when she opened her mouth to swallow the broth spilled out the sides of her face and streaked her cheeks. It was as if there were a round ball of air in her throat, repelling anything that tried to pass through it. She could speak, but her throat was scratchy. Maria gave her mint to chew and this at least called forth some saliva.

"You were attacked by the pigs, little mouse," Nonna Maria told Stella.

But Stella remembered. "No, I wasn't. They just wanted the bread. I had bread and they just wanted to eat it."

"Silly girl," Maria said soothingly. "Next time you just give them the bread."

"There won't be a next time!" Assunta said. She knew what she thought of pigs now.

"I tried to give them the bread." Stella's words were puffs of air. "But I couldn't give it to them."

"What do you mean you couldn't give it to them?" Maria asked, petting Stella's head, which was the only piece of her that bore petting.

Stella was relieved that she could explain what she'd felt, that someone was going to take this fear from her. "There was a hand. Like this." With her right hand she seized her left and squeezed so the fingers bunched together like grapes, slowly ripening before the women's eyes as the blood swam in fruitless circles. "A hand was holding me."

"Whose hand?" Maria asked. "Concettina's?"

"No, Cettina was over there." Stella gestured to her left. How freely her arms moved, without any pain! The rest of her was a burning belly. "It was an invisible hand."

Maria and Assunta were quiet, because this sounded awfully supernatural to them. Eventually, Maria thought to take out her rosary, and the two women started a soft chant of the Hail Marys. Cettina sat on the floor and stared up at her sister, who lay quietly on the bed and stared back. They didn't have to say anything to each other, nor did they have anything to say. Stella had been the one who was trampled, but Cettina had had to watch it.

When the suffering child was finally asleep, Assunta admitted, "I don't think it's the Eye, Ma."

Maria did not respond to this. Sitting on the bed with her palm on her granddaughter's forehead, she frowned with half of her mouth.

On the sixth day, the doctor allowed Assunta to take her daughter home. It seemed she had escaped infection. After the doctor reswaddled Stella's midriff and torso, Assunta handed him a packet of *lire*—his fee, the cost of the surgery, five nights' lodging, the price of one chicken, the entire bill paid in full, no installment plan needed. The once-beloved pigs had been sold to Zu Salvatore, who ran the store in the *centro,* and in whose basement their haunches were currently suspended. Between the cost of their food for the year and this set of medical bills, the pigs had almost paid for themselves.

As the thick crust of a scar formed over the wound that split her abdomen, Stella was bed-bound for many weeks—very trying for a child of six. During this time her godmother Za Ros entertained her by teaching her various womanly handicrafts. She taught her to embroider handkerchiefs and to crochet increasingly elaborate decorative lace. Stella, naturally competitive, focused her bored energy on mastering these tricks, then basked in the adults' admiration. Everyone told her how clever she was.

On an unseasonably warm day in February, after four arduous weeks of only being allowed to leave the bed to use the chamber pot, Stella convinced her mother that she felt well enough to go outside. Assunta clutched her daughter's arm as they walked the forty steps to the church *chiazza*—that was as far as Assunta would let Stella go. They stood on the plateau and looked down over the mountain together, silently appreciating the panorama. Weak March sunlight cut through the veil of gray clouds and splashed the olive valley below them, a yellow puddle of springtime between the mountains.

Stella's ancestors had stopped here on this plateau three hundred years earlier to build the village of Ievoli because of this incredible view. From the *chiazza* where these ancestors erected their church, one could see all the way to the Tyrrhenian Sea to the right and the Ionian Sea to the left. The volcanic island of Stromboli smoldered perpetually at the edge of the lichen-green bay, and Stella and Assunta watched together as it emerged from the hazy horizon when the sun began to sink behind it.

This was Stella's world, this mountain hers to live on despite everything that tried to kill her. Her belly aching, Stella slipped her hand back into her mother's and they walked home for supper. But she would come back to watch the sun set again tomorrow.

DEATH 3
Bludgeoning (Education)

The third almost-death of Stella Fortuna coincided with the end of her formal education. It was August 16, 1929. Stella was nine and a half years old.

In general the Ievoli schoolhouse was not a very dangerous place, because the children didn't spend much time there. In Mussolini's Italy, elementary education was compulsory through third grade, but it was hard to enforce this law in villages like Ievoli, where there was limited benefit to sending one's child to school.

The school was a boxlike wood and stone edifice on the far side of the church *chiazza*. It had a vaulted twelve-foot ceiling and tall windows to let in lots of light, and got very cold in the winter, so there was no school between Advent and Easter. There was no school during the month of August for Ferragosto, the celebration of the Assumption, or in September, for the festival of the Madonna Addolorata—Our Lady of the Sorrows, Ievoli's patron saint—and when the olive trees needed to be harvested.

When school was in session, there were two teachers, Maestra Giuseppina, who taught the boys, and Maestra Fiorella, who taught the girls. Maestra Giuseppina, who had finished upper school in Nicastro, was married to a university graduate she had met before the Great War. They lived in the apartment above the school, where he wrote history books while she taught the sons of Ievoli.

Maestra Fiorella was a bit of a different story. She lived alone, for both her parents were dead. She was only twenty-three but was already a spinster in the eyes of the village women, who felt sorry for her. It was not an easy life, being a spinster without hope of a match, and Maestra Fiorella really had none—there were no unmarried boys of her generation left, between the Great War losses and the wave of emigration that had made white widows of so many a Ievolitana. Besides, Fiorella wasn't wife material. She did not know how to cook and she was a slovenly housekeeper—ladies paid calls on her during the afternoon siesta to appraise the level of grime on her walls and to sneakily wipe down her counter. Fiorella had terrible skin, probably a product of her constant illnesses (to accommodate which the girls' side of the school was often closed without explanation). Although she had a patient disposition, she was not clever. She had pursued the position of village schoolteacher because it had become evident she wasn't going to be good for much else.

Usually the girls' lessons consisted of the *maestra*'s reading aloud from her primer, omitting the words she didn't recognize. The passages were mind-numbing and often unintelligible, what with the missing words and the fact that the primer was written in Italian, which was very different from the Calabrese language the girls spoke at home. There was only one broken slate for everyone to share, so after the morning reading the children who had taken the trouble to come to school that day—because, let's be honest, it is not always convenient to come to school, especially when there is a good chance of discovering the teacher has not come, either—would take turns writing the letters of the alphabet on the slate. Since Fiorella disliked math, the girl students never learned multiplication or geometry. This was too bad for Stella, who was good with numbers; she probably would have caught on quickly.

Stella started going to school the Easter of 1927, when she was seven. Assunta had wanted Stella to wait until Cettina was big enough to go with her. The sisters sat at one desk and kneeled together on pebbles in the corner when the *maestra* caught them whispering to each other. Stella was smart and enjoyed being admired and envied by the other students. But the *maestra*'s lessons were boring, so sometimes she and Cettina would only pretend to go to school. They'd dress, kiss their mother good-bye, then spend the morning picking cherries off other people's trees, or sitting on the rocky ledge above the algae-filled cistern trying to catch the bergamot-green lizards that peeked out to sun themselves.

When they did go to school, the school day lasted from 9 a.m. until noon; sometimes they adjourned earlier. During chestnut or strawberry season, Maestra Fiorella would have the whole class stump out to the fields and collect fallen fruit, which she'd take home for her own dinner. The children were not supposed to tell their parents about this kind of recess, but of course people caught sight of the little girls all marching out of the *chiazza* together, and the parents gossiped unhappily about how Fiorella was stealing their children's labor when she was supposed to be teaching them. No one stepped in to stop her; it would have been too awkward a conversation.

On the other hand, Maestra Giuseppina, who taught the boys, was a devout fascist. Every morning when she stepped into the classroom at five of nine it was expected that the little *ragazzi* were already assembled in a row in their matching uniforms to perform the official salute to her and to the picture of Mussolini on the wall. But at least the boys learned to read.

There were so many things a girl needed to learn at home, anyway—cooking, horticulture, the tending of baby siblings, cleaning. There was endless needlework—linen to be spun, clothing to be stitched or mended. A girl needed to prepare her trousseau, all those bedsheets and kitchen linens and underwear she'd need for her marriage, and she started working on that grand project when she was nine or ten. That was the age, too, at which she would start taking part in the village's cottage silkworm industry, which would occupy her twenty-four hours a day for the month of July.

But for a little girl, the most important education of all was spiritual, so that she might grow up to be a good Christian wife and mother. Stella and Cettina had started catechism classes after Easter of 1928, when Stella was eight, a little on the old side, and Cettina was six, a little on the young side.

Catechism classes met on Saturday afternoons in the vestry by the church. In 1928 the teacher was Signora Giovannina, who owned the peach grove, and who felt the great weight of the responsibility of all of these children's immortal souls if she couldn't knock the fear of God into them.

Stella was good at catechism. She memorized the incantations and Bible verses as easily as she remembered folk songs. Cettina was not so good. She struggled to remember things from week to week. When Stella tried to whisper her sister prompts, Signora Giovannina yelled at Cettina, which made Cettina freeze up and abandon any thought that might have been in her head. This was a tricky moment; Stella hated watching her little sister suffer, but if Stella tried to help it would only get Cettina in more trouble.

Stella always thought of what her mother had told her—that she had to look out for Cettina, that Cettina was just little, not smart like Stella. It was hard to tell as they grew up if Cettina actually wasn't smart, or if it was just that she could never quite catch up with her older sister, even though she was always expected to follow by her side.

They were old enough now that their adult characters had emerged out of their baby fat. Stella already realized what kinds of things the women in the village said about her, and what kinds of things they said about her sister. They said Cettina was a good girl, an obedient girl, a hard worker, a bit of a brute because she had no common sense. Stella, meanwhile, was pretty and sharp— quick, clever, and hardheaded, *capotost'*, the most stubborn and willful little girl anyone had ever seen. She was proud to be called all those things. Stella wanted to be tough. She had survived, against all odds, two near-death experiences. She liked to think of herself as harder, stronger than anyone else around her.

They *said* Cettina was the better sister, but secretly they all were more interested in Stella. Stella was nine years old, but she had already realized that. And as much as she loved her sister, she did not mind it one little bit.

Stella made her First Communion the Easter of 1929. But Cettina was not ready to make Communion. She would need a second year of catechism, at least. This was very upsetting to Cettina, who felt left out. She loathed catechism and now would have to go without her sister, who was henceforth exempt. Making Communion, however, was not optional; Cettina's place in God's kingdom depended on it. She would have to figure it out on her own.

Cettina cried the whole day she learned about Stella's upcoming Communion. She was still crying when she and Stella got into bed.

"You'll be all right, little bug," Stella told her, fanning her legs in the cold blankets to warm them up with body heat. "You still have Marietta and Vicenzina to keep you company."

Cettina snuffled into the pillow. Stella imagined it was covered in snot.

"I wanted to wear a white dress," her little sister said when she was ready to talk. "I wanted to carry a . . . what do they call it? With the flowers?"

"A bouquet," Stella answered.

"I wanted to carry a bouquet and walk into the church with you and make Communion."

"You'll make Communion with the other girls your age, next year. If I don't go this year I'll be too old. The biggest one."

Cettina was sobbing again. "What if I never make Communion because I'm too stupid?"

"Eh!" Stella said, a reprimand. She'd learned this noise from her mother. "Enough. Everyone makes Communion, and you're smarter than lots of those other kids."

The most upsetting thing was, if Cettina had gone this year, she would have had her own white dress to wear in church. Instead, next year she would have to wear the white dress Stella had already worn. But that's just the way it is, being the second sister.

"Chi tutto vo', tutto perdi," Assunta reminded her daughters. A favorite of her many proverbs: whoever wants everything loses everything. Assunta's enemy was still the *invidia;* she did what she could to teach her daughters not to be jealous, especially of each other.

Stella had a new white dress; Cettina did not. "But look what you have." Assunta gave Cettina a lemon, the sour kind with the thick skin. Other citrus wouldn't grow this high up the mountain. "You have a lemon, and if you want, you can have a lemon tree."

Cettina loved plants, and she wanted to love a lemon tree. Stella had a white Communion dress, but Cettina had a future lemon tree, maybe.

Spring passed into summer, and the little sprout grew. In July Assunta helped Cettina transfer it to the garden. She made a special spot for it right by the house, where Cettina could see it from bed if the window was open.

After she had made her First Communion, Stella stood up with her mother to get the Eucharist at mass; meanwhile Cettina had to sit in the pew and hold Giuseppe so he wouldn't climb down into the aisle. Stella also now went to confession with Assunta each Thursday.

It was at confession the last Sunday of July that Father Giacomo mentioned the Verginelle to Assunta. Stella was just within earshot, outside the confession vestibule, where she was sitting, absolved, and saying her rosary.

"I want to invite Mariastella to join the Verginelle procession this year," the priest said to Assunta. "Would you let her?"

"Of course," Assunta said immediately. She felt proud heat in her chest and her eyes had already filled with tears. On the eve of the Assumption, thirteen little girls between the ages of nine and twelve would lead the annual pilgrimage down into the valley and through olive groves to the ancient shrine to the Virgin at Dipodi, which had been built in the year 314 by the Emperor Constantine. The Verginelle, dressed in white, would kneel and pray by candlelight all night, offering their sweet virgin prayers to the Madonna. The faithful would file into the wooden benches behind them and together they would pass the whole night chanting the liturgy. At dawn, they would begin the journey back to the mountain villages, where upon arrival the women would immediately start cooking because the feast itself would commence at midday, everyone in a euphoric sore-footed delirium.

The Verginelle was especially close to Assunta's heart, as she was herself dedicated to the Madonna's Assumption by her name. She had never missed a pilgrimage except that one year she was seven months pregnant with Cettina and had been in such a horrible state. Assunta herself had been selected for the Verginelle when she was eleven years old. She cherished the memory—she had felt like an angel for those holy hours. Now she pictured her pretty little daughter Stella with a crown of white flowers on her head. No doubt this delightful image had also occurred to Father Giacomo.

At dinner, when Assunta made the announcement of Stella's selection for the Verginelle, Stella let her aunt and grandmother's cooing die down before saying, "Mamma, I can't be in the Verginelle." She put her arm around her sister, whose eyes were darkly shining with misery. "Not if Cettina can't be in it, too. Please tell Father Giacomo."

"Stella!" Assunta laughed. "Cettina is little. She'll be picked some other year."

"No, Mamma," Stella replied. "We are sisters. We're supposed to be together."

Stella had been turning this idea over since she'd been in church and was extremely pleased with herself for thinking of it. By taking this stance, she would look like a martyr of selfless-ness, which would be even better than just being selected for the Verginelle. She would be a hero—a saint.

Assunta was worried about offending both the priest and the Madonna by heading back to negotiate for her daughters' participa-tion in the pilgrimage. On the other hand, she was overwhelmed with pleasure at the way Stella took care of her sister. She would figure out a way to convince the priest, a special offering of some kind, although she had no money this summer. She had not heard from her husband in six years. But she could probably spare a chicken.

Stella was glad her mother didn't seem to realize how conniv-ing this plan was. If she could convince her mother of her good intentions, she didn't need to convince anyone else.

On August 14, 1929, leading the pilgrimage to the shrine of the Madonna for the feast of her Assumption were fourteen, not thirteen, little girls in white dresses, with crowns of white paper flowers. One of them was too young, not even eight years old. She fell asleep during the all-night prayer vigil and snored in her sister's lap. Everyone was very happy.

Maybe the Madonna knew the truth of Stella's dark little heart, because it was the day after the Assumption that Stella almost died for the third time.

It was an oven-hot August afternoon, and the *chiazza* between the church and the school was full of children. Stella and Cettina joined the fray after they had finished their lunch, keeping an eye open for their favorite all-black street cat. They played a hopping game across the courtyard with Giulietta, a sallow, birdlike girl who also had no father. She was five years older than Stella, too old to be playing in the *chiazza*, really, and a bit simple, but she was about Stella's size and she was fast, and Stella liked to race her along the forest paths.

The hopping game was adequate at first. But the joy of physical exertion passed, and Stella began to feel listless. She stopped and stood aside with her arms crossed over her scarred abdomen. After Stella had missed a rotation, Cettina paused by her sister. "What's wrong, Stella?"

"It's too hot to play here anymore," Stella said. She felt bored and itchy. The smell of cook-fire woodsmoke mingled with the sweat soaking her dress. "Let's go into the schoolhouse," she said. "It will be cool."

The school was supposed to be closed up, because it was vacation. But everyone knew the back door wouldn't lock, since the bolt connecting the top and bottom halves was broken. If you gave the bottom a good shove, it would swing in, and you could stoop in under it. Mothers told their children not to play inside the schoolhouse because older boys went into the deserted classrooms to do bad things. But the ceilings were so tall that the air inside was cold and moist even in August, and the village children often played there until Maestra Giuseppina scattered them.

Cettina, always the goody-goody, didn't want to break the rules. "That's naughty, Stella. What will Mamma say?"

"Nothing. Why would she say anything?" Stella now had a satisfying idea in her head of lying on the cool stone floor of the boys' classroom, where she wasn't allowed.

Cettina didn't like it, but she followed Stella, the way she always followed Stella. Stella leaned hard against the thick wooden door and nudged it open. Giulietta stopped hopping and trailed them in. Giggling, they pushed the bottom half of the door closed behind them and padded on their dirty bare feet into the silence of the dark chambers.

They passed an hour in the schoolhouse, rooting through the boys' facilities, trying to find what masculine secrets were hidden there. They lay on the classroom floor, just as Stella had imagined doing, feeling the cold stones absorb their body heat until they drifted off, napping in the dim afternoon light.

When Stella woke up, her skin was chilled, goose bumps standing on the side of her arms. Cettina was dozing beside her, Giulietta singing thinly to herself. The sun was descending into the olive valley, and as the grogginess cleared from Stella's eyes her vision fixed on a dark splotch on the wall, a disconcerting blemish in the thin lemony light. She felt a cold tickle race up her arms, and she tried to figure out what about the splotch was wrong. Then it moved, and she shrieked—it was one of those thick-bodied long-legged brown spiders that hide in stacks of firewood.

Stella did not like spiders at all. She was on her feet, and gave her sister a kick in the ribs, although Stella's scream had already woken Cettina.

"It's just a spider, Stella," Giulietta was saying, but she scrambled to her feet, too. They had all had enough of this adventure.

The three girls dashed out of the boys' classroom and through the main hall. Stella fumbled for the door's broken latch; the sun had sunk enough that no light fell along the doorframe.

She located the latch and gave it a tug, but the door didn't move. Stella felt an irate frustration mounting, a weird discomfort in her stomach and that creeping cold along her arms. She pulled again, adding all her body weight. This door had swung open easily earlier. Why was it so stubborn with her now? There was a flash in Stella's mind, an image that flared like a bonfire, of another hand on the other side of the door, its supernatural aura burning through the wood, holding it so that Stella couldn't wrench it open. Stella, taken aback by the image, released the latch and stared at her hands. She realized, as she blinked, that it had been her own hand she'd seen, the way silvery spots appear when you rub your eyes too hard.

"What's the matter, Stella?"

Stella looked at Cettina, who in the shadows was nothing but a pair of dark, accusing eyes.

"Nothing," Stella snapped. What was wrong with her, she couldn't even open a door? "The latch is just stuck," she said.

She reached up again and seized the latch, pulling with all her body weight, but this time the door was unresisting. She stumbled backward as it swept open. But there was Cettina's foot, under hers, and she slipped, overcompensating, throwing out her arms as she plunged toward the door.

That was it, just a little conk on the head. But as unlikely as it seems, this may be the closest Stella came to death in all her eight near misses, because no one knew how to bring her back from the brink.

The schoolhouse door was made of heavy oak, and Stella was exactly the right—or wrong—height. When she fell forward, her temple split against the sharp lower edge of the bolted top half of the door, and her head rebounded and she fell to the ground on her back, cracking her skull against the flagstones.

The screaming of the little girls brought Suora Letizia from the nearby priory. There was blood everywhere, as there always is with a head injury. The tiny nun wrapped her apron around Stella's gushing wound, scooped her up in her arms, and carried her home to Assunta. Stella breathed, but she did not wake up, not even after they splashed her with water. Her body was floppy and unresponsive. Cettina was hysterical and Assunta was tearing out her hair in panic. This time it was eighty-year-old Suora Letizia who made the run down the mountain to Fereleto.

The doctor brought his surgery kit, and for the third time he stitched Stella Fortuna up like she was a sock for darning. The gash on her scalp was long, and the skin up there is thin and difficult to bring back together once it has been parted. Although he made the tiniest stitches he knew how, the doctor's handiwork would leave a long silver crescent scar, faint but visible, and a hitch in her hairline.

Stella didn't wake up. It was a very weird thing that happened this time, everyone said. Stella lay unconscious for four days. On the second day, when she still hadn't woken up, Za Ros went down to Feroleto again to ask the doctor what to do. The doctor didn't believe her at first, and said Stella was probably just healing and would wake up soon. On the third day, when Ros came back again, he made a second trip up to Ievoli. He was not able to hide his reaction from Assunta; his face was as gray as liver. She had not been pulling out her hair for nothing; Stella was going to die.

The doctor didn't know what to do. He had never seen anything like it before. He tried every remedy he could think of to restore consciousness, but nothing worked.

For Stella the long twilight lasted only a moment. When she woke, her hunger was a fiery cramp in her gut. She sat up and was nauseated by her dizziness, a combination of dehydration, starvation, and concussion.

"I want a tomato," she croaked. The sun was yellow-bright on the walls, the open door, the flat surface of the table. Pain shot through her head as her unaccustomed eyes squinted defensively. There was her mother, and Cettina and Za Ros, all looking at her dumb with surprise. "A tomato," she repeated.

"She wants a tomato," Za Ros said, and swatted Cettina, who leapt to her feet and scurried out to the garden.

The dizziness—it was hard to fight. Stella put her hand against the wall, and the silver spots sliding across her vision reminded her of the ghostly hand she had seen on the other side of the school door. It was her most recent memory, the weirdly stuck door and the invisible hand.

"Stella *mia,* you're awake, she's awake." The women were ringing her bed now, blocking the bright sun. They were touching her and praying. She didn't care what they were saying. She was ferocious with hunger.

Cettina came running back with her small hands full of tomatoes. Their dark red flesh was hot with the August sun. They were perfect, wet and smooth and the flavor of the earth.

"Bread," Stella said, gasping, and they brought her bread, and water, and olives and beans. They fed her until she was finally satisfied.

Assunta couldn't talk; she was weeping with relief. Ros said to Stella, "Tell me, *amore,* why are you so unlucky? No one else I ever heard of has accidents like your accidents."

"I'm not unlucky," Stella replied. The vision of her ghost was vivid in her mind; three years ago, she'd suspected she was haunted when she'd felt that hand close around hers in the pigpen, but she was certain this time. "It's the ghost of the other Stella. She is trying to kill me."

Ros clucked her disapproval of this idea, but Cettina said, "She's cursed."

Now Ros laughed. "Cursed, or haunted? Is it a ghost or a hex?"

Stella shook her head, which pulsed with pain. "I don't know," she said. Her voice was like a goat's bleat.

"Maybe both," said Cettina.

After the door bludgeoning incident, Stella never went back to the schoolhouse. Neither did Cettina. At the end of their formal educations, at ages nine and seven, respectively, they'd learned how to make the letters of the alphabet. They'd learned some basic Italian. They could perform a Roman salute. They could add and subtract numbers, which their mother had already taught them at home, and they could sing Maestra Fiorella's favorite songs. They'd learned that it was important to segregate boys and girls, and that when resources were limited, the boys should get them first. They had learned by their teacher's example how to force charity, manipulate favors, and not feel guilty about taking advantage of any situation. Some of the lessons would have more impact than others.

The week after Stella's third almost-death, Antonio Fortuna showed up in Ievoli unannounced. His wife hadn't heard from him in six years. Assunta tried to hide her dismay, but she couldn't fool Stella.

It was the first time Stella was old enough to remember her father's visit. In general he created a very strong impression on her that life was better without a *capo famiglia,* a man of the house. His voice and smells were too big for their one-room home. He did not talk to his children much, but when he did have something to say it was always at the top of his voice. The girls endured rump-smackings for unladylike offenses, like running in the house and speaking at the dinner table. These had not been punishable before, and Stella's pride smarted and temper soured under Antonio's new regime.

Stella had been told she loved her father and that her father loved her, but now that they'd met they were two differently sized strangers with nothing in common except Assunta. Stella wasn't sure Antonio even knew her name, for the number of times she'd heard him say it. Most of all she disliked the change he effected in her mother. Assunta's face was pinched and her eyes drooped; she seemed simultaneously annoyed and exhausted. She cleaned up his extra messes and bowed her head when he shouted at her. She must have been lonely, because Za Ros and Nonna Maria no longer stopped by to visit. In general, the house was a dour, joyless place. Stella was exactly old enough to wonder what the point of having a husband or father was, when he seemed to be a source of arbitrary disorder and suffering.

I fear that the timing of Antonio's visit was very bad indeed. I wonder how Stella's life might have turned out differently if she had had a father earlier, when she would have been too young to be critical of his dominion; whether she might have grown into a teenage girl with more predictable desires who would have seen romance and marriage as a prize to be won and not a sentence to be endured.

The most disgusting thing about her father was watching him use her mother's body. It happened almost every night, in or near the second bed Antonio had built against the northern wall of the house on the first day he came back to the village. Stella was used to nestling into Assunta's fleshy bosom to be petted and caressed to sleep, but now her mother slept in the new bed on the other side of the room, and Stella would be dragged out of sleep by the whisper of her mother's voice: *Tonight, again? Aren't you tired?* or *Be quieter, the children will hear you.* These susurrations would blend into other noises, slap-slapping and suppressed grunting that Stella could hear even over her brother's and sister's heavy sleep-breathing. And Stella would watch whatever she could see, because it made no sense to her why her parents did this same meaningless thing over and over again, her father's yellow buttocks bobbing in the light of the summer moon and her mother's thighs jiggling in the wrinkles of her gathered nightdress. When she caught a glimpse of her mother's face in the dark, it always wore what looked like an expression of worry.

The week before the annual Ievoli *fhesta* of Santa Maria Addolorata, the Blessed Lady of Sorrows, was when the Thing happened. Somehow it had not happened before, in all the nights Stella had sucked on her cheeks and watched her father do the job to her mother—but that night, he looked up mid-exertion and he caught his daughter's eye. Stella's gut seized and she pressed her face into the mattress and pulled her arm over her head, but it was too late. When he finished with Assunta, Antonio came over to the children's bed.

"Tonnon," Stella heard her mother whisper from her bed.

"One minute."

"Let them sleep."

Peeking under her armpit, Stella trembled in sickened fear as she saw his bare legs come to a stop in front of her bed.

"I know you're awake," he said to her. "You little pervert."

Stella felt like she was going to vomit. She had heard the word before, although she wasn't sure what it meant. She tried to lie completely still.

"Look at me," her father said. Stella didn't move.

"Tonnon!" Assunta called with more urgency.

"Quiet, woman." His feet shifted on the floor. The black hairs on his calves were as wiry as a pig's. "Mariastella. Look at me or I'll whip you till you're dead."

There was nothing for it. Pretending she wasn't about to be sick, Stella removed her arm from her face and pushed herself up to a prim sitting position. She couldn't make herself say anything but she scowled up at her father. In front of her face was his penis, which she forced her eyes away from, although it shone slickly in the gray starlight from the window.

Antonio looked down at her for a moment. "You like to watch? Eh?" He grasped her chin and stepped closer so that the odor of his groin, sweat-thick and ferric, filled her nose. "You like to look at your papa's thing? Why's that? You like to dream about men's things? Are you growing up to be a little slut?"

Stella bit on the inside of her cheeks. Her mouth was sour with bile and she swallowed back a semi-solid reminder of her dinner.

"Are you gonna be a slut?" He dug his fingers into her jaw; Stella never cried, but the crush of his grip brought tears to her eyes. "You better not be."

"Antonio, leave her alone." There was an edge of panic in Assunta's voice. "She's just a child."

"A child whose mother has been raising her to be a slut," Antonio said. "Good thing I got here when I did. No daughter of mine is gonna be a slut. You hear?"

Stiff with terror and fury, Stella said nothing. She focused on fighting down the bile, on willing the tears pooling in her eyes to be reabsorbed.

"I said, did you *hear* me?" Antonio repeated. Then in one abrupt motion, he bent over, jammed his hand up the skirt of her nightdress, and pinched the tight, delicate skin of her private area. Stella cried out in shock as much as pain.

"Antonio!" Assunta shrieked.

"Do you?" Her father was pinching her so hard she could feel the blood throbbing in her soft tissue. "This is for your husband. No one else. You let anyone else touch you here and I'll kill you myself."

He released her flesh and pulled his hand away; the removal was awkward and his arm became tangled in Stella's nightdress for an absurd stretch of moments. Stella's mind and body were a murk of fear and disgust and rage and pain and fluids. She was barely aware of her mother's embrace as Assunta climbed into the children's bed, wrapping her arm around her daughter's shivering torso.

"You must not upset your father, my little star," Assunta whispered in Stella's ear as she stroked her hair. "You must not be stubborn with him or make him angry so he hurts you."

Stella wasn't listening. Her shaking grew worse, into uncontrollable spasms. Her tender private skin ached and swelled, and pain shot up through her pelvis and into her gut. She never would let *anyone* touch her there again. And she would never again wonder if she loved her father, or if he loved her.

It wasn't clear how long Antonio was staying. Was he going to be a permanent part of their lives now? He spoke of America as if that were his home, so maybe he would eventually leave again. But the days dragged by and still Antonio stayed.

Every night since he'd pinched her, Stella was terrorized by the idea that her father might attack her while she was asleep. It kept her awake past the point of exhaustion. If Stella woke during the night she would hear her father's snoring and be unable to think of anything except his presence across the room. She slept on the outside; she felt obliged to use her body as a vanguard to protect Cettina, who Stella knew would be too stupid to protect herself.

When September came, Stella went to work at her first job, down the mountain in Barona Monaco's olive groves. It was Stella's idea to go to work, but Cettina came with her, of course. They weren't going to school anymore, and there was no point sitting at home when they could be making money—especially if it meant they could avoid their father.

To get to the *barona*'s groves, you crossed the stone bridge over the gully, but then instead of continuing right toward Feroleto, you headed straight down the steep forested hillside, following the winding mule path. And then in one breath the wet, spicy fragrance of the forest gave way to the hot, soily smell of the cultivated fields, the gray-green expanse of *uleveti*. The olive trees were like bushy animals huddled together, furry with their slender two-tone leaves that changed color in the wind. When Stella crossed her eyes the valley became a soft, uninterrupted blanket of blue-gray-green, the color of the lichen that grew on the cistern where she helped her mother wash their clothes.

Gaetano and Maurizio Felice, neighbor brothers who were a few years older than the Fortuna girls, introduced them to the *barona*'s overseer. The first day, Stella and Cettina helped the Felice boys, but the second day they knew what to bring for themselves: old blankets, bread for lunch, one empty glass bottle apiece, a small cloth purse. The boys demonstrated the technique: you shook a tree, hard. The olives that were ripe enough would fall to the ground. Stella and Cettina knelt to pick them up and stashed them in their cinched-up aprons. You had to be careful not to pick up any that weren't firm to the touch, and which might have been lying on the ground before the tree-shaking, because even one rancid olive could leave a greasy smear on the millstone and poison the flavor of the oil in that batch.

Around 4 p.m., when the day was noticeably cooling, the girls would knot the olives in the harvest cloths, balance the loads on their heads, and follow the path through the groves down to the press, which was near Barona Monaco's enormous house. A good day of picking would yield olives enough for five bottles of oil. As the miller inspected their olives and scattered them evenly over the great stone plate of the press, the girls would siphon off their own single bottle of olive oil—their pay for a day's labor.

The cloth purse the girls brought to the fields each day was, of course, for stealing. At stopping time, as they knotted their bundles, they also each packed a fat pouch with smooth, firm olives, which their mother would either serve fresh with dinner or would preserve for the winter. Stella and Cettina knotted their pouches under their skirts, making sure no telltale bulge would arouse suspicion if they were stopped by the pinch-faced overseer on their way home.

Stella loved fieldwork. She loved the leaves and the sweat and watching her progress build on itself, apronful by apronful. Her mind became empty, like a long prayer, as if God were speaking to her through the warm dirt on her hands and the burn in her thighs. She relished the disorienting moments of putting down her foot too quickly and feeling a cool, smooth olive splay her bare toes.

After the war, a land reform bill would force the heirs of the absent Barona Monaco to sell off this land. *Contadini* who had harvested for her could harvest it for themselves, now, if they could scrape together the capital to buy a piece. Stella would be long gone by then, but a second cousin she never met would own the very acre of olive trees Stella worked in on her first day.

Autumn became winter, and Antonio stayed and stayed. Eventually all the olives would be harvested and Stella would be trapped at home with her father. She hoped by then he would have moved on.

It was too late for Assunta, anyway, who had begun to swell with another baby. She became bloated and would have to lie down for the whole afternoon. Her legs were cinched with bulging veins and her feet wouldn't fit into her church shoes anymore. An unfair consequence of her father's lust, Stella thought, the price her mother had to pay for something she hadn't wanted to do in the first place.

The night before Antonio finally left, in February 1930, Assunta prepared a going-away feast of thick *tagliatelle* pasta with garlic and her *peperoncino* olive oil. Antonio didn't like beans—he said no one but poor people ate them in America—which put a limit on Assunta's cooking, given what was available in the winter.

Over this dinner, Antonio informed his family he was never coming back. "I'm done with this garbage way of life," he said. "No meat to eat, no running water, worrying that the wolves will come for you when you take a shit in the woods. It's so backward here and you don't even know because you live like animals, you can't even imagine anything better than animals." Antonio downed his wine and refilled his glass. "I waste so much money going back and forth, giving up jobs and having to find new jobs. This is it, this time. A one-way trip."

Stella tried not to let her hopes rise too much that he was telling the truth. She had known her father to bluster before.

"That's why I stayed so long this time," he was saying. When he ate, he pushed pasta onto his fork using a piece of bread. "To spend some time with my mother. I'll probably never see her again, unless she comes to America."

Assunta adjusted the rag tied over her hair. She was studying her husband, who hadn't looked up from his food to tell this lie. Cettina caught Stella's eye, and Stella shook her head so her sister wouldn't interrupt. Stella picked up pieces of pasta between her fingers, one at a time, and watched her parents, waiting for something to happen.

When it had been quiet for long enough, Antonio said to the table at large, "We'll all be Americans soon. The first thing I do when I get there, I'm going to take my citizenship test, and then I'll bring you all over to live with me."

"I'm not leaving," Assunta said suddenly. "Ievoli is my home. My family is here."

Stella was as shocked to hear her mother talk back as she was disturbed by her father's threat.

"*We* are family, woman," Antonio replied. "One flesh, before God and man. These are my children I gave you."

Stella felt dread spreading across her chest. *Please don't cry, Mamma.* He would beat her, he would beat them all.

But Assunta didn't cry. "I meant *my* family," she said, her voice as hard as a chestnut. "Who will take care of my mother if I leave? Who will take care of the baby's grave?"

Antonio shrugged. "You all will come to America and we'll be a family there. I will buy a big house on an acre of land and we will drive from place to place in an automobile. You'll never have to see a donkey again."

This was a mean thing to say. They all loved their donkey.

"I don't need another house. I have a house," Assunta said. "This is my house, which you're eating in right now."

For the first time, Antonio seemed stimulated by the conversation. He brought his hand down flat on the broad planks of the table. "Eating food you bought with my money that I gave you."

"I have a house already," Assunta said again. She stood and began stacking the children's dirty dishes. "I fed your children for years when you didn't send any money. We have everything we need right here."

Antonio laughed angrily. "You think I need *you*? You think there aren't plenty of women in l'America? I have all the women I want over there. Women who give me less trouble."

Assunta looked as if she had been struck. She placed one hand on her belly, perhaps subconsciously, perhaps making a point.

Stella felt the masticated paste of the pasta congealing into an uncomfortable clump in her gut. She was only ten, but she knew what her father meant. She had the picture in her mind, the shining buttocks waving in the moonlight, his expression of concentration fixed on the back of some woman besides her mother.

Antonio understood that he had behaved badly, but he was not a weak man, as he would show them, and it was his prerogative to upset them when there was disorder and his wife spoke back to him. He stood up so that his stool fell and he gripped his wife's chin with one hand.

"Listen," he said. "I don't need you and you don't need me. But *you* promised God to obey and serve me." He released her chin and she took a step back. "I'm offering to take care of you and of our children, which is the right thing to do. Now *you* decide. You can come be my wife in America, or you can stay here and not be my wife. But I'm not going to argue about it anymore."

And he left to go drink with his friends.

Stella did not need to say good-bye to her father because the carriage for Napoli took him away so early in the morning she could pretend she was still asleep. She assumed, relieved, that she would never have to see him again.

Part II

 # YOUTH

I wanted to come to America because I heard the streets were
paved with gold. When I got here, I learned three things:
One, the streets weren't paved with gold. Two, the streets
weren't paved at all. Three, I was expected to pave them.
—"Old Italian Story," Ellis Island

Cchi vue, a vutte chjina o la mugliere mbriaca?
Which do you want, a full bottle or a drunk wife?
—CALABRESE PROVERB

DEATH 4
Drowning (Immigration)

December 9, 1988, when she was just short of sixty-nine years old, was when Stella Fortuna almost died for the eighth and final time, the episode our family refers to as the Accident. As you already know, some things were never the same after her life-saving lobotomy. Since her prefrontal cortex had been removed, she no longer had inhibitions or impulse control. When she pinched an adorable child's cheek, she might draw blood. She refused to wear any color but red. She developed a compulsive need to mop up standing liquid—so, for example, one must not leave her unattended with a bowl of soup, or she'll ball up her paper napkin and stick it right in. Worst of all, Stella woke up from her coma in a furious rage at her sister, Concettina.

I have a lot more to say there, but that's for later. For now I want to tell you one strange little story.

Since they'd arrived in America and learned that a birthday was a thing to be celebrated, the Fortunas had always celebrated Stella's birthday on January 12, the birthday listed on her passport and her social security card. When she woke up from her coma, she was adamant that her birthday be changed to January 11. She struggled with the words to explain; her language skills were coming back only slowly. She got frustrated, clammed up, and scowled. She told them she wouldn't go if they held a party on January 12. The family had rented Mount Carmel hall; they would have to eat the deposit. "My birthday is the eleventh," Stella said. End of conversation.

Crazy Stella, with her red outfits and her perforated reality. Everyone threw up their hands; they moved the birthday party up one day. What were they going to do, argue with her? Every year since then, for the last thirty years, they've laughingly gathered for "Stella's new birthday" on January 11. They tap their temples and roll their eyes. "Who knows what goes on up there."

In Ievoli, I went to the *comune* office to pull the family genealogy. The registrar officer was most generous with her time, photocopying the whole long family record, which dated back to 1826.

You, clever reader, know already what I saw next, in the eeriest moment of my life. There, on that registry next to the name *Mariastella Fortuna (seconda)*: the birth date *11 Gennaio 1920*.

Stella Fortuna had been born on January 11, not January 12. So after her Accident, Stella woke up crazy. Except on this one point, her birthday—a point on which she was correct, and everyone else was wrong.

Why had she let her family make that mistake for all those years? And what, after the Accident, made her finally put her foot down and correct it?

I visited Auntie Tina after I returned from Calabria and asked her if she had any recollection of when or why her sister Stella's birthday was changed.

"It was always January twelve," she told me. The fact that the birth registry mistake matched crazy Stella's new birthday, she said, was just a coincidence.

But it wasn't a coincidence. Tina misremembered. Which can happen, when a person lives with a revised history for so long it erases its antecedent.

Stella, crazy Stella, knew the truth, when no one else took her seriously. What other truths were locked in her head? What else were we misremembering?

Here, after much research, I am able to present to you the explanation of why Stella Fortuna's birthday was changed, and why she kept it a secret for so long—forty-nine years—that even her sister forgot it. It is also the story of the fourth time Stella Fortuna nearly died, when she almost drowned during her attempt to emigrate to the United States.

The fourth death is the most controversial, because it is the most ambiguous—the danger was only recognized long after it had passed. It may not be completely truthful to list it among the almost-deaths. It's the best legend, though, and sometimes a good legend is truer than the truth.

Antonio Fortuna is a rather inscrutable villain. After years of ignoring his family, why was he interfering with their lives now and forcing them to join him in America?

Antonio had his reasons, obscure though they may seem. Some of them might even have been altruistic. Nowadays, all we remember about Antonio Fortuna—rightfully or wrongfully— are the nasty things he said and did. But the whole picture is more complicated than its fragments, which are so simple and ugly in isolation. To be honest, there are sections of Antonio's life I can't tell you anything about; he was a forceful man but not a prolix one, and many of his secrets were buried with his bones.

Not all of his secrets, though. I know some.

Tracci, as you know, was a hamlet south of Ievoli. There is a mountain-hugging road that connects all the villages like beads on a necklace. If you follow the road from Ievoli about half an hour past Polverini, you'll get to the crumbling *campanile* of Tracci's chapel, which is barely as big as a two-horse stable. Tracci no longer exists; the houses that are still standing are empty and its last inhabitants have moved away, but at the turn of the twentieth century it was home to fifty people or so. There was once a time when Tracci drew pilgrims because of its Madonna statuette, which had been known to accomplish minor miracles—she famously protected a priest who was transporting her when he was beset by wolves. Now she lives, somewhat slimy with glistening moss, in a cave cut in the mountainside. A rusted iron gate protects her little grotto, and some locals must still visit her, because there are offerings of plastic flowers nestled among the rocks at her feet.

In 1896, Antonio's father, Giuseppe Fortuna, was eighteen years old and engaged to be married to a Tracci girl named Angela Gaetano. That September, two months before his wedding, Giuseppe went to stay with his maternal uncle Luigi Callipo in Pianopoli to help with the olive harvest. There were four Callipo first cousins; Mariastella, the oldest, was a year older than Giuseppe. Mariastella never told a soul what had happened between her and her cousin Giuseppe, whether she had been weak of will or whether Giuseppe had taken advantage of her, but eight months after he went home to Ievoli and married his fiancée, Angela, Mariastella gave birth to Antonio.

There was nothing that could be done; the baby's father was already married before God to a good Christian woman. Mariastella's father made his wretched daughter, still sore and torn from her labor, carry her mewling infant up the mountain to Tracci to confront the exploiting cousin. Luigi Callipo demanded Giuseppe take the baby off his hands, but Giuseppe's pregnant wife, Angela, whose marital happiness was destroyed forever that day, refused. She became so crazed with rage or betrayal that she couldn't stop hyperventilating and everyone was afraid she would go into early labor. Luigi demanded money in restitution for his daughter's lost honor, but Giuseppe didn't have any money, and neither did his father. Mariastella's honor was the Callipos' problem, not the Fortunas'.

For the next ten years, Mariastella lived in her father's house, an unmarriageable ruined woman whose presence was a reminder of her abomination. Not every family would have been so cold; some would have raised their daughter's bastard child in loving embraces and hoped for the passage of time to erase the shame. But the Callipos were strict about female virtue, and Mariastella was never allowed to forget her sin. There's not much else I can tell you about the first decade of Antonio's life, except that it was not a happy one.

Angela, Giuseppe's wife, died giving birth to her fifth child in 1909. She was twenty-six years old and such a shrunken, cowed woman that her memory was entirely lost by the time of her children's children, who grew up calling Mariastella Callipo *Nonna*. For when Angela died, Giuseppe took his fallen cousin as his second wife, rescuing her from an otherwise unredeemable life of ignominy. He needed a woman to care for his four young children and Mariastella was the right choice—a chance to make peace with God over past indiscretions, to heal a family wound.

Even in 1909, Tracci was already in decline. The Fortuna house Mariastella and her son moved into was old and shabby. The well was a mile away, so it was difficult to keep the house clean or do laundry. But at least Antonio was now a legitimate son with a last name.

Antonio was thrown together with four half siblings. Mariastella would drop another two babies before she became too plagued by prolapse and uterine infections to be a desirable sexual partner to her husband. She would in fact die of a urinary tract infection in 1950, at age seventy-three. No one recognized the signs of blood poisoning, even when she walked around in the *chiazza* wrapped only in her blanket and the skin God gave her. Everyone just thought she was crazy.

That was forty years on, though. In the meantime Mariastella had children to raise, food to grow and cook, water to fetch, laundry to wash in the cold stream. She was not destroyed by her circumstance, as Angela had been. But she was a very hard woman, hard as the cast-iron pan she used to discipline her children and stepchildren.

I know it becomes difficult to follow our Calabrese family stories because of all the repeat names. Our family trees are taxonomically mind-boggling, Linnaean nightmares with roots not quite numerous enough to support their trunks, where an unwhole-some bloodline can be muddled by overlapping names. In the Fortuna family, you don't have to go far back to find tangled roots—they are right here, in the generation of Antonio's siblings.

Giuseppe Fortuna and his family lived, as you already know, in a one-room house with one square bed. The children were made in that old square bed, and then they had to sleep in it. Of course it became too much, but it became too much incrementally, a little at a time, each of the children growing one pound bigger, and then one pound more, a swelling symphony of fat baby limbs and sharpening toddler elbows. It is hard to isolate the breaking point, the day things went too far. It is especially hard when you have no spare money for more furniture, or anywhere to put it. Sometimes the best solution is to just think to yourself, Sure, it's getting bad, we'll have to do something about that, and go back to the cycle of the plow and exhaustion and sleep.

Did you wonder why Antonio Fortuna, the restless, the play-boy, had gotten himself married to Assunta Mascaro when he was only seventeen years old? Now you know why. Marriage was his easiest solution for escaping that dingy, grotesque house and the communal bed. Not everyone else was able to escape it.

This is the core fallacy of the famous southern Italian sexual jealousy, the poetic inspiration for the world-renowned machismo, the revenge knifings and the disciplinary patriarchy. There was no need to be jealous of a spouse or inamorata. There was no bed for them to be unfaithful on, no moment of the day not full of back-hunching blister-rupturing physical labor. The place a woman was most likely to have the job done to her was at home.

In the summer of 1918, Antonio's half sister Mariangela gave birth to a baby girl, whom she named Angela. The mother was twelve years old; the father was one of her two brothers who had been living at home, either Anto or Domenico. It was impossible to say which for sure.

Despite her lost virtue, eventually Mariangela was able to find a husband; we pretend virginity is everything, a woman's only asset, but the truth is the only thing about a woman that matters is whether she can work. None of Angela's still-living half siblings, who are much younger, seem to know what happened to her after the war, when she vanishes from any written historical record. (To be frank, it is not easy to bring her up as a topic of conversation; even my most forthright interlocutors have steered the subject away from her.) I wonder if Angela ever left the village where she was born, and if she did, whether the story of her origins followed her. I wonder whether she went on to have children with too few great-grandparents. I wonder if she struggled, or if it was all just taken in stride, the way things are and always have been.

I am curious about a few other things, but there is no one to ask. For example:

How was Mariangela allowed to be raped? How, above all, did their parents not know what was happening? Or did they know and turn away? Did Giuseppe, the patriarch, beat his sons for their atrocity, or did he beat his daughter for giving up that one precious asset?

And then—what happened? Did they go on all living together, and for how long? Did Mariangela have to go on sharing a bed with her rapists? How did her attackers live with their shame as they watched it bear fruit?

And then—did the rapists suffer as a result of their behavior? Or was this a youthful transgression—boys will be boys, let's all try to put it behind us? Does a rapist look at his infant daughter with love? Is there a desire to protect, to care for, when the same man-boy felt no such desire to protect or care for the infant's mother? How, exactly, do the laws of humanity work in a situation like this?

I know that eventually Anto ended up moving to California, and Domenico left for South America, but no one is sure where. Perhaps the brothers were driven out for their bad behavior, or perhaps, as Mariangela told Assunta, they had been avoiding the draft. The siblings did not keep in touch.

This history is taboo, so no mention must be made of it, under any circumstances.

Except I know as much as I do, which goes to show you only certain secrets are for keeping. I admit I haven't been able to quite figure out the difference between the two. Maybe that's why I'm writing this.

That, in any case, was the childhood Antonio Fortuna was leaving behind—when he married and moved to Ievoli, when he left Ievoli for war, when he left again for America. I'm not saying Antonio Fortuna wasn't a monster. I'm just telling you where the monster came from.

As much as he wanted to escape his upbringing, Antonio did not go to war by choice. He was conscripted, like most of the five million Italian men who fought.

It is hard to read about the Great War in Italy. Hard to read because material is hard to come by—the truth was obscured by Mussolini, buried under propaganda—and also hard to read because the facts are devastating. The price of the war was absurd: hundreds of thousands of men sent to die over a few miles of unarable snowy mountains at the Austro-Hungarian border.

The fighting was a bloodbath, the ratio of blood shed to territory gained worse even than on the Western Front for most of the war. The soldiers advanced up mountainsides, climbing over the corpses of their own dead, and into previously unimagined technology—poisonous gases, barbed wire, machine guns, grenades—their own military police's guns trained to their backs, forcing them forward.

This went on, day in and day out, for more than three years.

They fought in a wintry wasteland of the snowy Alps, under the constant threat of avalanches—the White Death—that killed more Italian soldiers than the Austrian shells did. There were never enough helmets or weapons. The water bottles were made of wood and full of mold. The gas masks, which most soldiers didn't have anyway, weren't effective against chlorine or phosgene, which passed over battalions in poisonous clouds and left rows of crouching corpses clutching their stomachs and foaming at the mouth.

The Italian soldiers were so dehydrated because of the poor supply chain that their feet became too swollen for their boots, so they marched barefoot and frostbitten. Their uniforms were so mud caked and lice ridden that they resorted to wearing women's clothing they ransacked from abandoned villages. They ate dead horses and rats they caught in their trenches. They shat in the same holes they slept in because they were too afraid of snipers to go to a latrine. They died of typhoid and cholera. They went deaf from explosions, lost their balance stumbling over broken ground and fallen comrades. They charged toward their deaths in total confusion. There were gruesome incidents of friendly fire.

They answered to a general who was ignorant, egomaniacal, stubborn, and indecisive, all at once, an idiot man with unchecked authority who placed no value on his soldiers' lives. The general's name was Luigi Cadorna, and I only write it down here because I believe his monstrosity should be more widely known. For those who might make the argument that Cadorna was incompetent, not evil, I will offer my opinion that it is the moral responsibility of the incompetent to identify their own weaknesses and not accept positions of power.

What makes the truth even more wretched is that they died for nothing at all. Whatever promises had been made to Italy for entering the war were null in the grimacing face of peace. At the end of four years of bloodshed, 1.5 million Italians had been killed, an additional seven hundred thousand soldiers disabled by injuries. There is, as with all wars, the missing statistic of how many women were raped because they lived in the contested territory. Another half a million Italian civilians died of the Spanish flu the soldiers brought home from war hospitals, the highest influenza mortality rate of any nation.

The casualties extended beyond the years of the war, extend even to today. It took Italy fifty years to pay off its war debts. The country's economy was destroyed, and industrialization shifted irrevocably to the north, which was the kiss of death for any meaningful development of Italy's south. It is the reason that, today, Calabria still sends its youth to work in faraway cities, where they settle and don't come back.

Somehow, Antonio Fortuna survived the war.

He was drafted with the very first class at age seventeen, and he lived to bring his body home, uninterrupted by bullets or shrapnel. He survived the November 1915 offensive on San Michele, where half the Catanzaro brigade was slaughtered. He survived his brigade's assault on the Asiago Plateau, a disaster in which the Italian soldiers were trapped in muddy sinkholes and barbed wire, where the Catanzaro 141 lost three-quarters of its men and where the soldiers not mowed down by gunfire had to spend the freezing night playing dead among the corpses until they could escape at dawn.

They say war is a crucible, where men are forged. I would venture that a monster is forged in a crucible as easily as a man is. Some men go to war and find God; others lose God forever. Antonio was one of the latter.

But he survived.

Maybe his daughter Stella's ability to survive death was inherited. She never liked her father, but maybe she owed him that much.

When Antonio Fortuna came home after four years in the army, Ievoli was too small for him. He sailed to the United States for the first time in February 1920, following in the footsteps of four million other Italian immigrants. Most of them came from the south—Sicily, Campania, Puglia, and Basilicata as well as Calabria—where Italian unification had hurt the most, where war and taxes had squeezed the already impoverished *contadini* dry. The south was emptied of adult men; in Calabria, 30 percent of households had no *capo,* no male head.

Italian men emigrated because they wanted to work, to make better lives for themselves than the poverty and exploitation they had left, although there was plenty of poverty and exploitation in l'America, too. Italian laborers—almost always men, often illiterate and with no recourse to aid or advice—crossed the ocean in steerage to be herded onto trains bound for coal mines in West Virginia or for jobs laying railroad track in the forests of Pennsylvania. They left unpaved, unplumbed, deforested, and malarial villages; they left starvation, cholera, entrenched feudalism, an inescapable class system. They left their families, in hopes of reuniting with them under better auspices. They brought their love of food and orderly gardens, their languages and their prejudices, their mysterious triple god and their myriad saints, their rites and their songs and their pageants. They brought their worship of their mothers; they brought their mothers. In many cases they intended to go back, which made our Italian ancestors unusual among would-be American immigrants, but in many cases they never did go back, which made us the same as everyone else.

Antonio was on the late side for American admittance—if he'd been just a few years later, after 1924, when the U.S. government passed the National Origins Act and ethnic quotas were instituted, Antonio would most likely have had to pick some other destination, perhaps Canada, Argentina, Australia, or France, where many Calabresi would end up.

The first time Antonio emigrated, he knew nothing about where he was going. He spoke no English, but he wasn't worried.

He had learned in the Austrian Alps, where the officers and the men they commanded had barely been able to communicate with each other, to think of self-preservation as a physical choice, and he was a strong man.

Antonio was lucky, because others had already paved the way for him. By 1920, there were microcities of Italians embedded in every American metropolis. For those who had emigrated one generation earlier, the dangers had been acute. Without knowing how to read or write, Italian men signed away their souls, at the mercy of their employer's unregulated sense of humanity. Many were killed by overwork, accidents, and explosions. Some simply disappeared. Some were prey to the nascent Italian American organized crime syndicates that flourished by creating protection and extortion rings among their own disenfranchised and fearful countryfolk.

But as I said, Antonio was lucky. His boat arrived at Ellis Island. Over the years of human history, many people have made the choice to get on a boat to go to a strange and hostile place—can you imagine the desperation they must have felt in order to step onto that boat knowing there was a chance they would not reach their destination? Most recently, these people have been emigrants trying to get into Italy, not emigrants trying to leave, and their passage is no easier or safer than that of their antecedents. Thousands of refugees from Syria, Libya, Eritrea, Somalia, Ghana, and Nigeria have died off the coasts of Italy in the last ten years, capsized, drowned, sunk in flames. History marches on, and names and destinations change, but not the injustices we let one another suffer.

Antonio Fortuna arrived in New York in February 1920 on a ship called the *Providence*. You can see for yourself, if you like—it's right there in the Ellis Island manifest.

He had sailed from Napoli with an army buddy from Catanzaro named Nico Carbone. When the young men arrived in Napoli, they had no friends in the world besides each other and only a notion that by going to l'America they would be able to become rich men. They'd obtained prepaid tickets and labor contracts from a *padrone* and spent the spring and summer laying railroad track in western Pennsylvania. I can only assume this first period in America was difficult, because Antonio sailed back to Italy as soon as he could afford to.

He returned to Ievoli in November 1920 with the clothes on his back and a change purse of American coins. He had very little to show for his time in America; he'd barely been able to pay back his passage debts. But he had learned many things about how the world works, and he was alive. The railroad hadn't been worse than the war. It hadn't been worse than Tracci.

The second time he emigrated, Antonio did not fall for a *padrone* scam; he paid for his own ticket using the stash of money from his first trip. He found his own way to a railroad job, seeking out the Reading office in New York's Pennsylvania Station. He knew enough English this time to explain that he had some experience. He got a job right away rebuilding the mid-Atlantic corridor.

His second trip was even shorter than his first, because Antonio rushed home for the birth of his first son—you already know that story. But this time, there were witnesses to his time in America. One of them was a soft-spoken, dapper Abruzzese man named Tomaso Maglieri. Tomaso was twice Antonio's age and only two-thirds his size, but they were on the same track-laying team, digging, clearing, anchoring the sleepers and connecting the rails. Antonio Fortuna and Tomaso Maglieri had little in common, but Tomaso, too, had served on the Austrian front.

In May, after they had been working together three months, Antonio and Tomaso received letters from Italy on the same day. Antonio's letter said that Assunta was pregnant; the baby was due in October. Tomaso's letter said his wife, Cristina, had been safely delivered of a baby boy on Easter Sunday. She had named him Carmenantonio.

"Maybe you will have a daughter," Tomaso Maglieri joked, "and someday my son will marry her."

"No, the first two were daughters, so this one must be a son," Antonio told him. "But your son Carmenantonio can marry my Mariastella."

"Eh, an older woman!" Tomaso laughed. "Every man's dream. Here, let's shake on it right now, and then we won't have to worry about betrothing them later."

Tomaso and Antonio didn't see each other again for twenty years. They didn't keep in touch, and probably never thought of each other in the interim. It was all a joke, I think—we all think. Well, Carmenantonio "Carmelo" Maglieri always loved a good joke, even if Stella didn't have the same sense of humor.

When Antonio Fortuna made his third trip to the United States, he joined his old army buddy Nico Carbone in New York City. Nico lived on Mott Street in Little Italy in a windowless tenement rooming house in which eight young men took turns in bunk beds and cots. There was a job on Nico's construction crew waiting for Antonio when he arrived; Manhattan was sprouting like a vegetable garden in June, buildings stacking on top of one another, and there was plenty of work for Italian boys. Over the next seven years, Antonio built a bank, a church priory, a subway station, and a palatial stone edifice that turned out to be a university dining hall.

In the blizzarding colder months, when New York paused its frenetic contracting, Antonio hung around the Elizabeth Street bars with Nico. The Roaring Twenties were Antonio's own roaring twenties and, to be blunt, he forgot his family. He wasn't used to fathers who loved their children, and it didn't occur to him to love his. Between construction jobs and protection sidelines, he must have been making quite a bit, but he sent none of it home. While Assunta was jarring every last wrinkled fruit so her children wouldn't starve through the winters, Antonio was growing fat on beefsteak and the bathtub gin they served in the speakeasies. He spent what was left on women.

But Antonio was reminded of his patrimony in the spring of 1928, when he attended the funeral of Rocco Scavetta, the tall, round-bellied old Mott Street grocer. The entire neighborhood came to pay respects, even the mobsters Rocco had tussled with over the years. As Antonio sat in the church's second-to-last pew, he surveyed the hundreds of bowed dark heads and thought about his own funeral. Signor Scavetta was a man with a legacy, seven sons and two daughters, grand- and great-grandkids, and all of their friends mourned him now. Antonio understood, finally, what children were for.

Only a few weeks later, a man from Pianopoli tracked Antonio down. Tony Cardamone was the younger brother of Assunta's sister-in-law Violetta. Since Antonio hadn't spent much time in Ievoli since his marriage, his and Tony's paths had seldom crossed.

The two men sat at the heavy marble-top table of one of the Mott Street cafés, drinking cloudy percolated coffee so strong its steamy aroma obscured the smell of the illegal anise liquor the proprietor had tipped in. Tony Cardamone was passing through New York on his way home to his wife in Hartford. He had worked on the railroads for a while but was settled down now with a construction job. He didn't seem to want anything from Antonio, although Antonio was on his guard.

"When it's time to bring your family over," Tony Cardamone said meaningfully, "you should think about coming to Hartford. You can live in a real house, not like here, everyone piled up like chickens in a coop."

Antonio shook the man's hand and they wished each other well; Tony Cardamone had to catch a train home and couldn't stay for dinner. "Come to Hartford," he said again before he left. "We'll take care of you. Get you set up."

There was no particular reason for his generosity that Antonio could see. Most likely Tony Cardamone felt compassionately toward Assunta, who was, as everyone knew, a saint, and who had been abandoned for a very long time. But he didn't press; if something was meant to be, it would be.

A year passed. In August 1929, Antonio was out at a Lower East Side saloon with Nico Carbone when they were involved in a bar brawl in which a man was killed. I don't know whether there was any deeper history behind the episode or it was just a particularly unlucky drunken night on the town. But I know that the murdered man's name was Johnny Mariano, that he was one of Frank Costello's personal goons, and that it was Antonio's knife that ended up in his ribs. Antonio escaped the scene, leaving Nico, who'd been knocked unconscious, to take the rap. Antonio hid in his landlady's coat closet for two days until he could sneak onto a ship bound for Napoli. Nico Carbone was given a fifteen-year sentence for Johnny Mariano's murder, but was found dead in his jail cell only two months into his incarceration. Your guess is as good as mine whether or not it was really suicide.

Antonio knew he couldn't return to New York anytime soon, but he was chagrined to be back in Ievoli, this place he thought he'd put behind him. Tony Cardamone's offer was on his mind as he bided the winter of 1929. As soon as he felt it was safe to set foot on American soil again, Antonio asked his sister-in-law Violetta for her brother's address in Hartford.

Assunta's last baby, the one Antonio planted during his final trip to Ievoli, was born in the beginning of July 1930. Stella helped her grandmother deliver him.

Assunta was kneeling in the garden, supervising as Stella and Cettina poled beans, when she felt her water break, the liquid sliding down her thigh and into the soil below her. For a moment she considered just sitting there and letting the baby be born right in her garden under the boisterous summer sun. How could she even stand up? The church bells had recently rung noon and the rag over Assunta's forehead was crusted with dried sweat. The baking sun on the globe of her belly made her think of a round brick bread oven, the baby cooking inside. Whole minutes passed as she lingered on this thought, but she finally pushed herself up, the baby's juice sliding down her leg. "Cettina, go tell your *nonna* and Za Ros that the baby's coming. Stella, help me inside."

Stella, nervous with anticipation, walked Assunta back into the house as Cettina took off down via Fontana. Cettina would end up spending the night with Za Ros and the silkworms, who needed round-the-clock feeding at this molting stage; better for Cettina to be out of her mother's hair.

Stella, meanwhile, was ten, old enough to assist with the birth. She sat her mother on a wooden stool and followed Assunta's taut but level instructions until Maria arrived. Do this. Go get that. Assunta would not scream or cry out during the whole process, because it was best the neighbors only learned what had happened after it was all over and decided. Best not to bring down the Eye.

Stella obeyed her mother. She spread the old brown harvest blanket over the bed to catch the worst mess. She brought a fire to life from the coals, the scars on her arms pulsing in resistance to the heat. She had never seen a baby being born before, had been too young to remember the last time her mother had labored. She stared at her mother's face during the contractions. Assunta's skin was swollen and her eyes bright red, the veins on her temple and neck standing out. Stella was old enough to understand; if things did not go smoothly, her mother might die. She realized as she scurried up the hill to the cistern that these might be among the last minutes she had with her mother, and she fought to keep her mind calm, to move carefully but faster so the moments might not be wasted.

Nonna Maria arrived with her pouch of mint, her face pink from climbing up the steep hillside in the midday sun. Stella felt only a fraction of the relief she wished to feel upon seeing her grandmother. Maria looked old and weak to her. Suora Letizia was away in Nicastro today; it was only the two of them, Stella and her little grandmother, to help Assunta bring the baby out.

In fact, it was an easy labor, less than five hours. But Stella, who had no context, was shaken by the experience. She was mature enough to understand that this was the one time in life when the taboo womanly area must become not taboo, when it must be exposed to other women for the baby to come out. But to see the purple-brown skin of her mother's vagina, layered like the leathery folds of an enormous fig, part convulsively around the hairy head of the baby—Stella was so sure the baby was dead, its head was so still for so long—and the yellow-brown snake of fecal matter that squeezed out under the baby's head, which Maria snapped at Stella to wipe away with a rag and which was still hot and soft in her hand when she dropped it, rag and all, in the chamber pot—the slime-sealed eyes of the baby when it finally emerged, the strange blue and white cord wrapped around his little shoulders—Stella was not ready for this. She was not a child and she should have been stoic, prepared to assist in whatever way she could. It was what you did, when you were a woman; this was her induction into the secret world of adult women, and Stella's heart and mind were rejecting its ugliness. She had seen her precious mother reduced to an animal, a sow in a sty, with no control over her own destiny in this terrible moment.

This was a formative experience for Stella. This was the origin of her second phobia, the horrifying repercussion of the first.

Three very bad things happened in 1931.

The first was that Za Ros moved to France, where her two sons had been living. "Their life is good over there," Rosina explained to Assunta. "They will never come back here, not even to see me. So I have to go to them."

Assunta understood missing your children—of course she did. But Ros had stood in for Assunta's dead father, for Assunta's absent husband. Ros was her moral fiber, who made her a better and more holy person. Assunta could not imagine her own daily life without her tiny sister. She cried from the time Ros told her until Ros boarded a train north two weeks later. She wasn't wrong to cry—she would never see her sister again. Neither would Stella, who loved her godmother.

Ros was one of the good ones, as they say. I wonder how things would have been different for the Fortunas if she had stayed. But she made a good decision for herself. The village southwest of Marseilles where her sons installed her was a charming place where people were kind to her. Ros got along so well with the locals that she got married to a French widower, even though she was over sixty years old, and became the stepmother of five grown children. She drank grappa every afternoon of her life and lived to be 105 years old. On her centennial birthday, in 1972, the town newspaper printed a picture of her smiling toothlessly on the front page.

It was lucky for Ros that she left Ievoli when she did, because if she had waited just a bit longer she would not have been able to convince herself to go. The second bad thing that happened was in September, when Assunta's brother, Nicola, was using a horse-drawn plow to turn over the earth to plant new trees. Nicola lost control of the temperamental horse and was knocked down, and the plow blade dragged over his thigh. Nicola, who had none of his niece Stella's luck, bled to death out of a severed artery no one could stanch.

So in six months, Assunta had lost her sister and her brother. Nonna Maria had lost her daughter and her son. Maria was a tough woman, much tougher than Assunta. But I think both of them only held on to sanity after Nicola's passing because they had each other.

In December, the third bad thing happened: a letter from Antonio.

Wife Assunta

It is time for you and our children to join me here in America now. Write to me with their birthdates so I can apply for a family passport. I will send for you when the paperwork is ready.

Antonio Fortuna

She had not heard from him since he had left with his declaration that he didn't need her if she didn't want to be a wife to him. She'd thought her world was safe from his further interference—that she would live as a white widow in her beloved village and raise her children in peace. She had Suora Letizia read the letter to her until she had it memorized, but she didn't write back. Maybe if she didn't write back, Antonio wouldn't be able to send for her.

The following spring, Nonna Maria was splitting firewood behind her house when the ax blade struck a knot and a wedge of wood flew up and hit her in the eye. It was a strangely precise hit, fast and clean. The pain was delayed by shock, and it took Maria several moments to figure out what had happened. She dropped the ax in the dirt as the pulsing in her face became more intense. It wasn't until she looked at the ground and saw her own eye there looking back at her, round and yellow and surprisingly large, that she understood.

She bent down and picked up the eye between her finger and thumb, turning it over in her hand—it filled her whole palm. With her eye in one hand and her walking stick in the other, she climbed up the hill, calling, "Assù! Assù, I have a problem."

It was the first family medical emergency since Stella's bludgeoning in the schoolyard. This time, Assunta sent Stella down to Feroleto so Maria wouldn't be left alone.

"You'll have to get the doctor to come up here, Stella," Assunta said. "Do you remember where his house is?"

Stella was sure she could find it. "What if he won't come?"

Assunta shook her head. "You have to make him come, no matter what."

While Assunta put Maria's eye in a bowl of water to keep it moist, Stella tied up her skirts and went hurrying down the mountain. A work detail sent by the government in Catanzaro had put a proper road in, including a bridge that stretched over the gully to Feroleto, but Stella stuck with the donkey path she knew.

She found what she was looking for by instinct. There was the doctor's house, with its yellow stucco finish, seven doors up on the left side of the cobblestone road that ran through the center of town. The nameplate said DOTTORE and underneath that MASCARO AGUSTINO. She hadn't known the doctor had the same name as her mother.

The house was empty, but Stella knew where to go next. It was the afternoon rest hour, and pretty much all of the men in the entire town were gathered in the *chiazza* in front of the bar, their backs to the valley. Some looked at Stella askance, but no one asked what she wanted. Thinking of her grandmother bleeding at Assunta's kitchen table with her eye in a soup bowl, Stella took a large breath and bellowed, *"Duttore! U duttore è ca?"* She remembered the good Italian she had learned in school, appropriate, she thought, for this public occasion, and tried again, *"Il dottore è qui?"*

The men fell silent as they took their own inventory, but the doctor was not there. Then a fellow with a large gray mustache remembered the doctor had gone to Nicastro to restock his medical supplies. Stella would just have to wait.

Stella sat in front of the chestnut tree in the middle of the *chiazza,* where she wouldn't be able to miss the doctor if he passed. The men chattered around her, but her blood was ringing in her ears and she couldn't hear anything they said. It was possible her *nonna* would die. Time and again she considered running back home to be with her grandmother, and each time she heard her mother's voice: "You have to make him come, no matter what." So she waited, fingering the ribs of the suture scars on her left arm, wondering if the doctor remembered sewing her up, even though she couldn't remember it herself.

Stella was lucky, because it was two hours to Nicastro and the doctor might have decided to stay the night, but in fact he only kept her waiting an hour and a half.

"I'm Stella Fortuna," she told him. "You saved me three times and now you have to save my grandmother."

He was probably tired from his travels, but he followed her back up to Ievoli as the bells of Santa Maria Addolorata were ringing the first call to evening mass. Maria was lying on Assunta's bed with a folded cloth pressed over the right side of her face. Stella's stomach clenched at the sight of it; although she couldn't quite place the memory, she remembered viscerally the feeling of pulling away a bandage; she pictured the doctor removing the cloth to reveal blood squirting afresh from her grandmother's socket.

This did not happen. It had been a clean wound, as woodsplitting wounds go. The doctor rinsed the raw flesh with a solution that caused Maria to jerk back in pain. He rebandaged the socket with a white cloth that he secured by tying a handkerchief loosely around her head.

"You need to rest and let it heal," the doctor said, looking Maria in her good eye. "Don't touch it, whatever you do." He said to Assunta, "The most important thing is to prevent it from getting infected. There's a lot of open skin there"—he circled his hand in front of his own eye—"so lots of opportunities for infection unless you keep it very clean."

Assunta nodded. "Understood," she said, although words were difficult.

"What do I do with my eyeball?" Maria asked. Her voice, Stella thought, sounded just like it always did.

The doctor shrugged. "Whatever you want." And he left to go home to his wife for dinner—at least he was married now.

By the following afternoon Nonna Maria's whole face had become hot to the touch and it was clear the doctor's warning about infection hadn't been an idle one. For five days the house was full of the scent of mint and purifying chamomile blossoms, which Assunta boiled in the water she used to clean Maria's wound.

The infection passed, but not before it had spread to Maria's left eye. When her fever finally lifted, she was completely blind.

After Maria lost her second eye, Assunta prayed nervously for guidance. She received no specific revelations, and after hemming and hawing she paid the Pianopoli postman Mancini to write a letter for her to Antonio in Hartford. In it, she explained that she could not leave Ievoli because her mother was blind and would die if there were no one to take care of her. She was sorry that she couldn't obey him about coming to America but she would always be his wife, married before God. She stuttered when she had to say this to Signor Mancini, and she left the post office crying.

Antonio never replied to the letter. In fact, he never wrote to Assunta again.

There was no money coming from America for the Fortuna family. Meanwhile, around them Ievoli was built up and emptied out as young men headed to Argentina and France, sent money home, then came back to take away wives. The women of the village bought things at the store with money that came to them by post; they no longer went barefoot, or without undergarments.

Stella watched the culture of the village change around her as she entered her teens. Her neighbors grew chubby and made bigger tithings; the church was stuccoed and painted yellow, its *chiazza* refurbished with round flagstones. Families built new two-story houses. Mandevilla climbed neatly up their charming pastel façades and children stayed in school until they knew how to read.

Meanwhile, the Fortunas still had Assunta's house at the top of the hill, a cube of stone with naked mortared walls. Everything up here was just a little shabbier. The Fortuna children sat barefoot in the last pew at mass. Stella looked down from her mother's mountaintop garden onto the neighbors below, neighbors she had the suspicion were looking down on her mother.

Stella was old enough to see her run-off father as the source of their hardship. Well, they didn't need him or his American money. Stella and Cettina pulled their own weight. They harvested green olives in September and black olives in January. In March and April, the sisters picked oranges in the hills down around Feroleto. After oranges were done, the spring was devoted to their home garden. July was taken up morning and night by the *baco da seta*, feeding and then boiling the silkworms, and then there was a rest, for the feast of the Assumption in August, and then it was back to the olives.

In between the olive harvests, they worked Don Mancuso's chestnut farm. The girls arrived at dawn to beat the squirrels, who were formidable opponents. The sisters scoured the stringy grass around the bases of the chestnut trees for the spiky, pea-green husks of ripe fruit that had fallen during the night. They flicked the burs into baskets with a stick so as not to prick themselves. When the basket was full they would dump their findings on the harvest blanket, then shuck them and toss the empty burs into the woods, where they couldn't be confused with tomorrow's harvesting. They were allowed to keep one-quarter of what they picked; the rest went to Don Mancuso's overseer, Pepe.

The girls each had a pair of old chestnutting mittens their Nonna Maria had given them. The inside was stitched with a rectangular patch of cracked leather. The mittens weren't impermeable, though, and the girls' fingers and wrists were always red with pricking. Cettina shucked quickly and gruffly, as though she took pleasure in the pain, and Stella would surreptitiously flick the trickier unsplit burs to Cettina's side of the blanket, letting her sister do the dirtiest work. Cettina was either stupid or contrary enough that she never complained about it.

It was in Don Mancuso's chestnut orchard that Stella became a woman, October of the year she was thirteen. She'd been feeling sick since the afternoon before, sore in her abdomen and nauseated, although nothing ever came up. This feeling, the unique unpleasantness of a menstrual cramp, would be instantly familiar the next time it crept up on her, but this first time it was frightening and not something anyone had given her any reason to expect.

When she and Cettina set off up the mountain just before dawn, Stella had thought she'd be able to bear it, but the pressure in her stomach had increased over the morning. She'd wondered if there was something seriously wrong with her, if maybe there was another cholera epidemic coming and she'd be the first to fall. It had, after all, been four years since the last time she'd almost died—that was on her mind lately, that her curse had been suspiciously inactive. Where was the malicious little ghost hiding? Part of Stella was looking for death around every corner—maybe this was it, today. As she stooped to pick up the chestnuts her torso pulsed with pain and she felt as if her spirit were seeping out of her body, a great weight she couldn't see pulling her into the ground.

At midmorning, after the sisters had gathered the fallen chestnuts and crouched on the blanket to shuck them, Stella noticed she was feeling much better. Her relief lasted only as long as she sat in one place; when she shifted because her left foot was falling asleep, she realized her leg felt damp. Her calf, which had been tucked under her, was covered in blood. Her heart pounding, she rubbed at her leg with her dirty and pricker-sore hand, thinking she might have absentmindedly scratched open her flea bites, the way her mother always scolded her not to. She was unable to discover any cut or break in her skin, but she did find that her thighs were smeared with blood as well, as if it were coming from her belly.

Cettina had not paused her shucking. Stella was glad her sister hadn't noticed anything awry; she couldn't deal with Cettina falling to pieces right now. Keeping her voice calm, Stella said, "I have to go home, Cettina." Although she wasn't sure she would make it—what if she dropped dead right on the donkey path, like Nonno Francescu had?

"What?" Cettina looked up. "You can't. We have to get these to Don Pepe."

"I don't feel well," Stella said. Actually, with each breath she took she became more certain she was going to die. "Something is wrong. I have to see Mamma."

"What's wrong?" Cettina pulled herself up to her feet. "What's wrong, Stella?" Her voice was climbing in pitch and volume.

Stella wanted to be annoyed with her sister, but the bigger part of her wanted to cry. She had to remind herself that she wasn't weak. She would die alone on the donkey path before she would cry. She stood up, too, and Cettina saw the blood on her hands and gasped.

"Stella! Stella, there's blood!" That was all it took, Cettina was sobbing.

Fortified by her sister's hysterics—the reminder that someone had to be the adult—Stella said, "It's going to be fine. I just have to go home so Mamma can see if I need a doctor." She wouldn't need a doctor, because she would be dead, but it would be no help to tell Cettina that.

"I'm, I'm coming with you," Cettina said, wiping snot off her face between sobs.

"Don't be stupid! Finish these and take them to Pepe."

But Cettina couldn't do that—she was weeping with panic at the thought of being left behind—and so the morning's work was abandoned there for some other enterprising harvester to claim. Later Stella would wish they had at least thought to steal some of the shucked fruits, but no, a whole day's labor wasted.

They ran home down the mountain, which took half an hour. Assunta was sitting on the bed, nursing Luigi, who was three years old and should have been weaned a long time ago. Somewhat guiltily, Assunta pulled her breast back into her dress and stood up, leaving Luigi looking sullen.

"Girls," she said. "What's the matter?"

Cettina, out of breath from running and shuddering with tears, needed comfort and threw her arms around her mother. Stella, standing uncertainly in the doorway—would she infect her little brother?—lifted her skirts with her bloody hands, showing her dusty brown and red feet. "I'm bleeding, Mamma. It's coming out of my legs and my stomach. Everything hurts."

"Oh, Mariastella," her mother said. What was that tone in her voice, reproach? *How could you let this happen to you?* As an older woman, Stella would revisit this vivid moment, the memory of her mother's face, and reread the dismay: *How could this have happened to my baby already?* But that conclusion required the wisdom of age. In the moment itself, there was nothing to fish her out of her pool of shame as her mother, unconcerned about contagion, guided her to a stool and patted her head, making her feel young and dumb for being afraid.

"You're going to be fine," she said, and then those words every girl has to hear at this same barbaric, uncomfortable moment in her life: "It means you're a woman now." Stella felt herself flaming red from her collarbone up to her forehead as her mother showed her how to wad a rag and explained how she needed to stick it up into herself. "You have to do that for about a week," she said. "And remember that no matter what, you must never let any man see the bloody rags. Hide them until you can clean them. You should start wearing panties now, so it doesn't fall out. Can you make some for yourself?"

"I can make some," Stella said, her mind dull with her humiliation. She had nothing else to do for the afternoon, since they had lost all their chestnuts.

As she sat on the stool, the rag jamming up inside her where nothing had ever been before—a wet, heavy reminder that Stella couldn't control her own life—her shame began to give way to anger. Her mother had known this was going to happen—she could have given her some kind of warning. There was no reason Stella had had to crouch in the chestnut fields thinking that today would be the day she died. This one thing Stella never quite forgave her mother for.

Cettina got her first period one month after Stella, even though she had only just turned twelve. She couldn't stand to be separated from her sister in any way; even their womanly cycles matched. What a frustration this was to Stella—aching and indisposed at the same time every month. She knew Cettina wasn't personally responsible for that, that it wasn't as though she'd had a choice. But honestly.

Cettina was good in the kitchen and helped Assunta in her self-sacrificing way. Stella would watch somewhat jealously as her mother and sister giggled and chopped and stirred. Stella consoled herself with the knowledge that she was more precious to each of them because she was aloof, turning up her nose at kitchen activities. They teased her about being a princess, but they spoiled her, brought dinner to her already cut and laid out on a dish, complained to each other about how lazy she was but cleaned up after her.

Well, that was all fine with Stella. She was no kitchen slave; she had other, more refined talents. She was the best needle crafter in the village. This was how Stella spent the heat of the day, her blind grandmother Maria reclining next to her on the bed incanting old rhyming stories as Stella made perfect things with her hands. The tiny complex patterns came as naturally as counting to ten to her. She made tablecloths, doilies, and dress lace, and she was so clever at it that other Ievoli girls asked for her help as they prepared their own trousseaus. Their mothers paid Stella in chickens, in cheese, in oregano pizzas big enough to cover half Assunta's kitchen table and which Giuseppe finished all on his own when no one was paying attention. The brat.

"Too bad none of these girls can pay you back by helping with your trousseau," Assunta lamented. "But no one is as smart as my Stella." This was an unlucky thing to say, so Assunta immediately performed a *cruce*.

"That's all right. I won't need a trousseau anyway, Ma."

"No trousseau?" Assunta snorted. "What blankets are you going to sleep on after you're married? Are you going to feed your husband dinner on a table with no tablecloth?"

"I'll never get married," Stella said. "Not if I can help it."

"Madonna have mercy on my daughter." Assunta clicked her tongue and crossed herself. "Don't even say those things, Stella. You think it's a joke now, but you'll curse yourself someday if you have bad luck."

Stella let it drop, because there was no point in getting her mother upset. But she had already started to make up her mind about her own future. She wasn't interested in marrying a man like her awful, braying father, or having her body torn open to bear him a child. The more she thought about it, the less she could imagine being married to any man at all.

After the midday meal, while Stella stitched with intense focus by the lemon tree window, the whole of Ievoli shut itself up until the first call to mass at five thirty. Houses were silent and dark, the bougainvillea blossoms bobbing genially in the breeze the only sign of movement. The fountain, the village's source of life, burbled unmolested by laundry-scrubbing housewives. The garden plots were as empty as if they had planted themselves, the shiny faces of the tomatoes and chili peppers glinting red on their righteous stakes. A foreign traveler passing through at the wrong time of day might think the town had been abandoned completely, that it was haunted by the ghosts of perfectionist horticulturalists.

The Fortuna house was among the shabbiest now. The Fortuna girls were at a social disadvantage, with their missing father and no dowry. But by 1935, when Stella was fifteen and Cettina about to turn fourteen, they had established themselves nonetheless as the Ievoli town beauties. They were good-looking to begin with, all clear skin and plump lips. But Stella had made them the most beautiful by making them the best dressed.

With the little bit of extra money she'd made from selling silk and lace pieces, Stella had purchased cloth from the peddler to make herself and Cettina fine new dresses. She experimented with stylish puffed sleeves and narrow, tailored waists. The girls changed into these dresses for mass in the evening, which was a vanity the Lord surely sanctioned because it gave everyone in town a reason to come to church, to gossip about the pretty, vain Fortuna girls.

Ever ambitious, Stella spent the summer of 1935 making herself and Cettina each a *pacchiana,* a festival costume. They were enormously complicated, as Stella was learning piece by piece. Most women commissioned a *pacchiana* from a specialty dressmaker. Fathers saved up for years for a daughter's *pacchiana,* which would last the rest of her life, albeit with a changeable second skirt—green for the maiden, red for the married woman, black for the widow.

Well, Stella didn't have much money, but she did have a will to conquer this task. She and Cettina were going to the festival this year—they were going all the way to Nicastro for the first time in their lives. Her neighbor Gae Felice had told her the Nicastro festival was much bigger than Ievoli's, two days of dancing and music and vendors selling everything from anise candy to gold jewelry to painted postcards from the monks of San Francesco in Paola. Assunta had promised she would allow her daughters to go to the Nicastro *fhesta* if Stella could make the costumes, which seemed safely impossible, but she should have known how stubborn Stella was when she wanted something.

Stella needed a model to base her project on. Assunta's *pacchiana* was not ideal. It had been made cheaply the year Assunta was courting, when her father had dropped dead and left Maria with so little money for Assunta's dowry. Instead Stella modeled her work after her Nonna Maria's well-made *pacchiana,* which was nonetheless fifty years old and needed a little modernization. Her blind grandmother put on the pieces one by one, showing Stella how they must attach. Together they ran their hands over the seams, Stella studying and reconstructing in her mind, her *nonna* spinning to demonstrate how the skirt should lift, how the shawl should drape. Maria's wilted eye socket disappeared behind her cheeks as she smiled like a carefree girl.

There were many pieces to a *pacchiana,* and Stella had to make two of each, one for herself, one for Cettina: long white underskirt, then the second linen skirt, bright green like the leaves of an orange tree, which a girl wrapped voluminously around her waist to create a bustle. Then the black wool bodice, which fell in a knee-length fringed apron. The torso must be close-fitted over the rib cage; here Stella had the opportunity to show off their figures. Black sleeves hung to the elbow, below which Stella would attach the eyelet lace she was crocheting. Above the bodice, demurely covering the cleave of the breasts, the costume allowed a single vivacious strip of red cloth to peek out from the swaths of black and white.

Cettina's contribution to the costume was the belt. It was the width of a fingerprint and would be cinched as tightly as possible to reinforce the hourglass effect of the waterfalls of cloth. Cettina was a patient embroiderer as long as she had a pattern to follow, and Stella stitched some flowers and vines that her little sister copied in tiny detail.

The week of Ferragosto, after their pilgrimage to the shrine of the Virgin at Dipodi, Stella finished the costumes. Cettina helped her lay them out on the bed for their mother to see. Assunta wasn't satisfied; "You have to make sure it all does what it's supposed to do, Stella," she said. So the girls helped each other dress. Even though they had tried on the pieces one at a time over the last few months, it still felt strange, like crossing a bridge, when Stella put on the entirety of the costume and saw the way her mother and sister were looking at her. And there was her little sister in the full regalia of an adult lady—her little sister, an inch taller than Stella herself, her bosom exploding so energetically from the tight-fitting bodice that it was impossible not to look. Well, that's what the dress was supposed to do. Stella looked down at her own bosom, standing forth so buoyantly proud of itself. People would be looking at that, too.

"*Fhijlie mie,*" Assunta said. She was crying, her open-eyed tears. "My girls, you are ladies." She touched Stella on the forehead, creating the tiny cross three times with her thumb to banish the *mal'oicch'* before moving on to Cettina. "Now is when you have to be the most careful. Now is when everyone will be jealous."

The Fortunas left for the Nicastro *fhesta* at dawn, the girls sitting stiffly in the Felice brothers' cart in their bosom-plumping *pacchiana* corsets. Stella's heart was racing with anticipation at the thought of visiting bustling Nicastro, of a festival attended by thousands of people. As the cart wended down the rutted mountain road, Stella's breasts bounced ostentatiously—much closer to her chin than they usually were, which was both thrilling and unsettling. Men would look at her. Was that something she wanted, though? The memory surfaced, inexplicably, of her father's naked injunction, of the way he had pinched her in the dark. As the sun rose on their party, pinking the silver undersides of the olive leaves, Stella tried to shove away the nauseating thought of her father.

Gae and his brother Maurizio jovially walked the whole way beside the cart, chatting with Assunta like they were old friends.

The Felice boys had a knack for flirting with older ladies, and Assunta didn't mind pretending she wasn't onto them. She had her habitual black hair cloth tied over her head—no getting too festive—but her face was bright with excitement, which smoothed away the worry lines.

Nicastro was an ancient city, cascading down a mountain below the ruins of a Norman castle. All the streets were paved with flagstones and lined by crumbling but immortal mortared Norman walls. The central *corso* was a grand boulevard, wide as a field. By the time they arrived, it was already roaring with hawkers and music. There were more people than Stella had seen in her life, or even imagined. Black skirts and men's long black cloaks eddied between the carts and wooden stalls filling the cobbled *chiazza*. There were rich, cream-skinned girls with gold crucifixes or *cornetto* charms sparkling on chains that lay weighty on their bosoms, rising and falling to catch the sunlight. Stella tried to imagine how much those necklaces must have cost.

The Fortuna women walked timidly among the vendors, with Gae leading them like a friendly sentinel. Giuseppe had taken his allowance from Assunta and followed Maurizio off into the crowd, and they didn't see that contingent again until it was time for lunch. By then, Stella had grown accustomed to the hot energy and loosened up, happy to drink wine and clap along to the music.

The throng of black *pacchiana* skirts was interrupted by splashes of unexpected color. Stella first noticed a woman in an eye-catching dress as pink as mandevilla. Stella stared—she could not even imagine what dye might make that color. The woman's black hair was uncovered, and—Stella realized—she was coming toward them.

Assunta, who was holding on to Cettina's elbow, also saw the woman approaching and tugged her daughters around in a quick about-face.

"*Zingara,*" Assunta whispered to them. *Gypsy.* In fact, Assunta would not have felt confident making such a pronouncement if she hadn't overheard another woman alerting her companion a moment earlier.

Cettina's head whipped around for a second look, and Assunta smacked her daughter's hand. "Don't look at them or they'll steal your purse."

Stella felt her heart speed. Real Gypsies. She tried to sneak a look without turning her head.

"Just look away," Gaetano told her. "And mind your money at every moment."

"Why are they here?" Cettina whispered.

"To beg," Gae said. "And to take advantage of people who don't know any better."

Cettina's face was red. "No, I mean, why are they here, in Nicastro, if nobody likes them? Why don't they go somewhere else?"

"No one likes them anywhere," Gae said. "There would be nowhere to go."

Cettina spent her allowance on an oil-fried batter pastry. Stella watched, rapt, as the vendor dropped liquid batter in the skeeching oil, fished out the fluffed dough, dipped a spoon into a jar of chestnut flower honey—how much must a jar of that size cost!—and shook amber droplets onto the hot pastry. He served it to Cettina on a thin piece of pinewood. Cettina shared with Stella, of course.

Stella chose for herself a piece of anise candy, *liquirizia*. It was salty and spicy and made her tongue curl, Stella who could chew the hottest chili peppers without shedding a tear. She browsed with longing through the wares of the cloth vendors, through tables of ribbon and glossy threads and buttons. It was good to understand what she was missing by only buying from the peddler, and also whether there were items she could haggle harder over in the future.

Assunta bought a few things: a special hard cheese; dried Sila porcini mushrooms that were said to be more delicious than meat. There was a fat bareheaded gold seller with a retinue of swarthy young men protecting his table. Assunta stopped and inspected every piece on display. She was looking for something particular.

"How much is this?" she asked the man behind the table.

Before the fat man opened his mouth to answer, Gaetano stepped forward to stand at Assunta's shoulder, tipping his hat respectfully to the gold seller, who tersely quoted a price. Assunta looked at Gae, who nodded; it was fair.

Stella, grudgingly impressed by Gae's gallantry, moved in closer so she could see what the prize was. It was a tiny *cornetto*, to protect against the Evil Eye, shaped like a pepper and carved from white bone.

"This is what you need now, at your age," Assunta said. She hadn't turned around, but Stella knew her mother was talking to her. It was because of all that cleavage Stella had on display. "To keep away the fascinations." Assunta asked the vendor, "Do you have another one?"

"No, *signora*. Just what you see here." The vendor leaned over his own belly to point to another piece on the table. "There's this one that's carved bone, as well, but it's black, not white."

Assunta considered the piece, stooping over the table so her nose was inches from it. "It's different," she said.

"Yes, the color is different." The fat man's voice sounded both patient and tired. "Otherwise, same thing, carved bone, same price."

Assunta straightened and turned to Gae. "Please tell the man I want to buy both." She patted her right breast a little more energetically than was appropriate in public, not realizing she was letting everyone around her know where she kept her money. "We'll come back for them in a minute."

Stella and Cettina retreated with their mother to the closest alley, where, looking very suspicious, Assunta crouched to retrieve her wealth from between her bosoms and spread the coins in her palm for Stella to count. The two charms would cost almost all their money. On the other hand, wasn't this what festivals were for, splurging on the things they couldn't get every day?

They returned to the gold seller's table, where Assunta handed her money to Gae, and Gae presented it to the fat man. The charms were strung on leather thongs before they were passed along to Assunta.

"Someday someone will buy you a real gold chain for this," Assunta told her daughters. "Maybe me, maybe your husband." She tied a charm around each of their necks, the white one for Stella, the black one for Cettina. "Remember, when the time comes, the big gold chain looks shinier, but the little chain actually has more gold in it, because there's less space between the links. You'll know you've found a good man if he buys you a very small chain."

In the afternoon, the music took over, and the shopping gave way to singing, drinking, and dancing. Stella felt shy watching the other girls dancing at first, but also felt envious of their comeliness. It was impossible not to look at them with their smiling cheeks and swirling hair. Soon any shyness had melted away and Stella and Cettina joined the circle of laughing girls they had never met before, spinning on the bare balls of their feet to the sharp, endless music of the concertina and violin—that was the secret of the tarantella, to keep dancing so the spider had no chance to bite you. Stella especially enjoyed sneaking glances at the concertina player, a handsome and animated young man in his mid-twenties, with a friendly face and curling hair. The music he made with his hands stirred her blood and almost wiped away the tainted memory of her father that had been dogging her all day.

Stella was off her guard, indulging her warming thoughts, when a voice behind her said, "Hello, *bella ragazza*."

If she hadn't been so startled, she might have reacted differently—defensively, or sarcastically. Instead she whirled around, her eyes wide, and said, "Me?"

The young man who stood there behind her, close enough that she'd heard him over the music and laughter, was five inches taller than Stella, and maybe three years older. He had curling dark hair and unruddied skin. He lifted his black cap and bowed.

"Ah, I should have said beautiful *girls*," he corrected himself. Stella felt Cettina breathing heavily, excitedly at her shoulder. "Beautiful sisters?" Neither sister said anything to affirm or deny. "You're not Nicastro girls. I would never forget your faces if I had seen them before. Where are you from?"

"Ievoli," Cettina replied, and probably would have said more except Stella pinched the skin of her sister's forearm hard enough to make her squeal.

"You don't just tell strangers where you're from," Stella chided.

"Your sister is right," the man said. Without looking, Stella knew Cettina's eyes would be reddening with embarrassed tears. The man might have sensed it, too. "But anyway, I'm not a stranger, so you shouldn't feel bad." He indicated with his chin. Gae Felice, their chaperone, had somehow drifted into the conversation. Moments earlier he had been half the *corso* away with a group of young men, but he must have been watching his mice like a hawk. "Are you related to this man? He is my friend."

"Not relatives, but they are like sisters to me." Gae stepped forward and clapped the dark-eyed man on the shoulder. "Stefano. How is it?"

"Oh, not too bad, Gae." Stefano smiled at Stella, who felt goose bumps rise on the warm skin of her arms. He liked her, he was making no secret of it. He said to Gae, "Aren't you going to introduce me to your sisters here?"

Gae smacked Stefano's chest—not gently—with the back of his hand. "Like sisters, I said. Let's not go too far." To Stella and Cettina, he said, "Ladies, allow me to present Stefano Morello, of Sambiase. You know Sambiase?" The girls shook their heads, and Gae pointed toward the far side of the *chiazza*, where the

Nicastro road led toward the sea. "If you go on in that direction, it's the next *paese*."

"A pleasure," Stella said, although since she didn't know anything about this man she was careful not to sound too sincere.

Stefano removed his hat and bowed. "And may I ask the names of your mysterious lovely friends?" he asked Gae.

Gae did not answer immediately; he stared at Stefano, a territorial challenge. "Mariastella and Concettina Fortuna. And just over there"—he gestured to the rock where Assunta was leaning, clapping her hands to the music, happily unaware that young men were imperiling her daughters' virtue—"is their mother, Signora Assunta Mascaro."

"I look forward to being introduced," Stefano said, unaggressive, confident. Under the pressure of his attention, Gae's gentlemanly chaperoning had taken on a new flavor, a proprietorial one. Stella couldn't decide whether the two men were good friends teasing each other or if there was something more at stake.

Gae and Stefano chatted for a few minutes while Stella and Cettina stole glances at each other, not quite communicating their opinions. It was impossible not to compare the two young men. Stella knew Gaetano was admired by all the Ievoli girls, but Stella rather preferred Stefano's look, slender and clean and dark. His face was small and fine under the shaking array of black curls.

"Now," Stefano said, and the music was shifting as if to help him along, "might I have the honor of a dance with you *belle*?"

"We don't dance with men," Cettina said. The rules were one thing she was secure in.

"Oh, no," Stefano said. His face was exaggerated chagrin, but he was not surprised. "Well, then, perhaps we can join your mother and enjoy the music together?"

That was what they did. Assunta was wary of the new man but happy to be his friend the moment Gae, who was very high in her esteem, gave Stefano his endorsement. Stefano bought them a flask of wine, which they shared as Giuseppe ran among the dancers, madcap as a street cat with everywhere to be. As Stella relaxed, she decided she rather liked Stefano Morello, who was smart and smooth and who wasn't chasing down other dance partners but was content to spend his holiday charming her mother. Would she want him to court her? To hold her hand, to kiss her? Her mind reeled away from that idea, and she focused on the music.

They stayed at the *fhesta* until the bells rang for the six o'clock mass, then took Communion in the cavernous Nicastro church and set out for home. As the Felice brothers escorted them up the mountain path, Mauri walking ahead of the cart with a lantern so the donkey didn't take a turn off the road, Stella, who was exhausted and exhilarated all at once, dozed and awoke again. She had a song in her head, "Calabrisella Mia," a song the musicians had sung twice that day. It was the story of a young man whose heart is broken by a beautiful dark-eyed girl who does not love him back.

You looked at me with such passionate eyes, the lyrics went, *and I stole your beautiful handkerchief. My Calabrisella, let us make love. I am dying of desire.*

It couldn't have been the first time she had heard the song—it was the quintessential Calabrese folk song, sung in love or in jest by every wooing Calabrese boy to his every blushing or irritated lady target. But for the rest of her life Stella would think of this night when she heard the song, whose chorus filled her ears for days.

Tirulalleru lalleru lala! Sta Calabrisella muriri mi fa!

Two weeks after the *fhesta,* Stefano from Sambiase came all the way to Ievoli on Saturday afternoon. He must have traveled through the heat of the day to arrive for dinner. He stayed with the Felices and on Sunday morning, after attending mass at Santa

Maria Addolorata, he knocked on the door of Assunta's house and asked if he could visit with them for the afternoon.

"You came so far," Assunta said.

"But not too far." He smiled at her. "Not too far to come again."

All the Ievoli women whispered about the handsome, well-off young scholar who came all the way from Sambiase because he had been bewitched by Stella's beauty. She was the envy of the town, and Assunta often performed the Evil Eye hex to protect her from the other girls' jealousy, but it was true Stefano must have been very smitten. He visited four more Sundays over the course of the winter, even in early January when a surprise storm hit. That day, there was an inch of snow lying over the flat surfaces, and it was still there when Stefano arrived, unexpected, as mass was letting out. He had brought the Fortunas a tiny jar of real coffee. They brewed it in a saucepan over the open fire, then let it cool on the snowy stones outside the front door. Stefano led the giggling Fortunas down the white-dampened street, tipping clean snow off tree branches into a bowl. They drizzled the collected snow with the almost-cool coffee and two teaspoons of precious honey, and ate this rare treat, *scirubetta,* passing around three shared spoons. Five-year-old Luigi, who had a sweet tooth, managed to get the lion's share.

Besides coffee, Stefano brought the Fortunas other gifts—a bottle of grape brandy, a carved serving spoon. Eventually, he brought a chain for Stella's *cornetto*—a fine gold chain, with interlocking links the size of the head of a needle. Stella wondered if he'd overheard Assunta's advice to her daughters all those months ago at the festival, or if he just had parents who'd taught him the same.

That was the visit when he asked Assunta's permission to be her daughter's *fidanzato*.

"Well, I'm not her father. So it's hard to say." Assunta didn't feel secure in her own judgment on this matter, but it wasn't her place to destroy an opportunity for her daughter, so she said, "But yes, you have my permission."

Another parent might have added "If she agrees," but this did not occur to Assunta. Stella was grateful for her mother's absent-mindedness, because at least she'd never had to make any promises about her own cooperation. She was confused and uneasy about Stefano's attention, and spent his visits torn between enjoyment of his wonderful company and fear that he wanted to make a wife out of her. Why did she fear being his wife? She couldn't answer that question for herself, either, but the idea made her stomach twist. She liked him and thought he was handsome. But the closer she felt tugged to him by his charisma, the more acute her aversion. If she let him get too close, he might touch her; he might put his hands where her father had, bind her to him, fill her with his seed. Handsome as Stefano was, Stella couldn't imagine she'd ever like a man enough to make entering into the servitude of marriage worthwhile.

"I'm not going to be a *contadino*," Stefano told her. He couldn't have guessed that saying so only made Stella think of her father. "You wouldn't be a farmer's wife who is hauling firewood on her back and plowing fields like an ox."

"I'm happy to work," Stella said. "I'm a good worker." She didn't want to give him false confidence. "Besides, what will you be if you're not going to be a *contadino*?"

"I'm going to own land," he said. "Not farm someone else's."

Stella turned this over. It sounded nice, but she thought a chicken might as well say *I'm not going to lay eggs anymore. From now on I'm going to be a rooster.* "How are you going to get land? You'd need so much money."

"Mussolini is making changes. He is going to take Italy away from the rich princes and give it back to the Italians." He tossed his head; his dark curls had a great effect on the Fortuna women. "I might move to Catanzaro, or maybe even Rome. I am thinking that maybe I can get involved in politics."

Stella exchanged a glance with Cettina. The girls weren't sure what "politics" entailed. "You want to be a mayor, something like that?"

"I want to be part of the new world," Stefano answered, his dark eyes narrow. "Maybe a government minister. But to get there I need to build up a reputation, respect. So first I am going to become a soldier."

"Ooo, a general, I could see him." Assunta leaned over Stefano to present him with a bowl of doughnuts she had just fried. "He would be so handsome in a uniform."

Stella was quiet for the rest of his visit. Her mother was very sure of Stefano, and Stefano seemed very sure of Stella. Here was a clever, ambitious man who wanted to take care of her. He was certainly a prize—clean cut, well groomed, educated, willing to travel hours from another, richer village to visit her. Stella realized no one was waiting to hear what she had to say. It seemed that the world was accelerating around her while she slipped deeper into a pool of unease.

She was never forced to assert her position because the letter came.

Antonio's letter, which arrived in early April, was addressed to Cicciu Mascaro, Nicola's older son, who as closest living male relative was to act as his Aunt Assunta's chaperone and representative. The letter explained that Antonio had obtained a five-person passport for his family, despite his wife's unhelpfulness. The passport was waiting for them in Napoli with a Signor Vittorio Martinelli, who also had prepaid tickets for their passage on a ship called the *Monarch*. They would be leaving in five weeks, on May 18. Cicciu would put the family's affairs in order and sell the donkey, the goats, and the furniture. If they could not find someone to buy the house in that short window, Cicciu should look after it until a sale was arranged. Cicciu was to chaperone Assunta and the children as far as Napoli and help her meet up with Signor Martinelli—Assunta would pay for all related expenses.

How did Antonio have the right to arrange such a thing? "It can't be, Mamma," Stella said. "He can't sell your house. He can't make us do any of this."

Assunta was speechless with grief, but Maria replied sadly, "He can. He is her husband." Everything Assunta owned was in fact Antonio's to dispose of as he would. A house that one woman, Ros, had given to another woman, Assunta, subsumed by the patriarchy, snap! Just like that.

I probably don't need to tell you that Assunta was distraught. She incapacitated herself in a two-day breakdown during which she lay in bed and sobbed, a kitchen towel pulled over her eyes.

What would happen to Nonna Maria? She was not included on the passport. Assunta was sure her mother would die, what with having no eyesight, no source of income, no one to bring her food or to help her wash her clothes. Well, there was Za Violetta, but that was hardly comforting.

During this period, while Assunta was prostrate with ruinous emotion, Cettina cooked all the meals. She and Stella weeded the garden, although they reflected together that they wouldn't be there to eat what they'd planted.

Stella was numb with ambivalence; her heart was foggy, cold, locked. On the fringe of her emotional void—like Gypsies circling at the *fhesta,* waiting for their chance to approach—were splashes of regret, relief, heartache, hatred for her father, anger at her village for not being more prosperous, harder to leave behind. Together they didn't make sense. Stella was a person who preferred black-and-white distinctions, so she shut them all out. She couldn't bear the thought of leaving Ievoli—her grandmother, her perch on the church *chiazza* where she liked to watch the sunset, the stray cats who stopped to visit with her in the sun-baked alleys. But budding, flowering inside her heartache was something else—ambition for another life. Despite the cold shock of it—of learning that with one snap of his faraway fingers her good-for-nothing father was upending their existence—Stella wondered if this was a gift from God. She would go to America, and she would not have to make a decision about marrying Stefano.

Cettina, fourteen, vacillated between tearful and stoic; she always took her emotional cues from her mother and sister, so this was an especially confusing time for her. Stella knew Cettina would suffer more than she would, in the end, because Cettina wasn't as tough. Stella wouldn't make things worse for her mother and sister. Instead, she bottled up her grief, compressed her frustrations into compassion, brushed and braided their hair, rubbed their backs, turned over the logistics—the reality—in her head.

Someone had to be in charge of tying up all the loose ends. As Assunta cried into her blind mother's lap, Stella decided she herself was going to have to be that someone. There was no time to sell the house, so they didn't try. Cicciu would send the money to Antonio whenever the sale was finally made. The Fortunas' clothes all fit in one trunk, which Stella bought from Zu Salvatore's store. She carried the trunk up the hill alone; it was unwieldy and heavy and halfway home Stella was in a sweaty rage at herself for not having accepted help. When she got it home Cettina lined the bottom with basil and mint, to keep away the insects and disease and bad luck, and together the sisters folded and packed.

The pork cured in January would go to waste, so they ate as much as they could, *suppressata* sliced up with every dinner. The widow Nicoletta had heard the Fortunas were leaving and asked if she might have their chickens. She had no money to exchange, but it was one thing taken care of. They were good layers and

Stella hoped Nicoletta wouldn't kill them and feed them to her layabout son.

The donkey, who was thirteen years old, Stella gave to Gae Felice. She didn't want to sell the poor thing, not to someone who would try to put the wilted beast in front of a plow. But she thought of Gae as softhearted and believed he would care for the *ciucciarijllu* fondly. She had to arrange it behind Assunta's back or there would have been a great show no one wanted.

Stefano came to say good-bye on their second-to-last Sunday. He wasn't ruffled by the departure; he, too, was leaving to join the army in the fall. "We will be together soon," he told Stella, who was even more uncertain that was what she wanted than she'd been before. "The ocean is not so hard to cross. When I have enough money for a nice house, I'll send for you. You won't have to be gone long."

When Stella said good-bye to Stefano for the last time, she let him kiss her on the cheek. She wanted to do him that little favor in case she never saw him again.

Five weeks—it is no time at all, especially when it is followed by "forever."

The entire family made a trip to Nicastro to have their passport photos taken. When Stella saw the developed picture of herself, she was surprised at what her own face looked like. It reminded her, dismayingly, of her father's.

Stella and Cettina washed and perfumed their hair with lemon for their last Ievoli mass, and they wore their fanciest dresses. Stella wanted the village to remember her at her best. The sun shone hard on the black wool and she sweated into the puffed sleeves as they knelt in the Fortunas' family pew. She had tucked basil leaves into her armpits to disguise the body odor, but she would still have to wash the dress before packing it for the journey. She could hardly guess she would never wear it in America, that nothing American women wore looked anything like her best dress. She couldn't keep her mind on Father Giacomo's homily, and instead prayed to the statue of the dolorous Virgin that the boat they were about to get on wouldn't sink in the middle of the ocean.

That Monday, with little Luigi tagging behind, they took their last load of dirty clothes up the mountain to the laundry trough. As Stella scrubbed her clothes against the stones, she thought about Antonio's world, where water came into houses all on its own, like having your own private fountain in your own kitchen— a world where you never carried a bucket down the mountain on your head, or scrubbed laundry against stones in a stream. She wouldn't be unhappy if she never had to do laundry again, she decided. She had no way of knowing how badly she would yearn for the cold, clean taste of the Ievoli cistern's mountain water, or that in the years to come, the rest of her adult life, there would be nothing she would do more than laundry.

On May 15, the day before the journey to Napoli, Stella snuck out of the house—alone; she did not want Cettina coming with her, for once—and climbed the mountain toward Don Mancuso's chestnut groves. The trees were full of rosy-silver catkins, and the flat, knife-shaped leaves buzzed with bees and fruit flies. There was no human but Stella for miles, no reason for any human to come here as the trees did their summer business. She found the tree where her first period had come—she was almost sure it was the right tree—touched its bark, which was striated like wool.

She would never again split open her finger pads on a chestnut husk, or accidentally drive a spine into her nail bed. Her days of farm labor were over. She didn't know where Americans got their chestnuts, but she knew that it wasn't from Don Mancuso. She sat under the tree and closed her eyes, trying to absorb the hum of the grove and the scent of the warm summer wind.

At dusk, as she was coming back down the mountain, instead of going home Stella continued down via Fontana past their house, past the alleys of stone and stucco buildings. Without letting anyone catch her eye, she crossed the *centro* and took the dirt road down toward the cemetery.

Stella hadn't been inside in years. She remembered coming with her mother when she was a little girl to care for the lost Mariastella's grave. Now Assunta prayed every day in front of the shrine she'd made at home, but Stella didn't know if she visited the grave often at all anymore.

The bougainvillea was in bloom, the magenta lanterns of the blossoms tapping against the cemetery's wall in the breeze. Bunches of flowers balanced on the ledges beneath nameplates, making it easy to see who was missed most. Stella passed them all, turning down the last aisle, shadowy and chill. She started as a lizard scuttled off a late patch of sunlight. She tried to guess if she was alone.

There it was, her name carved in the marble, the most expensive thing her young mother had ever purchased. There were no flower offerings. Did her lost sister feel neglected? The priest would say there was no one here to neglect, that the first Mariastella was with God in heaven. But if everyone believed the priest, why were there so many flowers on the other graves?

"Mariastella," she said out loud, her voice sounding dry and powerless. How strange it was to say your own name to someone else. She swallowed to wet her palate and tried again. "Mariastella."

Was she there?

Goose bumps had risen on Stella's bare, scarred forearms, but she'd made herself so nervous she didn't think it was proof of anything.

"I wanted to tell you—" But she didn't, she didn't *want* to tell her. "I thought you should know, we are leaving here." The breeze seemed loud in her ears. Because she felt she was supposed to, Stella extended her hand, ran a finger along the wedge-shaped indents of the carved letters. "We have to leave you. I'm so sorry."

It was as she said it—*I'm so sorry*—that Stella felt the cluster of pressure in her sinuses, saw the wetness at the edges of her vision. She had not cried in many years, and of course she wouldn't cry now.

When she had come back in control of herself, she said, stiffly, "We will never forget about you, though. Please don't be afraid of that."

Her voice echoed off the stone without any warmth. Feeling confused and not knowing why, Stella wrapped her arms around herself and left.

Assunta had to say good-bye to Maria the night before they left—it was too difficult for the blind woman to make the journey to the Feroleto train station. Stella had never seen her mother as silent as she was that morning. Assunta looked like an old woman herself, harrowed by her separation.

None of the Fortunas had ridden a train before, nor had cousin Cicciu, who would accompany them to Napoli. They were all a little awed by the concept and keen to do it correctly. It was a hazy day for May, a weird dampness rising up out of the marina. They were too early, and milled in the Feroleto *chiazza* for two hours. When it was finally time to board, short, round Za Violetta pinched Stella's cheek affectionately. "I'm going to miss you, Stella," she said plainly. Looking into her aunt's clear brown eyes, Stella believed she meant it.

"God bless you, Zia," Stella said, and she meant it, too.

The train had come from Catanzaro, and there were already people on board. Nervously Stella waited, holding her silent mother's elbow, as Cicciu tried to find them seats. "We must not take our eyes off our bags for even a moment," he warned them. "There are thieves everywhere."

They would spend today on the train, which would arrive in Napoli late tonight. Tomorrow they would meet with Signor

Martinelli and have their medical exams, and the day after that they would sail with the *Monarch* at first tide. Stella had portions of food allotted for each of the meals between now and their departure, and kept the coin purse with all the family's *lire*. She'd waited for Cicciu, the chaperone, to ask her to hand over the family funds, but so far he had not. Stella thought Cicciu was just as nervous about this journey as any of the Fortunas.

The train descended, somewhat jerkily, from the mountain villages, the roads and groves Stella knew so well, and into the less familiar yellow plains of lower Nicastro, where they stopped for half an hour to pick up more people. Some passengers took the opportunity to walk their goats up and down the train platform. After Nicastro, the scenery changed drastically. There, so close she felt she could touch it if she stuck her hand out the window, was the sea.

Stella had seen the marina from the top of her little mountain, watched the far-off bowl of water change color, silver under a passing rainstorm, gold at sunset. But now, as the train waddled by on its tilted tracks, the sea filled the entire window. There was no horizon, only ripples of turquoise waves that turned white as they curled against the beige sand of the shore—Stella had never imagined the waves of the sea, or the endlessness. The day after tomorrow she would sail out into that nothingness. She was filled with an eerie but familiar sense of dread.

They reached Napoli two hours after sunset. Passengers crowded and pushed to exit, bumping Assunta with their elbows and packs. The Fortunas assembled their belongings, Cicciu entreating them worriedly to hurry, hurry before the train pulled away with them still on it, until one by one they tumbled down the wooden steps onto the platform. Stella's eyes struggled to fix on a single face in the unending blur of hats and kerchiefs. She stood dazed for a heartbeat as the crowd pressed into and past her, everyone headed in tacit union toward the exit, before her survival instinct shook her awake and she grabbed Giuseppe's arm. "You stay close by me," she snapped, then called, "Mamma!" Assunta, her face still blank with her grief, came to Stella's side, Luigi clutched in one arm. Cettina, the good girl, followed Stella without instruction, hugging the Fortunas' satchel to her chest like a fat toddler. "Zu Cicciu, we'll follow you," Stella told her cousin pointedly, and he rallied his wits, hefted their trunk, and led them into the rush.

The Fortunas were sleepy and sore from twelve hours on the train, but they were not too tired to be overawed by the terrifically strange scene they met outside the station. The night streets were lit by glass-globed lanterns, the buildings rising as tall as trees. It was warm and muggy here by the sea, where the air felt wet and dense. There were people everywhere, despite the hour, walking, loitering. Clusters of Gypsies, whom Stella recognized now, stood in the shadows under the station's arched stone porticos. Neapolitan men of all ages strolled arm in arm on their evening *passeggià,* or chatted with women with uncovered heads and dresses in all colors. Stella assumed they were Gypsies, too, and wondered why any men were talking to them—were they not worried about being robbed? Cicciu saw her staring and bent to whisper, *"Puttani."* His voice was almost gleeful. Maybe Cicciu had never seen a whore himself and was as fascinated as Stella was. These were the fallen, the defiled, women who *chose* to do the job with men, who took money for it. Were they born deviant? Or had men made them so? Could she see the difference in their faces?

A horse-drawn cart clattered to a stop in front of her. "A ride?" the thick-accented driver shouted at them, shaking Stella out of her reverie. How stupid, to stand there staring like idiots, hanging themselves up like an offering to the thieves and con artists of this famously dangerous city.

"You need a ride?" the driver shouted again. Stella looked at Cicciu and saw the uncertainty on his face. She felt her gut clench. Cicciu didn't know what to do.

"I'll take you," the driver said. "One *lira,* wherever you're going."

Stella looked at Cicciu again, saw the stress sparkling in his eyes. He was paralyzed with his own doubt.

"Come on," the driver said, stern now. "Don't you know how dangerous this city is? Anyone can see you are new here and will take advantage of you. Let me get you to wherever you're staying before someone comes along and robs you or worse."

"One *lira,*" Stella said, surprised to hear her own voice. "One *lira* to anywhere?" This city was massive and strange; Stella would have no way of getting them to the right place when she couldn't trust anyone she spoke to. She had to hope the driver was not one of the evil ones.

"One *lira,*" the driver repeated.

Stella looked at Cicciu again, and her cousin nodded. "One *lira,*" he said, and they all got in the carriage.

Cicciu told the driver the hotel's name and the road it was on—all information from Antonio's letter. The carriage driver made small talk, turning over his shoulder to shout questions at them in his baffling Napolitano dialect. Cicciu and Assunta said nothing, and Stella felt obliged to answer at first, where they were from and that they were going to America. She felt increasingly uneasy about sharing personal details with this stranger and stopped responding, letting him fill the silence with his own halfhearted chatter. The moist air bore a sour tinge, like the smell that hits you when you uncover a rotten squash at the bottom of the vegetable pantry, only saltier. As they passed shops and dark alleys, her heart pounded at the notion of wasting a whole *lira* on a carriage ride to the hotel, but she reasoned they never would have been able to find it on their own.

When the driver pulled his horse to a halt, Cicciu checked the name on the hotel's sign against his paper. It took him a long time to check, Stella thought. She saw that his hands were quaking. The Fortunas climbed down from the carriage, and the driver helped them unload the trunk.

Stella took out her purse, which she had been hiding in the folds of her skirt. As she pulled out the coin to hand to the driver, she thought of Cicciu's quaking hand and tried to quell her own nerves.

"One *lira* per person, *signorina*," the driver said.

Stella's heartbeat accelerated. She knew that was not right, a full day's wages for this short carriage ride—he was trying to cheat her. "I believe it's supposed to be one *lira* for all of us, *signore*." As soon as the words were out of her mouth, she scolded herself for saying "I believe," for letting herself sound soft. She glared at him. "Six *lire* is far too much money for this short journey."

"*Signorina*, you are misinformed." The driver's deep-set eyes were earnest. "Maybe you don't know about the road tax? All the prices have gone up these last two months. If I don't give the officials the exact tax money for each person I transported I pay a huge fine, maybe lose my whole business—and they always know who's coming through, those *carabinieri*, nothing better to do than spy on honest people all day. If anyone saw me with a cartload of six people and I can't pay the tax—*ffft*." He made a slicing gesture with his hand, as if he were cutting off his own head.

Stella looked at Cicciu, who was looking at the ground. He would not help her now. She was seething in anger and drowning in doubt—she was sure the driver was cheating her, but at the same time she wasn't sure. And there were her sweet little mother and Cettina and the boys looking at her with wide, worried eyes. She was the one with the money. She had to make the decisions. Well, soon they would be in America; they wouldn't need this money anymore, anyway.

She dug back into her purse, trying to find a five-*lira* coin. "I'm sorry it's this way, *signorina*," the driver was saying. "I know it's hard for you *emigranti*, coming from the countryside where things are so different. I'm a country person myself." She felt her pulse calming as she handed him the coin. The expression in his deep-set eyes did seem heartfelt. "But you live here in the city a long time and realize how the world works, you know?" He looked down at his hand. "And the rest, *signorina?*"

Stella, who had been letting down her guard, was instantly angry again. "What do you mean, the rest? Six isn't enough for you?" She felt her family shifting in their shoes around her; felt the pressure not to make a mistake for them all. "You want to rob us of even more?"

The driver laughed, not unkindly. "No, *signorina,* six is quite enough. But you only gave me two." He stuck out his palm, showing her two one-*lira* coins.

"Oh," she said gruffly, feeling sheepish for her anger. *Could I have been that stupid?* "Sorry." She took back a one-*lira* coin and exchanged it for a five-*lira* from her purse. His fingers closed around it before it could even clank against its companion. Already her doubt had set in again, but the driver leapt up on his seat and tutted his horse away.

Inside the hotel, the Fortunas stood together by the door, forming a protective ring around their trunk and bags, as Cicciu approached the desk to speak to the hotelier. They were in the right place, it seemed; there was a very long conversation between the two men. How could there be so much to explain? Stella, still jumpy from the confrontation with the driver, stood by her mother, a comforting hand wrapped around her arm, feeling Assunta's stuttering pulse in the thick, hot vein that throbbed in the crook of her elbow. Eventually Cicciu summoned Stella to pay the hotel fare, two rooms—one for Cicciu, one for the Fortunas—for two exorbitant nights. They had been expecting this, though; Stella counted out the forty precious *lire.* As she set them on the counter, she looked at what remained, that unease in her gut rising again. There was too little in the purse.

"*Scusi, signore,* could you tell me, how much should a carriage ride from the station be?" she asked the hotelier. "For all six of us?"

The man shrugged. "One *lira,* no more."

One lira. "But what about the . . ." Stella tried to remember the driver's words. "The road tax. That the . . . the *carabinieri* check?"

"There is no road tax, *signorina.*" The hotelier shook his head. "I'm so sorry. The *truffatori* of my city. They give us all a bad name."

The man showed them to their rooms, where they settled in sullenly. Stella was so angry with herself she couldn't speak. As her mother distributed their dinner, Stella poured out her purse and counted all her money. Sure enough, she was four *lire* short.

"He cheated me," she said out loud.

"Oh, Stella," her mother said. "It's too bad, but there's nothing we can do now. Five *lire,* but all past."

"No," Stella said, the fire roiling in her belly. "He cheated me *again.* I *knew* I gave him six, but he must have switched the coin really fast, and he tricked me into giving him *another* five." She was so furious—with the man as well as with herself—that her vision clouded with a silver fog. She blinked to clear her eyes and saw that Assunta and Cettina were looking at her blankly. "So altogether," she explained, "I gave him a one-*lira* coin, a five-*lira,* and another five-*lira.* Even considering I took one *lira* back, I still paid ten *lire* for what should have been a one-*lira* journey."

Having wrapped her head around the tragedy now, Cettina gasped. Assunta clucked her tongue and said, "Madonn'." Cicciu was intent on his *suppressata,* or perhaps on not meeting Stella's eye.

Stella took in a lungful of air. She needed to calm herself down. "How can a man be that evil? Stealing from people who can't protect themselves?"

"The world is full of evil people, my little mouse," Assunta said. Her eyes were red from crying about her mother, but now she was focused on her daughter. Stella tried to swallow, but her mistake was caught in her throat. "You can't trust anyone in this world, no one but yourself. You have to know exactly what you believe, so you can stick to it. Otherwise people will always try to cheat you or confuse you." Assunta patted the bed beside her. "Come sit, Stella, and have some bread."

Stella turned to the wall to gather herself, but regarded her mother from the corner of her eye. Assunta's advice to trust no one was an adage everyone repeated without thinking about what it meant. But Stella *was* thinking about what it meant. About knowing what you believe—she had believed she had given the driver six *lire,* and he convinced her her beliefs were wrong. It was her fault for being weak of mind and will.

That night, Stella lay in the uncomfortable bed, head to foot with her mother and sister, and polished the crystal of rage and shame in her heart. She would not be weak. She would know what was what—she would never allow self-doubt again. She would be ready for every situation; she would never, ever let anyone take advantage of her. If they did, it would be because she deserved it.

A boy only a few years older than Stella met the Fortunas at the hotel at eight o'clock the next morning to bring them to Signor Martinelli, the emigration agent. He checked to make sure they had brought their passport photos, then led them on a short walk through the stony streets, down a wide boulevard and into the agency office. There were fifteen other people already waiting. There was room on one of the benches for Assunta, but not for anyone else.

"It's a busy day, with the boat leaving tomorrow," the boy explained. "Wait here and Signor Martinelli will call you." Their escort left, Stella guessed to pick up other families at other hotels.

They waited for perhaps an hour. Periodically the door to the private office opened, emitting a family, and Signor Martinelli would read another name from a list. The crowd in the waiting room ebbed and replenished itself with new arrivals. Assunta, who had cheered up a bit, sang songs to little Luigi. Cicciu taught Giuseppe the rules to a new card game. Cettina was mostly quiet. Stella didn't broach conversation with her sister, though; she was beset by a distracting anxiety that overwhelmed even her exhaustion.

Stella had begun to grow hungry by the time Signor Martinelli called them into his office. He sat behind a beautiful shining wooden desk and Assunta and Cicciu took the two stools before it. The children stood, Cettina holding Luigi, who was really too big for it, on her hip.

Signor Martinelli, a balding man whose face was dominated by a fluffy gray mustache, examined a sheaf of papers. For Stella, the bad feeling had already set in—the conviction that something was wrong. His expression was confirmation.

"You're the Signora Fortuna," he said at last. He had the same Napolitano accent they had been hearing since they arrived, but he spoke slowly and clearly. He must have been used to emigrants speaking dialects from all over the southern provinces. "Assunta Mascaro, yes?"

"She is," Cicciu answered.

"And you must be Mario?" Signor Martinelli asked.

There were several beats of silence. "No," Cicciu said finally. "I'm their cousin Francesco. I'm just their chaperone."

"You're not traveling."

"No, *signore.*"

Signor Martinelli raised his eyes to examine each of the standing children. "All right. Which of you is Mario?"

Another silence descended on the room. Stella was the one to reply, finally, when Cicciu did not. "There is no Mario, *signore.* We are Stella, Concettina, Giuseppe, and Luigi." She indicated each Fortuna as she spoke their names.

"Stella?" Signore Martinelli repeated. "Stella who?"

Stella blinked, the anxiety humming in her ears. "Mariastella Fortuna," she said. "That's me."

Signor Martinelli sighed loudly. "A problem, my friends. A big problem." He turned the papers as if for them to see, not that most of them could read what was written there. "Your visa is for the wife of Antonio Fortuna, Assunta Mascaro, and her four minor children: son Mario, age sixteen; daughter Concettina, age fourteen; son Giuseppe, age thirteen; and son Luigi, age five. It seems to me someone replaced you, Signorina Stella, with a son with a different name. The whole visa is incorrect. I'm sorry to say you're not going to be able to travel."

This time, the silence was a long one. Stella felt Cettina shivering beside her. Finally, Stella said, "What?"

Signor Martinelli repeated himself. It took him many words' worth of repeating to explain.

"This doesn't make any sense," Cicciu said. Stella was relieved he was speaking up at last. "This has been planned for a long time. Zu Antonio paid to have all this paperwork taken care of. They have left everything behind. Za Assunta and the children must be on the boat tomorrow."

"I'm sorry," the agent said. "It's very unfortunate, but the rules are strict."

"This doesn't make any sense," Cicciu was saying again. "This doesn't—"

"How can we fix it?" Stella interrupted. Cicciu was trapped on the problem; she needed a solution, and fast, before Signor Martinelli kicked them out of his office.

"You can't fix it," Signor Martinelli said, addressing Cicciu, as if he had been the one who'd spoken. "This visa is no good. I can't do anything because the visa is issued by the American government. Antonio Fortuna must reapply for a visa."

Stella's mind was frantically turning through options. She remembered what she had heard about telegrams, which could deliver a letter far away in only hours. Maybe she could still contact her father in America in time? "If he can fix the passport today, we can come back tonight with our—"

"*Signorina,*" the agent said, curt but kind, "this will take many months to fix. Maybe years. Your father must reapply for the passport with the United States government, and they have strict quotas about how many passports they issue."

"Quotas," Stella repeated. The word sounded familiar, but she wasn't sure what it meant. Her mind was numb. "It was one small accident that made this mistake." She thought she might explode into delirious laughter. "One tiny, tiny change, which no one noticed. Can't you just change it back?"

Martinelli's mustache flared as he sighed. "I'm sorry, *signorina*. They are very strict about visas. They can turn your whole family away if there is any discrepancy, and then you and I are both in very big trouble." His face was sympathetic, rueful—but then so had been the face of that swindling carriage driver. "I cannot let you on that boat."

"What do we do?" Cicciu asked Signor Martinelli. Assunta, beside him, was crying.

"Go home to your village," the agent said. "You go home to your village, *signore*."

What was there to do?

The Fortunas turned around and went home.

At the Napoli station, Stella counted coins for the return fare. She'd had mixed feelings about going to America, but now that they weren't going anymore she was subdued by a sense of futility. Dumping all their earnings into that dirty ticket man's palm just to go back to where they had started—what was the point?

Cettina, whose face was glinting with nervous sweat, was thinking the same thing. "So many things we could have bought instead," she whispered to Stella, in that whisper that could be heard ten paces away. "So many pairs of shoes."

"We don't need shoes," Stella said darkly. "We have nowhere to wear them."

The worst part of bad news is sometimes not the bad news itself but having to explain the bad news over and over again, to have to endure the reactions of people who are sometimes well-meaning and sometimes only pretending to be well-meaning, and sometimes not even that.

A big mistake. Whose mistake? And no one could fix it? Did you try everything? Why didn't you do this, or that? All that money. What a waste. What is your husband going to say? He's going to be so angry, what will you do?

Yes, other people are sometimes the worst thing in the world.

At least the Fortunas had somewhere to live, since they had been unable to sell the house on such short notice. But being back was strange. They had only been gone for a few days, but Ievoli now seemed small and pitiful. Stella had seen a train, a sea, a city; she had encountered businessmen, whores, and thieves. Ievoli was both the only safe spot in a maelstrom of disparate fates and also no longer enough to keep her safe from it.

Three thousand miles away, Antonio Fortuna was irate. He had paid extra money to have Signor Martinelli handle all the paperwork so that it would be sure to be done correctly; instead it had been absolutely done incorrectly. Had it been Antonio's own handwriting that was to blame? He had been the one to decide on "Maria" instead of "Mariastella," which sounded long and un-American to him. He had thought a common name like "Maria" would make processing the immigration papers easier. Had he introduced the error by trying something new and not quite true? Had he been scammed?

After five years of waiting in the visa queue, Antonio's efforts had failed. But he was Calabrese; his head would only become harder and harder until it cracked like a pumpkin. He refiled the paperwork, painstakingly hand-lettering the forms. It was May 1936; if the mysterious visa lottery took as long as it had last time, he might be reunited with his children, one of whom he'd never met, by 1941. By then, three of them would have achieved majority and would need to file separate requests for adult passports. But that wasn't something he could plan for, so he sent the papers off to molder at the bottom of whatever office pile they would molder in for almost too long to do any good.

The news about the *Monarch* reached Ievoli in July. The ship had been lost at sea—caught fire in the middle of the Atlantic and went down with all hands and souls.

"You almost died again, Stella," Giuseppe pointed out. "You almost drowned in the ocean. Now that's *four* times you almost died."

She hadn't even known her life was at stake until two months after the fact.

Assunta said many rosaries for the people on the boat. She couldn't get over the thought that she had sat among the dead in Signor Martinelli's office, that those little babies who had played on the floor by her feet were at the bottom of the sea.

"God gave you the mistake with Stella's name to save you," Nonna Maria said. "God bless. It seemed like a bad mistake at the time, but it was really a gift from God."

Stella thought of the prayer she had said kneeling in the church that last Sunday before they left for Napoli. Had she called down the hand of God? She thought of her visit to the cemetery to say good-bye to her little lost sister, the seizure of regret she had felt at the idea of leaving her alone. If the Fortunas had been lost at sea, not even their remains would have been able to keep the little ghost company.

On a windy Sunday afternoon Stella snuck out of the house while Cettina was busy with her weekly hair wash and delousing. Stella had questions, and she needed to be alone to ask them. She hurried down via Fontana to the cemetery and stood in front of

Mariastella's grave, arms crossed protectively in front of her chest. The eeriness of her previous visit had dispelled, but not her sense of danger.

"I know you're there," Stella said to the cold marble plaque. There was, naturally, no response. "I just want to know one thing. Did you sink that whole ship just so you could get me? Did you kill all those people because you hate me so much?" She waited in the silence for as long as her patience lasted. "Or was it the other way around?" she asked. "Did you save me by messing up my passport?"

The sun beat down on her hot black braid and the wind stirred the grit between the mausoleums. Stella had known there would be no answer, but she was still frustrated. "I know you're there," she said again. She gave up and went home.

Waiting—years of waiting. The opposite of having only five weeks to say good-bye was having an indefinite amount of time to say good-bye, knowing you would be pulled away but never knowing when.

This was how Stella passed the ages of sixteen to nineteen—waiting. In many lives, these teenage years are the most vibrant, of greatest impact on the person one becomes as an adult. Stella watched as young men and women around her fell in and out of love, fought, bore children. She watched as they cemented their characters and their roles in society, as she and her sister sat by, waiting, waiting, waiting for news.

Months and seasons ticked by, measurable by crops, by feast days, by the increasing rambunctiousness of Giuseppe, who had plunged into the rage of adolescence and found much to challenge him in his one-room world of women, by the stretching limbs of baby Luigi, who was not a baby anymore. Stella herself had stopped growing taller when she was eleven years old, but her bosom did not stop swelling. Cettina had outgrown her by an inch, and had strong shoulders and sturdy hips—a born breeder, Assunta joked. The girls looked good, very good; Assunta blessed their *cornetto* charms every day to ward off the jealous thoughts of their neighbors. But what good was being the town beauty when everyone knew you were going to leave?

The girls Stella's age were getting engaged and married. Lately it seemed like Cettina was constantly helping the brides make *mustazzoli* to hand out after the ceremonies. The girls of Ievoli were scrambling to nail down the boys, and the mothers of Ievoli to nail down their sons by saddling them with wives and children, because the boys all wanted to emigrate. Stella watched the frenzy with aloof amusement—the girls' machinations, the public flirting, the theatrics of one- or two-sided wooing. Immigration had imposed an inverted economy on the village marriage market—it was still the boy's prerogative to choose what he liked, but now he expected the girls to chase him for the honor instead of the other way around. The whole charade was irritating, especially because it was not a charade, and would become many people's realities for the rest of their lives. Stella was not friends with girls outside the family, not like Cettina was—Stella didn't need any friends besides her mother and sister—but from afar she marveled at their desire to leave the nests they were born in and make different lives with a man. It was the way things were done, must be done, as God's dictates about fruitful multiplication required. Stella was untroubled by the priest's insistence that good Christian women married—after all, weren't virgin nuns holy?—but she was alone in the village on this point. There was a piece missing inside her, the piece that all the other girls, even her sister, had.

Kind, genteel Stefano visited every Sunday that summer of 1936. It was an arduous trip, but he wouldn't admit to tiring of it. Everyone had grown very fond of Stefano, including Stella, who had decided it wouldn't hurt her to be nice to him because he was going to be leaving soon for the army anyway. Later she would be glad she had given him that much, at least.

In the autumn, as Stella split open chestnut burs, she remembered her May visit to the chestnut grove, her wrong thought that she would never break the pads of her fingers on a spiny husk again. She felt foolish for not having seen that it wasn't going to work out. The plan to emigrate had never made sense; why had they all gone along with it as if it had?

November came, and Stefano left to join the army. He sent Stella his first letter two weeks after he left. Stella was not a good reader, but she could tell Stefano was an elegant writer. Assunta kept the letter on the shelf with her special dishes, where it couldn't be ruined, and she took it down to show anyone who came to the house.

Spring. Artichokes. Beans. Lent. Easter. Tomatoes. Squash. Summer. Silkworms. Mulberry harvests, long nights. Ferragosto. Pilgrimage to Dipodi, feast of the Assumption. Autumn. *Fhesta*, olives, chestnuts. Winter. Olives. Christmas, the feast of San Salvatore. Olives again. The pig slaughter. Fennel. Oranges, tangerines. And artichokes.

Blisters, fleas, broken nails. Mass, mass. Praying for visas, praying for blind mothers. Other girls' weddings. Other girls' babies. Boys disappearing, to Africa, to Rome, to France.

Waiting.

And waiting again.

And again.

Three and a half years went by. It was late October 1939. The world was going to war, and I really can't tell you how Antonio managed to secure visas for his family in the precious last batch before all emigration was halted. Some of the people I've interviewed assume that money must have changed hands.

There were three passports this time: a wife and dependent children visa for Assunta, Giuseppe, and Luigi, and two solo adult visas for Mariastella and Concettina. They were to sail on December 16 from Napoli on a ship named the *Countess of Savoy*. Antonio had bought second-class tickets; they would not sleep in steerage, as he had, but would come over to their new home in style. The voyage would take seven days; he would meet them on December 23 at New York Harbor.

Za Ros's older son, Franco, who lived in France, bought the house on via Fontana so he could give it to his son, who wanted to come back to Ievoli to find a wife. Stella knew Assunta was happy the house was staying in the Mascaro family, even if she had gone from owning a house to having nothing at all with a few strokes of a faraway man's pen. That is how things work, so. Why worry about it?

"Whatever happens," Cettina told their cousin Cicciu, "please. You cannot let Zu Franco cut down the lemon tree." She pointed out the window at the little lemon tree that stood in the sunny spot between the house and the stable, the one she had planted when she was a little girl.

"Of course they won't cut down the lemon tree," Cicciu told her. "That would be bad luck." They did, though, of course. They cut down all the trees and filled in all of Assunta's land to build houses they sold to other men's sons.

Assunta and her four children made a shopping trip to Nicastro at the end of November with a packet of money Antonio had sent them. Everyone was to buy a traveling outfit. Nine-year-old Luigi was adorable in his first good shirt and a pair of brown short pants. Stella and Cettina picked out ready-made dresses at a shop, dark blue dresses the seamstress assured them were appropriate for American sea travel, with wrist-length sleeves that would cover Stella's scars. Assunta could not be talked into any color but black for herself.

From the post office in Nicastro, Stella sent a note to Stefano's mother in Sambiase so that Stefano would have the Fortunas' mailing address in America. He had been deployed with the Infantry Division Catanzaro to Africa. During his years in the army, Stefano had written letters periodically, although Stella never wrote back. She didn't know what to say, and besides, her writing would only have been an embarrassment to her. When he'd joined the army, Stefano must have thought he'd be out already by 1939; Stella couldn't believe he had imagined he would be twenty-two and Stella almost twenty and still neither of their futures had come about. Stella prayed for him, but he was so far away, in a place she couldn't contemplate, and her prayers felt empty and directionless. Or maybe it was that her prayers felt tainted—tainted by her secret hope that the army would keep him away indefinitely, that she would never have to be his wife.

Stella did not visit the cemetery the second time she left Ievoli forever. She counted down the days until December 14, when they would catch the train for Napoli, and she kept thinking, *tomorrow, I'll go.* But she didn't.

Napoli was wetly cold in December, damp winds gusting off the open harbor and sticking to the shabby waterfront buildings. Stella felt no wonder this second time in the port city. She had not been able to shake off her sense of hopelessness, that there was still a great thing that was going to go wrong. She was queasy with nerves, thinking about the last attempt they had made, of all hands and souls at the bottom of the sea.

The Fortunas arrived in Napoli on the evening of December 14. They went first thing next morning to the ocean liner's ticket office. The tickets were in order, and the names matched the passports this time.

When the ticket agent showed Stella her visa, she noticed the birthday written next to her name: 12 GENNAIO 1920. She was about to point out the mistake to the agent—her index finger was already hovering over the page—when her heart started pounding crazily in her chest at the idea that she would be the reason, again, that the entire family was turned away. *No, Stella*, she told herself. *No one needs to know.* She had to cough to cover the words that had half emerged from her throat. *"Scusi,"* she said politely.

She didn't say anything to her mother or Cettina about the mistake on her visa, not until they were safely through the immigrant processing at New York Harbor—either of them might have been unable to cope with the news. By then it was already on all of her government-issued paperwork. January 12 was her new American birthday.

After acquiring the tickets, they went to the doctor's office for the medical certificates they would need to board the ship. The line snaked out the door and into the chilly street, but the Fortunas only waited half an hour; the examination was very quick, an inspection of eyes and tongue and a general up-and-down.

In their hotel, they shared the bread Cettina had packed. Cicciu took them out for a walk in the evening, but they were all anxious about getting lost in Napoli, so after ten minutes he brought them back. It was a long, dreary evening. The three women lay head to toe in the sour-smelling bed; Giuseppe and Luigi slept on the floor and made restless sounds all through the dark night. When the knock on the door came before dawn the next morning, Stella was awake, head aching.

It was Cicciu, but he hadn't come to tell them it was time to take their things down to the dock. No—he was holding a newspaper, and his face was red as a cherry pepper. There it was, across the front page—Stella felt like she had been waiting for the headline Cicciu read out to them. Mussolini had halted all transatlantic voyages; the country was preparing for war. No more boats would be departing from Napoli harbor. No more Italians would be allowed to leave.

The ticket office was already thronged with people by the time the Fortunas got there. The clerk would not give anyone their money back, dismissing threats and curses with a weary wave. Everyone needed to settle down, they were trying to see if the ship might be allowed to leave, even though the orders from Rome seemed unambiguous. Hours dragged on and panicked anger stretched into exhaustion. People sat on trunks, strutted, shouted, picked fights. There were some women weeping, although for once Assunta wasn't one of them. Stella watched her mother's shrewd eyes and wondered what she was thinking, if maybe she was hoping to be sent back to Ievoli a second time.

They waited in the drafty ticket hall all day for news. Assunta sat on her trunk, because the varicose veins in her legs, which had never stopped swelling after Luigi was born, were sore from standing. Stella braided and unbraided Assunta's long hair. Luigi was a good boy; he worked off his bored energy walking in laps around the ticket office, and eventually squatted on the floor to nap with his head in his mother's lap. Giuseppe, meanwhile, was nowhere to be found. Stella imagined him running free on the streets of grungy, crime-ridden Napoli. She wondered how far he could possibly get in this city where things cost ten or a hundred times what a person expected them to.

"What if the boat leaves while he's gone?" Cettina said.

"Would serve him right," Stella replied.

When the bells sounded in the piazza outside for evening mass, the ticket agent made everyone leave. "Come back tomorrow!" he shouted over the murmuring, fretful people. "Same time, same place. The boat leaves tomorrow morning, eight o'clock."

Would-be passengers, stupid or intractable with mind-numbed exhaustion, looked dully at one another, trying to decide if they were going to trust and obey. The agent's boys made rounds, shaking dozers awake and repeating the instructions in loud, slow Italian to old people and country bumpkins.

The hotelier checked them back in for another night; luckily he had two rooms, which the Fortunas paid for with the coins the ocean liner agent had given them. Cicciu offered to go out and buy them some food, but Assunta waved him off. She knew he needed what he had to get back to Ievoli. They went to bed early without supper.

"What will we do if the boat doesn't leave tomorrow?" Cettina whispered to Stella. She didn't whisper softly enough, because Luigi's heavily lidded eyes slanted toward his sisters. "We don't have any more money for a hotel for another night."

"Don't worry," Stella said, making her voice deadly serious. "It will be fine, although we might have to sell Giuseppe to the organ grinder."

"The what?" Cettina, always a little late on the pickup, was taken aback.

"You know, the man with the little monkey in the *chiazza*," Stella said.

"Oh, that's terrible, Stella," Cettina said. Stella was rolling her eyes at her sister's obtuseness when Cettina added, "You know Giuseppe is too old to be an organ grinder's boy. We'll probably have to sell Luì instead." The sisters shared a smile as Luigi squealed into his mother's skirt.

For the second night in a row Stella stared at the black ceiling as Cettina and Assunta snored on either side of her. She was jealous of them—they could blubber themselves to sleep when they were tired, knock themselves out like babies with their own intemperate emotions. The blood vessels under Stella's eyes pulsed and her head rang with exhaustion, but God gave her no gift of peace of mind. Instead, hallucinating through the night, she saw an ocean that stretched forever and she imagined a boat breaking to pieces and disappearing into the waves.

* * *

The *Countess of Savoy* sailed at eight o'clock the next morning, one day later than scheduled. It ended up being the last emigrant boat to leave Italy until after the war.

This is what the Fortunas would miss by evacuating Italy when they did.

Six months after they departed, in June 1940, Mussolini would declare war on France and Britain. Before the Italian state crumbled in September 1943, four million Italian troops would be deployed to theaters all over the hemisphere, from Somaliland to Russia; half a million Italians would lose their lives, a third of them civilians.

For the average Italian, this was a time of privation and fear. Soldiers—Mussolini's fascists, American and British "liberators," and then, most cruelly, the German forces that had until 1943 been Italy's allies—took turns occupying countryside villages, including Ievoli, where, one woman hesitatingly told me, "They took advantage of the beautiful daughters." I met a man who was born in 1943, smack in the middle of the six years his father was gone as a soldier, then prisoner, in Russia. "We didn't talk about it," he told me. "My father had to accept that my mother didn't have a choice."

Nonna Maria, at least, would not suffer during the war. She would die only a few months after Assunta left. So would the *ciucciu,* whom no one loved anymore.

In 1956, Cettina would go back to Ievoli, on a trip she and her husband took on their tenth wedding anniversary. When she visited her home village, she was distressed by how changed it felt to her—empty, listless, wounded. She let a cluster of vaguely remembered cousins dress her up in a fancy *pacchiana* and take pictures of her, *Calabrisella bella,* standing in front of the church. Cettina would smile through her disorientation and bring her negatives home to develop and pass around among her Italian American friends.

But Stella would never go back to Ievoli. She would never again see the early-morning sunlight reflecting off the shiny ripening rinds on the lemon tree, the lemons themselves not as lemon-yellow as the sun. She would never again stand in the church *chiazza* and watch the smoking volcano Stromboli appear on the orange horizon at the last moments of sunset. She would never again walk down the fog-thick mountain path after a January cold snap to see steam rising off the ilex trees as the frost evaporated in the wintry Calabrese sun, or worry that a *cinghiale,* a gray-tusked wild boar, might come charging out of the low-lying mist, leading its snorting brown babies to snuffle for bugs and mushrooms among the olive tree roots. She would never again sit on the red earth mound at the top of the olive grove and watch the leaves turn over in the wind, blue-silver green blue-silver.

You step on a boat knowing it is forever, one way or another. But understanding what forever means—that is something your heart tries to protect you from.

The ocean is vast. You and I might forget its formidability; we can close our eyes and cross it in a few hours. For Stella, it was seven days of nothing but water in any direction, of watching anxiously every time a fellow passenger tapped the ash out of his pipe, of thinking about all hands and souls.

On the morning of the seventh day, Stella and Cettina stood at the bow, hands gripping the rail so that they weren't jostled loose by the throngs of people who had collected to see the harbor come into view.

One of the crew chattered to the gathered travelers in fast Italian and Stella struggled to pick out words she understood. A middle-aged man standing near them caught Stella's eye. "You don't have Italian?" he asked in Calabrese.

"Only a little," Stella said. She knew she shouldn't talk to the man, but this felt like a moment she could shrug off rules.

Besides, her mother was far away, hiding from her queasiness in their berth.

The Calabrese man with the gray fedora translated what the prolix young crewman was saying to the crowd. The boat was arriving three hours later than expected; your families who are waiting have been informed. It is Christmas Eve, Merry Christmas, everyone. The Lord has given us the gift of His only begotten son and also of a safe crossing to America. Up ahead on the left you'll be able to see the statue.

"The statue?" Stella and Cettina echoed together.

"The Madonna of New York Harbor. Just wait," the man with the fedora said, then added kindly, "You wouldn't believe me if I told you, anyway."

Of course you know what New York Harbor looks like, can imagine what it looked like in 1939. But now imagine you come from a world where the tallest building is two stories and where glass is used strictly for church windows. Imagine that you have a father who never thought to send you a postcard.

The kind Calabrese man helped with the trunk as they disembarked. He explained what would happen as they progressed through the emigrant processing stations. Here there is a medical exam, but it is short, and there won't be any problems because you've already had an examination back in Napoli. You can all go in together, I'll be right behind you. Here is where we wait to be entered in the register. We'll be here for a little while, just be patient. Your family is waiting on the other side of that wall. Now is when they give you your certificate of arrival. Whatever you do, don't lose that form. You'll need it when you apply for citizenship.

And last, as he left them—his *paesan* from his village was waiting for him in the antechamber—he tipped his hat and said something to them in English. "That means *buon natale*," he said, and winked.

"Say it again," Giuseppe demanded.

The man repeated himself, slowly, and in chorus they answered back: "Me-ri Cris-mas!"

The Fortuna family was feeling buoyant as they stepped into the waiting room, their new U.S. residency papers in hand, happily feverish from a stranger's kindness and eager to start their new life.

But Antonio wasn't there.

Stella searched the crowd of hopeful and tired faces. It had been nine years since she had seen her father, and she had been a child then. She could conjure a strong visceral memory of him, but she wasn't sure she would know what he looked like if she saw him. She glanced at her mother for guidance. Assunta looked worried, but she didn't say anything to her children.

They stood, awkward with their trunk, by the exit door until a young man approached them and, speaking unintelligible English, guided them to the side so they would be out of the way of foot traffic. He wore a neat black shirt and trousers that looked like a military uniform to Stella. Still, Assunta said nothing, not to the man in the uniform, not to her children. Her mother was completely helpless here, a child among her children. Stella's heart twisted, in compassion for her mother and also under the pressure of the idea that if something needed to be done, Stella would have to be the one to do it.

Where was Antonio?

The large clock on the wall, elaborate with filigree, had said three thirty-five when Stella had first checked its time. She watched as the minute hand moved up and then down again. Newly papered United States residents emerged and were absorbed into the tearful hugs or uncertain handshakes of the people who had come to wait for them. On the other side of the wall was New York, but Stella could see nothing of it but the thin white light that came down from the high windows. As she stood still she noticed the chilly air creeping up her arm. It was cold in here, as cold as the middle of a January night in Ievoli. How cold was it outside?

Eventually Cettina managed to settle Assunta on the trunk so that at least her sore legs wouldn't bother her. What would Stella do if Antonio never came? Where would they go? Stella played through possibilities. They had his letter with his address on it. Could they find his house on their own? Would they be able to walk to Hartford? Most likely not, especially now that evening was approaching. They had no money; they couldn't hire someone to take them. They couldn't rent a hotel room for a night. Stella's gut roiled with anxiety and anger. She'd spent her whole life trusting chaperones—now that there was no chaperone she was helpless.

As the clock hand rose again, the man in the militaristic suit crossed the almost empty antechamber toward them. He spoke in English again, pointed at the clock, the doors, and through miming gestures succeeded in communicating that the building would be closing at six. Stella nodded, trying to look competent, and said in her best Italian, "Thank you, mister. We'll wait here until six." Assunta, looking small on the trunk, nodded as well.

The white light at the high-up windows had turned gray, then disappeared. The antechamber was even draftier, and Cettina had nestled into Stella's side so they could share body heat. Luigi and Giuseppe, both of whom the sisters had had to scold for raucousness, were asleep on the floor, heads in Assunta's lap. Stella's feet hurt from standing in her new Nicastro shoes.

Five thirty came and went, and Stella's heart began to pound. One by one the station agents, the doctors and record keepers who staffed the facility, had left, pulling knee-length wool coats over their uniforms and tucking scarves under the lapels as they passed through the antechamber and into the wind whistling outside. At five of six, the black-shirted man came out again and said something to them. Stella, her stomach sutures pulsing with her panic, smiled brightly and nodded. He repeated himself, and so she nodded again. He sighed, and walked back to his office box.

The overhead lights were turned off at six, but the uniformed man kept the light on in his office. The sisters were silent, Cettina trembling but for once keeping her silly mouth shut. Stella stroked her mother's head like a cat's to keep them both calm. She watched the minute hand descend again. There had been an innocent mistake, and Antonio had gotten the day wrong. Antonio had gone to the wrong place and would find them here when he figured out where he needed to go. Antonio was not looking for them. Antonio was dead. Antonio was in jail. The tickets had been a hoax. The journey had been to punish Assunta for being a bad wife and now they would all live homeless in a foreign country. The minute hand passed the six and began its ascent toward the twelve again. Any minute now the guard would kick them out.

It was 7:20 p.m. when Antonio Fortuna finally came to collect his family. He came with another man who looked familiar but whom Stella couldn't place.

"We went to see a movie when we heard the ship was late" was the first thing Antonio said to his wife after not having seen her in almost a decade. "But we got up so early this morning to drive down here that when the lights went out in the movie theater we both fell asleep."

"You must have been so worried," the strange man said. He had a warm face and a friendly-looking mustache. "You poor things."

"This is Zu Tony Cardamone," her father announced. "Your Za Violèt's brother. He's going to drive us home in his car."

Stella and Cettina exchanged glances. Car?

"Zu Tony, you know my wife, Assunta. These are our children. Mariastella, Concettina, Giuseppe, and this must be Luigi." Antonio stooped to look in the brown eyes of the son he had never met. "Luigi. I'm your Papa."

"I know," Luigi said. His face had flamed.

"Are those all the clothes you have to wear? Short pants?" When Luigi, confused, didn't answer, Antonio turned to his wife, his voice rising. "You let him wear short pants in December?"

Assunta didn't reply, either, and Stella could only imagine the disorientation she must be feeling, knowing she had made a mistake but not sure where she'd gone wrong. Stella's gut rippled with anger at her father for humiliating her mother like a child. She swallowed to stop herself from saying anything.

Antonio took off his long coat and wrapped it around Luigi's shoulders. The hem came down to the little boy's ankles. "There," Antonio said. "Hold that closed so you don't catch cold. It's even colder in Hartford."

Dazed and apprehensive, they followed Antonio Fortuna outside and into the darkened park that abutted the harbor. Stella peered through the murk and shadows, trying to see what was different about this place. The air felt hard on her skin, the cold wind so strong her cheeks tingled. Stella shivered and focused on the pain in her feet to keep warm until they reached a plot of land that was full of parked cars, their glass headlights a row of winking eyes in the dim light. Stella was silent in awe, imagining how much money all these cars could be worth.

"We all have to fit in here," Antonio told them. He opened one of the car's doors and pulled out a coil of rope. "Giuseppe, help me tie the trunk on top. Assunta, you get in the front with me and Zu Tony. Stella and Tina, you ride with the boys in the back."

"Cettina," Stella said sharply.

Her father turned to look at her. He knew she was correcting him. "What?"

"She goes by Cettina, not Tina," Stella said, because she knew Cettina herself was going to be too shy to speak up.

"She'll be Tina here," their father said. "Cettina is such an old-fashioned name." He held Stella's gaze with his narrow own, and then, deliberately, let his eyes case her body, sliding down over her hips and then back up to fix on her famous breasts. Stella remembered, suddenly, the night he had pinched her, and she felt an oily bristle run up her torso, tasted a mouthful of bile. "Tina is a better name for an American," Tony said.

As Stella and now-Tina huddled into the cold backseat of the car, Stella understood that she hated her father even more now than she had as a child.

There was so much to see, and yet it was dark. Stella must have fallen asleep. Tina shook her awake as the car descended a hill toward a sparkling clot of tall buildings. "This is Hartford, Papa says."

Electric lamps, tall as trees, hung over the pavement, each bedecked with a ribbon-bound green garland. Stella marveled at the opulence as Tina shook the boys awake to gawp. Was there so much wealth in this city that everyone had electric lights and paved streets? Was one of these tall buildings their house?

"See here," their father said. "See this big store? That's G. Fox. My construction company did renovation work on it last year."

Stella tried to imagine her father having something to do with the arches of glittering glass, the monolithic stonework.

"Is it a church?" Tina asked, staring at the bright lights.

"What?" Antonio guffawed. "No, *stupida,* I told you it's a store. It's the largest department store in the whole country, right here in Hartford." He craned his neck over the passenger's seat to look at Tina. "Why would you think it's a church?"

But Tina had recoiled at being called stupid. Stella didn't speak up, because she was still woozy with sleep, but she knew what her sister had meant. Tall, white-skinned ladies, statues but somehow more alive than statues, stood frozen behind the glowing glass, lit by the most fiery, brightest lights Stella had ever seen. They looked like angels stepping out of boxes of heaven.

It was past midnight, but they stopped at Zu Tony Cardamone's house. Zu Tony's wife, Za Pina, who looked sleepy but was cheerful, had made a huge *antipasti* spread. There were eggplant cutlets, provolone cheese, pickled mushrooms, and oil-cured roasted peppers. There was lots of fish—anchovies and sardines and breaded *baccalà*. It was Christmas Eve, after all. There was a basin of chewy *fettuccine* and extra *raù* Pina had kept hot to pour over the top. This, Stella would learn, was what American Italians ate. This was what made them think of home, although they had never eaten anything like it when they'd lived in Italy.

Stella was ravenous, the dread she'd felt during the endless wait in the New York terminal finally lifted. As soon as she had eaten, she became so sleepy she thought she might sit down right on the fancy cloth-covered chair and sleep through the night. Just as keeping her eyes open had become painful, Antonio herded them back out to the car so Zu Tony could take them to their own new home.

The building they pulled up to was much like Zu Tony's, but the street was darker. They trudged up two flights of mold-flecked stairs, Zu Tony insisting on carrying Assunta's trunk before bidding them all good night. Stella sleepily marveled that this kind man was in any way related to needle-eyed Za Violetta.

Antonio opened one of two doors on the third-floor landing with a long silver key and let them into the drafty apartment that would be their home. He hit a switch on the wall, and electric light illuminated a shabby sitting room. No woman had been here to take care of the things that made life more worth living.

Stella and Tina followed their father down the hallway. "This is your bedroom," he said. "You'll have privacy. Isn't that much better than back home?" Neither of his daughters responded. He pointed out the bathroom, showed them how to use the toilet. "We don't have to share it with nobody. Our own toilet. Just you be careful not to get it clogged up, all right? The plumber is a fortune."

Stella and Tina looked at each other, not knowing what a plumber was, or how to clog a toilet. Stella hoped it was something they could figure out in the morning.

When they were alone in their new bedroom, Stella toed off her shoes and sat on the mattress of the single bed, rubbing one sore foot and then the other. Tina opened the trunk and stared inside, until Stella said, "I'm too tired, little bug. We'll do that in the morning."

"Yes." Tina closed the trunk again, then noticed the curtain. "Oh, Stella! We have a window!" She drew back the curtain and fell so dumbly silent, Stella came to look.

There, three stories below them, leaning up against a chain-link fence with spiked wire on top, were rows—or maybe more like piles—of shanty houses. Lit by a bonfire in the middle of the garbage-filled lot, roofs of rusty scrap metal shone dully among beams of broken wood. Around the fire were dirty people wearing what looked like rags in the bitter cold. Stella thought of the Gypsies in Nicastro, of their bright colors and watchful eyes. She felt sick in her stomach.

"This," Tina said, her breath leaving a fog on the glass. Her voice had caught in her throat. "This is where we live now?"

DEATH 5
Rape (Marriage)

The fifth death began in a dream.

One July morning in 1941, in the hanging lavender of predawn, Stella Fortuna rose from the bed she shared with Tina, leaving her sister to her last minutes of wet late-sleep snoring before their grueling day in the tobacco fields.

Stella took their ceramic washbasin to the kitchen, filled it with warm water, and brought it back to their nightstand. This was the girls' beauty area, safe from the hectic imperialism of the boys' barging and odors. This morning in her dream—for this was a dream—Stella watched her own face in the scuffed blue mirror nailed to the wall above the basin as she guided her washcloth over the areas that needed the most attention. She didn't recognize herself, but that didn't seem strange.

She only realized the man had entered her room when she heard the door tick closed. At first she was annoyed; she wrapped one arm across her breasts and cupped the washcloth between her legs, waiting for the man to apologize and depart. He did not—he stood solidly, his outstretched arms creating a cage between Stella and the door. In that moment, she understood he was not in her room by accident.

Stella called out, "Tina!" The tenement walls, so permeable when her brothers were shouting, seemed to absorb her voice. "Tina!" But Tina was not there—something that would only ever happen in a dream.

The man lifted a finger to his lips. He was a gray shadow in the stingy light, but his black irises were shiny. Stella felt a cool

171

ripple under the skin of her buttocks, where his gaze had fixed. She was helplessly exposed.

Racked by trembles of revulsion, her naked dream body buckled uncontrollably. (In the real world, her sleeping self spasmed, kicking Tina hard in the thigh.) The man crossed the floorboards that separated them, his calloused palms encasing her. The touch was sickening but sensual; Stella felt a tingle of response in her flesh. At the same time, her stomach began to throb, low and tight behind the suture scars. No man with a calloused hand had ever touched her skin like that. How did her dream self know what that touch felt like?

He gripped her shoulder, turning her toward him. She tried to resist, but her limbs were sleep-paralyzed, disobedient. She mashed her concealing arm so tightly against her chest that one of her breasts was forced out from under it. In sickened dismay she saw her areola spring free, her frightened nipple curling inward.

Her fear rallied her. Not bothering to hide her nudity anymore, she shoved him away with all her might. There was nowhere else to go, so she climbed into the window frame. She parted her legs for the shortest possible interval, then quickly crouched into herself, enduring the unfamiliar sensation of air sweeping over her most private skin. The man was shaking his head, stepping toward her again. Everything was wrong, so wrong, perversely wrong. His hands closed around her arm.

Her vision was whited out by panic. She struck out and lost her balance, felt herself tumble sideways. Her chin hit the floor and her jaw jammed up into her skull, teeth singing with the reverberation. The hands tightened, and she screamed. The world was invisible; she could only feel—hands on her arms, then her leg, the beads of blood rising, the bruises beginning to form. The dream shattered. She was awake.

The dim early morning in the bedroom was the exact same lavender it had been in her dream; Stella's senses stuttered. *"Tina!"* Her father's bellow. *"What the hell are you doing?"*

Above her, curling rags ringing her sister's swollen face. The fallen rod on the floor by her legs; one blue cotton curtain threaded through the two sisters' arms.

Stella felt her shoulder muscles constrict around the pain in her socket. She realized the hands clenching her arm were not the dream-rapist's but her sister's, gripping so fiercely she left white ovals in the shiny pink of Stella's burn scar. Stella reached up to touch her jaw, and the skin leapt with fiery tenderness.

Her father's silhouette crossed the shadowy room. "You little bitch." He hooked his elbow around Tina's neck and Tina went careening toward the wall, catching herself against the bed just in time to receive the back of his hand across her face. "Little whore. What the hell were you thinking?"

Tina sobbed, incoherent. Stella lay dazed on the floor by the window, her body surveying its various pains: the bruises on her arm, her tailbone, her cheek; the bleeding open skin in her gums; the torn feeling in her shoulder. Their father loomed, enraged as ever, waiting, exhaling wet, irregular breaths into his mustache. Long seconds passed as Tina gasped and coughed into her nightgown. She was not going to answer.

Antonio turned on Stella. "What the hell is going on?"

Stella pushed herself up to feel the flat safety of the wall against her back. She tasted blood, and located with her tongue the fissures where teeth had been.

"She tried to push you out the window?"

Tina's head popped up, and she lifted an arm to protect her teary face. "No, Papa, she was trying to jump out the window. She was going to kill herself. I was just—"

"You shut up!" Antonio was leonine, roaring, his curling hair wild in shadowy silhouette. "Stella, I asked you did she try to push you out the window? You were fighting?"

Stella's stomach rippled, a residue of the trapped feeling from her dream. "No." Speaking was difficult; her mouth was swelling fast. "No, Papa, it was a dream."

"A dream? A *dream*?"

Stella swallowed a mouthful of blood. "A bad dream." She felt the burly arms closing around her naked rib cage again. "There was a . . . a bad man, and I was trying to get away."

"She was going to jump out the window, and I stopped her," Tina put in. "She was about to fall, and I pulled her back down."

From Antonio's disgusted expression, Stella could tell he didn't quite believe them. "What kind of idiot are you, Stella?" he said finally, still loud enough to be heard down the hall. "You going to kill yourself over a bad dream?"

A sunflower of yellow fury burst in her mind, and she blurted, "A man came into this room to rape me, Papa." The word "rape" had the effect she intended; Antonio's forehead tightened in a fur of eyebrows. She stood, pulling down her nightgown and rubbing her sore shoulder. "I was scared to death. I have a right to get away from a man who's trying to rape me."

Stella could see that Antonio was turning this over. She forced herself to meet his eye steadily.

"Ah, *mannaggia*." If he was swearing, the violence was over. "What was all the screaming?"

"That was Stella," Tina said. "That's what woke me up, thanks to God, or I wouldn't have seen her about to fall out the window."

Assunta came into the tiny bedroom then, her field kerchief already knotted over her hair. "What's happening? What's the matter?"

Tina had conquered her tears. "Stella dreamed she got raped, Ma. She tried to jump out the window."

"Raped?" Her mother's voice was shrill enough to cut through Stella's nausea.

"It was a dream, Ma."

"Who was it?" Assunta was patting Stella on her shoulder and breasts, verifying she was still intact.

"Yes, who was it?" Tina echoed.

The sisters' eyes caught like magnets. The sparkle in Tina's eyes struck Stella as lascivious. She averted her gaze, stared into her lap at the bruised heel of her left hand. This was the kind of conversation that could escape her control.

"Who was it?" Tina said again. She had never been artful in her voyeurism. "Was it a colored man?"

At the words "colored man" the dream appeared again in Stella's mind's eye. She saw the rapist's dark eyes flashing, the stretch of flannel over his shoulders. And the words were right there; it was so easy to deflect the truth, she did what so many other Italian Americans before and after her have done: she blamed a black man. "Yes," she said. "A colored man."

"Who?" Excited, Tina knelt beside Stella, clasping her shoulders. "Was it the delivery man from the shop?"

"Was it one of the Jamaicans from the truck?" her mother suggested. "Was it that man Donny?"

"No." Stella felt sick enough already from this ordeal; she didn't want to think about what would happen if her mother and sister fixed on a name for the imaginary culprit. "Just some regular colored man."

Antonio began to shout again. "You're never to talk to colored men. If I catch—"

"*Papa!*" The room fell silent at her shout, and Stella was relieved. She was on the verge of vomiting. "Get out of our room. We have to get ready for work now, or we'll miss the truck."

For a moment, Antonio looked like he might raise his hand to show her what speaking like that to her father got her. Instead he turned for the door, and Assunta followed, sniffling faithfully. As Tina closed the door behind them, their father called, "I'm gonna nail that window shut."

As the sisters stood near the blue mirror, Tina dabbing at the cut on Stella's cheek with the wet washcloth, Tina whispered, "Tell me the truth, Stella. Who was it? Was it Donny?"

"I don't know who it was, Tina," Stella lied. "Stop asking."

She dressed as quickly as possible, trying not to feel the rapist's eyes on her naked back. What she didn't tell Tina was that the man in the dream—a dream she would relive again and again over the next decade, a dream that would terrorize her sleeping patterns and haunt her waking relationships—the man in that dream who had pinned her naked in the bedroom window hadn't been a colored man at all. It had been her father.

That was the fifth time Stella Fortuna almost died—that was the time she almost committed suicide by jumping out of a third-story window.

The first time Stella had the nightmare was in the summer of 1941, eighteen months after she arrived in Hartford. Those eighteen months had been the easiest and the hardest of Stella's life.

Tony Fortuna, as he was known here, lived in a tenement apartment in downtown Hartford, not the house he had promised his wife. The apartment consisted of a living room; a kitchen with a gas stove, which had to be explained; and three narrow bedrooms. There was no garden anywhere on the street—nowhere to grow tomatoes. Assunta had to buy them from the peddlers who parked their wooden carts along Front Street.

Tony said the tenement arrangement was temporary. There was a house he was going to buy on Bedford Street, in a nicer part of the Italian East Side. The owner, an old Napolitano, had promised to give Antonio two years to save up the agreed-upon two thousand dollars. "He likes me," Antonio said. "He trusts me."

In some ways America was better than Ievoli, even if it wasn't what Stella had been imagining. In the bathroom was a toilet with a flush; water was somehow pumped all the way up to the third floor and swirled everything away. They ate meat twice a week—Tony insisted. Assunta had no experience with cooking meat; she had never eaten beef in her life before arriving in America. Pina Cardamone, Zu Tony's wife, accompanied the

Fortuna women to the frightening huge grocery store and showed them how to pick from the pink and red orgy of dead flesh at the butcher counter. Za Pina taught Assunta and Tina how to pan-fry a beefsteak and oven-fry pounded chicken cutlets. At first the meat menus were nerve-racking—one small mistake would ruin the whole expensive piece, and Assunta cooked in fear of Tony taking the strap to her. But she acclimated. She was an excellent cook, because she liked to eat and knew how to taste. Tina was another natural cook and would make some man a good wife—Za Pina liked to repeat that, especially and pointedly in Stella's hearing. Stella smiled and waved Za Pina off—she didn't let the teasing get to her. But she wasn't going to fry a beefsteak no matter how many blood vessels Za Pina burst trying to teach her.

The other *zia* who came over to give them lessons was Filomena Nicotera. She tried to coach the Fortunas through her U.S. citizenship handbook; she and her husband, Zu Aldo, ran a delivery service and their English was very good. She was frequently accompanied by her daughter, Carolina, who was sixteen. Carolina Nicotera had a pointy chin and flashing dark eyes, which she rolled in an American fashion at her pushy mother. Carolina bundled Stella and Tina up in woolly scarves and took them on excursions along Front Street, teaching them the rules. She brought them a bottle of nail polish and showed them how to cut their cuticles.

Luigi was enrolled in an American school. Schooling was mandatory here until age sixteen—Stella couldn't even imagine what children could study for that long. Luì was so small that it was months before he realized he was two years older than most of his second-grade classmates. He was "Louis Fortuna" now, but in American, the nickname "Louie" sounded just like what they had always called him anyway.

The winter in Hartford was like nothing Stella had ever imagined. It snowed almost every day, fat white clusters so heavy-looking, Stella couldn't understand why it took them so long to fall out of the sky. From their drafty bedroom the girls watched a burly ragged man with a plywood board sweep snow off the buckling roofs of the shanties in the back lot.

Closed off in the dingy little apartment, Stella sought distractions from her intense homesickness. She was cold and miserable and she missed her grandmother, her *ciucciu,* her sweet little house on the top of the mountain. Her chest ached with longing—sometimes her throbbing heart felt so sore she would have to lie down to catch her breath. But she couldn't let her mother or siblings know. If she didn't hold it together, none of the others would be able to, and she'd be blunting their progress into their new life. She corralled her brothers into playing card games at the kitchen table, where it was warmer than the sitting room. She organized Assunta and Tina into crocheting blankets with her to supplement the meager cotton ones Tony had on the beds. She tried to keep them all chatting so their minds wouldn't dwell on what they'd left behind; when she couldn't think of anything to talk about, she sang songs Nonna Maria had taught her, hoping her mother and sister would join in; if her throat was too constricted to sing, she hummed.

The cold was unrelenting, and noses were always running. Stella learned about the unrelievable misery of chapped nostrils, endemic in Hartford in February and March. The air was not the same air she had breathed in Ievoli—it pierced her lungs and her throat when she inhaled. It carried illnesses the Fortunas had never suffered before—coughing that sounded like the barking of a dog; sweating fevers that lasted for four days, head-clouding pain behind the eyes. Strangers coughed their diseases into the air at church, on the bus, in the streets, filling the wind with the malice of their individual suffering.

None of the Fortuna children owned clothing that was warm enough. Their first month, January 1940, was a parade of visits from cousins and *paesan,* people Tony knew from Sacred Heart

Church and the Italian Society. Women brought bags of old clothes, coats, mittens, sweaters. Wearing secondhand dresses made Stella concentrate on how much her life had changed. The fabrics had been stitched together by machines, sized to fit someone else; they were tight around the shoulders or long in the arms. They were old, something someone else had thrown away, but they were still nicer than anything she had owned.

In the nine years since the Fortunas had last seen Tony, Assunta and her children had been poor but free; now they were prisoners of his will and whims. Tony had all the money; he was the only one who could speak English; he controlled every aspect of their lives.

Stella had never taken to being controlled by anyone, ever since she was a little girl and had told her Za Violetta she didn't respect her. Stella Fortuna was a grown-up woman now but clung to the same basic beliefs about who was worth her respect. Her father did not meet the requirements. He drank, he shouted, he was secretive about his comings and goings.

"What did you bring us here for?" Stella would shout at her father during their many rows. She fought back her fear of him and gave him lip whenever she could, for the sake of morale. "You lock us up all day like prisoners. You took us away from our home, our *paese,* our *nonna,* our relatives and friends, why? What was it all for?"

Antonio never answered her question. He would smack her face or her ass and tell her to shut up. Or he would say offhandedly, "If you like it so much better there, why don't you go back?" But of course that wasn't an option. Italy was at war; the Fortunas had escaped just in time.

Tony's presence made them all nervous. Assunta would crack her children on the behind with her fat wooden spoon if they broke one of her rules, but it was dispassionate justice and they always knew they deserved it. Tony's justice was mystical and anything but dispassionate, especially when he was drinking.

There was relief on the two nights a week, on average, that Tony didn't come home at all.

The first time was in late January, when Assunta and her children had been living in Hartford for four weeks. Assunta had fixed supper and they'd waited for Tony. When he hadn't come home by nine o'clock, Assunta gave up and served the cooled pasta. The children ate quickly. When the boys had cleaned their plates, Stella sent them to bed. Normally Giuseppe would have made trouble, but tonight they just filed out, taking the kitchen radio with them.

"Where's Papa?" Tina asked again when the boys were gone— she had asked four times already, as if Stella knew anything more than she did.

She suppressed her irritation with her sister. This wasn't Tina's fault.

"Don't worry about Papa," Stella said. "I'm sure he's fine. He's a big man." She watched her mother eat the last pieces of macaroni. Assunta's cheeks were wet, but her eyes were small and angry. Stella picked at her ugly memory from the summer when she was nine years old—watching as her father mounted her mother from behind, grunting like an animal. She shut the memory off before it could run its full course. How had this man, with such manly appetites, made do in the decade he'd spent away from his wife? The thing Stella must have already known in the back of her mind clicked into place, and any sense of worry vanished.

Tina was looking at her with that willfully stupid expression. She was waiting for Stella to tell her what to think, how to feel.

Stella stood. "Tina, why don't you go wash the plates now?"

"But what about Papa?"

"Papa can feed himself when he gets home." Stella squeezed past her father's empty chair. "Never mind, stay there. Sit," she warned her mother, who had started to rise. Stella had an idea.

Shivering with nerves—she had never done something like this before—she took down three short glasses from the cupboard and the jug of her father's wine from the sideboard. She set the glasses on the table and filled them nearly to the brim.

"There," she said.

Her sister and her mother were looking at her expectantly. She knew what they were thinking—*What is this? We don't do this*—because this was what men did, drinking after dinner, like smoking a pipe. Stella passed a glass to Tina and took one for herself. *"Salut',"* she said. She waited until the other women lifted their glasses, still watching her with misgiving. *"Salut',"* Stella said again, and took as large a swallow as she could. Almost immediately she felt better, as if the wine were a calming medicine.

"Salut'," Assunta echoed, and took her own large gulp. With no reason left not to, Tina followed suit.

Late into the night the women drank and played *briscola*. The tension eased as the wine opened up their respective angers and affections. Stella noted the feeling of the drunkenness setting in, reveling in it as the cards became harder to count and their mistakes became increasingly funny. The dining room had ceased to feel uncomfortably cold; she now appreciated the draft, which rippled sensuously up her arms. So this is why they drink, she thought. This happy softness.

"I don't care if he wants to go see a *putana*," Assunta said between deals. She hadn't cried since they started on the wine. "Oh, Madonn', you think I'm jealous of what some other woman is having done to her?"

Stella would never have been able to say the words sober, but here they were, tumbling out of her mouth: "What's it like, Mamma? When he does the job to you?"

Assunta waved her hand, dispelling the unpleasant thought. "Oh, just a big hassle, you know? Part of being a wife. You gotta be there for him when he wants to do it, doesn't matter how you're feeling, and then sometimes it makes a baby." Assunta was staring at the table, her eyes glazed, but she kept speaking, candidly—Stella tried not to move a muscle, afraid that any disruption would make her mother clam up. "And even if you think to yourself, we have enough babies, I don't want to be pregnant again, you can't say no to your husband."

The candle on the table between them flickered. Stella's heart was racing. Her imagination was damply alive with the alcohol and she couldn't stop a progression of visions, putting herself in her mother's place.

Tina was watching her mother with wide eyes. "Does it hurt?" she blurted.

"No, it doesn't hurt," Assunta said. "Not all the time. Only when you really don't want to. Or sometimes it hurts when he drinks too much, or if it takes a long time." Stella's mother wrinkled her chapped nose. "The best husbands are the ones who finish the job fast, and whose *pistola* isn't so big, so they don't hurt as much." She shrugged, her sheepishness overtaking her alcoholic immunity. "But you can't know that before you get married. You just have to take your chances."

Stella gulped down a glass of wine. She hoped she'd already taken all the chances she was going to have to in her life.

By the time they finished the bottle, they were too drunk to play cards anymore. It was one in the morning and Antonio still hadn't come home. Stella and Tina helped their mother, giggling sleepily, to her bed, then huddled together in their own—the cold had seeped in again through the filmy wine-warmth. The girls whispered to each other in the dark. Tina's breath was sweet and sour and thick; Stella wondered if her own was the same. Would Antonio beat them when he found out what they'd done? Why had he left to be with a *putana* when his wife was right here? Should Stella be happy he wasn't bothering Assunta, or offended he had broken God's law and chosen another woman over his wife? How grotesque, to know your husband was also doing grotesque things to another woman. Did that other woman also have his children for him?

Stella thought about the money Tony must spend to keep a *putana*. How much sooner might he have brought his family to America if he had saved that money—if he'd really wanted them there?

The darkness shrank and bulged around her. Stella was full of the memory of that hot summer night in Ievoli, of Antonio's naked ass thumping into Assunta's pushed-up skirts. She felt the pinch in her groin, the blood rising under her father's fingernails. Stella felt sick to her stomach—a mixture of the wine, the memory itself, the indignity her sweet mother had endured because she owed her obedience to a brute . . . Stella realized her thighs were throbbing; she was clenching them tightly together. That was never going to happen to her. Never.

Spring broke on 1940. Along the Fortunas' walk to and from mass, the trees were still naked, but gray, dry bushes burst into yellow flowers, root to tip. Forsythia—they were everywhere, living wildly roadside or manicured into thick, square hedges that separated the houses. Stella would learn that forsythia was how you knew winter was over in Connecticut. The spring air was still colder than Christmas back home, and Stella couldn't believe the flowers didn't die. But they didn't, and they were followed by more.

Home in Ievoli, Stella thought, the camellias and the daffodils would be blooming. She hoped someone picked a bouquet for Nonna Maria, who loved their smell.

There was a problem with the house Antonio was going to buy on Bedford Street. Although he'd been promised a terrific deal, there was no way he would ever have the two thousand dollars he needed. He made no mention of money he'd already saved before bringing his family to Hartford; Stella was certain no such money existed. He made eighteen dollars a week working his construction job. The rent on the Front Street tenement was six dollars a week; one dollar went into the church basket at mass. Five dollars went into the grocery jar on the kitchen counter. Even if Antonio was putting the remaining six dollars in the bank, which Stella doubted, he would only be able to save three hundred dollars a year.

His wife and children would have to find jobs.

This was how Assunta, Stella, Tina, and Giuseppe found their way to the tobacco farm in the summer of 1940. Antonio's friend Vito Aiello had worked there when he'd first arrived in the country, tenting and harvesting large-leaf shade tobacco, the kind they use for fancy cigar wrappers. In April, Antonio brought Zu Vito over for dinner to explain how it would work. They'd catch a truck on Farmington Avenue and it would take them to and from the farm, which was outside Hartford in the countryside. The tobacco season ran from May through August. Anyone could show up for fieldwork; as long as you did a good job your first day, they let you come back again.

Tina cried in bed that night, little hiccuping sobs. Stella was swimming through her own confusion and dismay, thinking of the oranges she would be harvesting back home. She let Tina cry for a while, imagining the tears were tapering off, but they never did. Finally, tamping down her own nasty thoughts, Stella stroked Tina's long hair and said, "Don't be upset, little bug. Come on, stop crying. You'll wear yourself out."

Tina coughed to clear her teary throat. "I thought we were going to live real nice here," she said. "We were going to live in a nice house, have nice clothes. But instead he made us give up our own house and come live where we have to share with other people, and he made us give up our own land and come work on someone else's farm like *cafoni*."

This was all true. Stella stroked her sister's hair quietly for a few minutes. Don't waste sadness on the problem, she scolded herself. Sadness is weak. Think of how to fix the problem, instead.

"We're not *cafoni*," Stella said. "It's the opposite. Anyone can own land here in America. Yes, we're going to work in a field, but then we'll have money to buy our own house. All right? Forget Papa. We're going to work hard and buy a house for Mamma."

Tina's blubbering had stopped. Stella guessed what her sister must be thinking—how surprising, the idea that girls like them, Tina and Stella, could buy a house. They had worked for chestnuts and olive oil, but they had never worked for money before.

"You really think we can buy a house?" Tina said eventually.

"We're going to work really hard," Stella said. "You know how good we are at working hard, little bug. We can do it."

"We can do it, Stella," Tina repeated. "We'll buy Mamma a house."

Each day, in the twilight before dawn, Assunta, Stella, Tina, and Giuseppe walked down to Farmington Avenue and waited with the other day laborers until the tobacco truck came; then everyone climbed up the metal steps to the flatbed and sat thigh to thigh on the splintering benches, clinging to their neighbors. The truck carried them out of Hartford on a wide, painted highway, then along narrower streets lined with magnificent houses, one after another, as if everyone here were some kind of minor nobility. And then on to the shade-leaf tobacco farms, acres of thin cotton tenting stretched between eight-foot-high stakes. In the summer breeze, the dark green leaves, wide as your hand, beat gently against the cloth cage, dancing shadows you could see from the road.

The sun would just be rising as the laborers were sorted into field hands and stitchers. The fieldwork involved pulling weeds, mending tents, and harvesting mature leaves, ten hours under the beating summer sun. The air was heavier and wetter here than it had been in Ievoli, and amplified the discomfort of the heat. The shade under the tobacco tents was no relief, it was so stifling and humid. Stella's and Tina's smooth pink cheeks burned so badly the skin cracked and peeled off in itchy sheets. Stella learned to look out for little green snakes in the dirt and for thin-legged brown spiders, sometimes as big as her palm, nesting near the holes in the netting, where the bug hunting was best.

In the barns, the leaf-stitching team sorted through the baskets brought in for drying and separated the leaves by size. Each leaf was strung into a graduated stack that would later roll into a single cigar. The foreman, who was courteous to the older ladies, never selected Assunta to do fieldwork, which was a blessing, what with her varicose veins.

Everyone else waiting for the truck in the morning was black. Stella was scared almost out of her wits the first day to be surrounded by black people, and none of the Fortunas would have gotten on the truck if Vito hadn't been there with them.

"Just keep your hands and your eyes to yourself and they won't bother you," Vito told them. "Joe, you can take care of your mother and sisters, right?"

"Yes, sir," Giuseppe said, although he was more of a symbolic chaperone. He was seventeen and still boyishly slender.

Fortunately, many of the black people were women, which was much less worrisome than being surrounded by black men, whom Antonio had warned his wife and daughters to be very afraid of, although Stella thought if it had really been so important to her father that their virtue not be subjected to strange men, maybe he shouldn't have made them go to work in the fields in the first place. Many of the women were friendly and tried to chat with Assunta and the girls. Some of the black ladies were not Americans, either, Stella learned. They were Jamaicans, from an island they said was hotter than the hottest day of Connecticut summer.

"You make test?" Stella asked two of the ladies in the English Za Filomena had taught her. She never learned their names. "For *sitizenscippu*?"

They shook their heads. They were only in America for the summer. When the tobacco season was over, they'd go back to their hot island. "That's home, and we love it."

Stella indulged in a short, jealous fantasy in which she would sail home to Ievoli at the end of the tobacco season. "Then why you come here? If you just go back home."

The ladies laughed. "Money, girl," the thinner one said. "Same as you."

The money in question was sixty cents a day per person, two quarters and a dime. The foreman paid them as they boarded the truck at the end of the day. Zu Vito had warned them they'd be easy robbery targets when they got off the truck in Hartford at sunset, obviously coming home from day labor, so they walked quickly and kept their eyes down. When they'd made it safely to the Front Street tenement, they filed through the kitchen and dropped their coins into a washed-out bean can on the narrow shelf where Assunta had perched the photo of the first Stella. When all the Fortunas had made their daily deposit in the bean bank, Stella counted up the total, making a tally mark for each accrued dollar on a paper ledger she tucked in the can. She kept the can where they could all see it to inspire them; she maintained the ledger as ostentatiously as she did so that Giuseppe—or Joey, as he was going by now—would know he couldn't steal from it for candy or cigarettes.

On Friday night after dinner, Stella and Tina stacked the week's quarters and dimes and rolled them into the paper wrappers the bank gave out. There were forty quarters in a ten-dollar deposit roll, and every week the Fortunas made at least one such roll. Five-dollar rolls of dimes were rarer accomplishments, a roll every other week. On Saturdays, while her children worked a sixth day at the tobacco farm, Assunta went to the bank to make the weekly deposit in their house savings account.

The whole cycle should have been miserable, toiling away in the sun to save money for the house they'd thought their father had already bought them. But . . . no. That sound of the coins echoing hollowly in the empty can, less and less hollowly as the can filled—it had become Stella's favorite sound. Assunta and her children were buying themselves their own house. They were a little army led by a haphazard but lovable general, and together they were taking care of business.

Start to finish, the tobacco season lasted four months, and by the beginning of September there was no more work. Then Stella and Tina were back to being stuck in the Front Street apartment all day.

To make matters worse, the news that Nonna Maria had died finally reached Hartford. It came in a letter from Antonio's younger brother Zu Egidio, who wrote to relate his intentions to emigrate to Australia, and who in passing offered condolences. Maria must have died months earlier; Za Violetta had not gotten around to sending them a letter.

As one would expect, the news was debilitating for Assunta. She had been sure that by leaving Ievoli she had written her mother's death sentence, and now her guilt was irrefutable. She vacillated between silent, sobbing prayer and hysterical anger. In her grief, Assunta's awe of her husband vanished. She blamed Tony for snatching her away in a time of need. She shouted into his face, and when he struck her to silence her she shouted more. The neighbors downstairs banged on their ceiling when the fighting got too loud; the blond-bunned woman who lived on the other side of the third-floor landing came over armed with a rolling pin to say she'd appreciate it if "you screaming wops" could keep it down. Assunta did not care about being called a wop, but Tony did, and it made him even angrier.

Stella wanted to comfort her mother, to mourn and pray for Nonna Maria together, but she wasn't going to step into the battle between her parents. Instead, she and Tina hid in their bedroom, crocheting and watching the shantytown dwellers move among their bonfires. Stella crossed her eyes at the dismal façades of the tenements behind the *sciantinas,* pretending that beyond them on the obscured horizon was her little mountain overlooking the marina, that in a stone house at the little mountain's peak there was a bowl of fresh olives, just harvested, sitting on the table and waiting for her to bite into their tender green flesh. Stella thought of the first Mariastella. With Nonna Maria gone, there would be no one left to remember the baby or to clean her grave.

Stella also received a letter from Stefano's mother in Sambiase. Stefano was still away in Africa. She begged Stella to send a letter she could save for him.

Stella was torn between guilt at not having written—she owed it to Stefano; he had no other girl to write to him while he was at war—and misgivings about not knowing what to say to this man she had realized she would never marry. In the end she had little Louie, who had learned good penmanship in the American school, write a message for her. *Dear Signora, We are praying for Stefano every day, and for your family. We are well here but we are working hard and we think of our family in Calabria. We send you our best wishes. Sincerely, Stella Fortuna.*

After that, the war must have become more difficult, or perhaps the censorship was stopping communication, because the Fortunas had no other letters for a long time.

Stella and Tina were only trapped in their dingy tenement room for a few weeks before they found another job. One of their new friends from the Italian Society, a sweet, thin Pugliese girl named Fiorella Mulino, had found jobs for them in a laundry on Front Street. It was no good for Joey, because they only hired women, or for Assunta, who couldn't be on her feet for ten hours, but

Stella and Tina arrived with Fiorella the first Monday of October and the manager let them stay. They were put in Fiorella's group, ironing and starching, up on the second floor.

Instead of paying a day wage like the tobacco farms, the laundry paid by the piece, which put a kind of performance pressure on their employment. Stella liked it. Each shirt starched and ironed was worth two cents. After a frustrating first day, she got the knack—dipping the shirt, stretching it across the board, pressing and alternating irons. She experimented with stroke rotations to permeate the heat more quickly and evenly through the cloth. She could fit four or even five shirts in an hour, and sometimes came home with eighty or ninety cents a day.

Tina, on the other hand, did not respond well to the time pressure. She was a person who liked to do things thoroughly—whatever anyone else did, Tina did it more, and harder. For example, she had once washed Assunta's good ceramic pitcher so energetically that the handle had broken off in her hand. This aggressive task approach did not combine well with the anxiety of counting accomplishments against the clock; under pressure, Tina could not harness the required finesse. The first time she got in trouble was for a shirt so stiffly starched it had to be rolled to crack it, then sent down to the first floor and rewashed. Tina starched for four days, her face an arterial pink and streaming sweat, which descended her jaw like tears and spattered the bosom of her dress. On the fourth day, she overcompensated for her slowness by pressing too hard on the shirt she was ironing, leaving a devastating iron-shaped burn mark. The manager was enraged, but yelling at Tina was never any good, because she sobbed so thoroughly—as thoroughly as she scrubbed pitchers—that after a while you felt stupid yelling and ended up doing whatever you could to get her to stop. So Tina was sent home at three o'clock with no pay; she wasn't fired, although it took Stella all evening to convince Tina she hadn't been. Stella didn't tell her sister that she'd given the manager the seventy-four cents she'd earned that day to pay for the ruined shirt so he wouldn't count it against her little sister. Tina could come back to work the next day, but she had to be on the washing team on the first floor, with the Polish ladies. That was less desirable work to the Italian girls, but at least Tina couldn't accidentally ruin anything in the washing room. Maybe with her vigor she'd be able to get some of the tougher stains out.

Seeing his daughters had a taste for work, Tony harassed them to study English harder. He tried to impress them with the fiscal advantage of having papers—if they naturalized, they could apply for factory jobs. "I make five times as much money as you in one week," he said.

But the citizenship test was an insurmountable obstacle. Stella and Tina took turns carrying the study book around, but after months of turning the pages it was no more legible than it had been in the beginning. With much concentration, Stella could sound out the English words and guess their meanings, but Tina had had so little schooling in Ievoli that she could barely remember how any of the letters were supposed to sound even in Italian, never mind in this strange foreign language where nothing sounded the way it looked. Ten months in the United States had given them only a little English. They were surrounded by Italian speakers. Stella was shy of her accent; even when there was a chance to speak to an American—say, at the store—she found herself doubting words she'd been sure of a moment before, and resorted to pointing or blurting out Italian instead.

Nevertheless, she quizzed her sister like she used to for catechism. "You know this one," she'd say, then read in English, 'Where is the Statue of Liberty?'"

"I don't know," Tina said hopelessly.

"Yes, you do! You saw it yourself." Stella raised her arm and made a fist in the air, like the green lady with the torch. She repeated in slow English, "Statue of Liberty."

"New York!" Tina smiled. She got one!

" 'What is the name of the President?' " Stella read out carefully.

A pause for thought. "Rosa Vela," Tina answered. This meant "pink sail" in Italian, which Stella had thought up so Tina could remember Roosevelt's name. "Picture a fancy boat with pink sails," Stella had suggested. "It's so fancy the President sails on it."

But then things became very opaque, and the book's answers didn't help the girls understand the questions.

" 'Why does the American flag have thirteen stripes?' " Stella spread the book between them so Tina could see the picture of the flag.

"What is 'stripes'?"

"*Strisce.*" Stella pointed to the alternating white and gray in the sketch. Tina was silent. "It says here there are thirteen stripes because there are thirteen 'colonies.' "

"What is 'colonies'?"

"You know, like *colonia*," Stella said. "Cologne, perfume." This didn't seem right, but it was the best she had for Tina. "Maybe America has thirteen famous perfumes?"

The questions only got harder, full of words Stella had never even heard the Italian equivalent of. Who wrote the Declaration of Independence. How can an American participate in their democracy. What is the role of Congress. Under our Constitution, what powers are given to the federal government. How many times has the Constitution been amended. It was very hard to help Tina memorize the answers when Stella couldn't explain what the questions were asking.

Fiorella Mulino reminded them she had passed the citizenship test by attending night school at Hartford High. Classes were free; they started at seven, so you could come after work.

Stella disliked the idea of night school and would have preferred to keep trying to memorize the book on her own. She loathed putting herself in any situation where her weaknesses were on display; she also didn't relish the nightly walk out of their ghetto of *paesan*, past the shantytowns and dark alleys of lurking strangers.

"I'll escort you," Fiorella offered. "Stella, you're clever, you might be able to pass on your own, but Tina won't, no matter what you do, you know that. And if you go with her to the classes maybe you can help her catch up." She smiled slyly. "Plus, you might meet some nice boys."

"Oh, Madonn'." Stella clasped her hands and rolled her eyes heavenward in supplication. "Please don't put that idea in Tina's head."

The first class they went to was on a Tuesday in mid-November. It hadn't occurred to Stella and Tina to change out of the sweat-stiffened dresses they'd worn all day at the laundry, but after they saw how smartly some of the immigrants dressed up for class, they followed suit. The classes were boring and confusing, just like school had always been, only worse because now it was in English. Stella was often tired after a ten-hour day standing over the ironing board. But she went, feeling nagged and guilty about the money she could be earning if only she could get a better job.

Joey, who was working part-time as a janitor at the Italian Society, didn't seem to worry about his U.S. citizenship. But in general Joey didn't worry about anything. That was his gift. Sparkly brown eyes; bright, straight teeth when he smiled; and not a care in the world.

After their first American Thanksgiving, which they celebrated with the Nicoteras, Carolina talked Stella and Tina into cutting their hair. "You want to get it like this." She reached up and patted her own curls, which radiated from her head like saints' halos in church paintings. "And you want to get a permanent wave, if you can, so that you don't have to mess around with curling rags every night."

"Our father likes us to wear it long," Stella told Carolina. Tony had the notion that women with short hair were loose. They could move faster, dance more energetically without worrying about pins flying around.

"But he always says how he wants you to be real Americans," Carolina said pointedly. "Make him look around. All the American girls have short hair. The only girls with long hair are the country girls."

Stella knew what she meant by "country girls." There were some Italian families on Front Street who lived strictly, raising their daughters the way things had been back home—ankle-length skirts, veils, arranged marriages. Tony Fortuna had his rules and became explosive if they were disobeyed, but he didn't make the girls cover their faces to go to mass. Stella thought he was smart not to impose that kind of embarrassing stricture on his family; after all, they had lived most of their lives without him, and he didn't want to put himself in a position where they might stand up to him. He was a disgusting person, in Stella's opinion, but a wily despot.

Stella and Tina talked it over that night as they were combing out before bed. It was weird to think about parting with all that hair—the marker of their femininity. But Stella didn't want to be lumped in with the "country girls" anymore. Of course, Tina would do whatever Stella did.

The conversation with Tony began much as expected. "Papa, Tina and I want to cut our hair," Stella said during dinner that Sunday.

"Absolutely not," he said. "Women in this house dress respectfully."

"But Papa, you say you want us to be American. No American woman wears her hair long. Everyone will think we're . . . we're poor and new here."

Stella had been prepared for a protracted argument, but after several moments of hard thought, Antonio seemed ready to reverse his opinion.

"Yes," he said. "You're right. Short hair is better for life in America."

That seemed too easy. Stella watched his face to try to guess what kinds of private thoughts were passing behind it. "So you'll give us money for the hairdresser's?"

"All right," he said. "All right. You girls will cut your hair and then we should get a family portrait taken. That's what we will send home at Christmas." He slapped his thighs. "One year as Americans. Yes, we should take a portrait."

Her father had a vision in his head. Stella decided to press her luck. "Tina and I need five dollars each."

Antonio turned to look at her. His face was turning red, and she braced herself, but then he started to laugh. "If that's how much the hairdresser costs, you can figure out how to cut your own hair."

"No, Papa, it's for the permanent wave. We need to go and get it professionally done. They have to put chemicals in your hair to make it—"

"Absolutely no permanent wave. *Mannaggia,* give them a finger and they take your whole hand." Antonio had returned his attention to his food. "I'll tell you what, I'll give you each two dollars. You, too," he said to the boys. "You spend it on what you want, haircut, clothes, whatever. Just make sure you look good for the picture."

Two weeks before Christmas all six Fortunas dressed in their best and went down to G. Fox to get studio photos taken. The girls had each spent fifty cents on their new short haircuts, which they had practiced rag-curling and combing to frame their faces. The remainder of their budgets had gone toward blue cotton Stella sewed into matching long-sleeved dresses on Fiorella's mechanical sewing machine. Stella and Tina had begged Antonio for extra money for new shoes, but he had drawn the line.

The Fortunas posed with Antonio and Assunta seated in front, their sons on either side, and Stella and Tina standing behind them to disguise the old shoes they'd bought in Nicastro. Tina is one inch taller and a bit less bosomy, and of course there is that standout mole above her lip. Otherwise their smiles are identical, as are their dresses, their posture, the angles at which they hold their elbows—similar in the subtle and comprehensive ways only sisters are similar. Assunta's ankles are crossed and her feet tucked under her chair. She is smiling this time. Antonio may be smiling as well, but as with the Mona Lisa, no one can ever be sure what he is thinking; most of his expression is concealed by his mustache. Together, they are an impressive accomplishment of a family.

For fifty years, this portrait hung on various walls next to the grainier black-and-white of the first Mariastella. Somehow there is no other photo of the entire family, not even at any of the children's weddings. This was the first and last time they were photographed together.

Nineteen forty-one was better than 1940. Front Street was becoming less foreign. The Fortunas knew their favorite pushcart vendors; they understood the money and knew how much things were supposed to cost. They had learned to enjoy American food, its diversity and its rich ingredients. They'd learned a little more English. They worked hard six days a week, steadily setting aside money for their house; they had enough pocket money now that they could afford to dress American. They went to the Italian Society dances every Saturday night, meeting up in the evening with Fiorella Mulino, Carolina Nicotera, and Franceschina Perri to do one another's hair. Usually they met at the Nicoteras' house, because Carolina had no fresh brothers who would harass the girls as they tried to get dressed.

There was live music every weekend, usually a three-man band who sang songs in Italian and English. An ordinary Saturday here was a bigger party than the annual *fhesta* in Ievoli. Stella loved to dance and was good at it. Franceschina had taught her the fox-trot and the swing, and even Stella had been surprised by how quickly she shed her village-girl shyness about dancing with boys. It was thrilling to think of the scandal dancing like this would have caused back home, boys and girls moving so fast together, skirts flying, calves bare, uncorseted breasts bouncing—the freest and most joyful her body had ever felt.

Stella had her pick of partners. She danced often with Frankie D'Agata, who was very popular among the girls, until she decided she was spending too much time with him and started turning him down, which incited gossip. She said no to anyone who wasn't taller than she was. She rejected the wooing of Fiorella's older brother Vittorio, who she thought was greasy. She refused to ever, ever dance with either of the Perri boys on principle, especially the older one, Mario, who was particularly handsome and full of himself. He asked her anyway to spite her and tried to pinch her bottom. Sometimes she told boys no for no reason at all and danced with her girl-friends instead.

Franceschina admired Stella's attitude. "Ooo, you can be such a bitch!" she'd giggle, and the other girls would giggle with her at the naughty word.

"When you're pretty you have to be a bitch," Carolina said, and they giggled again. "Otherwise the men will take whatever they can get!"

"At least none of you have such a pretty sister." Tina said it as if she were joking, but she wasn't. "I'll always only be Stella's sister. People will always say, Oh! Pretty Stella is your sister? That's surprising."

The girls laughed again, protested—*no, silly, you're so pretty, you two look exactly alike.*

Stella, feeling complacent, smiled at her sister. "Don't be jealous, little bug. Jealousy will rot your heart."

"It's all right." Fiorella patted Tina's arm with her thin, smoothing hands. She winked at Stella and declared, "You're the good sister, Tina. Everyone knows that."

In the spring of 1941, Stella and Tina went back to work in the tobacco fields. Fiorella thought they were crazy to give up the laundry jobs.

"But this way we can be with Mamma," Stella explained. "And really it's actually more money, because it's three people's salary instead of two." Assunta hadn't worked all winter because of swelling in her legs. She had also miscarried a baby, and Za Pina had persuaded her to go to an American doctor. The doctor told her she had better not have any more children and had diagnosed early stages of rheumatoid arthritis as well as varicose veins. Assunta, forty-two, was an old woman.

The sweltering summer of 1941, when Stella had been living with her father's flying fists and leering sneers for a year and a half, was when the nightmare started—when she almost killed herself by jumping out the window. Who can say what poison had entered her mind and planted the dream there; maybe she'd brought down the Evil Eye on herself, showing off her prettiness too much, breaking too many hearts. Stella's life had been so comfortable, so happy lately. She must have been due for some pain. It had, after all, been six years since the last time fate had taken a crack at her.

It was like the nightmare had broken down a dam in her mind, because once she'd had it, the dream came back to her again and again—her father backed her into a corner, night after night, to molest her. The details changed; sometimes the dream took place in the tobacco barn, or in their old house in Ievoli. The story was the same every time, though—Stella was exposed, trapped, and touched; as the dream blossomed over time, she was presented with a male organ, which was rubbed against her. The dream never lasted long enough for her to know what happened after that. But she woke with a real knowledge of being touched in a way she didn't want to be. She woke sweating, in terror and disgust.

Tony did as he'd promised and nailed boards over the girls' bedroom window so that Stella couldn't try to jump out again, but other than that, the episode was mostly reduced to a joke. I've always wondered why no one took it more seriously; why later, when Stella told them, over and over, that she never wanted to get married, no one remembered that time her subconscious chose to die rather than be violated by a man.

Once the window was boarded up, the summer nights were stifling long hours of insomnia. Stella became a victim of her own subconscious, so tormented by her exhaustion she couldn't tell when she was drifting in or out of sleep. Even as the nightmare became familiar to her, she never got used to it, or overcame her paralyzing dread as the man extended his calloused hand. Her ten-hour days of field labor were an aching haze of misery; once she was so tired she had to miss work.

Stella would lie next to Tina in their narrow bed and press her fingernails into her palms, trying to keep awake. She prayed to the Virgin for respite, and also to the ghost of the first Mariastella, whom she'd realized she had not left behind in Ievoli. "Please make it stop," she'd whisper, over and over. "I know you're there. I know you did this. Please make it stop. Please let me be." But the dreams didn't stop.

What were they for? Punishment for being alive?

Or were they some kind of warning?

Stella couldn't talk about the nightmare to anyone, not even to Tina, because the words were too ugly. It had already taken its toll on her; she shouldn't let it take a toll on anyone else. So she kept it to herself. But the dream had an enormous and permanent effect on Stella's life. It taught her that some wounds couldn't be stitched up, that some bad things happen not once but again and again. This was the year Stella learned to smile with her lips closed, so no one would see the two missing teeth she'd knocked out in her fall. This was when she began to feel an uncontrollable revulsion for her father, to dread when he came too close to her, put his hand on her shoulder, let his eyes pass over her curves, as they so often did. Some days she trembled just sitting across the dinner table from him.

If Tony noticed his daughter's changed behavior, he never let on.

It was Carmelo Maglieri's bad luck that he met Stella only a few months after she started to have her nightmare. In a different version of this story, a version where the window stayed unboarded for a cross-breeze, or where Stella's catechismal education had allowed her to believe there could be a difference between sex and rape, or where the miasma of Tracci hadn't followed Antonio Fortuna halfway around the world—in those versions of this story, maybe Carmelo Maglieri wouldn't have been the villain.

Stella and Tina went back to the laundry in September. The leaves on the maples turned yellow and the leaves on the oaks turned brown and the air grew frighteningly cold, just as it had last year. Stella knew the parade of American festivals now; she was looking forward to Christmas. Stella knew what to expect from America; she had gotten used to it.

Then, in December, came Pearl Harbor.

The outbreak of war was terrifying, even though no one was surprised. Now that the U.S. had declared war on Italy, Italian Americans had a lot to talk about. At the Italian Society there were men who wanted to go home and fight for Mussolini and those who sent money to support his war effort. There were men who were glad to be in America, far away from Mussolini's fascism. On both sides of the argument people worried about their families back home. But the time for discussion was over—Italian Americans lived in and hailed from enemy states. They had to pick.

For the Fortunas, the only choice was America. Tony, their patriarch, had no love for his homeland and was proudly naturalized. He would never take them back to Ievoli. The world had already been changing when the immigrants left, and now the change had accelerated, the bombs dropping on ancestral villages and obliterating their old way of life. Stella feared the Ievoli she loved existed only in the rubble of her memory.

At night, airplanes roared overhead. The Fortunas lay in their beds wondering if bombs were going to fall. Like their neighbors, they put up blackout curtains so they wouldn't make their building a target. Hartford was a munitions production capital, and the Fortunas lived only ten minutes' walk from the Colt Armory, which operated twenty-four hours a day. The experience of Hartford at war was spooky, the abandoned streets, the furtive energy behind blackout curtains. Streetlights were against regulation; the girls had to walk to and from night school along unlit city streets.

It was too bad Stella and Tina hadn't become citizens already. Now all the Fortunas except Tony were enemy aliens. They had to go down to City Hall and register as such, have their picture taken for enemy alien ID cards, and get fingerprinted. If they were stopped and could not show their new identification, they would be in big trouble. They could be searched or interrogated at any time; police could come into their house and confiscate their belongings. Any letter they received from Italy could incriminate them. Some Italians were rounded up and sent to prison camps far away. They couldn't keep a radio anymore, because the police might think they were using it to communicate with German submarines.

"What would we tell a submarine?" Joey argued. He was angry he wouldn't be able to listen to *Crime Doctor* or Jack Benny, Louie's favorite.

For young men, there was one quick way out of enemy alienhood, one way to citizenship and all its perks: enlistment. If you were willing to risk death for the United States of America, you could get yourself naturalized lickety-split. Half a million Italian American men enlisted during the war. Which brings us to the next important moment in our story.

The first time Stella Fortuna spoke to Carmenantonio Maglieri, it was snowing. The Fortuna sisters were walking home from Hartford High after a night school class; it was January 1942. The blackout-dark streets were covered in a film of ice.

Carmelo—although of course Stella had no idea who he was at the time—slowed down his car, keeping pace with the girls, which made them nervous. Both he and the man in the passenger seat were dressed in olive-green U.S. Army uniforms.

Carmelo rolled down the window and called out, "Would you like a ride?" Those were his first words to Stella.

Her first words to him were "Go away."

But he didn't go away; instead he leaned head and shoulders out the window, a friendly smile on his face. Stella watched warily as wet snow clusters embedded themselves in his waxed black curls. Her stomach turned at the thought of men following her and Tina in a car. The girls were on Farmington Avenue, still twenty minutes from home, and the hard black heels of their shoes skidded on the slick pavement.

"Come on, hop in," Carmelo said. He spoke Italian with the generic southern accent some immigrant men adopted in order to communicate with speakers of many regional dialects; he could have been from anywhere in Italy. "Pretty girls shouldn't have to walk in the snow, in the dark like this. Let us take you home."

"No, thank you," Tina said. "We absolutely do not accept rides from strangers." She tugged Stella's arm and they resumed their slippery march, elbows linked, leaving wet snow to pool in the exclamation points of their footprints.

Carmelo rolled the car forward, catching up. "Very smart, not to take rides from strangers. But ladies! This weather is too much."

Neither Tina nor Stella replied, and the car tailed them as they shuffled on in silence. The cardboard shanties they passed were unsettlingly silent, the snow collecting on their pulping eaves. The moon was bright but diffuse, nestled among the storm clouds. Every night they made this trip Stella wavered between wishing it were better lit, so they would be able to see an assail-ant coming, and wishing it were darker, so they would have a chance of hiding.

"Come on, ladies," the man hanging from the window tried again. "It's not safe out here. I promise we'll take you straight home. On our honor as soldiers." He smiled and his cheeks became glossy marbles of joviality. Stella had twin thoughts that his face was handsome and that it was smarmy. He caught her gaze and she narrowed her eyes at him so he wouldn't mistake any invitations there.

"We know all about soldiers," Stella told him. She regretted it immediately; she didn't want to give him any ideas he didn't already have.

But he had ducked back into the car to consult the man in the passenger seat. After a moment, the curl-covered head popped back out again. "Your father," he said. "Tony Fortuna, right?"

"How did you know?" Tina said reflexively, and Stella elbowed her so hard Tina had to cling to her sister to keep her balance.

"So we're not strangers!" said the smiling young man, smiling afresh. "Your father knows us. Ask him when you're home, which will be in just a few minutes. He'll tell you all about us. I'm Carmelo Maglieri, and this is Rocco Caramanico." He indicated his companion with his thick thumb. "I worked with your father. We all worked together," he amended. He was so excitable he hadn't gotten his own story straight.

"We're not getting in the car," Tina insisted as Stella was saying, "Worked together where?" The cold had evaporated her mistrust. She wanted to get in the warm car.

"Construction, G. Fox," he said. "Two years ago, in the summer."

It was true, Tony had worked on the G. Fox site. But Tina said, "If you really knew our father, you would know he would *never* let us get in your car."

"Come on, Tina," Stella said. Her ankles hurt from walking on the ice. "This is stupid. They're just going to give us a ride home."

"Stella!"

"Fine, walk. I'm taking the ride." Stella made for the curb, and the driver—Carmelo—stopped the car. "Try not to slip and break your neck," she told her sister.

"But Stella!" The expression on Tina's face was simple despair. Her red lipstick appeared much darker in the dimly moonlit street, and with the snow catching on her hair Tina looked like a still from a movie.

Stella slid across the car's tan leather seat and called, "Come on, Tina. Get in." Then again, more tenderly, "Get in. It's going to be fine." And Tina got in.

The girls arrived home without incident and their father did not even yell at them about it. The trouble is, no matter how cold and dark the night, if you accept a ride from a man, you are allowing your entire circle to start gossiping. Stella made her own bed by getting in that car.

You might have been waiting for Carmelo Maglieri to make his appearance ever since his father, Tomaso, met Tony all those years ago on the railroad. Well, Stella wasn't waiting for him—she'd never heard of him. Nevertheless, I should tell you a little more about him here, since he won't be going away, no matter what Stella told him or how many times.

Carmenantonio Maglieri, known as Carmelo, was born in March 1921 in an Abruzzi mountain village called Sepino, a maze of medieval cobblestone alleys that sits on top of the ancient Samnite city of Altilia. Despite the Abruzzi's rich history and adorable brand of stone-and-flower idyll, there was no work there. During Carmelo's entire childhood, his father, Tomaso, had been sending home money from America. But in 1935 Tomaso was almost sixty years old; he wouldn't be able to support the family with his own physical labor for much longer.

Tomaso had applied for a visa for his son to join him when Carmelo was ten, but four years had passed and it hadn't come through. Meanwhile the family farm in Abruzzi was struggling; every year was poorer. Plus, Tomaso Maglieri did not have good feelings about Mussolini's government; it was one of the reasons he had tried to persuade his xenophobic wife to move the whole family to America. She never had to put her foot down, though, thanks to U.S. immigration restrictions.

In the end, the Maglieris decided to smuggle Carmelo into the United States without a visa. He took a two-day train journey north to Genoa, where he boarded a Spanish cargo ship bound for New York. Other young men from his province had made similar undocumented migrations, disguised as cargo or blending in with international sailors long enough to disappear, unannotated, at a foreign harbor. Carmelo had instructions about who to ask for at the Genoese docks, and enough money to grease all the necessary palms of the ticket agents and hustlers on the Italian side of the journey.

Being fourteen, Carmelo possessed that teenage fearlessness we all look back on with grim awe. It served him well, because he couldn't speak to anyone on the boat during the ten-day crossing. There were two other stowaways, but they were Greek, and the crew spoke only Spanish. So when the critical moment came—the landing in New York—the stowaways had to be removed before the docking inspection. A small boat rowed them to shore in the dark of night—a nerve-racking journey for a boy who had never learned how to swim. The rowboat grounded in the sandy shoals of an unlit beach and the Spanish sailor indicated for the stowaways to disembark and splash through the last shallow meters of frigid water to shore. That was the end of his emigration.

Carmelo wasn't sure what to do next. He needed to find the place he was supposed to meet his father. Tomaso hadn't known exactly when Carmelo would arrive, so he had given Carmelo the address of a *paesan*, a dockworker who lived in Brooklyn. Carmelo didn't know what Brooklyn was, never mind how to get there.

Carmelo bid the Greeks an awkward good-bye and started walking. He followed the first road he met and continued until he had reached a harbor. That seemed like the right place to settle down for the night; he would search in the morning for someone who could point him toward his next destination.

The trouble was, Carmelo was no better off in daylight. He was scruffy and smelly in his grimy travel clothes, and no New Yorker would have wanted to talk to him even if he spoke any English. He had a little money, but no idea how to use it, and no common sense about his situation except to know that he must, must, must not be detained by the police. This was how he spent nine days. Nine days! He slept on a dock bench, hesitatingly approaching unhelpful strangers with his best Italian, ducking out of sight whenever he spotted someone in a uniform, and accepting scraps from the pushcart vendors, for whom he performed chores. Eventually it was one of the vendors who brought an Italian-speaking friend to the dock to see if they could solve the homeless boy's problem. The Italian escorted Carmelo on the ferry and then on the underground subway to the address Carmelo had for the *paesan*'s house. Carmelo was so relieved that his dockside ordeal was over that he only realized later how generous the Italian stranger had been. He learned English quickly so he would never be caught speechless again.

Tomaso came to pick Carmelo up in Brooklyn and brought him back to his railroad team in Pennsylvania. At first Carmelo was only allowed to be a water boy; he earned half wages for running errands. By the time he was fifteen, though, he was a full-fledged railroad man. He was popular with the other men, gregarious, good-natured, and happy to be the butt of a joke. The railroad men taught him to cook and to read English. They played folk songs around the fire every night, any man who could sing contributing tunes from his own village in his own dialect. Carmelo learned the concertina from a man named Otello from Cosenza. When Otello went back to Italy in December 1936, he left his concertina with Carmelo.

Carmelo and Tomaso traveled wherever Reading sent them until 1937, when Tomaso fell in a ditch and broke his leg. The Maglieri men settled in Hartford for the old man's convalescence, sharing a couch at the tenement apartment of the Carapellucci family, Abruzzesi friends who lived on Front Street. Carmelo, still without papers, talked his way into a job on a construction team. This was where he met Rocco Caramanico, who would become like his brother. This was also where he met Tony Fortuna. When they figured out Tony knew Carmelo's father—it didn't take long; the first thing Italians do when we meet other Italians is to run through all possible family connections—they had a laugh about Carmelo's infant betrothal to faraway Stella.

The men might have become good friends, who knows, but the flood of 1938 came, and the Carapelluccis' tenement was destroyed. Tomaso went back to Sepino, but Carmelo stayed on, renting a room in a men's boardinghouse. He told his father he would work hard, save carefully, and do whatever he could to reunite the family.

Carmelo enlisted as soon as the U.S. entered the war so he could be granted citizenship with active duty. When the recruitment officer asked to see his documentation, Carmelo said—not untruthfully—that he had been very young when he'd come over from Italy, and that he hadn't been able to find his papers. The U.S. Army was hardly going to turn away a young man who was willing to fight and die for the Land of the Free just because he had no right to be there.

Under the church in the central piazza of Sepino, Carmelo Maglieri's hometown, there is a grotto dedicated to Santa Cristina, the patron saint. The shrine is lined with gilded chambers illustrating the stages of her life, her miracles, and her martyrdom, each chamber endowed by an emigrant far away. One of those grotto chambers bears Carmelo Maglieri's name on a gold plaque. It is an old cliché about Italian American immigrants that they kept the homeland in their hearts, but Carmelo never stopped thinking of Sepino, even when it was clear he would never return.

What can I say. Carmelo was a little bit of a sap. The type of guy who would tear up when his grandchildren came to visit. He was the opposite of Tony Fortuna in every way—well, in almost every way. Maybe this is why the betrothal joke was such a terrible one, if women are supposed to marry men who remind them of their fathers.

The second time Stella and Carmelo met was the night Rocco decided to marry Tina.

"You want the one with the mole on her lip," Rocco's older sister,

Barbara, advised him. The Fortuna sisters were wearing matching blue dresses, so the mole was the best way to distinguish them.

"The one with the mole is Concettina," Rocco said. It was two days after he and Carmelo had picked up the girls on Farmington Avenue. Rocco had asked Tony's permission to call again—it was plain he wanted to see about the sisters. On this second visit, he'd brought Barbara along as his consultant, and to represent his parents in Italy. Carmelo Maglieri had come along in support, or maybe with motives of his own.

Rocco meant to ask Tony's permission to marry one of the Fortuna girls before he left the Front Street tenement that very night. Rocco and Barbara had discussed this matter. In four days' time, Rocco would be sent to the Pacific with his unit, and it was best to have someone waiting at home for him, someone who could send him letters and care packages.

Now Rocco and his sister were standing in the doorway to the Fortunas' kitchen for this private conference. All the Fortunas, turned out in their Sunday best, sat or stood around the folding table Antonio had set up in the living room less than ten feet away, pretending they weren't wondering what the Caramanico siblings were discussing.

"Concettina has the makings of a wife," Barbara said. "You can tell she is hardworking just by looking at her."

Brother and sister watched the nervous party scene for a few minutes. Tina, who was indeed hardworking to look at, stood at her mother's elbow, shoveling pasta onto plates and refilling wineglasses. Tony sat at the head of the table; then came Joey, nineteen, and Louie, eleven, and Tony's friend Vito Aiello, whose wife was in Italy and who sometimes came over to play cards. Carmelo Maglieri was telling a story that had the boys laughing. Like Rocco, Carmelo had come in his full army uniform. Stella, the only woman sitting at the table, had her mouth set in a pout. Rocco saw his irresistibly charming buddy failing to charm her, and it made him want to try.

"They are both hardworking," Rocco told Barbara. "They work six days a week at the laundry. They give all their money right to their father, he'll tell you." Rocco always took Barbara's advice obediently; she was sixteen years older and she looked after him well. He was pushing back now because some little spark inside him was interested in Stella Fortuna, not in Tina. He was hoping Barbara would change her mind.

Barbara was not to be convinced. "But see how Stella is sitting while her mother and sister do all the work?" Yes, he saw; it was hard not to see. "Tina there, she's obedient. Those sturdy Calabrese legs," Barbara pointed out, and from this vantage Tina's calves in particular looked quite sturdy. "She'll bear you lots of sons and then still be strong enough to run after them." Barbara would be wrong about the first part, although Tina would run after many other people's children.

Rocco made one more stand. "I prefer Stella. Stella is prettier."

"Listen to me, Rocco. You don't choose the woman you are going to spend your whole life with by what she looks like. That's thinking like a man." When Barbara said "thinking like a man," she meant "thinking with your cock," but she would never have said the word "cock." "Pretty girls are for running around with. Strong, hardworking girls are for marrying." Maybe she was proud of being the marrying type herself. Or maybe some sisters set aside their female sympathies and hope for a docile caretaker wife for their baby brothers. "You're about to go off to war," Barbara reminded Rocco. "You want the one who is still going to be waiting for you when you get back."

The table was completely obscured by piles of whatever food Assunta had been able to produce on such short notice: an eighteen-inch bowl of fresh *tagliatelle* she and Tina had rolled out that morning; a plate of *pizzelle* left over from last weekend. There was an array of pickles: the last of the wood mushrooms Assunta had picked over the summer; a jar of yellow *lupini;*

roasted peppers in garlic oil. There was a bowl of egg-size beef and pork meatballs, soaking in still-hot tomato *raù*. They were dense with cheese and perfectly fried. It was hard to imagine that their maker had never seen a meatball only two years earlier. How quickly and completely things change, and then change again. Later Stella would remember these as some of the last meatballs they ate, without any special appreciation, before wartime meat rationing.

Stella was enjoying the party, but complacently. She watched Rocco across the table as Tony told him a long story. She tried to imagine whether the girls at the Italian Society would think he was a catch—she personally did not find him attractive, although he certainly was well-groomed, his clothing impeccable. His hair was clipped short on the side and tightly curled. She detected a hardness in him, a nervous energy—she guessed he would reveal himself to be a strict personality, a perfectionist. He was like her father in those ways. She wondered if her father would like Rocco for those reasons, or dislike him.

With the men's conversation humming around her—mostly they spoke about soldiering: the boys' enlistment, Tony Fortuna's time in the Alps, the strangeness of young men going to war against Italy when their fathers had fought for Italy only twenty-five years earlier—Stella made herself think about whether or not she was nervous. It was the first time someone had come to talk to Tony Fortuna about his daughters. Stella was twenty-two and Tina twenty; it was only a matter of time before this happened. She wasn't sure what her father's response would be, whether he would scare suitors away, or whether he would want to speed his daughters out of his house to the first respectable interested party. Maybe he would wave off courting requests in the American way and say it was up to his daughters. In which case Stella would say no, and that would be that.

What if Rocco was here for Tina, not Stella? Would he take Tina away? Stella imagined sleeping alone in the bed they'd always shared, Assunta standing alone in the kitchen over the steaming pots. But that *would* happen eventually. Tina would get married; she would make her life with a man and have lots of babies. And Stella would be left behind. Because she wanted to be left behind—didn't she?

Having worked this through in her head, Stella ate silently, drawing herself back into the atmosphere of the party. Carmelo Maglieri, who sat next to her, was telling Louie and Joey stories about basic training. Joey was saying he was thinking about enlisting, which was the first Stella had heard of it. Her brother seemed transfixed by Carmelo's charisma. Compared to his stiff, careful friend Rocco, Carmelo was expansive, pink-cheeked and energetic. He was handsome, indisputably; his black hair was thick and glossy, and his eyes were a brilliant light blue—the kind of blue eyes all the Italian girls talked about wistfully. Yes, he was handsome. Stella would admit that. Not that she cared; she was not interested in men. But *could* she like him? If there were reason to?

She thought back, deliberately, to her first ambivalent impression of him, head, neck, and shoulders hanging out of the car window that snowy night. She let herself remember and savor her wave of distrust—there are no good good-looking men, for no good-looking man needs to be good. This old adage settled comfortably into her consciousness. He was here as part of his buddy's game.

"And how are you tonight, Mariastella?" Carmelo asked, turning the conversation on her.

"Just fine," Stella answered, sitting up straight and narrowing her eyes. She had been being too friendly before. "And call me Stella. Mariastella is my dead sister."

She watched as his face softened in compassion. "Your sister died? I'm sorry, I didn't know."

"It was a long time ago," she said after a moment, relenting under Joey's critical gaze. "And I never knew her." As she said the words, denying her little ghost, cold air rippled up the skin of her burnt arm. But she was sitting by the window, and it was likely just the January night air.

"Stella almost died, too," Louie told Carmelo. "Five different times." Joey snorted.

"What? Five times?" Carmelo raised his bushy black eyebrows to prompt the boy to tell more.

Stella listened as her kid brother bragged about her bad luck— the favorite family story. *Attacked by an eggplant! Pigs, intestines . . . Lying there like she was dead for four days . . . We all could have drowned, actually . . . Didn't even know she was about to jump . . .* Louie was able to dwell on the grossness and the danger, the most entertaining pieces, without any concern for his listeners' discomfort. Carmelo made the expected horrified faces and Stella waved it all off, smiling. Louie's accent had lost most of its Calabrese inflection as he spoke to Carmelo, as though he had picked up the young man's neutral accent over the last hour.

"What do you expect?" Joey said to help Louie wind it all up. "What do you expect, with a name like Stella Fortuna?"

"Stella Fortuna," Carmelo repeated. "What a name."

Now that Stella had been drawn into the conversation, Carmelo focused his attention on her. He asked her about her work at the laundry, about whether she and Tina ever went to the Saturday dances at the Italian Society. She couldn't decide if he was being courteous or flirtatious, so she leaned back in her chair, crossed her arms on top of her belly, and answered coolly.

Joey enjoyed this less than when he had been the center of attention. "What about your buddy, eh?" he said. "Kissing up to my father over there. Did he come to try to court my sisters or only my father?"

"You know the rules, Joey. If your father doesn't like him, it doesn't matter if your sister likes him." Carmelo shrugged. "Rocco is a serious guy. He does things the Italian way. His family, they try to keep traditions."

Stella wondered about Carmelo's family. Young men on their own were dangerous because they had no fear of consequences, no family pressure to do the right thing. It was so easy for them to prefer the "American way" with the girls and then move on to another job in another city if things got too hot; everyone said that was what happened with Adelina Rossi, who got sent back to her father's village in Vibo Valentia last year. Stella watched Carmelo Maglieri break a meatball in half with his fork and push it onto a heel of bread. Can you tell a playboy by looking?

"Well, which sister is he even here for?" Joey was saying. "I haven't seen him talk to either one."

"I don't know. But," Carmelo added gallantly, "either one is such a catch, when he chooses, I will ask your father if I can court the other one."

"Hmph," Stella said.

Joey was incredulous. "He didn't even tell you before you came over?"

"Well, maybe it's hard for him to decide. You have two very pretty sisters." This time it was Louie who snorted. Eleven-year-olds disparage that sort of observation.

Joey lifted his wineglass, a warning little toast in Carmelo's direction. "Don't say that where they can hear you. They're already stuck-up."

Stella gave Joey a demure nod. She was happy to be called stuck-up.

Carmelo, of course, protested. "They're not stuck-up at all."

"They sure are," Joey said. "Don't go wasting your time being nice to them. They think they're too good for any of the guys around here."

"That's a really rude thing to say about your sisters," Stella said.

"Well, why don't you ever have boyfriends then?"

"I do so have a boyfriend," Stella said.

"No, she does not," Joey told Carmelo.

"Yes, I do." She was calm now, her position unimpeachable. "You know I am engaged to Stefano Morello." She turned to Carmelo and smiled. "He's away at war in Africa now, but he writes me letters." It had only just occurred to Stella that if she fudged some of the details of her tenuous and halfhearted courtship with faraway Stefano it might protect her from the more aggressive intentions of any Hartford skirt-chasers. "We have an arrangement to get married," she said. "After the war."

"After the war—that could be a long way away," Carmelo said. Did he look disappointed? She thought he did. Well, good. Better disappointed now than later.

But she had a flash of pity for him, now that he was no longer any risk to her, this very good-looking man all alone in this country and maybe just on the hunt for a family to be part of. She looked him in the eye and gave him her best, happiest smile. His cherry-round cheeks were pink as he smiled back.

After dinner, as the two young men collected their coats, Rocco Caramanico asked Tony if he could speak to him alone. Tony led him to the kitchen.

"I'd like to marry your daughter Concettina," Rocco told him. Everyone in the hallway could hear every word.

Antonio had been waiting all night to deliver his line.

"If you come back alive," he said, "you can ask me again."

The first Saturday of May 1942, Joey escorted Stella, Tina, and Fiorella to the Italian Society spring ball. There were fresh bouquets of carnations on every table and the crowd was both celebratory and jittery. The roar of conversation was so loud that Stella wasn't always sure what song the band was playing.

Boys had come in their new uniforms, because everyone was enlisting. Opinions about homeland, duty, and opportunity were strong and contagious and became more so with the distribution of alcohol. Joey had been bragging about thinking about enlisting for months now, and had plenty to talk about with the khaki evangelists. Stella knew Joey was especially attracted to the uniform itself, the effect he'd seen it have on women.

There was a separate sense of urgency among the ladies. Now that so many of the Hartford boys were going off to war, the screws were tightening on relationships and engagements. Some girls had sweethearts or approved family matches back in the villages; others were hunting with fresh voracity, collectively agitated by the feeling that something needed to be set into action with some young man before they all shipped out.

The Fortuna girls were above it, Tina armed with her standing promise from Rocco Caramanico, Stella with her artfully embellished half-imaginary fiancé in Africa. She was amused by the romantic fervor infecting the Italian girls. What sense did it make to put yourself in a position to be widowed by a man you barely knew? Better a widow than a spinster, apparently. That had always been the way of the world, hadn't it? Well, let them all prance around like fluffy roosters in their spring dresses. It was pure joy to be the only two people in the crowd with no agenda.

Stella and Tina were themselves celebrating: the Fortunas had bought the house on Bedford Street. The old Napolitano had decided to move back to Italy and had sped up the deed transfer. He had been angry, or maybe scared, when the FBI agents had come to his home and confiscated his transistor radio. He accepted $1,860 from Antonio in cash for the house, together with the promise that Antonio would send along the rest to an address the Napolitano would forward. In fact he would never send Antonio his address, and so the balance of $140 would sit untouched in the Fortunas' bank for five years. They assumed he must have been killed in the bombings.

In any case, they had a house now. As a reward for their accomplishment, the girls had new three-dollar dresses from

Sears with capped sleeves and large buttons up the front. Stella felt extremely American in her dress, which was watermelon-red. Her forearms were bare, but she didn't feel self-conscious about her scars, which seemed to match her dress, pinkly unobtrusive.

Fiorella had brought them congratulation presents: enamel brooches shaped like little butterflies. "After all your hard work!" Her long, gentle face was bright with her smile. "I have so much respect for you girls. *Tanti auguri!*"

Carmelo Maglieri strolled up as Stella and Tina were pinning their butterflies on their dresses. At first Stella didn't recognize him in his plain gray suit. Her brain turned over on the flash of familiarity— this good-looking blue-eyed man, who was he? Oh yes. But what was he doing here, and without his uniform? He bowed to them, pressing his fedora to his chest. "Good evening, beautiful ladies."

"Carmelo!" Tina almost shrieked.

Carmelo kissed Tina's cheeks warmly but did not try to kiss Stella. "What are we congratulating you on, Stella?"

"Stella bought us a house," Tina said, a little giddy at seeing him. "Three stories, on Bedford Street!"

"I didn't buy it, we bought it together." Stella was irritated with herself for not recognizing Carmelo immediately, and for having found him attractive.

"Oh, Stella, give yourself some credit," Tina said. "You were so smart with the bank, and the savings . . ."

"Our Stella, the smartest girl on Front Street," Fiorella said, squeezing Stella's arm.

"That doesn't surprise me at all to hear," Carmelo said. He inclined his head toward Fiorella. "Stella, would you do me the honor of introducing me to your friend? I don't believe I've had the pleasure." It felt so staged, Stella was certain he was acting out some scene he'd liked in a film.

"This is Fiorella Mulino," Stella said, keeping her voice dry. "Her family is from Puglia." Carmelo bowed again and Fiorella, blushing, replied, *"Piaccere."*

"May I bring you ladies something to drink?" Carmelo said. "Have you tried the punch?" They shook their heads. "Stay right here." His voice was as warm and animated as she remembered it. "I'll bring you some from the bar." With a third bow, he turned and stepped into the mass of frocks and suits.

"What a kind man he is," Tina said. Stella had nothing to say in response, and neither did Fiorella, who seemed a little star-struck. The girls pretended to listen to the band until Carmelo returned, four glasses of red punch clutched together between his large hands. He distributed them carefully and the four young people clinked, wishing one another health. The punch tasted like red wine but fizzed with carbonation. Stella felt a happy ripple through her nerves—they were toasting like adults, drinking alcohol with a strange man.

Her cheeks warm, Stella asked, "Carmelo, where is your uniform?"

Carmelo smiled that big, friendly smile. "Oh, didn't you hear? The army kicked me out. I'm unfit for service." His blue eyes were shining; even his bad news was something he'd admit good-naturedly. "Flat feet."

"Flat feet?" Tina said. "What does that mean?"

"Flat feet, just what it sounds like." Carmelo lifted his hand level with his nose, curling his fingers into a dome. "The middle part of your foot is supposed to arch like this. If it doesn't, it makes problems when you have to walk or run for a long time, like soldiers do. Now, God gave me feet like this." He splayed his hand flat and peered, smiling, across it at Tina, who smiled back. "Flat as a pancake," he said in English, and Tina and Fiorella giggled. "So much for me as a soldier."

"So much for your papers," Stella put in, then felt her face heat up—that had been aggressive, undignified.

But Carmelo shook his finger. "Aha, no, no, *signorina*. I served thirty days in the U.S. Army. I'm a naturalized citizen of the United States now. No going back."

218

"Really?" Stella couldn't believe it. "Why didn't they check your feet at the beginning?"

Carmelo shrugged. "It's just my luck. I'm a very lucky man," he said. "Even when I'm born with bad feet it turns out bad feet are good."

"*Truffatore,*" she said, *con artist*, and she meant it, but she smiled to take the edge off.

"That's what Rocco said," Carmelo replied, rueful. "Oh, he was mad. It was my idea to enlist in the first place, and here he is going off to war on his own."

Stella watched Tina's expression, waiting to see this all come together for her sister. "What did he say?" she asked.

"He tried to get out, too," Carmelo said. "But he's got perfectly good feet. Nice arches, Tina," he said, as though complimenting her on her choice of man.

They chatted for another ten minutes or so, Carmelo asking Fiorella about her family. As they were almost done with their punch, Carmelo bowed and took his leave. Stella felt a pang of jealousy as he left; he had not, then, come over to try to flirt with them, he had only been paying his respects. Well, his respect was all she wanted. It was just that she had enjoyed thinking that he liked her and could not have her.

Stella saw Carmelo one more time that summer, when Joey invited him over for his enlistment party at their new house on Bedford Street. It was the second Saturday in June, and the weather was beautiful. All of the Fortunas' friends—the Nicoteras; the Perris, whose boys Mario and Mikey were also enlisting this summer; the Mulinos; the Cardamones; Zu Vito Aiello—packed into the freshly painted rooms and spilled out into the backyard, where they could admire the tomato garden Assunta had planted the week before.

Into this mix came Carmelo Maglieri, for all the world like he was already part of the group. He had brought with him a bulky black box, which he left by the coatrack. Joey strolled Carmelo through the aunties and uncles, introducing him, and Stella eavesdropped on their friends' reactions to the Abruzzese boy's handsome smile and sparkling blue eyes. The mothers with daughters were practically squealing in delight to find this shiny fish swimming in the pool.

"What's the matter with you, Stella?" Franceschina Perri whispered. The girls huddled together in the kitchen, watched over by Assunta's somewhat sanctimonious new Blessed Virgin figurine, which stood on the wall shrine by the photo of the dead baby Stella. "Why are you playing around? Someone else is going to snap him up."

"Snap him up if you want him," Stella said. She certainly didn't want to get herself into a jam where her father thought she was encouraging Carmelo's courtship. "I give him to you. My gift, you can thank me later."

"Those eyes, though!" Franceschina clucked her tongue. "To die for."

"In Calabria lots of men have blue eyes," Stella said dismissively. "It's nothing special to me. I prefer dark eyes anyway."

After everyone had eaten, Carmelo opened the black box he'd brought and revealed a concertina. "May I play you a song, Signora Fortuna?" he asked loudly, because people had already started to assemble to see what was going to happen.

Assunta was giggling at the attention; she actually had to press her hands to her mouth to contain herself. "Oh, Carmelo, don't be so formal. You can call me Assunta."

"Well, lovely Zia Assunta, may I play you a song?" He had shouldered the concertina's strap and pressed a few chords—the living room was full of the anticipation of live music. "I know just the one I want to play. It runs through my head every time I see you." He made moon eyes and covered his heart. What a ham, Stella thought.

Assunta, still giggling, nodded. Carmelo's foot tapped triple time on the wooden floorboards, and before he even played the opening chord Stella already knew what he was going to sing. Her heart was pounding in her ears; she knew her face was red with emotion. The words were a little different than the words Stella knew, a dialect more northern sounding than the one spoken in Ievoli, but they were Calabrese—where had Carmelo learned to sing in Calabrese?

I saw her at the water doing her washing
My Calabrisella, with her dark eyes

By the time he had reached the second line, everyone was squealing and clapping with joy, because "Calabrisella Mia" was every Calabrese's favorite song, especially here, so far from home. Even cranky old Zu Aldo was smiling. Carmelo had won over a whole room of stubborn, distrusting Calabresi with one song on his concertina. Stella's heart was still pounding, caught in the memory of the *fhesta* in Nicastro all those years ago, dancing around the bonfire among the swirling *pacchiane* and the Gypsies, the night she thought of as the happiest in her life. The song had taken her home.

Carmelo's voice was clear and sweet, and was completely overwhelmed when the entire room joined him for the chorus:

Tirulalleru lalleru lala! Sta Calabrisella muriri mi fa!

As the last bar to the song closed and all the gathered friends were clapping and cheering, Carmelo turned to Stella and winked.

Fiorella had a new job in the fall of 1942, in a factory where she made mortar shells. They paid her thirty cents an hour—twelve dollars a week, since they were strict and only let you work eight hours a day. "If you get tired and don't put the pieces together exactly right, someone can get killed," Fiorella explained. But anyway, twelve dollars a week! She would never go back to the laundry.

Hartford—home to Pratt & Whitney, which produced aircraft parts, and munitions factories like Colt—had converted itself into a war engine. The factory owners were desperate to fill their payrolls so they could meet their government contracts. They were hiring girls galore, and even girls had to be paid minimum wage for these jobs.

Stella and Tina, meanwhile, were enemy aliens and were not even allowed inside any factory related to the war effort. Their four dollars a week from the laundry, which they turned over to their father, seemed especially paltry now.

Antonio, who had given up his construction job to go work at Pratt & Whitney building propellers, said to them, "Don't you wish you'd listened to me, and studied and gotten your papers?"

Rocco Caramanico wrote to Tina regularly from his post in New Guinea. He wrote two or sometimes even three times a week, which the girls could tell by the dates at the top, but the letters arrived in packets about once a month. If there was a gap in correspondence, Tina knew it was because the letters were lost, not because he wasn't writing them; he had revealed himself to be a consistent young man. If too much time went by between packets, Tina assumed Rocco was dead, and Stella would have to console her sister with reminders that he hadn't been dead any of the previous times.

The letters were always addressed to "My Friend Tina":

To My Friend Tina,

Thank you for sending me presents. It was very kind of you. The cookies were very good. Only a little stale, although I think you must have mailed them more than a month ago. Thank you for making them for me. It is raining here right now and I should go to sleep. Please give my regards to your family.

Your friend, Rocco Caramanico

Louie showed them where New Guinea was on a map from his geography textbook—farther away than they had been able to imagine, near Australia—and translated unfamiliar words that pertained to army life, like "mess" and "KP duty."

"That's Kitchen Patrol," Louie explained. "So he cooks for the other soldiers."

Rocco wrote often about KP, and especially about boxes of chicken parts. The chicken arrived in a box that had once been frozen, although by the time it came to Rocco it was a collection of thighs and organs and pieces of congealed blood sloshing around in a slimy yellow liquid. Rocco's job was to dump the box into a pot and cook it all together as it was, and that was what the unit ate, day in and day out. Sometimes he found feathers still in the box.

The letters never mentioned combat, enemies, or what work his chemical engineering corps was doing. The women had no way of knowing to what degree he was censoring himself so the letters could get through to them.

Barbara, Rocco's sister, found the idea of her brother in a kitchen hard to believe. "Rocco doesn't know how to cook anything," she said. He was very traditionally minded about those things; it was one of the reasons it was so important he found a wife who could cook and keep house.

Tina and Barbara put together care packages that they sent to New Guinea at the beginning of every month, homemade cookies and knitted socks and whatever else they could think of that would survive the journey.

Of the thirty packages they sent during the years Rocco was at war, he received eight.

In October 1942, the Fortunas received a letter bearing the Nicastro postmark. Stefano Morello from Sambiase had been killed in North Africa.

Tina only waited for Tony to finish reading before bursting into noisy tears. "He was such a nice boy," she sobbed. "I'm so sorry, Stella, I'm so sorry, he was such a nice boy." Assunta, too, had begun to cry, lifting her apron to wipe her face.

Stella, who of course could not cry, even now, held her mother and her sister and stroked their backs as they took turns sobbing into the bosom of her dress. In her heart she'd known she would never marry Stefano, but after six years of letting people believe she'd intended to, she was overwhelmed with melancholy. She thought of the day they'd met at the Nicastro *fhesta,* of his winter visits to Ievoli, gathering snow in the garden for *scirubetta* and feeding little Luigi with his spoon.

Stefano had died never knowing she'd intended to break off the engagement.

That evening, lying still in their bed after Tina had cried herself to sleep, Stella worked to construct a mental image of Stefano, of his hands, his hair, the way he dressed. Even the face was indistinct to her. Maybe she would have thought of him more often if she'd had a memory aid, like her mother's photo of the lost Mariastella.

Feeling a little bit disgusted with herself, she relaxed into a sense of relief. Stefano had given her a gift by dying—an excuse for spinsterhood. No one would expect her to let anyone court her; she was grieving. Stefano had bought her time—perhaps enough time. She could legitimately drag out the mourning for five years, she thought, and by then she would be twenty-seven. Far too old to marry.

She said a prayer for Stefano now.

The Christmas Eve party at the Society was the pivotal event of the year and had required much preparation. Franceschina Perri had her eye on a boy named Frank Carapellucci and had enlisted all the girls to help her run him down. Stella had never seen a girl go so unabashedly crazy for a boy like that. But Franceschina was a red-blooded American girl; she pooh-poohed the rules of decorum the Italian girls had been raised to follow. You did what you had to to get what you wanted.

Franceschina had met Frank at his welcome-home party at the beginning of December. He'd enlisted, was shipped off to the Pacific, gotten shot in the spine, and been sent back home, all in six months' time. The bullet was extracted and Frank was given his discharge papers, a free man with a little bit of a limp. Franceschina was determined to get her claws into the handsome war hero before some other girl got the same bright idea.

Unfortunately, Frank was a cool cucumber, and thus far had resisted Franceschina's flirtations. She had contrived to get her mother to invite the Carapelluccis over for post-mass luncheon, but the whole party had been for naught because Frank had only stayed for a sandwich and then left to meet some friends. Franceschina had hinted she would say yes if he asked her out on a date, but he had not picked up on the hint.

"I don't understand," Franceschina whined. The girls had each dropped by the Perris' house after their own various post-mass luncheons to see how it had gone, and now they were locked in Franceschina's room. "He seemed like he liked me, like he was making eyes at me, but then he didn't ask me out! Why? I made it so clear I like him, it's embarrassing!"

"He probably has another girl he's not telling you about," Stella said. "That's the reason he acts like that."

Fiorella, always erring on the kinder side of human nature, defended this man she hardly knew. "I think he's just shy."

"I do, too," Carolina piped up. "With the shy ones, you have to go after them hard or they slip away and someone else gets them."

"Ugh, Carolina." Stella smacked her on the arm. "Don't tell her that! She's already throwing herself at him. That's not how men work at all."

"What do I do, Stella? Tell me," Franceschina begged. "How can I make him pay attention to me?"

"You can't make him pay attention to you," Stella said. "That's the point. He has to *want* to pay attention to you. Otherwise you have nothing but trouble."

"Okay, then how do I make him *want* to pay attention to me?"

From where they sat on the bed and carpet, Carolina, Tina, Fiorella, and the forlorn lover Franceschina herself all turned their faces to Stella, waiting. Stella was the group expert in boys, since all the boys wanted her, and she had the girls' utmost respect because she didn't give a damn.

Stella was quiet for a minute, thinking about what she had in her arsenal for this situation. "Well, if we got you a really good dress . . . Carolina, do you still have that pattern you wanted to try? The one with the, you know." She waved her hand in her bosom area. They did, indeed, all know. Carolina nodded. "If you get me the fabric, I can make you that dress to have for the Christmas party at the Society."

"You can use my sewing machine, Stella," Fiorella offered. Stella had been counting on that already—she was the best sewer of the group but wouldn't have been able to finish a whole dress in that time without Fiorella's better equipment.

"What if he doesn't go to the party, though?" Tina said.

"That's our job, to make sure he does," Stella said. "We'll stop at nothing to make sure he's there."

Stella assigned the tasks. Fiorella would have Stella and Tina over for dinner every day after work for the next week so Stella could make the dress. Carolina was in charge of the gossip ring: she was to find out who Frank Carapellucci's friends were, and she was to lure them into making sure their buddy came to the Christmas party.

"You don't have to be sneaky," Stella advised. "Tell the friends there's a girl who's expecting him." Stella thought for a moment, then added, "Flirt with the friend if you have to. Give him some reason to cooperate, you know?"

Carolina tossed her glossy dark hair. "Anything for the cause."

"If you get married, you'll be Francesco and Franceschina," Tina pointed out.

Franceschina's eyes flashed. "So cute! It's too perfect."

Stella felt bad for this guy if he was planning on trying to say no.

The evening of the party, the girls reassembled at the Nicoteras' house. Everyone prepared their battle positions, pulling out last-minute hot rollers and passing a bottle of Fiorella's mother's perfume.

"There's something I have to tell you, Stella," Carolina said. "But before you get mad at me, you remember you told me to do whatever I had to do to make sure Frank went to the party, right?"

"She did," Franceschina said solidly.

"What is it, Carolina?"

Carolina smiled an evil little smile. "Well, guess who is Frank's *paesan*?"

"He's Abruzzese," Franceschina remembered. "What's the name of the village?"

But Stella already knew the answer before Carolina chirped, "Carmelo Maglieri! So, Stella, I told him you were going to be at the party, and that if he made sure Frank came that you would dance with him."

Fiorella and Tina squealed.

"Ooo, Carolina! You are such a crook." Stella's heart was pounding. Handsome, smug Carmelo Maglieri—she did not want to see him again, and she certainly didn't want to have to endure a dance with him. "You wait until now to tell me? I don't even have time to think of an excuse to get out of it."

"I would have called you, if you had a phone." Carolina paused to put on a bright red lipstick that matched her bright red Christmas dress. "Anyway, Stella, there are much worse people to have to dance with. Wait till you see who I promised Fiorella here to." She winked and all the girls hooted with mirth.

Stella knew she wouldn't be able to explain why she was so dead set against Carmelo's attention—they thought he was a catch, with his twinkling blue eyes and his concertina voice and his smart gray suit. She could hardly explain it to herself, but her gut instinct screamed out against him.

Stella solved her problem by sticking tightly by her mother throughout the party instead of mingling with her girlfriends. Tina, regretful to miss the romantic high jinks but reluctant to leave her sister, stayed in their corner. The Fortuna women watched Carolina, Fiorella, and Franceschina attack the Abruzzesi boys, pinning them in a cage of skirts, and soon the whole group was laughing and chatting. Stella congratulated herself for the excellent appearance of Franceschina's bosom, which Frank seemed to be having trouble not looking at.

"Well done, Stella," Tina said.

"Thank you," Stella replied.

"Franceschina should pay more attention to her *minne* or they're going to fall out," Assunta worried.

Carmelo Maglieri was not to be shaken off, though, and when his *paesan* Frank was safely dancing with his huntress Carmelo stepped through the crowd to join the Fortunas, bending low to kiss Assunta's hand. Stella saw how the gesture charmed her mother, her simple mother who had never seen a film in the cinema. Carmelo's necktie was holly-green. It was hard to ignore the brightness of his eyes.

Tina had dozens of questions for Carmelo about Rocco, but it quickly became clear that he had little to tell her; Rocco was not sending Carmelo letters from abroad. When Tina fretted over this, Carmelo laughed. "Why would he send letters to me?" he said. "It's much more important for him to write to his special girl."

Predictably, Tina's face began to turn fuchsia at this. "Am I really his special girl, do you think?"

"I'm sure Rocco thinks of you every day."

The idea passed through Stella's head that maybe Carmelo was checking up on Tina for his pal, keeping her loyal. She felt a new flare of distrust for him.

"We pray for him every day," Tina was saying. Her eyes were wet and energetic in her flushed face. "You should pray for him, too."

"I will," Carmelo said. His voice was serious now. He turned to face Stella. "I was sorry to hear about your fiancé. My condolences to you and your family."

Stella's wariness toward Carmelo coalesced into a cold nausea. Why would he be sad about Stefano, whom he'd never known? No man was that tenderhearted. No—by bringing up Stefano, Carmelo was alerting her to the fact that he saw her as on the market.

"We're very sad," Stella said stiffly. "He was a good man."

"He was a good man," Tina repeated, her voice breaking. Oh, not at the party, Tina, Stella thought, but Assunta was reaching out to grab Carmelo's wrist, an intimate gesture that surprised both her daughters into silence. "*You* are a very good man," Assunta said to Carmelo. "Thank you for thinking of us."

Suddenly the nausea overwhelmed Stella, and she was half-blinded by silvery spots of panic swimming over her field of vision. "Excuse me," she said. She twirled away from them and walked briskly toward the ladies' room. She had to escape. Let them think she was upset about Stefano. Luckily there was no line of waiting women. She locked herself in a stall and sat right down on the toilet in her dress, gulping lungfuls of urine-scented air, trying to calm herself.

She had been shaken by a vision of being married to Carmelo, too-smooth Carmelo, with his patient jokes and his unknowable agenda. Once the thought was in her head, she couldn't fight off the related thoughts it spawned. His hands on her, which set off ripples of phobic chills. Her body swelling with his baby. Her legs splayed like an animal's, like she had seen her mother's when Louie was born, that awful purple fig slimy with blood. Stella felt her body cramp, a ripple of fear and revulsion that started in her mons and shot up into her stomach. She couldn't banish the vision. She clutched her stomach, feeling the suture scars through the cloth of her dress. She had already been broken open once. It wasn't going to happen again.

When Tina came in and called under the stall doors for her, Stella ignored her. "Stella. *Stellll*-la. Come out. *Stellll*-la." Stella was stubborn in her silence. Finally, after the attempted interference of several other women, Tina went away.

Stella closed her eyes and tried to draw her mental picture of the mountain, the blue-silver olive leaves rippling like water in the breeze. She waited in the stall until the roiling in her stomach had subsided. Before going back to the party, she took the opportunity to pee. When she pulled down her panties she found blood in them—she must have lost track of the days again. She pulled down a handful of toilet paper from the roll, squashed it into a wad, and plugged it in, feeling better already. Perhaps it wasn't a premonition that had given her chills, just regular cramps.

Nevertheless. She couldn't let Carmelo Maglieri get too close.

"Did you ever think," said Stella to her mother the next morning as they were setting the table for lunch, "that blue eyes, like Carmelo's . . . that you need to watch out for *mal'oicch*'?"

"That's silly," Assunta said immediately.

"You know what they say about blue-eyed men," Stella said. "Nothing to stop the devil from looking out."

"That's superstitious nonsense," Assunta said. "You know that's not how it works."

"I know," Stella replied, chastised.

But before bed that night Assunta pronounced the fascination banishment over each of her children.

The war was a hard time, a literally dark time, a world muted by blackout curtains. Between the curfews and the absent young men, the social gatherings were short, stultified. There was no more meat; there was no more sugar. There were memorial masses for the boys who wouldn't come home.

Meanwhile, the Fortunas worked hard and got by. Tony rented out the second and third floors of the Bedford Street house to paying tenants, so there was rental income on top of their salaries. He still took his daughters' pay, but he gave them spending money for movies, haircuts, soda fountains. They were becoming more American by the day.

Every year, Stella's yearning for Calabria faded a little more, the pain of her separation softening into nostalgia. She felt guilty when she noticed, but she couldn't help herself. Ievoli was healing over, an old wound Stella, the survivor, had overcome. There was plenty in America for her to love—her colorful dresses, the delicious rich food, the cinemas and cars and toilets that flushed.

You work hard, time passes. Even hard times pass. For Stella, this wasn't hard times—she would have happily lived this way, working hard, eating her fill, spending her evenings with her mother and sister and friends, for the rest of her life.

Joey had enlisted in the army in 1942, and after two years of preparing for deployment he was shipped out with his unit to Europe in late autumn of 1944. He sent one letter, a single sad page addressed to Assunta and written in censor-proof English. The letter ended with one line in poorly spelled Italian: *I wish I was home.* No one heard anything else from him for six months, until the day in March 1945 when the Western Union boy came to Bedford Street.

Stella knew why he was there as soon as she saw him through the curtain. The uniform, the high-brimmed hat with the gold seal—they only sent a telegram for one reason.

"I'll get the door, Ma," Stella shouted to the kitchen. Her mother must be protected from this—at whatever cost Assunta must not answer the door. Stella took a deep breath as Tina appeared at her elbow.

"Stella. What is he here for?" Tina's voice was already ragged with tears.

Stella took another breath. Her heart was pounding. She was about to be told her brother was dead. She had to prepare herself.

Stella opened the door three-quarters and stood solidly in front of it, blocking Tina from running out onto the porch. "Yes?" Stella said to the messenger boy. Her throat was tight.

He was probably only fifteen years old, with an acne-blistered forehead and thick, rimless glasses. "Ma'am. Is this the home of Anthony and Assunta Fortuna?" He pronounced Assunta's name "Uh-suhn-ta."

Behind her, Tina was squeezing Stella's arm so tightly it hurt. "Yes," Stella said. "Those are my parents."

"He has a telegram," Tina said in Calabrese, and began to sob.

"Ma'am, I have a delivery for them."

"I will take it." Stella pressed her weight into the palm that was bracing her against the doorframe, letting the sharp edge of the wood cut into her skin. Behind her, Tina's sobbing had risen to high-pitched gasps.

The boy rubbed his nose uncomfortably. "I'm supposed to deliver it to either Mr. or Mrs. Anthony Fortuna."

Stella stepped forward and snatched the telegram out of his hand. "My brother is dead?" She felt the knot in her stomach convulse as she pictured Joey, in his uniform as she'd last seen him, dashing, handsome Joey, then her mind's eye flashing to his little fleecy head nestled against her shoulder in the bed they had shared as children. She heard the smack of Tina's hands on the foyer tiles behind her as her sister collapsed, wailing.

The messenger boy took a step backward and Stella seized his wrist so he couldn't leave. "What does this say?" she demanded. There were only a few lines of text, but Stella couldn't understand anything except Joey's name and the date. She searched for "dead" or "kill" but the English in the telegram was unfamiliar, too officious. "My brother Joey—he was killed?"

"Uh." The boy leaned forward and studied the text. "Not dead, no. Is she okay?" he said, pointing to Tina, who was prostrate weeping, her open mouth pressed into the floor tiles.

"She's fine." Stella's dark tunnel of dread began to recede. "My brother's not dead?"

He shook his head.

Still squeezing the boy's wrist, Stella turned to Tina. "Get a grip," she said. "Joey's not dead."

Tina instantly stopped sobbing. "Not dead?" She hiccupped. "Then what?"

The boy said English words Stella didn't understand. When she looked at him blankly, he repeated himself, and pointed to the telegram.

"He's hurt?" Stella tried. "Hurt bad?"

"No, geez," the boy said impatiently. He had a whole sack of visits he still had to make. "Is there someone in your house who speaks better English?"

After several months in a military hospital in France, Joey was sent home to Hartford. He'd been recovering from a self-inflicted gunshot wound in his left forearm. At least, that was how his discharge papers described the injury; Joey himself would never admit it, so people would always shrug and say, "We'll never know exactly what happened."

After two years of army training, Joey had apparently not been mentally prepared for combat; when his unit landed in France, his misgivings overwhelmed him. The rest of the 103rd headed north to invade Germany, but Joey Fortuna never made it out of Marseilles.

The army had court-martialed Joey as soon as he was released from the military hospital and sent him home with a dishonorable discharge. Despite his criminal act of self-mutilation, the Hartford veterans' hospital offered him an operation to fix his arm at no cost. Joey declined the surgery; he was afraid that if he were able-bodied they would send him back to war. A pointless sacrifice—if only Joey had been smart enough to ask around a little, he'd have learned DDs were never redeployed.

Despite his long sojourn in the French hospital, Joey's arm healed incompletely; the radius and ulna had both shattered on the bullet's impact, and the arm had been somewhat sarcastically reset by a harried military surgeon who only suffered malingerers because of his Hippocratic oath. Joey had avoided jail time, but the dishonorable discharge together with his new physical impairment became a long, dark shadow over his life and prospects.

Furthermore, as was protocol for a noncitizen soldier who had been dishonorably discharged, the INS had terminated Joey's naturalization application.

Tony dragged Joey down to the army office on Asylum Street to protest. He made Joey wear a suit. "You can't do that," Tony roared at the soldier on desk duty. "He went to war for you! The paperwork, it's already done. He's a citizen."

The soldier had no sympathy for cowards. He was cold and calm. "In the event of dishonorable discharge, they can put a stop to the naturalization application, even retroactively."

"Retroactively?" Tony repeated.

"Meaning even if it's already done. They can undo it."

Joey stared at the linoleum as Tony became outraged. "He fought for your country!"

"My country?" the soldier said neutrally. "Look, Mr. Fortuna, your son committed a crime against the U.S. military during a time of war. He's lucky to not be subject to more extreme disciplinary measures." For clarity, he spelled it out: "You're lucky he's not in jail."

That was the end of that negotiation. Tony stormed off to the bar without anything further to say to his son, who walked home alone.

If Joey had died during active duty, his whole family—parents, siblings—would have been immediately eligible for United States citizenship. But that was the root of the problem; Joey had been unwilling to die, or even get too close to risking death. And now he was a disgraced small-time criminal with no GI benefits and a bum arm.

Tony would never forgive his son for his cowardice. Tony, who'd spent four years in combat on one of the bloodiest battle-fronts in human history and who'd never shot himself in the arm, resented the weakness he saw in Joey. A son was meant to be proof of a father's manliness; Tony's son was unmanly. He was soft and spoiled and scared, a man who could earn no respect. As long as both men lived they were never able to heal this breach. Tony ignored his son if they were in the same room. If they did speak to each other—if Joey, restless for drama, forced a conversation—it ended in shouting, taunting, and a xylophone of slamming doors.

Joey was physically unfit to perform many of the construction and factory jobs the other noncitizen immigrant men took, and the truth of his situation was a black mark against him, quickly sussed out by interviewers whose own boys were off being brave. *You're injured because you served, but you don't have American papers or veteran benefits . . . ?* After four or five anemic attempts to find a job, Joey gave up and spent his time in his room at Bedford Street. He drank from the time he woke up—usually around noon—until he eventually fell asleep. He went through gallons of Tony's wine. Drinking was a habit he had picked up overseas, and he intended to live the rest of his life in a wine-dulled haze.

"You don't need this," Assunta would say to him when he sat down at the kitchen table in his undershirt and long johns. She'd say it as she poured him a tall glass of red wine from the jug she kept ready on the counter.

"Trust me, Ma, I do need it," he'd reply. He'd wait for her to set a dish of breakfast *pastina* in front of him. "This is who I am now, your pathetic drunk failure of a son. This is how it's gonna be."

The presence of this replacement monster—a different person entirely from the mischievous, affectionate, pretty-faced Joey who'd gone to war—was a continuing shock to Stella. The sight of him at the wine-stained kitchen table—it made her feel sick. He was her brother, the baby she'd learned to hold when she was just a baby herself, who'd cried for a whole day when his favorite stray cat disappeared, who'd wink as he cracked open chestnuts for her with one sharp, deft bite. Her baby brother—still so handsome now, despite his red eyes and nasty smile. But he was a monster who didn't care whom he hurt, as long as he could celebrate his own damage. She didn't see his suffering, like her mother did. He was an agent of corruption in their house, a perfect thing that had rotted and was determined to rot everything around it.

Joey's return was particularly annoying for Louie, who was fifteen and had had the boys' bedroom to himself for three years. Louie was a straight shooter, neat and polite, with subdued manners his teachers appreciated. He was on track to graduate from high school—the first person in his family to do such a thing—and had done well on the football squad. The sour-smelling and maudlin older brother in his bedroom was cramping his teenage style. In the summer, when school was out, Louie started sleeping at friends' houses and sometimes not coming home for days at a time.

Assunta cried about this, because Louie was her favorite. "You know he's the best of you kids," she would tell Joey as he sat at the table in a hanging-open bathrobe. "You let him take care of you like he's the older brother."

"I'm old in my heart, Ma," Joey would say. "I'm so old I don't have any reason to go running around doing shit to impress people. I know there's no point."

Carmelo Maglieri sometimes took Joey out for a beer. It seemed to be what Joey needed, and he would come home in a better mood.

"You should marry him, Stella," Joey told the whole family one night at dinner. "You know he's got it for you. He's been waiting for three years for you to come around."

Tony looked up from his food, appraising his oldest daughter. Stella felt herself flush so violently the skin on her neck began to itch.

"Good for him," she said shortly.

"Come on, Stella, you could do a hell of a lot worse."

"Shut up, Joey," she said in English. It sounded much stronger in English. "You're an idiot." She knew her father was still watching her.

"And you're a snot." Joey was shaking his head. "What about you you think is so great you could do better than Carmelo? Good-looking guy like that? Any one of the girls at the Society would say yes in a heartbeat."

"Well, let them fight over him, then." Stella focused on the cool air around her, willing away the burn in her face and neck.

"You should be thinking about your prospects, Stella," Tony said. "You're twenty-five. You never know who is going to come back from this war."

"Papa, Tina hardly needs more of a reason to worry about Rocco," Stella said. It was mean to turn the conversation that way, but the strategy revealed itself to be a stroke of genius. The focus was now on the latest news of Rocco Caramanico. No one said anything else about Carmelo Maglieri that night, but Stella knew the seed had been planted in her father's head. Carmelo had just become her enemy.

Carmelo worked at Pratt & Whitney, like Tony, but in the engine unit. After Joey brought up Stella's marriage prospects at the dinner table, it somehow came about that Carmelo was picking up Tony in the morning and driving him to work in his Plymouth. Stella wasn't sure if her father had sought out Carmelo or if Carmelo had made the offer. Either way it was bad news.

When he dropped Tony off after work, Carmelo would come in for a glass of wine and then end up staying for dinner. He was not subtle about his interest in Stella. She was being courted, and her father, who was old-world enough to believe his opinion mattered, was pleased. Stella was aware of the danger. Little innocent-looking lifestyle changes, like the commuting arrangements and the dinner drop-ins, were going to pile on her gradually until she found herself the mother of Carmelo's ten children and not sure when, exactly, she'd been broken down.

Stella was besieged in her own house, and her supposed allies were sympathetic to the enemy. Everyone liked Carmelo. He flirted with Assunta, who would chuckle and swat him with her kitchen towel. She invited him back night after night for dinner. "Poor thing," she'd say, "living in that awful bachelor building with a bunch of men." Stella didn't feel one bit sorry for him; the man was hardly starving and could easily charm some other doting mother into feeding him.

Carmelo gossiped with Tina like they were old girlfriends. He taught Louie card games. On nights Carmelo came over, Tony and Joey would both stay in, and the men would play cards at the kitchen table—a rare rapprochement between Joey and his father. This was the year Tony began to go out less in the evenings; it might be when his relationship with that other, unknown woman ended. As much as Stella resented Carmelo's infiltration of her family, she knew her mother was happier, free of the anxiety and sadness she'd had to rally against every night her husband hadn't come home.

Carmelo read and wrote well in both Italian and English; he read the newspaper every morning, he told them, and that was how he learned everything he'd ever known. It was Carmelo who enabled the Fortuna girls to pass their citizenship tests, at last, in July 1945. Carmelo read the study questions aloud, interpreted them into Italian, and quizzed the sisters until, finally, it felt like Stella was memorizing something she understood. He spoke to

Tina in English, knowing she struggled with the language, prompting her kindly.

Carmelo now used Calabrese expressions he must have picked up from the Fortunas. Was he working so hard to fit in with them that he even changed his speech? Stella wondered, was he doing it on purpose or subconsciously? And—which would be worse?

It would come eventually, the direct confrontation. "Eventually" turned out to be the week after Stella had become a United States citizen.

"With your father's permission," Carmelo had said during dinner, in front of the whole damn family, "I would like to take you out on a date, Stella."

"A date," Antonio said, repeating the American word. "What kind of date?"

"Dinner and a movie on Saturday night," Carmelo said. He seemed calm and confident. Meanwhile Stella was full of dread, looking down at her plate of pasta as the rest of her family stared at her. Their glee was palpable; it filled the dining room and clamped around her like an invisible vise. How could she fight against his charisma?

"Well, Stella?" Tony said.

"No, thank you," she replied in her politest voice. She could not break down under this pressure. She would not be subjugated. "I don't go on dates."

"Now's a good time to start," Tony said. "Or you're going to be an old maid."

"No, *thank you*," she repeated, sitting up straight and looking her father in the eye. "I do not date. I am mourning my lost fiancé."

"Horseshit," said Joey in English. Assunta would have smacked him if she'd understood.

"*Enough!*" Tony had escalated to his roaring mode already. "She accepts your invitation," he said to Carmelo. "You can pick her up here on Saturday at six o'clock."

Stella's hands were vibrating in fury. She was not in control of this situation. What could she do? "Tina, you'll come with me as a chaperone," she said.

Tony said shortly, "You're twenty-five years old. You don't need a chaperone."

Stella looked around the table, at her brothers and sister and parents and suitor all watching her, waiting for her to say something. With Joey filling the chair on one side of her and Tina on the other, there was no way she could stand up and storm out of the room with any dignity. She contemplated throwing her plate of food, but she wouldn't be proud of herself for that kind of melodrama.

So instead she gave them as little satisfaction as was within her ability. She picked up her fork, tined a collection of *ziti* pieces, and put them in her mouth. Her tongue was dry and her stomach tight. The moment dragged on, everyone waiting for her reaction, as she made her way steadily through the plate of pasta.

"Well, all right," Carmelo said after too long. "I'll pick you up on Saturday."

All his pretending to be a gentleman—a real gentleman would have backed off when she made it clear she didn't want to go out with him. No, he was like all the rest of them, the exhausting conspiracy of men working together to make women do what they wanted them to. She would tuck this away, this definitive proof that Carmelo wasn't as nice as he seemed.

That night, and every night leading up to her date, Stella had her nightmare. It had been more than a year since she'd had an episode and she'd hoped it had gone away. But here it was, back again—her imprisonment, the rapist's hands on her naked skin, her helplessness. Sleepless and exhausted, she'd go sit at the kitchen table under the first Stella's shrine and try to nap on her folded arms. She tried to rub away the feeling of the rapist's erection pressing into her thigh, rubbing until it bruised. She prayed to Mary for protection and forgiveness.

Dogged by insomnia, harassed, and unwilling, Stella refused to make any special effort with her appearance for her date, which was very upsetting to Assunta.

"Why can't you just do this, Stella?" her mother sobbed. Friday night had become a full-scale screaming match. "Why can't you be just a little nice to him so you don't spoil your chances?"

"For God's sake, Mamma, why can't *you* just listen to me?" Stella's voice cracked with rage. "I'm saying I *don't want* to marry him. I don't care about spoiling my chances because I *don't want* him."

"Yes, you do!" Assunta shouted. "Yes, you do, and you know it!"

"Mamma. Why don't you believe me? Why don't you *listen?*" A fight like this with her father would have been easier—he was just a brute and Stella hated him. But coming from Assunta— this was betrayal by the woman Stella loved most in the world, who apparently didn't care about her daughter's hopes or opinions. "When have I ever lied to you about anything? Never."

Assunta's sobs transitioned into howling. She was incoherent, the situation helpless. Stella, worn out by her anger, went into the bathroom and washed and curled her hair. She needed to for church, anyway. It was just one day early.

Carmelo, on the other hand, had made a good effort for their date. When he came to pick her up, his black curls were dampened and combed down along a neat center part. He wore his gray suit and a sky-blue silk tie. He had a new fedora pressed to his chest when she met him at the door.

Carmelo chatted, obviously a little nervous, during the short car ride, and Stella rode in depressed silence. Her fight with her mother lay heavy on her still. She was enervated by frustration.

No one believed she knew what was best for herself; everyone wanted to control her.

Now she was alone with Carmelo and the weight of the situation was hers to bear. Stewing in her bad feelings was not going to save her hide. She needed to focus on Carmelo, on ending the courtship.

She hadn't picked her tactic yet; was she going to be cold and polite and very distant? Or outright mean and rude? Or should she be normal and friendly, since it was so hard to not warm up to Carmelo, and just tell him plainly that she appreciated his effort, but she was never going to say yes and wouldn't it be easiest for them both if he would stop trying? She still hadn't decided when they arrived at Tom's Restaurant, which Carmelo had chosen for dinner.

Throughout the meal—she ordered a hamburger, and Carmelo followed suit—she vacillated. Every time she realized she was chatting too warmly, she would get angry with herself and retreat into a sulk, but then she would feel stupid and weak. The meal was exhausting whenever she remembered she wasn't supposed to be enjoying herself.

And Stella felt shabby sitting across from him in this brightly lit diner. She imagined the other diners looking at them, a handsome, well-dressed man and a barely groomed woman wearing no makeup, not even a little lipstick. She suppressed flashes of regret. Vanity, she would not let vanity be her downfall. The opinions of strangers meant nothing.

Carmelo was undaunted. In fact, he became increasingly comfortable and confident over the course of the meal. He talked to her about his twin sister in Montreal, his parents and brother back home in the Abruzzi. He asked her polite questions he already knew the answers to; she was disadvantaged because he had spent so much time trying to get to know her.

"Next time," Carmelo said as Stella folded her napkin and placed it on her empty plate, "I can take you down to the rose garden."

Stella had enjoyed the hamburger; she was feeling content. She shook herself out of that stupor. "Carmelo. There isn't going to be a next time."

"Yes, there is." He winked at her, so self-assured.

She felt a rile of hatred—yes, that was good. Nurture that. "I'm here because my father made me go out with you. You know that. I don't like you, and I never will."

"Oh, you'll see. I'll make you like me." He winked again. "I think you do already anyway."

"Carmelo. Listen to me." The wink disgusted her. She bit down on her frustration, spoke clearly and slowly so that maybe this time he would hear what she said. "This—you and me— isn't going to go anywhere. You can chase me all you want, but I am never going to get married. Not to you, not to anyone."

"Bullshit," he said jovially. "Every woman wants to get married."

"Not me." Her chest was tight. The fury of last night had come back, and now it was all directed at him.

"Yes, you do," he said. "Even if you don't know it yet. You'll change your mind. Just watch."

She stared at him across the table. For the first time, she noticed he had several unruly eyebrow hairs that splayed out of formation, poking up like insect antennae. "Carmelo. I'm telling you I don't love you, and I never will. You're not listening."

He shrugged, counting money out of his wallet, but his smile had tightened. "You think you know what you want, Stella, but you're going to realize you're wrong."

Her fury bubbled in her throat. It was like talking to a wall. "Why are you so persistent?" she asked. "There are a hundred other girls who like you. Quit wasting your time on me."

Carmelo's eyes were bright as he met her gaze. "Stella, I've seen our future together. It's a good one. You'll see it, too. We're meant to be together, we have been since we were born." She scoffed. Was he serious? "Listen. My friend Rocco is going to come back from the war and he's going to start a family with your sister. Think about how nice it would be if you and I got married. Our children would grow up together like brothers and sisters."

She'd teetered through years of ambivalence about Carmelo Maglieri—was he genuine or dangerous, sweet and gentle or cagey and manipulative? Now she understood: as kind as he seemed, Carmelo was as macho and controlling as Tony, just in his own way. Carmelo didn't love Stella—how could he, when he couldn't even listen to what she had to say? All he loved was his own dream of his own future, which he needed her for. He had no interest in trying to understand why she wouldn't want to be a part of it.

She needed to drive him off. Do something drastic to disrupt his fantasy. She looked down at her arms, resting near her plate, and rotated her left wrist so she could study the flat surgical scar, thinking hard. Her heart was beating in her ears. "You know I don't cook. And I never will."

"Oh, well, then you absolutely better marry me. I'm a great cook." He dipped his chin knowingly. "Not a lot of other men would put up with that from their wives."

There was her bubble of fury again. "What's wrong with you?" she said. She stood up from the table and raised her voice. "Why do you keep chasing me when you know I don't want you? I could never respect a man like that. It's pathetic." She took two steps toward the door, then turned around and made herself shout, "That's right, I said you were pathetic!" Let the other diners think she was a noisy wop. She didn't care. Let Carmelo think she was a noisy wop. Let him focus on that.

Carmelo stood, too, but she didn't let him get a word in. "You want a wife who would never respect you?" she shrieked. "You like being made a fool of?"

His face had flushed pink. "All right, Stella. Let's go."

"Pathetic," she said again. A horrible feeling was settling in her gut. The waitress was coming toward them, a broom clutched in one hand. She would have had no idea what the shouting was about, Stella realized.

"Come on." Carmelo gestured toward the door, and she walked ahead of him out onto the street. She felt sick. This was so undignified. She tried to steel herself. It would all be worth it if he would leave her alone.

"I want to go home," she told him. "I don't feel well."

He walked her to his car and opened the door to the passenger side. His face was still bright red as he got into the driver's seat. Was he mad? Embarrassed?

They drove back to Bedford Street in silence. He got out of the car to let her out, and then escorted her up the steps. Assunta scurried to meet Stella in the foyer. "What's the matter? Weren't you supposed to go to the movies?"

"Stella's not feeling well," Carmelo said. He didn't step into the house, just stood on the doormat.

"Not feeling well? Stella, are you all right?" Her mother was shaking her shoulder.

"I'll be fine, Ma." Stella fought back waves of mortification and anger. Was that all he was going to say? Was this over? "It's just an upset stomach. I'm going to bed."

Carmelo tipped his fedora as he bowed to Assunta, then to Stella. "Thank you for a lovely evening." His voice was flat, affectless. "I hope you feel better soon." He pushed his hat down over his ears and walked back to his car.

Assunta was wild eyed. She was probably trying to imagine what terrible thing had happened on the date. "What's the matter, Stella?"

Stella didn't answer. She pushed past her mother and went to the bathroom, where she vomited her hamburger into the toilet.

After her ruined date with Carmelo Maglieri, Stella lived through the nightmare four more times in as many days. She'd become so afraid of having it that she couldn't fall asleep, despite her exhaustion. Then, for some reason, it stopped.

Carmelo no longer stayed for dinner. When he dropped Tony off after work, he rarely even came into the house to say hello. She had successfully ended the courtship.

Tina and Assunta both harassed her and Tony gave her a black eye she wore proudly for a week. But the damage was done, and Carmelo didn't want her anymore. She was safe, until her father latched onto another suitor. What with the stiff competition among the East Side Italian girls for the returning soldiers, Stella wasn't worried. Carmelo had been her most dangerous brush with marriage, she was sure; it would be much easier from here.

Now that they were citizens, Stella and Tina went to work at the Silex factory, on a coffeepot assembly line. The day they went in for their interview, Assunta came along with them. She brought a tray of ravioli to bribe the foreman. Whether or not the ravioli were a factor, the Fortuna girls got the job.

Carmelo Maglieri broke his moratorium to visit Bedford Street one night in August. He sat at the kitchen table to chat with Assunta as she cooked, acting as if weeks hadn't passed since he'd last sat there. Stella had been keeping her mother company, sorting and tailing long beans, and when Carmelo sat down across from her he nodded polite greeting. His expression was serious today, none of his cherub smiles. The top buttons of his tan shirt were open, a gold cross on a chain hanging in an array of chest hair at which Stella had trouble not staring.

Carmelo accepted a glass of wine from Assunta, who was so overjoyed to see him she stumbled over things to say. Stella loved her mother for her affectionate heart, even if she was a traitor.

"I have some news, Za 'Ssunta," Carmelo said, but he was looking at Stella. "Zi Tony and I already spoke about it, but I wanted to tell you in person."

Carmelo's older brother, Gio, had bought a grocery store in Chicago from a *paesan*. Apparently Carmelo had been sending home so much money that Gio had been able to take care of their parents throughout the war with enough left over to buy a grocery store.

"He says since it's my money, he bought the store in my name," Carmelo explained. How did he manage to look humble?

Gio was in Chicago already. He'd run the store until Carmelo got there. Then they would run it together. Carmelo had brought his brother's letter, and Assunta was turning it over, studying the writing as if she could read it. "How nice, a store. But you're going away, Carmelo?"

He shrugged. "A store is a great thing. Hard work, but if you're a smart businessman you can make good money. The factory work here is good, but all the men are going to come home from the war and want their jobs back."

Tina, who'd been working in the garden, came into the kitchen, her hair sweat-frizzed around her pink face. She gave Carmelo an excited wet kiss on the cheek and he had to tell the whole thing all over again. Stella listened to her mother and sister's alternating sorrowful and ecstatic disruptions.

"But I came to talk to you, Stella," Carmelo said, taking the letter back and pointing it at her like a threat. Assunta and Tina immediately fell silent.

He was staring at her. Stella stared back.

"Listen, Stella." When he said her name a second time, her heart shuddered. "All you have to do right now is say the word 'maybe.' Maybe someday you will marry me. Just say maybe and I'll tear the letter up right here in front of you and I'll stay on Front Street. Maybe, just say maybe, Carmelo. Maybe someday."

She met his gaze steadily. "Never." She was intensely grateful that her father had not joined them in the kitchen for this conversation.

"Stella!" Tina squeaked.

"Never?" Carmelo asked her.

"Never."

She was startled by a fast, hard blow to the back of her head. She reached through the ringing to touch the source of the pain and her fingers came back wet—slicked in olive oil. It took her a moment to realize her mother had hit her with the thick wooden spoon she'd been using to sauté the garlic.

"*Stupida brutta*," Assunta said. "What is wrong with you? What kind of game are you playing?" She looked both angry and hurt. It was as though Stella had rejected Assunta's own son. "How many more times do you think he's going to ask you before he gets tired and finds someone else?"

Stella rubbed her scalp. "Mamma, how can you take his side over mine?" Seeing the way Assunta was gripping the spoon, she braced herself for another blow.

"I would have given you anything you wanted, Stella," Carmelo interrupted. "I would have given you the world. All I wanted was to make you happy."

The ripple of thought-pictures—his hands on her flesh, swelling pregnant belly. "You could never make me happy," she said, her mouth dry.

His face had hardened. "What is it you think you want in life, exactly? What do you think I could never give you?"

Stella was at a loss for words. How had she ever been unclear about what she wanted? How many times had she already told him—told them all? "I want to be left alone," she said finally.

The kitchen was silent for a moment. Carmelo shook his head. "You are a cold woman, Stella."

As if he had put a curse on her, she felt a chill ripple up her arms and torso. "Maybe so," she said. "But that's no business of yours."

"You think you're ever going to find someone who would love you more than I would have loved you?" He was staring at her so intensely she had to avert her eyes. "You are a fool."

After a throbbing moment of silence, Carmelo stood and bowed his little bow to Assunta and Tina. "I tried, Za 'Ssunta," he said. "I would have liked to have been your son-in-law. But I think I had better go home now."

Assunta and Tina tried to convince him to stay for dinner, but it was a hollow effort. Carmelo gave Assunta and Tina each a solemn kiss and wished them health. "Stella," he said to her, nodding his saline good-bye.

Carmenantonio Maglieri had left their lives.

Rocco Caramanico did, in fact, survive the war. He was gone for almost four years, like many men who were shipped to the Pacific theater, doing things unknown and wholly misunderstood by their families. Rocco kept a framed photo of his Engineers Chemical Corps unit hanging in his hallway for the rest of his life, but what had happened in New Guinea was anyone's guess. Had he shot a gun? Had he killed a Jap? Had he seen atrocities, been exposed to hazardous chemicals, watched his friends die? Had he been in any combat at all, had he ever felt any danger? He came back with no exterior scarring, no shrapnel spatter or purple hearts. What had he been *doing* all that time? Well, that is the mystery of war. The only thing Rocco made clear was that he would never eat chicken again. Otherwise, he never told anyone anything more than had been in his sterile, correct letters to Tina.

Rocco and Tina both kept their promises. Rocco returned to Hartford in January 1946, once his unit had been deactivated and he'd been released from a lengthy quarantine. He arrived on a Saturday and the next afternoon, when everyone was back from church, he telephoned Tony and requested permission to visit that evening.

He arrived with his sister at six o'clock. Barbara brought a plate stacked high with *mustazzoli*. Rocco carried a dozen red roses. Stella, who answered the door, was grudgingly impressed.

The Fortunas gathered around the coffee table, on which Assunta arranged Barbara's cookie platter and small glasses for wine. Stella could see Rocco was much thinner than he'd been when he left—perhaps thirty pounds thinner. He wore a black suit that must have predated the war, because it was too big on him, but otherwise he was immaculate.

Tina and Rocco greeted each other, after almost four years apart, with a handshake and shy smiles. Tina sat clumsily in a woven-backed chair near the couch, Rocco's roses spilling off her lap. Stella stood in the doorway, listening silently as Tina and Rocco made bland, compulsory small talk. The lamp on the round table between them had a Tiffany-style stained-glass shade, gold with green and purple grapevines; in its tinted light, Tina's complexion looked particularly tawny, Rocco's particularly jaundiced. Stella thought of all the things that could have happened to him during the war. How lucky Tina was that none of them had.

Assunta poured wine, then announced she was going to make dinner. Tina stood and followed; Barbara stayed where she was on the couch. She would be part of the negotiations. Stella, who would hardly be expected in the kitchen, took a silent step backward so she stood in the hallway, tucked into the shadow of the doorframe, hoping no one would think to wonder where she was.

"Well, I came back alive," Rocco said to Tony without preamble. "I would like to ask for your daughter Tina's hand."

It was really happening, right now. This was what a man proposing looked like.

"I'm glad to see you, Rocco," Tony said. "I'm glad it went well for you."

"I was lucky."

"God watched over him," Barbara corrected. There was a lull as they murmured thanks to God, and then as Tony lifted his glass and they drank a toast.

"I would like to marry Tina," Rocco said again when they had swallowed. "I think she would make me an excellent wife."

"But would you make her a good husband?" Tony shot back.

Rocco sat up even more rigidly. "I believe I would be a husband any smart, good girl would be happy to marry."

Tony chuckled. "You would, would you?" Stella wasn't sure whether he was teasing Rocco or not; Rocco wouldn't know, either.

"Yes, sir."

"All right, all right, so you think you two would be a match. I think you might be right, myself, from what I've seen. Writing letters to each other all this time."

"So I have your permission to marry her?" Rocco said.

"You have my permission to *ask*. This is—" Tony coughed into his hand. Rocco and Barbara sat at attention as Tony took a sip of wine and wiped his mustache on his wrist. "This is America, boy. I'm not just going to arrange something for her. It has to be her choice."

One beat of silence. Stella wondered if her mother and sister in the kitchen were straining to hear; she didn't hear any pot-banging, tap-running, or garlic-frying.

Rocco extended his hand. "Thank you, sir. It will be my honor."

Tony hesitated, or maybe just waited, before shaking Rocco's hand. "Well. Good luck."

"Thank you, sir," Rocco said again. God, he was so stiff.

Now was Barbara's turn. "About the matter of the dowry," she said, and that was all she had to say. She'd hit Tony's switch.

"Dowry?" he roared. "*Dowry?* Is that what this is about? You think I'm going to *pay* you to take away my Tina, the backbone of my house? *Pay* you, from the scraps I've saved slaving away for the last twenty-five years?" He shook his head, blowing like a bull. His hair had expanded into a halo of rage. Stella felt the natural gut terror at her father's anger—fists could very well fly—but she also recognized this as a performance. "I think you have the wrong end of the stick there, *signora*. How about *you* tell *me* how your brother is going to provide for *my* daughter?"

Barbara was tough; she'd been screamed at by men before. "*Scusa*, Zio, but you know very well it is the bride's responsibility to provide a trousseau. Otherwise what are she and her husband supposed to start their lives with?"

"My daughter has an excellent trousseau, don't you worry." Stella could hear him fuming so hard he was gasping for breath. "Not that that's any of your brother's business, if you're asking me for money here. Where I come from, a man proposing marriage to a woman has a home to take her to live in. Does your brother have a house for my daughter to live in?" And to Rocco, "Well? Do you have a house?"

A hesitation. "Not yet, sir."

Barbara said bravely, "It is custom for the bride's father to help a groom buy—"

"Custom!" Tony was roaring again. "*Custom* where I come from is for a man to be a *man*. It seems to me in your family men count on their women to take care of them."

Stella had leaned forward, dangerously out of the shadows, to see the expressions on the siblings' faces. Barbara had crossed her arms and her legs tightly. Rocco was still sitting in an attitude of military attention. His mouth was a dark yellow line.

Barbara's voice was even, but angry. "*Custom* is that a *man* supports his daughters when it is time for them to wed."

Tony was silent for a moment. "It sounds to me like you're not ready to make a serious offer here."

Stella felt her heart pounding at the suspense. Was Tony backpedaling on his permission? Would he really give Tina nothing for her new house? Or was this just bluster? Stella tried to imagine how her sister, listening in the kitchen, must be feeling.

"If——" Barbara began, but Rocco lifted a hand and she fell silent. He'd sat so still for so long his movement surprised Stella.

"I am quite serious," Rocco said. Stella realized he was radiating anger, as well. What kind of person did he become, she wondered, if things didn't go his way? "I will buy your daughter a house. I have all of my combat pay saved. In another two or three years I will have enough."

"What kind of house?" Tony asked. He gestured broadly, taking in his own castle. "My daughter's children will grow up better than this, if their father is a retired American soldier. It will need to have at least three bedrooms."

Rocco blinked. Stella waited, too tense even to take a breath. "I will promise her a house with at least two bedrooms." Rocco was negotiating, Stella realized. It was just like buying a donkey at the animal fair.

This seemed to satisfy Tony. "All right," he said. He uncrossed his legs and leaned forward, poured them all refills. "Well, in that case——"

Rocco raised a hand again, this time silencing his future father-in-law. "And," he said. "And you will buy all of the furniture. All of it." He ticked off items on his fingers. "Two beds, one for each bedroom. Two dressers for clothes. A sofa for the living room, and a coffee table. A kitchen table, a dining room set." Tony had been laughing scornfully through the list. Rocco, waiting for a response, added, "And a refrigerator."

At this Tony stopped laughing. "A refrigerator? In the house?"

"Yes."

"Do you have any idea how much a refrigerator costs?"

"Soon every house will have one," Rocco said. "Your daughter will need one to run her kitchen."

There was silence for what felt to Stella like a long time. Finally Tony said, "Once you have bought the house, I will buy two beds and one sofa. I will buy your dining room set, but how my daughter furnishes her kitchen is her business, so you will buy your own refrigerator. That is my whole wedding gift to you, two beds, one sofa, and the dining room set."

Rocco said, "All right, Tina will pick out her own kitchen things and I will buy them for her when we move in. And I will not ask you for a coffee table. But you will provide the dressers, one for each bedroom." Stella felt a wash of relief; they were reaching a denouement. But then Rocco added, "And you will buy two lamps for each room in the house. Good lamps." Stella heard a thread of vitriol. "And you will buy the lightbulbs to put in the lamps."

He was making a joke, she thought. It must be a joke.

Tony laughed again, this time with what sounded like genuine joy. "No, boy, you can buy your own lightbulbs." Still chuckling, he extended his hand. "I think we are done here. You may go speak to her now if you'd like."

Rocco stood, ignoring the offered handshake. "You will buy the lightbulbs, or you can keep your daughter."

There was a moment of shocked silence. Barbara's eyes were wide; she liked Tina, Stella knew, and probably wasn't sure if she should say something or let her brother fight his own battle.

"That's it, Signor Fortuna," Rocco said. "I am done here. If you think your daughter can do better, then I wish you both the best." He wiped his hands on his pants; perhaps they were sweating. "I know plenty of good girls who would be happy for any husband right now, never mind a U.S. Army combat vet with a good service record. I don't need to settle."

A nervous thrill ran through Stella, a thrill at the viciousness of it. Was this really the man Tina wanted to marry? Would he really have exchanged her for eight or ten lightbulbs? Even after four years of letters and care packages? Or was this bluster, too?

Tony stood, too. He said soberly, "All right. I will buy the lightbulbs. Two for each room."

"The lightbulbs, *and* the lamps," Rocco said.

"Yes," Tony said quietly. "Lightbulbs and lamps."

Rocco and Barbara did not stay for dinner. It would have been excruciating to have to sit through a meal after that, and for the girls not to be able to rehash. And Joey might have emerged stinking from the boys' bedroom at any time; Stella was relieved he hadn't chosen to do so during the shouting earlier, since he was sometimes drawn out for drama. Instead, Rocco asked Tina to join him in the hallway for a private conversation. They had to pass Stella in the hallway, but Rocco didn't seem to notice her.

Still not sure how much Tina had heard, Stella decided she didn't want to hear the proposal itself, so she walked through the living room, nodding coolly at her father, who looked irritated and confused, and joined her mother in the kitchen, where the women silently poured, toasted, and each drank down a tall glass of wine.

The wedding would be on August 17, 1946, a ceremony at Sacred Heart and a reception at the Italian American Home on Platt Street. Tony Fortuna paid for everything, as the father of the bride should. He accompanied Tina to the G. Fox bridal boutique to pick out the dress and the veil. They were one hundred dollars and twenty-five dollars, respectively. The dress was made of stiff white linen; although silk wasn't rationed anymore, it was still expensive, so Tina hadn't even tried on any silk dresses. Stella would have at least tried one on.

Stella would be the maid of honor, of course. She swam through a strange mix of emotions, heart-twisting pride and excitement to help her baby sister in this wedding, even though Stella had private misgivings about the marriage Tina was making. It was the second time Stella would be maid of honor, after Franceschina Perri's wedding to Frank Carapellucci last fall, so Stella had some good ideas about how to celebrate her sister. She spent fifteen dollars, carefully saved from her factory pay and hidden from her father in a pink sock she kept in her underwear drawer, to throw Tina a beautiful shower luncheon. She bought pastries from Federal Bakery on State Street and even made tiny "tea" sandwiches like the ones they sold at the café at G. Fox, triangles of American bread with cheese or jam inside. It was the closest Stella had ever come to cooking anything; she wouldn't have done it for anyone but Tina. All the ladies who attended cooed over their daintiness. Stella had spent a month of evenings making party favors—a handkerchief with a multicolor crocheted lace edge. She bought herself and Tina both new summer dresses, as well as new shoes, to wear to the party. And finally, Stella got Joey to buy her a bottle of anisette, which the ladies passed around after their tea. Everyone was laughing as they kissed Tina good-bye, and everyone left a cash-stuffed envelope in a pile on the table. A grand success of a shower; Stella was satisfied she wouldn't be shown up as an East Side hostess for a long time.

Stella's maid of honor dress was yellow and mimicked Tina's in its puffed shoulders and sweetheart neckline. The other brides-maids would wear an identical dress but in baby blue. For the bridesmaids, Tina had Fiorella Mulino, Carolina Nicotera, Franceschina's younger sister Loretta, and a girl named Josie Brandolino, who was the daughter of Tony's new Abruzzese boss. Tony had been laid off from his factory job in March—they had to make room for the boys coming home—and he was working odd jobs for a construction company. He wanted to make a good impression on his new boss there and made Tina invite Josie to be a bridesmaid even though the Fortuna girls barely knew her.

Tony booked a band and arranged the catering, sandwiches and pizza. Stella would have wanted to weigh in on her own wedding menu, but Tina didn't complain. Tony was paying, and he could choose whatever food he wanted.

Good for him, Stella reminded herself. This was the only wedding he'd get to host.

Rocco's sister Barbara volunteered to make the cake, a four-tier fruitcake dense with raisins, figs, prunes, and honey, sweet work-arounds to the ongoing sugar rationing. Barbara needed all the sugar she could get her hands on to frost the three-foot-tall sixty-pound behemoth a suitably angelic bridal white. This was not Barbara's first wedding cake—it was a gift worth at least thirty-five dollars, and she'd become a specialist over her years in Hartford. But decorating, she felt, was not her forte, and she conscripted Stella to help. Two Thursdays before the wedding, Barbara and Stella walked down to State Street and stood on the sidewalk outside of Federal Bakery for two hours, watching the white-aproned professionals decorate a wedding cake in the front bay window for everyone to see, as they did each morning. Stella shifted on her sore feet—she'd worn her nice shoes so they might convincingly pass as actual shoppers, not just snoopers—while Barbara stared, unabashed, and murmured things like "Aha! Did you see what she just did with the knife?" and "Well, we're not going to be able to make flowers like *that* at home, are we, Stella?"

The week after he proposed, Rocco had bought Tina an American-style engagement ring, a band of yellow gold with a half-carat diamond in the middle. She wore it everywhere, even to work at the coffeepot factory, every day for the rest of her life, until the day she was washing dishes and the diamond dropped out of the setting and down her sink. She had her nephew Artie take the pipe out, but they never found the diamond. This happened in April 2006, months shy of her sixtieth anniversary, and two weeks after Rocco had died.

The week before Tina got married, Louie, who had just turned sixteen, went into the woods by Keney Park with two of his friends from school, Bobby Minghella and Danny Peach. Danny's father, a Hartford police officer, had either given Danny his handgun to try out or had left the gun unattended where Danny could find it—this part of the story fluctuated—and the boys were going to practice firing at squirrels. They didn't even get off a single practice shot before the gun misfired—either Danny or Bobby had been trying to load it—and the bullet lodged in Louie's heart, in the muscle wall between his left and right ventricles.

It was a precision accident; a quarter of an inch in any direction and the bullet would have stopped his heart. Bobby and Danny panicked at the sight of the gushing heart's blood, a surprisingly dark maroon color. They dropped the gun and ran, assuming Louie was as good as dead, although they did stop the first person they met in the park—a middle-aged man who was walking his German shepherd—and pointed him toward the clearing where they'd left the body.

The dog walker rushed back to his house and called an ambulance in time to save Louie's life. He was pumped full of other people's blood, sedated and bandaged, but there was nothing else that could be done. The doctor explained that if he tried to take the bullet out, the surgery had a 50 percent chance of killing the boy. They could only wait and pray. The heart with the bullet in it would probably never work quite right, but it might heal over with careful convalescence. Forty-three years later, Louie would undergo a triple bypass during which his cardiac surgeon would pull out the old bullet, no problem. In the end, it wouldn't be Louie's heart but his kidneys that would kill him.

So, although the Fortuna-Caramanico wedding had been much anticipated, in the making for four years, in the end it was just one confusing day in a stressful week. Tina thought maybe they should cancel the wedding, but everything had been paid for and Tony wouldn't hear of it.

Assunta refused to leave Louie's side. She slept in a chair that was terrible for her circulation and she kept a vase of mint on the bedside table—she performed countless incantations every day; this was a fairly classic example of the Evil Eye at work. After a week in the hospital ward, she hadn't even been home to change her clothes. The night before the wedding, Stella, who had spent the whole day helping Barbara embed a lace pattern of tiny silver balls in the cake frosting using a pair of tweezers and whose hair still smelled like confectioner's sugar, came to collect her mother and sister at the hospital, but Assunta wouldn't leave. Louie's doctor tried to step in helpfully, to reassure Assunta everything would be fine while she was gone. The scene escalated quickly, Assunta weeping and the doctor yelling. It was plain to Stella, watching with the dawning embarrassment of the newly bilingual, that Louie's doctor thought her mother was crazy, an insane and dirty peasant with childish ideas about witchcraft who rejected his commonsense medical advice. Tina, who should not have been allowed to come to the hospital on the eve of her own wedding, realized her mother would not be attending and collapsed on the floor, which must have been covered in who knows what kinds of diseases. Tony brought an end to the spectacle by saying to his wife, "It's fine. You stay here with Louie. Tina doesn't need you." Assunta quieted down right away, cowed into hiccups.

That night she came home to Bedford Street, bathed, set her hair in rag curls, and slept in her own bed, then got up in the morning to fix the girls breakfast before they got ready for the photographer. The pronouncement that her daughter didn't need her seemed to have done the trick.

In all the drama of Louie's accident, Tina had been completely distracted and so had forgotten her panic about her impending sexual encounter with her husband-to-be. Which was just as well. Stella had been about at the end of her rope listening to her sister speculate and fret.

The wedding went smoothly, and there were many compliments paid to Tony Fortuna, who had hosted a lovely event.

Stella had seen many American weddings by now, and she knew what to expect. But seeing Tina come down the aisle looking so serene, so holy, she felt her heart pound with melancholy. Tina was leaving Stella to make her own family.

Carmelo Maglieri hadn't come from Chicago to be Rocco's best man, but he sent the newlyweds a card with eight dollars in it. In Carmelo's place, Rocco asked another *paesan* of his, a squirrelly young man named Jack Pardo. Among Rocco's other groomsmen were Joey, Mikey Perri, and, excitingly, a Portuguese man named Jimmy whom Rocco worked with at his new factory job. Rocco and Tina had Jimmy escort Josie Brandolino, Tony's boss's daughter, who wasn't very pretty and who they assumed would be grateful for a date even if he wasn't Italian.

Fiorella Mulino caught the bouquet, but she wouldn't be the next to get married. In fact, she would never get married at all. She would die of breast cancer two years later, when she was twenty-six years old. She must have already been sick at the wedding, although the girls didn't know it yet. In the bridal party photo that still hangs on Tina Caramanico's wall, Fiorella's eyes are ever bright, her sweet smile full of youthful perfection.

In the evening, the new Mr. and Mrs. Rocco Caramanico rode away in a limousine to a fancy hotel near the train station. Their bags were already packed and waiting for them there; the next morning they would board a train for Washington, D.C., for their weeklong honeymoon.

That night, for the first time in her life, Stella slept alone. She woke up many times during the night and would have to struggle out of her sleepy confusion to remind herself why Tina wasn't there.

Washington was very hot, apparently, and full of large white buildings. But that wasn't what anyone cared about.

"It hurt so much, Stella," Tina told her. "I was so scared. And then he wanted to do it so many times, every night and sometimes in the morning."

Stella wasn't surprised Rocco had turned out to be a goat with all those sexual appetites. She wasn't sure how much more of Tina's honeymoon gossip she wanted to hear—she was as curious about Tina's experience as Tina was eager to discuss it, but the details made Stella's stomach roil. She didn't say anything, just let Tina continue.

"He made me take off all my clothes, even my brassiere." Tina hadn't ever worn a brassiere, or even heard of one, until she came to America, but now that the girls knew what the undergarment was for, the thought of not wearing one was perverse. "He wants to suck on my nipple, like a baby." Tina's deep-set eyes were round with scandal. "Have you heard of that? A grown man sucking like a baby?" Stella grimaced. She imagined grown men did all kinds of abhorrent things. "And then, when he puts his liquid in you, it's all sticky and it makes your skin itch. You want to wash it off because it smells, but I don't know if I'm supposed to wash it off, because maybe then I won't get a baby. Then sometimes I can smell it on myself even outside, when we're walking around, and I wonder if other people can smell it, too."

"That's disgusting," Stella said.

"Yes," Tina said, chastised, and her face assumed a propitiating expression. "Maybe if I get pregnant soon he'll stop."

Rocco Caramanico had a good job working at the Gillette factory, where he was a foreman on the production floor, but he didn't have the money yet to buy the house he had promised his new bride. In the meantime, the Caramanicos moved in with the Fortunas to save money.

The sleeping arrangements needed to be reorganized. The newlyweds required their own room, certainly, with a door. The only solution was the room the sisters had shared. But where would Stella go? She couldn't sleep with the boys, and Assunta's living room was not an option. All the fancy things Assunta had made Tony buy for her were on display there, the doily-covered marble coffee table, the gold upholstered couch—all the symbols of her better life here in America, the things that set her apart from the dirt-sweeping village girl she'd been. No one would be sleep-sweating or drooling on that couch.

"If you would just get married and move out, this wouldn't be a problem," Tony told Stella, both with humor and without.

Assunta was hoping the tenants on the second floor would move out soon so that the Caramanicos could take over up there and Stella could have her room back. The Bedford Street house was designed for three families; if Assunta managed it right, she could have all her children living under her roof indefinitely. But she couldn't just kick the current paying tenants out, especially with Tony so tight for money, what with his only working part-time and with all the wedding expenses.

"You could sleep with me on the bed and your father can sleep on the cot in our room," Assunta offered. Tony hadn't been allowed connubial rights since the last miscarriage, doctor's orders.

"No way in hell, Ma," Stella said, and Assunta smacked the back of her hand because of her bad language. Assunta didn't know about Stella's nightmare about her father. But Stella would have rather joined the shantytown behind Front Street than shared a bedroom with Tony.

Instead, Stella slept in the kitchen on the trundle bed. The house was noisy and stinky with too many bodies. At night Stella couldn't set up her bed until everyone had gone to sleep, or she would be underfoot in the kitchen. She was sleep-deprived and always on edge. She had no privacy at all, and now there was an extra man walking around the house. Stella had nowhere to keep her clothes in the kitchen, so they stayed in Rocco and Tina's room. Dressing in the morning became a quadrille of awkwardness, Stella trying to dart in to reclaim her clean underwear during the slender margin of time in which Rocco took his militarily efficient shower. She hated when he caught her alone in the bedroom, felt his searching eyes on her nightdress as he stood in his bathrobe.

Rocco's muted lasciviousness made her nervous. He was the type of man who had never trained himself not to stare at a woman's breasts, and she'd noticed his eyes wandered over whatever female parts they were presented with. Having had this thought—that her sister's husband had thought about her body, and that the man had access to her any time he liked—Stella found it difficult to let herself fall asleep at night. She would start awake, feeling terribly vulnerable.

In her perpetual haze of half-sleep, the nightmare came back. The days began to run together in a sleepy smear. Stella's work at the factory became listless and imprecise.

This, she thought, living like this might wear me down.

At this moment of weakness, the worst thing that could possibly happen happened—it was like the footfall of God stamping out Stella's future. She saw it descending on her, but there was nowhere to jump out of the way.

January 12, 1947, the Fortunas were celebrating Stella's twenty-seventh birthday. Tina had baked a lemon pound cake. Stella was warm with wine and pleased with the party. Everyone— the Fortunas, the Caramanicos, Zu Ottavio and Za Caterina Perri, the entire Nicotera family—was crowding around the dining room table, which had been set with Assunta's nice yellow glass dessert plates, when the doorbell rang.

Joey stood up to get the door, and then he was bursting back into the dining room, shouting, "Look who's here!"

There he was, wielding a dozen hothouse roses like a knight's sword. His cheeks were cold-bright, and snow ridged the shoulders of his overcoat and the brim of his fedora. Perhaps it was only the swath of cold air he brought in with him, but it felt like witchcraft when the temperature in the dining room dropped enough for goose bumps to rise on Stella's arms. *You're a cold woman, Stella*—she remembered his words the last time she'd seen him, a curse laid on her skin.

"Carmelo!" Assunta couldn't contain herself and burst into joyful tears. "What's the matter, Joey? Take his coat, he must be freezing, he must be soaked! Carmelo, what are you doing here? Give Joey your coat! Come sit down, get warm!"

"These are for you, Stella," Carmelo was saying, the arm of roses extended toward her as Joey wrestled the partially removed coat off Carmelo's other shoulder, scattering snow across the rug. "I apologize for disrupting your birthday party. *Auguri, tanti auguri.*"

Stella took the flowers from him, stunned, numb, her mind soft. A wine-rich smile was stretched across her face, and she only realized when it was too late, when Carmelo beamed his cherry-cheeked smile back at her, that she must have looked like she was happy to see him.

She didn't need to say anything, thank God, because everyone was falling on Carmelo with kisses and hugs and handshakes and shoulder slaps. Was he back? Was he just visiting? Stella sat quietly in the middle of the hubbub and rubbed a rose petal between her thumb and index finger, wishing the silky fibrousness would recall her to reality.

Assunta brought an extra stool and Carmelo was installed at the table with a slice of yellow cake as wide as a building brick. With a typical amount of audience interruption, this was the story he told.

The store in Chicago hadn't worked out so well. The business was good, people in and out all day, lots of sales, constantly restocking, but Carmelo's brother, Gio, was too generous, letting people buy on credit, and the brothers were barely breaking even. After a year and a half, Carmelo knew enough about running a business to realize he'd been wrong about wanting to. He decided to sell off his share and come back to Hartford. Gio was selling his share in the store now, too, and would follow in a couple months.

Carmelo had come back to Hartford before Christmas. He needed a job, though, and he wasn't getting anywhere asking around. Jobs were hard to find, with all the boys back from the war and the factories done with their war contracts. He was running out of ideas when he got very lucky.

He was walking down Franklin Avenue at five thirty in the morning—he'd gone out early to get a paper and check the wanted ads—and passed a bunch of men milling around a chain-link fence, a pile of shovels and picks beside them. On a whim he took off his long wool coat and left it by the fence, then strolled up and joined the men. He was freezing cold but less conspicuous without the coat. The timing was perfect, since the foreman hadn't given out assignments yet, and Carmelo grabbed a pick and followed where the guy pointed, to a white line painted on the crumbling concrete. He watched a couple other men set about work, watched how they wrestled up the old concrete and dug straight down on the white line, making narrow, carefully defined canals in the road—they were laying space for underground electrical wires.

Carmelo dug and dug; hours passed, the other men on the line chatting with him but no one asking where he'd come from or getting suspicious that there were too many men. He was just beginning to get into the swing of the work, beginning to feel like he was good enough that maybe he could talk them into letting him stay on, when he hit what turned out to be a live wire—someone had mispainted the line he was following.

"Suddenly I wasn't cold anymore!" Carmelo slapped his thigh and everyone at the table around Stella laughed or cooed in horror.

He woke up flat on his back in the hospital, nearly electrocuted to death, and that's when it came out—when they tried to do the paperwork for the hospital bills—that Carmelo Maglieri wasn't even a United Electrical employee. Everyone got very nervous about lawsuits and seemed relieved to learn Carmelo wasn't intending to take anyone to court—as long as they could give him a job. A job they gave him, and a slightly gratuitous chunk of change to cover his medical expenses.

Joey poured all the men more wine as the story wound down. Tina was smiling as she gathered plates. Her joy at seeing Carmelo was simple and pure; her friend was back. For once, Stella helped her take the dirty dishes to the kitchen. Seeing her sister so happy, Stella felt guilty knowing she had driven Carmelo to leave, taken him from people who cared about him. But Tina didn't think of things in those terms. At least, Stella hoped she didn't.

Over the sink, where Tina was running hot water into the basin, Stella whispered, "I can't believe he's here, Tina. I thought we were done with him."

"But he likes you, Stella." Tina slammed down the tap and squeezed the excess water out of the dishrag with two hands; her usual unnecessary force. "Can't you see that? He's here because he still likes you even after how mean you were."

Stella swallowed. "I wasn't—"

"He's a good man, Stella," Tina interrupted her. "You should stop teasing him. He doesn't deserve it."

Tina dropped the rag in the sink and left Stella alone in the kitchen.

In February 1947, Tina had been married six months. The first three, the ladies at the Sacred Heart socials joked about Tina's robust good health and how a little one was probably on the way, but when Tina blushed and waved them off they left her alone, because everyone knows it's bad luck to talk about a pregnancy before the mother is showing. By the holiday season, though, Tina was fair game. She'd been married long enough, and all the ladies who'd already had to go through it wanted a turn at her, to make sure she had to go through it, too. They'd come up to her after mass and pat her belly, right there in the church, and ask her if there was something cooking.

"We're trying," Tina would say, turning her dark pink.

The ladies would cackle and say, "You have to try harder!"

Now that half a year had passed, people asked Tina point-blank what she was waiting for, or if something was wrong. Tina didn't know how to answer these questions and became flustered and downtrodden. It was upsetting to watch. When she could, Stella would step in and change the subject; usually this meant offering herself as a sacrificial lamb, because most ladies were more disgruntled that Stella wasn't married than that Tina wasn't pregnant.

On Ash Wednesday, Tina made a huge dinner for the whole family, hot boiled ricotta *polpette,* parsley-baked fish, fresh *linguine* she had cut before work. But her six-month anniversary had just come and gone and she was so distraught by that milestone that she couldn't eat her own feast. Six months of being a wife and she hadn't been able to do the most important thing.

Stella rubbed her sister's back while Tina cried in the Caramanico bedroom. "What's wrong with me, Stella?" Tina asked, as if Stella could possibly have the answer.

"You know it can take time," Stella said. "You've heard all the same stories I have. It's only been six months."

"Maybe I did something wrong and God doesn't want me to be a mother." Speaking these words made Tina start sobbing again.

"Tina. Enough. You've never done anything wrong in your life." Stella scratched gently at Tina's scalp, which had always soothed her since she was a little girl. "Just give it time, little bug, and pray to Santa Maria. I promise I will pray for you, too. *Va bene?*"

Stella did not want to see Tina suffering like this. But she also wanted Tina to conceive as quickly as possible for selfish reasons;

if there was a grandchild for Tony and Assunta to concentrate on, there would be less pressure on Stella to marry Carmelo.

No one could accuse Tina of not working that particular chore as thoroughly as she worked any other. She had told Stella more than once that she hoped Rocco's enthusiasm would eventually wane, but behind their closed bedroom door Tina seemed not to suffer inordinately while paying her marital debt. That very night, only hours after she had cried too hard to eat her own *polpette,* Tina made so much noise, soft cries like a little baby's, that Stella, tiptoeing to the bathroom, paused in the hallway to listen in disgusted amusement. Rocco's voice was a low, coarse rumble, his words obscured, but Tina's were not.

Stella shouldn't have, but she did: she took a careful, silent step toward the door of her old bedroom and laid her ear against the wood.

"That's nice," Stella heard, then Rocco's low murmur, then "That's nice" again.

It was not the first time Stella had overheard the Caramanicos in the act—it would have been impossible not to, with Stella's sleeping just around the corner in the kitchen—but she still found it horrifying and fascinating, almost unbelievable, that her good-girl sister seemed to enjoy having such an awful thing done to her. Breathing shallowly, the door cool against her too-hot ear, Stella tried to guess what the sounds she heard could mean. She felt the familiar knot in her stomach, the ball of nausea that always accompanied her dream, as she imagined what Tina must be letting Rocco do.

Stella was so focused on not betraying herself by making any noise that she failed to notice her father's approach until his musty, garlicky night breath landed on her neck. "Jealous, eh?"

Stella coughed in surprise, choking on her own spittle as she whirled around, bringing herself eye level with a sweat-matted T of curling lead-gray chest hair.

Tony chuckled. "I always knew you were a little whore. You can barely hide it." Before Stella's half-asleep brain even caught up with what was happening, her father reached out and cupped her left breast in his hand, giving it a gentle squeeze. "Don't worry, we'll get you some *pistola* real soon."

For the first time, Stella thought of leaving Bedford Street. An unmarried woman leaving her parents' home—it wasn't done, but how could she go on living here? Once the idea had crossed her mind, she thought about it constantly. She just had no idea how she could do it, short of marrying Carmelo Maglieri, but that would be taking her body out of the jaws of one wolf and putting it naked into another's.

Becoming a nun seemed like a terrible idea to Stella—nothing but housework and praying all day, a prisoner locked away from everything that was interesting and delightful in the world. But how else did a woman make it on her own? She had no education and very little English. The problem was larger than Stella's limitations, though. In the world where the Fortuna girls had been raised, a woman never left her father's house until she was married. To run away was the same thing as to become a whore. If she did run, she would risk breaking herself away from her world forever. She would be shunned in church. Her friends might not be allowed to see her anymore. Her mother's heart might break. Stella shoved aside the dread of what Assunta's reaction would be—Stella couldn't worry about her mother right now.

Whatever form her escape would eventually take, she did know she would need money. She had some, a small savings she had been siphoning off her factory salary before turning it over to her father. One morning in February Stella dawdled getting ready so she could count the money after Rocco had left for work. She had fourteen dollars in change. Only fourteen dollars. She thought of the fifteen dollars she'd spent on Tina's shower with some chagrin, but then shook that off—that had been one of the happiest days of her sister's life, and her own. But other than the shower, there were dresses Stella hadn't needed to splurge on, the money she'd spent on movie tickets and soda fountains with the girls. Her mind was churning, a mush of frenzied strategic planning and self-recrimination.

"You're going to make us late, Stella," Tina said as they sat on the Caramanico marital bed and counted out the quarters and dimes.

"I wonder how much rent Papa charges," Stella said. She was thinking about Miss Catherine Miller, the tenant who rented the third-floor apartment from Tony Fortuna. Miss Miller was a retired schoolteacher and had never been married. Stella wished she could ask the woman how she'd left her father's house. But Miss Miller was an English-speaking American, for whom the rules were different. And the old lady had never been particularly nice; there was a risk she would repeat anything Stella said back to Tony. Stella knew better than to trust anyone but herself.

"He charges twenty dollars a month," Tina replied.

Stella eyed her sister, already buttoned up in her winter coat. "What? Why do you know that? He told you?"

"He told Rocco. You know he's trying to get a tenant to move out so Rocco and I can rent one of the apartments."

Stella felt a sparkle of relief. The end of her kitchen-sleeping nightmare was in sight. "When?"

"Maybe this summer," Tina said. "The husband on the second floor"—she meant Mr. Czarnecki, but couldn't pronounce the family's last name—"is looking for a new job now but they promised to move when they found it."

Twenty dollars a month. Stella made sixteen dollars a week at the factory. She chewed on this, and also on the fact that Tina had known about this plan and had not shared it with her. Stella had never known Tina to have a private thought in her whole life. Things changed after you got married, apparently.

"Come on, Stella. We're going to be late." Tina's face wore a sheen of anxiety, or maybe it was just overheated from wearing the heavy coat inside for so long.

As they walked toward the Silex factory, Tina asked, "What's the money in the sock for, Stella?"

Stella thought Tina should have been able to put two and two together. Spelling it out made Stella feel like the crime was closer to being committed.

"I want to move out," she said finally. And because Tina was grimacing at her, uncomprehending, Stella added, "I mean I want to go live somewhere else. Not with Mamma and Papa."

"With Carmelo?" Tina said. Her eyes were so round Stella could see white all around the coffee-colored irises. "Stella!" she squealed.

"No." Stella fought back her anger. "Not with Carmelo. By myself."

"What? Why?"

They walked in silence for a moment while Stella weighed how to answer. "I can't live with Papa anymore," she said finally. She couldn't mention how Rocco's wandering eye made her nervous; she couldn't mention that she had realized, even if Tina hadn't, that the sisters weren't a team anymore, that Stella had no allies in her house. "I hate Papa. You know that. I can't stand to live with him anymore."

Tina didn't say anything, and Stella glanced at her, followed her gaze. On the right they were passing the playground. Even though it was only seven forty-five, one young mother, a girl of perhaps twenty, was already standing listlessly by the sandbox where her toddler, bundled up in a blue scarf and red knitted cap, was digging with a toy trowel. Tina stared at them so hard that Stella, thinking of the *mal'oicch'*, gripped her elbow and sped them up.

"Anyway. I'm thinking that if I can just save up a little more, then I could go live by myself. Like Miss Miller upstairs." Stella was gratified that Tina was listening to her again, the dreary spell of the mother-and-child tableau broken. "Make coffeepots, save my money, live by myself—like Za Ros used to save her silk-worm money, remember?"

Tina was frowning. "Who would cook for you, Stella? What would you eat?"

"Oh, Tina. That doesn't matter. I just have to get out of that house." She felt the heavy heat of her father's hand against her breast as if it were touching her again right now. "I have to get out or I might die."

"So dramatic, Stella," Tina said. "Why don't you just marry Carmelo? Then you can leave, no problem. Papa can't stop you."

Stella's heart cramped, as though a hand even larger than her father's had reached into her chest and squeezed it. "I don't want to marry Carmelo, Tina." How could Tina say such things? How—after their lives spent together? Had she never once listened to anything Stella said? "Him or anyone. I really, truly—I promise you, I will never marry any man." Her pitch was rising. She felt on the edge of hysteria. "I mean this from the bottom of my heart, I swear to God our Father and the Blessed Virgin, I am telling the truth, Tina. I don't know why you don't believe me."

"I do believe you," Tina said, chastised. Stella knew, though, that Tina's faith in her would only last as long as this walk they were taking together, that the moment Tina spoke to Assunta, or Tony or Carmelo or Rocco or any of their girlfriends, Tina would forget that she had believed Stella and would shrug and tell whoever it was that she didn't understand her sister's stubbornness, either.

They walked in silence for a few minutes as Stella tried to calm the rage and hurt and frustration in her chest. As the factory came into view on the next block, Tina said, "But where could you go on your own, Stella?"

"I don't know. All I know right now is I need to save up as much money as I can."

"I'll help you," Tina said, and gripped Stella's fingers to cement her vow.

There were so many other questions Stella had no answers for, no information whatsoever. Where could she go? Did they have rentable bachelor rooms like the one Carmelo lived in, but for single ladies? Her English was so bad; would she be able to explain herself to a landlord? How would she know whom to trust? Was there anyone she could ask for advice without getting herself in trouble, without it all getting back to her father?

She thought she should be able to put aside two dollars a week without alerting Tony—she would have to be sneaky, think of excuses for where the money went. But she could do it. If she could save fifty dollars, that should be enough to leave, shouldn't it?

Would she make it on her own? Could she?

And if she couldn't, what was her next plan?

The last time Stella rejected Carmelo Maglieri was on Palm Sunday, 1947. It wasn't an encounter she had been prepared for, and it was not her finest work. But they should have realized what would happen if they trapped her in a corner like an animal.

The Fortunas had gone to mass down at Sacred Heart. They chanted along with the Latin liturgy, received their palm fronds, tithed, and took Communion. Afterward, they had lunch at the Perris'. Za Caterina served leathery fried *baccalà* and a nice spread of meat-free Lenten antipasto, provolone and pickles and *lupini* beans. They walked home in the twinkling March sun, everyone half drunk on homemade wine and happy to remember that Assunta had baked an orange cake for the afternoon.

They had only just arrived home when there was a knock on the door. Stella was put on alert when Tony, who did not generally answer the door, leapt to his feet and bellowed, "Assù! Make some coffee!"

Stella followed her mother to the kitchen. "Who's here, Ma?"

Assunta didn't say anything, but her hands were shaking as she tried to spoon coffee grounds into the percolator. Assunta was not good at secrets.

From the hallway came the sounds of a second knock, of the locks tumbling. *"Who is it?"* Stella mouthed. Her mother spilled coffee on the counter and hurried to wipe it up, but she still didn't say anything.

Never mind. Stella exited the kitchen, slid silently around the corner just as Tony was opening the door, and locked herself in the bathroom. She sat on the toilet lid and clenched her fists, listening for the inevitable.

And there it was—Carmelo's booming tenor, so sure the whole world wanted some of his cheer. "What a beautiful day!" she heard through the door. And then all the correct platitudes of a ritual visit—*Zi Tony, you are so kind to invite me to your house. Za 'Ssunta, I would love some coffee. The cake looks delicious.*

She realized her mother, the traitor, must have made that cake knowing Carmelo was coming over. How long had they been planning it? Had Tina known, too?

There was a tapping on the bathroom door. Stella, fuming so athletically that she was having trouble catching her breath, didn't respond.

"Stella, come out." It was Tina, of course. "Stella, Carmelo's here. Come out and say hello."

The naïveté of the entreaty made Stella angrier. "I warned you, Tina."

A disingenuous pause. "What? He came over to visit Rocco. Just come out and say hello."

"Bullshit," Stella said. This event had been planned; Assunta had baked a cake. Stella'd bet anything Carmelo had come over to propose to her. She'd bet anything Tony had already approved the suit—maybe even suggested it.

Tina tapped at the door again, as if any of her deep knowledge of her sister's personality led her to believe Stella was going to come out of the bathroom. "Stella. Come out and say hello, Carmelo's here."

Tina continued to tap and call for a few minutes before giving up and going away. Stella forced her breathing to even out, feeling the flush fade from her face. For a period she felt sick to her stomach, and she rubbed her *cornetto* and tried to drive away the bad feeling, until she realized it was not a haunting or a déjà vu at all, it was just a memory—the Christmas party four years ago when Carmelo had made her hide in the bathroom at the Italian Society, and she'd thought she was getting sick but it was just her monthly bleeding. To be thorough she checked, but it wasn't her time today; it was only the memory that had been about to overwhelm her. She splashed water on her face.

Time ticked by as she waited for Carmelo to leave. Stella rode out waves of muted fear every time she heard footsteps near the bathroom. She was waiting for the moment Tony would come and knock down the door, give her one or two for being fresh and drag her, disheveled, to the living room. But Tony never came.

Every fifteen minutes or so Tina would come by and tap on the door, ask her to come out. She didn't reply to her sister. Once there was violent banging, the manly kind, and Rocco's voice: "Stella, get out of the bathroom. I need to piss."

"Go piss out the window," she snapped, then regretted saying anything at all. She heard Rocco curse her but leave.

There was little to do in the bathroom besides lose herself in her anxieties. She found a bottle of red varnish in the medicine cabinet, and painting her nails kept her occupied for a while. She hummed to herself to force some equanimity, painting carefully. Usually Tina did Stella's right hand. She tried not to imagine the repercussions of this afternoon. How badly would Tony beat her tonight after Carmelo left? Was this going to be the rest of her life, hiding in a bathroom?

Carmelo seemed determined to prove he was as stubborn as Stella. Two hours must have passed, but she still heard his aggressively cheerful voice booming from the living room. Didn't he realize that if she were forced to come out at this point, she would be completely humiliated? Did he plan on not leaving her any dignity at all?

The last time Tina knocked, she had changed up her cajole. "Stella, come out. I have to do a number two. It's serious."

Stella didn't answer. She was engaged in a full sulk now, and ashamed of herself, but she saw no other way out. The sun outside the window was dimming and her head was filling up with a twilight ache.

Two minutes later, Tina came by again. "Stella! Please come out. I have to go." She rapped, hard. *Bang bang bang.* "Stella! Please, please, Stella, please. It's an emergency. Please come out. Or just let me in! You don't even have to come out."

Tina wasn't a very good actor. She was probably really suffering. Well. Served her right. She had chosen to be loyal to Carmelo, take his side over her own sister's. With genuine malice, Stella hoped Tina shat herself.

"Please, Stella." Tina's voice was breaking. "I'll do anything. I'll give you my gold necklace. Please, Stella." She rapped again. "All of my jewelry. I'll do all your chores for you. Please, Stella."

Stella looked down at her shiny drying nails. They weren't perfect, but they were pretty good. *You're a cold woman, Stella,* she heard Carmelo saying.

She sat silently until her sobbing sister went away.

Finally Stella heard Carmelo make his good-byes and leave. For good measure, she waited another fifteen minutes; she would hate to come out and find out they'd all been playing a trick on her and he was still there. Feeling prim, she exited the bathroom, her red nails smoothing the sweat-wrinkled skirt of her pink Palm Sunday dress.

Rocco, sitting on the couch, sneered at her. She hoped he had taken her advice and pissed out the window. Next to him sat Tina, whose back was slumped, eyes downcast. Stella didn't have to decide whether she wanted to ask Tina about what had happened, because her mother came into the living room to announce, "Dinnertime. I just have to strain the pasta. Get the table ready, Tina." Assunta shot Stella a malevolent look. "You, too, *stupida brutta*. Help your sister for one time in your life." She snorted and performed her version of a flounce back to the kitchen, wide hips lurching over her swollen legs.

Tina and Stella were silent during dinner. Stella was afraid to draw attention to herself, lest her frighteningly neutral father be inspired to take a position on her behavior this afternoon. Tina, meanwhile, stared darkly at her plate. Stella had begun to feel remorse about how vengefully she'd treated her sister, even if Tina had betrayed Stella. Stella wondered what had happened to Tina's number two.

When dinner was over, Rocco went to the Caramanico bedroom to change into his robe. The women could hear his shout all the way from the kitchen. "Tina! What's the matter in here? It smells like shit!"

Stella caught Tina's arm. "What did you do?" she whispered.

Tina shoved the pile of dirty dishes onto the counter and wiped her forehead, which had broken into prodigious sweat, on the sleeve of her good dress. "Oh, Madonna, Stella. When you wouldn't come out of the bathroom, I had to go *cacchi* so bad . . . my stomach was upset, I don't know what it was. Oh, it was so bad, there was nothing I could do! So I . . ." Stella handed her a dishrag, which Tina used to wipe her mouth—even her mouth was sweating. "So I went in the bedroom and took one of the bowls from the wedding china, you know, from the box under the bed. I went in the bowl, and—"

Stella almost choked on her scandalized laughter. "Tina! You made *cacchi* in your wedding china?" But even as she spoke she considered what else her sister could possibly have done. Gone outside in the yard?

"*Tina!*" Rocco was bellowing.

"A big bowl," Tina said urgently. "You know, the kind for fancy soups. There was nothing to wipe with, so I used my night-gown, the silk one from my honeymoon. But then there was nowhere to put it, so I put the *cacchi* bowl and the nightgown under the bed, and now the whole room stinks." Tina was crying sloppily. "What do I do? If Rocco finds out what I did . . ."

"*Tina!*" Rocco shouted.

"*Rooo-ccoo!*" Assunta shouted back, so loudly Tina was star-tled out of her tears. "Rocco! I need you!" She turned to give Stella a theatrically accusatory glare, then called, "There's some-thing stuck behind the stove, Rocco! I need you to move it for me!"

"In a minute," Rocco called back.

"No, right now!" Assunta was pushing the oven from the wall. "Hurry or it will fall on me!" It was like a vaudeville production, Assunta trundling herself down to her knees. But here Rocco came hurrying into the kitchen, after all, so maybe it wasn't so ridiculous. "Go, *stupida,*" Assunta hissed, smacking Tina on the calf.

Stella and Tina ducked past Rocco, scurrying down the hall-way and into the second bedroom. It stank like a butcher's slop pile in July.

"Ugh, Tina," Stella said, but they didn't have time to waste. She could hear the oven squeal as Rocco moved it with unfortu-nate ease. "I don't see why you thought it was going to fall on you," he was saying to Assunta. They only had seconds to solve this.

Tina bent down behind the bed and rose slowly, carefully, the china tureen sloshing brimful between her hands with a soupy yellow-brown liquid in which Stella could plainly, regrettably, make out the *lupini* Tina had been snacking on at lunch. Stella

278

heard Rocco coming back down the hall and in a flash of synchronicity she threw the window open just as Tina lunged toward it—for a moment they were perfectly connected again, like they had been as children, as if they shared the same set of eyes and hands and impulses—and Tina tossed the whole lot of it, nightgown, shit, tureen and all, through the open window, which Stella brought crashing back down onto the sash just as the china smashed against the driveway.

Rocco opened the door and looked from one flush-faced sister to the other. They smiled at him pleasantly.

"What are you doing in here?" he said to Stella after a moment of confusion.

"Just leaving," Stella said. "Tina was lending me her red nail polish." She wished she'd been able to think of something else to say, but what were the odds that Rocco would notice her nails were already painted?

"Huhn," Rocco grunted. Stella filed past him, followed by Tina, who went to wash herself off before her husband noticed the streak of brown across her bosom.

It was too good to be true, Tony's sitting out the whole charade peacefully.

Tina and Rocco had gone to bed; Stella was sitting at the kitchen table with her mother when Tony joined them. He seemed cheerful and youthful; Carmelo's demeanor had proved its contagiousness. He poured himself a glass of wine and topped off his wife's and daughter's.

"*Salut,*" he said, and Stella murmured "*Salut*" soberly as he clinked her glass. Assunta did the same, but she was peering up at her husband through her bushy eyebrows in a way that put Stella on alert. Her mother knew what was coming.

"I'm toasting the impending marriage of my oldest daughter, who all the world thought was doomed to be a spinster." Tony smiled at his women. "Congratulate me."

"Tonnon," Assunta said, warning.

"Congratulate me!" He slapped the table, indicating that his good-naturedness was not to be taken for granted. "It's a great thing for a father."

"Congratulations," Assunta whispered, making Stella apologetic eyes.

"Now, *fhijlia mia*," he said to Stella, "I think you have a lot of work to be doing on your trousseau." He shook his finger at her, almost playful. "I have a feeling you have been very neglectful."

"Papa, I'm *not* getting married." But Stella was shaking, tremors running up her arms. *You're a cold woman, Stella.*

"Oh yes, you are. I told Carmelo this afternoon. He's coming back tomorrow with a ring." Antonio shrugged, jovial. "Who knows, maybe he'll buy you a diamond, although God knows you don't deserve one."

Stella's mind was trembling with confusion; in this weird moment, her conviction had eroded. The cot in the kitchen; the recurring nightmare, recurring again; Carmelo's hothouse roses. Carmelo, Carmelo. Carmelo, who had purchased her from her father like he would have a cow, who didn't care whether he had her consent as long as he had Antonio's. But . . . She hated herself for thinking it, but . . . Would it really be so terrible to be married to Carmelo Maglieri? He was no Rocco Caramanico; he would never barter Stella for lightbulbs or ogle her sister. But marriage— to have her body broken open by a man . . .

"But Papa." Stella swallowed half her wine, a sour splash in her throat. "Remember when you told Rocco you weren't going to make Tina marry him? That it was Tina's choice if she wanted to get married?"

"You have a choice, too," Tony said. "You can choose to marry Carmelo Maglieri or you can go straight to hell, if I have to kill you myself."

For once in his life, Tony showed mercy and stood up and left the kitchen, a dramatic exit for the *pater ex machina*. At least

Stella didn't have to argue with him anymore; she had so little dignity as it was.

Not meeting her mother's eye, Stella drank down the rest of her wine, trying to sort through her feelings. *I would have given you anything you wanted, Stella,* Carmelo had said. *I would have given you the world.* Had he meant it? But what was the world to her, if her own body wasn't hers? The second glass of wine was spreading over her stomach. She stood and went to the counter for the flask.

Assunta followed her, reached up, and put her palm against the nape of Stella's neck. Her hand was warm, making Stella realize how cold the kitchen was.

Her mother had always loved Carmelo. Her mother, who loved Stella so much. Her smart, simple mother, who knew so much about survival. Assunta wouldn't wish this marriage on Stella if it were such a terrible thing.

Assunta touched the white bone *cornetto* hanging against Stella's chest. "You need this now."

Stella stood motionless at the counter for a long time after her mother went to bed. She needed a lot more than protection against the Evil Eye right now. She needed a plan.

Play along.

Stella remembered the folk adage that the best way to cover up a love affair was to get married to someone else—a girl suffered a lot less public scrutiny once her virginity was out of the way. Stella was adopting a similar strategy, although to opposite end: she was going to save her virginity by getting engaged. Instead of continuing to treat Carmelo as her enemy, she would enlist him as an ally—albeit without his knowledge—in her plot to escape Tony. The months leading up to the wedding, Stella had learned from Tina's experience, would be packed with frivolous expenses, which would offer her a cover for grafting money from her Silex salary into her secret stash. Meanwhile she would have to work out the logistics. She would have to prepare herself for the possibility that she might be disowned, kept away from her mother forever.

In any case, the first step in the resistance was entering into the engagement.

On Monday after work, Stella took great pains to look her best for Carmelo's visit, locking herself in the bathroom one last time. She changed into her watermelon dress, even though it was a little too early in the spring for the airy linen, and affixed Fiorella's butterfly brooch to its bosom. She didn't have time to wash her hair before dinner, but she fluffed it with a comb and pinned it prettily above her ears. It had been long enough between cuttings that the resulting curls bobbed against her cheekbones, which she rouged.

She was reapplying her lipstick when she heard Carmelo arrive, then Tina's nervous knock on the bathroom door. "He's here. Stella?" She must have been wondering if tonight would be another showdown.

"Just a minute." Stella took her time laying down one last coat. She felt quietly in control. It was the most peaceful, the happiest she had felt in months, since Rocco moved in—no, since before Louie got shot.

When she stepped out of the bathroom, the Fortunas were already noisily gathered around the spread Assunta and Tina had made: oven-fried chicken cutlets, hot artichoke hearts, still in the pan they'd been braised in, a two-pound bowl of *pasta aglio e olio,* and a dandelion salad from the backyard. Stella affected an air of chastised melancholy as she offered Carmelo her hand in greeting. She didn't want her father getting suspicious.

Carmelo didn't wait long, only until everyone but Assunta was seated. Although there was barely space for him between the table and the dining room wall, Carmelo pushed back his chair and took a knee at Stella's feet. "Stella Fortuna, I want to ask you a question," he said. He pulled a jeweler's box out of his jacket pocket, opened it, and set it on the table between them. Inside was a gold ring with three diamonds. Stella stared at it, distracted against her own will by the sparkle of the center diamond, which she couldn't help but notice was bigger than the single diamond Rocco had bought for Tina.

Carmelo, who was still kneeling, took Stella's hand, which she observed more than she felt. "Stella Fortuna," he repeated her name, and then again, "Stella Fortuna, I would be honored if you would be my wife. Will you marry me?"

He spoke to her in Italian, but the words were the American ones, a gallant appeal for her favor. As if this were her choice. As if this arrangement were any less of a business transaction than Rocco's bartering over lightbulbs with Tony.

"Yes," Stella said quickly, and was glad it was the only thing she was required to say. In this actual moment of the proposal, her calm vanished and unease prickled in her stomach. She wasn't a natural liar, even if she was good at putting on a show.

"Are you sure you want to marry me, Stella?" Carmelo's blue eyes were steady and searching, and she struggled to meet his gaze. The ring in the open box sat on the dining room table between them. "For a long time you didn't want to. Are you sure you've changed your mind?"

The unease that was simmering in her gut heated up to a boil. He was asking her point-blank what she wanted. Was it the right thing to lie to him, to use him?

But no, she reminded herself—he didn't really want to know. He had never taken her seriously before. Why would he now?

"Yes, I'm sure." She was shocked at the sound of her own voice, firm, neutral. There was no other way to win the war against her father; if Tony didn't kill her, as he'd threatened, he would at the very least find some other man. "Before, I didn't want to get married at all," she said. "Now I've decided I would never marry anybody else."

It was a six-month engagement, not too short, not too long. Carmelo's ring was just a little too tight on her finger and left a red mark when she slid it off to wash her hands. "You have to stop doing that, Stella," Za Pina warned her. "You're going to lose it. You gotta get used to wearing it all the time."

All the people who had nagged and pressured her for the last four years were suddenly kind and caring. They threw her parties and bought her gifts. They were genuinely happy for her, now that she was falling into line.

Carmelo came over for dinner three or four nights a week and everyone was very joyful now. He kissed her on each cheek now when he came and when he left, and she accepted his kisses. She made no trouble. She waited.

In the hot summer evenings of 1947 Stella sat at the kitchen table with a glass of wine, waiting for her cot, as Assunta scrubbed the stove and ran a lemon wedge over the counters to keep away the ants. When the rest of the house was asleep, they sat together and drank under the single naked bulb that hung over the linoleum. In the old days, Tina would have joined them, but now Tina was closed behind the door of her room with her husband. Nevertheless, this was the time of day Stella was happiest, sitting with her mother. On these sleepy summer nights, Stella could almost imagine they were home in Ievoli, in a world with no men to serve and service, just her and her mother, who loved her—that if she stepped out the back door into the warm evening air she would see not the picket fence that separated the Fortunas' garden from the neighbors' but instead via Fontana rolling down the mountainside into the breeze-bobbing valley of silver-green olive trees.

Stella loved her mother so much. Her chest ached with the idea that these evenings were the last they would spend together like this. Stella had forty-two dollars in her secret sock and six more weeks until the Fortunas thought she'd be walking down the aisle. She hadn't figured out where she could possibly go, but she was going to have to make her move soon. Make her move or be trapped forever.

"I'm so afraid, Mamma," she said. They had finished the entire jug that night. Stella's heart thumped, swelling painfully under the weight of what she wanted to say to her mother. "I'm not like you," she managed. It was the closest she could get to what she meant. "I can't be a mother."

"Of course you can, little star." Assunta wrapped her soothing hand around Stella's wrist. "Any woman can be a mother. It's natural. There's no reason to be afraid."

Stella fought back the grotesque image of a child swelling inside her. "It's not natural for me. I don't love babies the way other women do. I don't even like them."

"It is different when it's your own, Stella. You'll see. You love it more than anything. Everything will change for you."

"What if I'm not like other women, Mamma?" Stella's breath ran out before she could finish the question.

"You are," Assunta said. "All women are the same."

When her mother went to bed, Stella lay looking at the extinguished lightbulb, whose fiber seemed to give off a residual glow in the black and gray kitchen. Even her mother, the person she loved most in the world, didn't understand that Stella meant what she said. Even her mother didn't take her seriously.

One person did take Stella seriously: her enemy, her father. He'd been watching her carefully, waiting for her to slip up. Maybe she had been playing too docile; maybe that had raised his suspicions.

Stella was still a little hungover when she got home from work the next day. Her headache had fermented over the course of eight hours on the assembly line. The air in the Bedford Street house was swampy with late-August heat and heavy with the basil-garlic aroma of Assunta's *raù*. Unknotting her head kerchief, Stella followed Tina toward the kitchen, where they usually fixed a snack before dinner.

But Tony was home today, and he was sitting at the kitchen table. From the way Assunta was standing silently by the stove, staring into her pot, Stella knew something was wrong even before she saw what Tony had in front of him: a pile of coins; an array of crumpled dollar bills that had been smoothed flat; a flaccid knitted pink sock.

"Papa," Tina said.

"Why don't you leave, Tina," Tony said. "Go to your husband."

Bright red face hanging, Tina hurried out of the kitchen. She did not meet Stella's eye as she passed. In retrospect, it all should have been clear then, but Stella's mind was still struggling to catch up.

"Tonnon." Assunta was crying—why hadn't Stella noticed immediately?

"Quiet, woman." Tony didn't look or sound angry. He patted the pile of coins on the table in front of him. "Rocco gave me all this money," he said to Stella. "He found it in a drawer in his room. He was worried it might be stolen from me, so he turned it over. Do you know where the money came from, Stella?"

Rocco. The pervert, the thief, the betrayer. Stella felt a wash of guilt, guilty blood rising into her cheeks and drumming in her ears. She fought back the guilt with anger. "It's mine," she said. "It's my money."

"What do you mean, it's yours?" Tony's eyebrows were jumping. "You say it's *your* money but you mean it's *mine*, right? You're my daughter, and as long as you live in my house the money you bring in is my money."

Stella's mind was hot with stupefaction as she tried to think of a way to calm him down. Assunta was crying into her hands now, her whole face obscured.

"What is the money for, Stella?" Tony said. "What have you been stealing money from your father for? Your father who's been spending his every penny to give you a beautiful wedding?" His chair shrieked against the linoleum as he stood. "Thirty dollars just for the goddamn flowers, eh?"

Her money, spread out over the table. Irrationally, Stella tried to think of how she could take it back. Later, she couldn't explain to herself why she hadn't just bolted—hadn't recognized the hopelessness and run for her life. In the moment, though—well, it was one of those moments a person doesn't understand as it happens, only after it's over.

"Well?" Tony was standing in front of her now, he was gripping her shoulder, his wide uncompromising thumb driving into the soft partable flesh of her arm socket; he was forcing her up against the red-flowered wallpaper. Stella emitted an unintentional sound, a grunting yelp. Tony seized her loose curls in his left hand and bashed her head into the wall, knocking it into Assunta's shrine to the first Stella. Her vision smearing and then clearing, Stella saw that the wood-framed photo had tumbled to the floor, facedown. "Well, *fhijlia mia*? What was the money for? Was it to pay me back for your wedding cake?"

"It was to run away." The words came out of her mouth like a curse; then and later she would never know why she said them. Maybe it was because she was so angry she would have cut off her own head to annoy him. Maybe it was because she had never been a very good liar, or because she knew in her heart that her plans to run away were over forever now, and she lashed out in despair. Or maybe it was the little ghost who made her say it, facedown on the floor, taking this one last chance to get even. "I was going to run away," Stella said, "and I was never going to come back."

"Shut up!" Tony roared at Assunta, who was shrieking now, an earsplitting ululation that made Stella's skin crawl. "You," her father said to her, "you make your mother cry. Her oldest daughter says she's going to run away and live like a whore?" His fist full of her hair, he dragged her, hunched over and stumbling like a three-legged dog, out of the kitchen and down the hall toward his bedroom. Stella's whole body was hot with panic, her skin prickling as she tripped over herself to keep up with him. "You need to be taught a lesson," Tony was saying. "You're so damn stubborn you refuse to learn your place in this world. Well, this can't go on. I can't give you to your husband like this."

He threw her onto his bed and locked the bedroom door behind him, an oak safeguard between himself and his wife's bloody knuckles and clawing fingernails. "Take off your dress," Tony told Stella. "Your shoes. All your clothes. Take them all off."

"I—" She stood up, staring at her father, his tousled hair a black halo in the dim afternoon light. Stella was dipping into her nightmare—it was exactly like this. Paralysis settled on her limbs. She swallowed. "What?"

"I said take off all your clothes," Tony said. "You can obey me and take them all off nicely or I will cut them off you with my knife."

Her fingers vibrating, her conscious self retreating into the high-up window ledge of her mind, Stella turned away from her father so she faced the wall, toed off her shoes, contorted her arms to undo her own zipper. Her body undulated with shudders. She folded her dress and dropped it onto her shoes.

"All of it," Tony said. "Everything."

She unclipped her brassiere and watched it fall to the ground below the wealth of her hanging breasts, her elbows jerking, shivering as if she were freezing to death. Gooseflesh covered her arms, her scars rippling with cold fuzz. She hooked her thumbs into her girdle and, choking on saliva, peeled it down over her hips. Behind her the metallic click of her father's belt buckle, the *zzzziff* of the leather strap being pulled out of its loops.

But he didn't rape her, like the dream version of her father would have. Because whatever other forms Tony Fortuna's perversions took, he was not a man to throw away his daughter's only asset, her virginity. He might have stared at her breasts and pinched her fat and given her nightmares about his unquenchable desires, but Tony knew where he drew his own line. A woman's virginity was for her husband; that was a sacred rule. Tony had learned that rule from his own mother, whose father had not protected hers.

No, he didn't rape her, he only beat her. He told her to get on the bed, and when she resisted and screamed, he brought down his fist on her cheek, the same gesture as if he were slamming a glass down on the table. Later the molar and incisor he'd loosened with this blow would fall out, creating the third and fourth holes in Stella's gums. After this impact, which made Stella's head ring, she didn't resist anymore, but lay on the bed and took the beating, leather belt and metal buckle against bare ass and thigh and back.

"You're worse than a donkey," Tony said to her. She couldn't see him, but his breathing was heavy, staggered. "I have to break you like a donkey if I'm going to teach you to obey your master."

Staring at the wall as she absorbed the pain, turning herself over to the ordeal so that it might end faster, she thought of the *ciucciu* they had left behind in Ievoli and wondered if Tony would have really done the same thing to him.

That was when Stella Fortuna gave up. She gave up resistance. She gave up everything.

Stella missed two days of work because she couldn't walk normally or sit in a chair. There was broken flesh all over her thighs and back that seeped blood for days before scabs finally crusted over. She lay on her belly on a blanket spread over her mother's living room sofa, where she was allowed to sleep now because of the medical emergency. If anyone walked past her through the living room, Stella kept her eyes closed and her face turned to the upholstery.

When Carmelo came over for dinner, Tony entertained him in the kitchen. Stella lay staring at the stitching on the cushions, listening to Carmelo's booming laugh as the gray darkness within her spread. He brought her a bouquet of sunflowers, which Assunta arranged on the coffee table where Stella could see them, but the Fortunas didn't allow Carmelo into the living room. What had her family told him? That she wasn't feeling well? Or had they told him the truth? Soon he would own her broken body. The thought left her coldly empty.

Her mother brought her a bowl of *pastina* and stroked her hair. "Your eye will be all better by the wedding, *piccirijl'*," Assunta said. Stella didn't answer. She had nothing to say to her mother.

She had even less to say to her sister. Tina came in and sat on the chair next to Stella's sofa. "I'm so sorry, Stella," she said. "I didn't know Rocco was going to tell Papa about the money. I couldn't lie to him when he asked me. He's my husband. I had to tell him the truth."

Stella heard her mother's voice in her head, *Cettina's just little. She's not smart like you. Concettina* muscarella, *my little bug.*

"I couldn't lie to him when he asked me," Tina said again.

When Stella didn't respond, Tina gave up and left Stella alone in her misery. Tina gave up awful fast these days.

In some secret part of her suffering heart, had Tina wished this on her sister? Had Tina, with her controlling husband and unresponsive womb, desired to see her pretty, smart, charismatic sister thwarted?

This thought pricked at Stella's mind as she lay facedown on the couch. But she couldn't live with it, and she suppressed it— so successfully that it would not surface again for forty years.

Since Tina was already married, Stella's maid of honor was Carolina Nicotera. I can't tell you who the other bridesmaids were, because all the photos of the Maglieri wedding have been destroyed, and those details have been lost. If the photos had survived, though, Stella would have been smiling in none of them. She never smiled in a photo for the rest of her long life, because she now had four missing teeth to hide.

Stella's dress was made of white silk—a more expensive dress than Tina's stiff, formal linen had been. Tony bought Stella a floor-length lace veil, just like Tina's. What a waste, that she couldn't just wear Tina's. Of all things to throw away twenty-five dollars on—half the money she would have needed to run away.

Stella did not remember having her hair done, taking photos, or even saying her vows. She was numb, almost blind, with fear so potent it became an enfolding blanket, a protective layer between her mind and the world. To the wedding guests, she appeared calm, beatific with her close-lipped half smile.

The one part of the ceremony she did remember was their first kiss. Carmelo cupped her face in one white-gloved hand and leaned in cautiously, kissing her gently on her closed lips. Stella was shocked by the sensation of the kiss—its softness and electricity. She had never felt a man's lips on hers before and the impact was unexpected. Her body recoiled in a shudder of fear, and she gripped Carmelo's hand to regain herself. He was smiling into her face; he was so happy.

The reception was at the State Armory, which had just opened its Officers' Club, rentable as a special-occasions venue. Stella sat on the gold bridal chair on the head table dais. She sat and watched the dancing, and Carmelo sat beside her in solidarity. Seeing these happy people dance, this party ostensibly for her, Stella felt nothing but a sense of remove. She had no control over anything here. The feeling reminded her of one of her earliest memories, her child-hand clamped indelibly around a piece of bread as the pigs circled. She was about to be trampled, and there was nothing she could do, because someone else had seized her hand.

The hall was rented through midnight, but Stella left the party at nine forty-five. In the room cordoned off for the bridal party, Stella changed into her blue traveling suit, a large-buttoned jacket and trim-fitting skirt with matching pillbox hat, which Assunta had bought her at Sage-Allen. They were headed to Montreal for their honeymoon, where October could be cold. Her winter coat was folded on top of her waiting suitcase.

Her mother and sister, who helped her take off her wedding dress, cooed over the suit, smoothing the fine blue fabric over her shoulders and breasts with their sturdy, affectionate hands. She was glad there was no mirror in the room, because she didn't want to look herself in the eye. Her name was Stella Maglieri now, and her perfect blue-suited body was a package for a man to unwrap, to consume and interrupt and dismantle.

Assunta took Stella's arm; Tina took Stella's suitcase and coat. Stella was escorted down the hallway, which seemed so dark, the music of the band so far away. Outside, Carmelo and Tony waited by Rocco's idling Buick. Assunta and Tina, both crying, kissed Stella good-bye. Carmelo opened the sedan's back door for Stella, then walked around the car to get in on the other side. He was nervous, too. He kept his hands carefully in his lap so there was the whole middle seat of space between them. Tony sat in the front passenger seat and Rocco drove them away. Her father was there to make sure she got on that train, by use of his bodily force if necessary.

Stella had drunk nothing at all during the reception, lest alcohol make her even more vulnerable. Even wrapped in her numbing blanket of remove she couldn't think of anything but the threat of sexual intercourse. Her entire body was tense with anxiety, pulled into a hard curl like a snail disappearing into its shell.

The Maglieris' first night together as man and wife would be spent on a combination of trains. They would take the Boston & Maine Railroad service, which left Union Station at 11:15 p.m. In Boston they would transfer to another train, which would take them all the way up through New England to Canada. Carmelo kept the tickets folded in a leather travel wallet, together with a paper of instructions he had written down for himself. Stella stared out the dark window, feeling exhausted and hollow-eyed, until they reached South Station in Boston. It was almost as big as the train station in Napoli had been, although comparatively empty at this hour of night. For a bleary moment Stella imagined stepping on board a different train and riding it not to her own deflowering in Canada but instead home to Ievoli. There were no trains at the station, though, except the one she was getting off and the one she was about to get on; her choices were to carry on with her husband or go home to her father—not that she had any choices, or even a penny to her name. She had nothing at all except her traveling suit, two new holes in her mouth, and a cold invisible hand clamped around her own.

They arrived in Montreal at two in the afternoon on Sunday, worse for the wear. Carmelo's twin sister, Carmela, and her husband, Paolo, met them at the station. Stella's new sister-in-law was tall, maybe five six, trim but sturdy. The family resemblance around the nose and eyes was strong.

Carmela presented them with a basket of food she had prepared for them: ham sandwiches, apples, a jar of homemade wine. Paolo drove them to their hotel, a stately building that reminded Stella of the manors on Prospect Avenue in West Hartford, minutely attended to and fragrant with wealth. The cut glass of the front door glittered in the drooping October sun as a white-uniformed bellhop held it open for them.

Stella had never spent a night in a hotel before, with the exception of those awful nights in Napoli. A "hotel" in her imagination was shadowy and insidious, a place where men took a woman to do the job, where a girl's father or brothers couldn't walk in—a place where everyone knew what you were up to, a place full of complicit, smirking strangers. But this hotel was all marble counters and waxed floors, glowing with luxury—everything was finer than anything Stella had ever seen or touched.

Carmela used her French to help the Maglieris check in. The hotel stay, five nights, was Carmela and Paolo's gift to the newlyweds, and their apology for not attending the wedding. "Why don't you take some time to relax and freshen up?" Carmela said. "We'll come back at five o'clock and take you out for dinner."

Carmelo was given the key to room 6, which was on the second floor. As Stella followed her husband up the staircase, a roil of nausea swelled in her stomach. Her situation wasn't any different from that of any other woman going to any other hotel—no more subtle or mysterious than any whore's. Right now, everyone she knew—all the men she had ever rejected, all the women who had ever called her stuck-up—was imagining her checking into this hotel so she could have the job done to her. She imagined them imagining her indignity, how in that moment when Carmelo put his dirty end in her, she would have to think about the *paesan*'s collective amusement.

Her breath came in shallow, grasping whuffs by the time they got to 6. Carmelo turned to her at the door. He had probably been lost in his own sexual reverie, for all she knew, anticipating the consummation of his four-year courtship. There was concern on his still-smiling face. "Are you all right?"

Compulsively she waved off his arm. "Just lady troubles." That might mean anything to him—it had just popped into her head, but it could buy her some time.

The room would have seemed enormous if there had been any focal point in it besides the bed, which was fat with duvet and piled in red and gold pillows. The fabric on the pillows shone slightly. Strangers had drooled on those shining pillows, Stella realized. How could the hotel people clean shiny fabric like that? Carmela had sent a bouquet of white roses; they were waiting on the polished black dresser with a stiff gray card that said *Congratulations Stella & Carmelo Maglieri*. Stella thought of the money the Martinos had spent on her for this wondrous place. It was a shame she wouldn't be able to enjoy it.

"You want to lie down and rest?" Carmelo gestured to the heap of red and gold silk. "It's been a long trip."

Yes. "No." Her spine was creaking from the train ride. She couldn't look at him, began to pull off her gloves instead. "I—I think I better go to the toilet."

"Yes, yes." He bowed broadly and stepped out of her path. As she closed the door between them, she took a final look at her husband. He stood at the window watching the street, a square of sun lighting up his oiled black hair. He was still smiling.

Stella turned on the faucet for aural privacy and studied herself in the mirror. She tried to think about her situation. She wanted to feel nervous or angry or crafty, but instead she just felt tired.

After a few minutes she couldn't let herself run the water any longer; she felt guilty about the hotel's water bill. Tucking her gloves into her handbag, she sat down on the lowered toilet lid and stared at the dirt patterns her heels had left on the white tile floor. She was sweating from the climb up the stairs, but when she thought about undoing the buttons on her coat, she ruled it out. There was too much bed on the other side of the door for her to take off any of her clothes.

All right. All right. Now what are you going to do?

She was on her honeymoon. She had avoided a wedding night encounter by virtue of their travel arrangements, but every hour was borrowed time. It was going to happen, there didn't seem to be a reasonable possibility that she could avoid it anymore. She would endure the violation of her most private places, the bestial reduction of labor and childbirth, the tearing and stretching, maybe even death. The thought sprouted unhelpfully in her mind, like clover in a stone wall, that she had misjudged Joey, that she finally understood why he had shot himself rather than offer his body up to circumstances beyond his control.

Was *she* just going to let it happen? Let her whole life be the choices other people made for her? But she had never made a choice for herself—that had been her mistake. She'd never known what it was she wanted out of life, only what she didn't want. People can't understand negative convictions. A man who is willing to die for something is a hero, but a man who is passionately not willing to die for something is a coward. Maybe that was why no one had listened to her, thought she'd been doing anything but playing hard to get.

She hunched on the toilet in her wrinkled blue travel suit. A heaviness had settled low in her chest, a weight hanging from the bottom of her heart. She wondered if this was despair. What was she going to do? She had spent most of their courtship sitting on the toilet hiding from Carmelo. She doubted the same strategy would get her through an entire marriage.

Stella and Carmelo spent the afternoon walking through the cobblestone streets near the hotel. They stepped into shops and stopped for pastries. Stella let Carmelo carry the conversation, and she accepted his arm when he offered it. It was not a bad feeling, strolling through a pretty city with her hand resting on a good-looking man's elbow. But even as she enjoyed herself, Stella suffered a swelling nausea of fear. Those complacent thoughts were the dangerous ones. If Stella let herself like a piece of her marriage, she might succumb to the whole thing.

For dinner Carmela and Paolo brought them to a restaurant Tina would have considered "fine dining." There were pink cloths covering the tables and short candles in glass tumblers. Carmela took Stella's hand in her cold one for a long moment— Stella was wearing her gloves, but the cold passed right through them.

"My brother told us you were very beautiful," Carmela said.

Carmelo touched Stella's elbow, where her sleeve had creased into a pinch. "Now you see for yourself," he told his sister.

Paolo summoned the waiter and ordered for the table in French. They shared several dishes so Stella and Carmelo could sample them: sea mussels cooked in white wine, the giant bones of a cow split and served shimmering with their own marrow, long soft French-fried potatoes. Stella had never eaten such fancy food. She noticed only after she had gnawed all the meat off a duck bone that Carmela had left hers on the plate, separating the meat from the bone with her knife and fork.

Carmela and Paolo seemed to be kind, solicitous people. Paolo had a job at the docks, and Carmela was a cleaning woman at a university. Paolo was a soft-spoken man. He said little throughout the whole meal. Carmela, who looked so much like her brother, listened intently as Stella answered her questions about her family, about Ievoli, about presents she had received at her shower. She asked Stella if she needed anything for her kitchen, and Stella smiled sweetly and said, "Oh, I don't cook, so you had better ask your brother what he needs for the kitchen, instead," which shocked Carmela into silence. Carmelo laughed it off ruefully and his sister's expression lit up in a grin. "You're lucky he spent years cooking for all those railroad men," Carmela told her. "They made him a great cook. At least twice as good as me."

For dessert, Carmela ordered a small, soft chocolate cake that was hot on the inside. The cake, a surprise to Stella, arrived as Paolo was insisting on picking up the check for dinner. Carmelo fanned colorful Canadian bills on the tablecloth and made good-natured threats about never coming to visit again if Paolo was always going to pay for things. Meanwhile, the cake sat primly under its orange peel garnish, giving off a cakey aroma. Stella had eaten so much she had begun to feel turmoil in her gut, but Carmela insisted Stella try it. "Just one bite. Just one *forchetta*."

"Not *forchetta*," Carmelo interrupted. "That's Italian. We have to learn Calabrese now, Carmela." He winked at Stella. "You have to say, '*Na bròcc.*' "

The light from the table candles rippled in his smile lines, and Stella couldn't help but think that this man had done more than his twenty-seven years' worth of smiling. That was something someone else would have loved about him, but it made her feel sad. She did not love him, and she never would. Some other woman would have wanted badly to make him happy. But he had to be so damn stubborn. The thick chocolate coating her throat made her want to cough. How stupid Carmelo was, forcing them into this arrangement that would make them both unhappy.

The good news about that heavy chocolate cake was that it settled so poorly in Stella's stomach that when she and Carmelo got back to the hotel room she was able to make herself vomit. On this occasion she left the bathroom door open, so Carmelo might see the veracity of her indisposition. It was a shame flushing away that duck and those beautiful potatoes. But she'd saved her virginity for one more night. She slept in her blue suit again, not even taking off her stockings or jacket.

Montreal was lovely the first week of October, the leaves at the peak of their autumnal change. Chilly breezes cut through the stone façades so that Stella never felt overwarm in her thick new coat. As the hours ticked by, Stella's anxiety accumulated, gradually but inexorably, like sand in the bottom of an hourglass. Eventually she would run out of time.

They went to mass at the Basilique Notre-Dame—a cathedral, the meaning of which word Stella finally understood. The building was bigger than the emigrant ship *Countess of Savoy,* its distant ceiling supported by muscular piles of swooping stone. Stella would have happily sat through a second mass so she could continue staring at the sparkling stained glass.

After the mass, as they ate lunch on the Rue Notre-Dame, Carmelo told Stella about the great cathedrals of Italy, the inspiration of all church architecture. "This cathedral is beautiful," he told her. "But Stella, ours are ten times more beautiful."

She could not imagine even the Vatican more opulent. "You've seen them?"

"Only the cathedral in Genoa. When I was fourteen, the afternoon before I got on the ship to come here." He was squinting in the sun. "It is very old, Stella, eight hundred years old. Like nothing they have in the Americas." He paused. "I hope it is still there. After the bombs."

A sentimental man. Stella looked down at the crumbs of her sandwich.

"But Rome," he said after a moment, his voice clear again. "The Vatican, St. Peter's—they are the most magnificent in the world, *certo.* We'll go there someday. We'll walk through St. Peter's together."

Carmelo was wrong. They never would.

That second evening of their honeymoon, Stella and Carmelo went to see a movie with Carmela and Paolo at a cinema that looked like a palace. There was only one movie in English, a love story about two pianists. Stella didn't understand the fast-talking actors, but the movie was full of wonderful music.

On the walk back to their hotel, Carmelo took Stella's hand in his, and the anxiety she had set aside for the entire beautiful day came rushing back to her. She had let her guard down, she had been kind to him—how would she say no to him now? She was almost hyperventilating as Carmelo fumbled with the hotel key.

Still wearing her winter coat, she rushed to the drawer into which she had unpacked her clothing, scooped it all up and locked herself in the bathroom, as was her custom. Sucking calming breaths through her mouth, she assembled a night outfit for herself: her long-sleeved honeymoon nightgown over a pair of long underwear bottoms. She had the latter because Za Filomena had given her a married lady tip a few weeks before the wedding: when Filomena wanted to signal to Zu Aldo that it wasn't a good day for her, she wore long underwear to bed to indicate there would be no access down there for him. "It's not a problem anymore, now that we're old and I went through my change," Za Filomena had confided, "but when I was younger I sometimes put them on even when I wasn't bleeding, if I just didn't want to be bothered that day." Stella had made sure to include three pairs of long underwear with her final trousseau.

There wasn't much else with which she could armor herself, although Stella had the notion to pull a girdle over the long underwear, which made her pelvis feel protected. It would be quite a lot of work for anyone to get through—impossible without her cooperation, she thought. All right. That was the best she could do.

"I am very, very tired," Stella announced as she stepped out of the bathroom. She was alarmed to see Carmelo wore only his trousers and a sleeveless white undershirt. The contours of his torso, revealed for her now, reminded her of her father's; he had large, smoothly muscled arms, the arms of a strong man who would become stocky, not stringy, with age.

Stella's mouth was dry and her girdle throbbing. "I—I am very tired," she said again. Her voice sounded weak. She hated herself. "I am going to sleep."

"Stella—" Carmelo began.

"Good night," she said, and turned off the light.

Fearfully, Stella peeled the covers back in the darkness and tucked herself in. For good measure, she took the pillow out from under her head and put it between them in the middle of the bed.

No sound came from where Carmelo stood, and at first Stella was afraid she had failed to track him in the dark over the pounding of her heartbeat, which splashed over her eardrums like unrelenting waves against the hull of a boat. But after a long time he gave a noisy sigh, and she heard him undo his belt buckle and step out of his pants. She was paralyzed by panic, waiting to see if he was going to respect her or if he would try to touch her anyway, for the terrifying period until finally, finally she heard him snore.

She lay in the dark, her head flat on the mattress and her ankles throbbing from walking the cobblestone streets in her heeled shoes, and felt her heart race. It was an immeasurable amount of time, hours, before she fell asleep.

On Tuesday, she needed to escalate her efforts. She had come too close yesterday. Today she would have to be mean, to pick fights, to go out of her way to repel him.

She'd been so nervous even when she was asleep that she had woken with the first light of dawn and dressed defensively. In that meditative silence of morning, she'd hit on the idea that if the honeymoon went poorly enough, Carmelo might return her to her family when they got back to Hartford. If the marriage wasn't consummated, it could be annulled. There was a shred of hope—she just had to make him hate her.

For this third day of their honeymoon, Carmelo had arranged a surprise for Stella: he had hired a horse-drawn carriage to take them around the city. As they rode in silence, staring out opposite sides at the quaint streets and parks, Stella imagined Carmelo's internal monologue of disappointment, having wasted a week's salary on this silly experience his new wife refused to enjoy. She savored her own bad mood, nurturing her grievances and resentments, hoping that Carmelo would catch her malignance like a poisoned wind.

The day dragged, and even Carmelo was deflated in the face of Stella's sullenness. But the worst, for everyone, was yet to come, at dinner with the Martinos. Carmela's warm, solicitous chattering made Stella's head spin. She needed to clip any budding blossom of friendship Carmela perceived between them.

Stella refused to speak throughout the meal, ignoring questions and avoiding eye contact. Her most hostile behaviors were thwarted, though, by Carmelo, who shamelessly covered up for her, laughing and telling weak jokes, apologizing profusely to Carmela and Paolo for subjecting poor Stella to such a tiring day. Not enough damage was being done; Stella had to foment her aggression.

The opportunity came just after the arrival of the main course. Carmela was saying to her brother, "It is hard for us to get time off, but we will come and visit you in Hartford when you have a baby. I hope it's soon."

This was Stella's moment. Here she had the tools to be nasty. "I don't really see why," she said, surprising everyone with the bell-clear sound of her voice, "you're so interested in our future children when you haven't done the work of having your own."

The moment of silence stretched so long even Stella, the author of it, felt disoriented. Paolo looked down at his plate.

"We've been trying since we got married," Carmela said. The habitual warmth was gone from her voice. "I . . . I have had bad luck so far. But God knows what's best."

"Bad luck?" Stella put down her fork. Mean, she was going to be mean. Her stomach clenched in anticipation, in warning. She opened her mouth and willed the words out. "It's true God knows what's best. Maybe God doesn't think you deserve to be a mother."

"Stella," Carmelo said. He was shocked, his eyes wide. "How can you say that?" She knew that he was thinking of Tina, whose face Stella banished from her mind.

"I just think it's rude," Stella said, loudly enough that the tables around them hushed. She fixed Carmela with a stare, narrowing her eyes so that she would not accidentally blink or look away. "Attacking us with questions about our children. Some people need to learn to mind their own *cazzi*." Stella was glad for the low lighting, because she couldn't make herself use that vulgar expression without feeling her face heat up—she'd never said it out loud before, only heard her father and Joey use it. But it had the desired effect.

Carmela had turned to Paolo, her face haggard as an old woman's. "Is it all right if we leave?" She didn't wait for an answer, dropping her cloth napkin over her plate as she rose from her chair. Paolo was standing, too, pulling out his wallet as Carmela headed toward the coat check.

Carmelo stood in protest. "Paolo, please don't, we'll be fine."

"No, no," Paolo said, his voice as soft and unprepossessing as ever. "Please, allow me. Carmela only means well."

Carmelo tried to fend off Paolo's generosity, but Paolo dropped bills on the table and followed his wife out the door. Carmelo stood as if dazed. Stella's heart was pounding, her ears throbbing. They would have been hot to the touch, she knew. Some of the other diners were openly staring. Stella consoled herself that most of those French-speaking people probably had no idea how awful she'd been. She ate a small piece of her pork, trying to appreciate the flavor.

When Carmelo took his seat again, he was silent for several minutes. Stella persevered with her pork, but she had to cut tiny bites and chew them many times. Her stomach was tender, almost sore, because of what she'd done.

"Let's go, Stella," Carmelo said finally.

"No," she said, making her voice brash and disrespectful. She couldn't look at him. "Why should we waste all this expensive food? That doesn't make any sense."

They sat in silence as Stella steadily ate her way through her dinner, taking little sips of wine in hopes that it would unsour her stomach. The waiter came over to see if there was something wrong, and Carmelo bumbled through a short conversation, pantomiming paying the check. At that ugly picture, Carmelo's over-the-top miming in the moment of his own unhappiness, Stella felt a flare of disgust.

When the waiter left the final change, Carmelo drank down his full glass of wine, then reached for Paolo's glass. As Stella was finishing the last of her pork roast, he said suddenly, "She only meant well, I know because she is my sister, but maybe she overstepped asking about children. But you know that's something people do, even though they shouldn't," he was saying, talking quickly—to himself, Stella thought, not her. "She just meant to show she cared about her family. That's all. You should try to put the whole thing out of your mind." Now he *was* talking to her; he was touching her elbow again.

She looked up and saw his soft smile and sad eyes in the candlelight. "I hope you don't worry about this, Stella," Carmelo said. "I know she will be so sorry she upset you. She just wants to be your friend and she made a mistake."

Stella felt sick. How could he take her side? Why wasn't he leaping to his sister's defense, shouting invectives at his malicious, vulgar wife? In this moment Stella was sure she had just made the world a worse place and gained no strength from it herself.

"I'm ready to go now," she said. Her voice sounded like a child's.

When they got back to their hotel room, Stella was vibrating with remorse and fear. It was a terrible thing she'd done, terrible. Now she needed to be strong and make it stick. She rallied herself, cleared her throat, and told Carmelo she was too upset by what had happened, that she couldn't bear to look at him tonight, he looked too much like that woman. She stared at the floor. "You had better leave me alone now."

He didn't say anything, and finally she looked up to check his expression, which seemed to be one of disbelief, or suppressed anger. But he pulled his coat back on and said, "I guess I'll go have a drink." And he left.

Stella didn't see him again that night. She had trouble falling asleep, her conscience swirling with remorse and justifications. When she woke up in the morning the linens on the other side of the bed were still pulled to in a perfect nurse's corner.

Unsure of what to do with herself, Stella dressed in her fourth honeymoon dress, which was a muted green that reminded her of the gray-green of olive leaves back home in Ievoli. She went downstairs to the parlor area where the hotel staff served breakfast. She sat at a table and drank a cup of coffee the breakfast maid prepared for her. She ate a pastry. Her chest, the area around her heart, was sore with her guilt. Some other breakfasters came and went, and Stella had another cup of coffee. She couldn't get back into her room; Carmelo had the key, and she didn't know where he was. But this was what she'd wanted, to be left alone.

She looked down at her green dress, whose color soothed her. She thought of the maiden-green skirt of her *pacchiana,* which she hadn't worn in a decade. She would be wearing red, now, married lady that she was. But here she was in this virginal green. She carefully folded back the cuffs so that her scars were exposed. How far away was that dangerous, beautiful world where she had almost died so many times. It had been six years since her last almost-death, when she had tried to kill herself to escape a nightmare that had seized her mind—a nightmare that was simply a part of her everyday life now. How fast those last six years had gone by, like they hadn't mattered, a cycle of ironing and praying and hair-curling and doily-crocheting that both maintained and undid itself. There were some blemishes and some highlights, but even those ran together, as if her memories had stopped being important.

Stella was spared any difficult conversations because Carmelo came into the parlor when the grandfather clock by the fireplace read nine fifteen. He was dressed in a fresh yellow button-down shirt and his jacket was pressed; he must have pressed it himself just now up in their room.

"Good morning, Stella," he said, taking the seat across from her. His hair was washed and oiled into a smooth, shiny black sweep over his forehead.

"Good morning," she replied. She wondered where Carmelo had been all night. Had he gone to his sister? Another hotel? A whorehouse?

They didn't say anything else to each other through breakfast. Stella drank a third cup of coffee as Carmelo ate two pieces of toast with jam.

Two more days, she had to get through, and two more nights.

On Wednesday Stella suffered the products of her malfeasance, her entire body tightened around the coil of her guilty gut. Carmelo took them to the pier, where they boarded a tourist ferryboat that chugged them down and then back up the river. There was a bar on the boat, and Carmelo bought himself a bottle of beer. Stella felt too queasy to want even water.

They did not meet Carmela and Paolo for dinner. Carmelo took them to a restaurant near their hotel, where the waiter was unkind and made a show of not understanding the French words Carmelo tried to read off the menu. They ate in silence. Stella's groin was aching, a lancing pain like she sometimes got during her period, but she knew, unfortunately, that today's pain was the result of the guilt. What was Carmelo thinking? Was he giving up on her yet? Toward the end of the meal, Carmelo left the table to use the toilet, and Stella took the opportunity to drop her steak knife into her handbag. It felt melodramatic, but maybe she'd need to be melodramatic later.

The walk back to the hotel was too short. As Carmelo closed the door to their room, Stella said, "You better not think you are going to lay a hand on me now."

He turned to face her, removing his hat. His cheeks were pink and his eyes were angry. "This is ridiculous," he said. "Do you think I don't know what you're doing?" She didn't say anything. "We're married," he told her. "It is my right."

"If you try anything, you'll see what's coming to you," Stella said. She hated him in that moment and she was certain he hated her. "Even if I have to sleep with a knife under my pillow."

There was a strange pause as they each tried to think of what to say next. After waiting several beats too long, Stella opened the clasp of her purse, fumbling through her gloves, and produced the steak knife.

"This is ridiculous," he said again. "What do you think is going to happen? You think we're going to live out the rest of our lives and never sleep together?"

"Not if I can help it," she blurted.

Well, there it was.

"Just take off your clothes and get it over with." Carmelo was shouting. "You'll see it's not such a big deal."

Stella's stomach contracted, the coil tightening. "No. It's never going to happen."

Carmelo threw up his hands. The hotel room key went flying into the wall and bounced onto the carpet. "Remember what you said to my sister yesterday, about God punishing her? What's your plan there, huh? When people ask you why you don't have a baby?"

"It's none of their business," Stella said, her conviction collapsing into guilt about how she had treated Carmela.

"Right. Because people mind their own business. Because that's how the world works."

"It's easy." Stella cleared her throat to steady her voice before adding, "I'll just tell them your *pistola* doesn't work."

The last vestiges of kindness in Carmelo's face had fallen away. "All right, Stella. Why don't you think this through a little? Do you realize where this all leaves me?"

"I think . . ." Stella had to clear her throat again. "I think I want to go to bed." She made a show of lifting the pillow and placing the steak knife under it. "Maybe it would be best if you slept on the floor."

"No, thank you," Carmelo said. "I'm not feeling tired. I think I'll go have a drink." He tipped his hat to her and said in English, "Have a very nice evening, Signora Maglieri."

She had saved herself for one more night. She lay in bed, trying to dispel the panic of the encounter. Her heart ached from pounding; it had been pounding and pounding for so many days.

On Thursday she woke at the weak blond light of dawn, again to a half-empty honeymoon bed. She hadn't thought to close the blinds. She lay where she was among the cascade of decorative pillows and watched the ceiling change color as the dawn yellow deepened and brightened. What a bed this was; she would never sleep in another like it. She wished she had been able to enjoy it.

She finally got up when she had to pee too badly to put it off any longer. Locking the bathroom door behind her, she took a long shower, letting the hot water run over her wantonly, then spent some time reassembling her curls in the mirror over the sink. She would wear her last dress today, her pink Easter dress.

Stella had just pinned on her hat when she heard the key in the lock. She was standing by the window, emptying ticket stubs that had collected in her handbag onto the bedside table. Carmelo closed the door behind him, tossed his hat onto the bed, and took off his winter coat. He was rumpled-looking, his hair awry, like a man, Stella thought, who had slept in a chair.

"Take off your dress and get in the bed," he said to her.

Immediately Stella's heart was pounding in her ears again. Her fingers tingled numbly on her ticket stubs. She made herself laugh, as if he were joking.

"Take off your dress and get in the bed," he repeated. "You're not my wife until you do it, and I'm returning home with a wife."

"No," she said, turning her back on him. The knife was far away, and he was coming toward her; she could hear the compressions of his feet in the plush carpet.

"You're my wife, Stella. Wives do what their husbands tell them to. And now I'm telling you to take off your dress." His fingers closed around her upper arm.

"Get your dirty hands off of me," Stella said, twisting out of his grip. She could have opened the door to the hallway and run down the stairs, but instead she did what was most familiar and ducked into the bathroom, throwing her weight against the door to close it. But no—he had jammed his foot in, he was forcing it open. She fought back with all her strength, her high heels sliding on the shower-wet tile floor, her mind white with panic. He was so strong—she was nothing in comparison. The door opened, inexorably, and he was there in the bathroom with her.

He shoved her shoulder so she spun around, her face to the mirror. He used his left arm to hitch her elbows behind her back; her shoulders twinged at the strain. He kept her pressed to the sink with his pelvis against her rear end as he yanked her dress up over her hips, then roughly jerked down her girdle and stockings. It took a long time, because the elastic was strong; when he tried to tear it, it pulled taut against her tenderest flesh.

Stella was trapped in her dream—it was the same listless helplessness, the hands rough and unstoppable as her mind sank into lassitude. Cold marble pressed against her belly, and she stared at her meaningless face in the mirror through that strange, terrifying moment of skin chafing skin, a dry, uncomfortable contact rub that was only a prelude to the real pain. Her mind was empty, a sleepy wipe the gray-white color of a dream.

You hold on to it so tightly and so fearfully for so long, and then it's gone so quickly, like a pot of water emptied into a stream.

She felt her own blood dripping down her left thigh in a fast-moving pearl, the sink marble heating up against her belly.

Carmelo's face in the mirror bore an expression of intense concentration as he thrust, thrust, and thrust toward a deliberately speeded conclusion. His liquid followed the pearl of blood down the same trail of her left thigh, and as Carmelo pulled away from her with a noisy sigh she looked down to see pinked-up semen had landed on the white tile floor, milky-clear like the albumen of a fertilized chicken egg. As Carmelo left the bathroom, shutting the door on her behind him, Stella knelt to the ground and began to clean up the sticky mess with a fold of toilet paper.

Part III

 # MATURITY

Fhijlii picciuli, guai picciuli; fhijlii randi, guai randi.
Little children, little problems; big children, big problems.
—CALABRESE PROVERB

U lupu perde llu pilu, ma no llu vizzu.
A wolf may lose his fur, but never his vices.
—CALABRESE PROVERB

Chi sulu mangia sulu s'affuca.
Those who eat alone choke alone.
—CALABRESE PROVERB

DEATH 6
Exsanguination (Motherhood)

One morning in September 1954, Stella Maglieri woke up alone in the bed she shared with her husband; he'd left for his 5 a.m. shift at the electric company several hours earlier. Dawn lay tangerine-orange on the slats of the venetian blinds. Stella stared at the sheet where it pulled taut over the perfect ball of her belly. Inside the ball was her restless fifth fetus; if she delivered it alive it would become her fourth child. In the crib beside her was her third baby, ten months old and fussing; in the converted closet were her first and second, stacked in bunk beds. As she watched the sun slide over her stomach, a voice sounded in her head: *You are nobody.*

For a moment Stella lay frozen, wondering if there was someone in her house. The voice was as clear as a factory boss on the claxon. *You are nobody.* But she hadn't had a boss in six years, and besides, the voice sounded just like her own.

You are nobody, it said again.

And she wasn't.

This is the story of the sixth way Stella Fortuna almost died, of motherhood.

Before the motherhood, though, there must be the pregnancy, which happened pretty much right there in that Montreal honeymoon hotel bathroom. The fact was, Stella Fortuna, who had survived five near-death experiences, had endured the thing she'd feared even more than death. This time, no one had any sympathy for her.

For the thirteen hours of their train ride home, as the New England foliage burned by along the waterways on the other side of the window, Stella had seen none of the loveliness. Her mind was gray, and it grayed out the entire world. Someone could have snatched her hat right off her head and she might not have noticed. In the grayness there was one circle of thoughts: she was not a virgin anymore. She had given up the *rosetta*. A piece of someone else's body was inside her even now. It was over, it was over, her choices, her chances to run. She could never have it back.

That was the beginning of her married life.

When they arrived in Hartford, Carmelo Maglieri took his new wife to visit her family before heading home to his tenement. Carmelo and Stella drank coffee at Assunta's dining room table, eating angel wings left over from the wedding. Tina had made an orange cake, and Assunta served them on her yellow glass as though it were a special occasion.

Stella sat through the visit feeling weary and ashamed. She let Carmelo do most of the talking, although she knew they were judging her for that, too—he's subdued her, they must be thinking to themselves; he's mastered her, finally someone has. The one thing everyone at the table knew was that Stella had been deflowered since they last saw her. They were marveling at how the act had changed her, the way people always talked about the change that came over a woman once she "knew." Stella just needed the job done to her, and now she acts like a wife. Stella knew there was no one here, even among her dearest, who felt any compassion for her. As Carmelo told sugarcoated stories of Montreal and forks clicked against Assunta's delicate dessert plates, Stella stole looks around the table, gauging. Her stooped, smiling mother, eyes wet with affection for her handsome new son-in-law. Her frankly curious sister, stealing looks right back. Her smirking brother-in-law, Rocco. She couldn't control what Rocco was imagining about her, and the fact that it probably wasn't far from the truth made her ache with weakness.

For once Stella wished Tina would hassle her, ask her too-blunt questions. She wanted to pour out her heartsickness, but she wasn't sure how; maybe plainspoken Tina could drag it out of her. But the sisters had no private moment.

As dusk fell Carmelo carried two boxes of Stella's clothes to his car. He opened the passenger door for Stella, who got in the car as her family saw them off. Stella belonged to Carmelo now, and her lot in life was to follow where he led her. Tina waved as Carmelo drove away, but Stella couldn't make herself wave back.

Carmelo's Front Street apartment was in a bachelor building, five floors of single-occupant rooms with a shared kitchen and a lone bathroom on the ground floor. The building was sixty years old and wasn't up to any of the current residential codes; it was mildew-damaged from the floods of the 1930s. The arrangement was temporary, but noxious. The corridors were low and dim; the kitchen was full of dark scurrying.

Carmelo's room was on the third floor. The bed was only a single, nailed to the wall. There was a dresser for clothing and shelves on which Carmelo kept his pots, pans, and food, so neither the roaches nor the neighbors would have the opportunity to get into it. The room's remaining space contained a card table and a folding chair that looked just like the ones they brought out from closets for parties at the Italian Society.

Carmelo had courteously cleared two-thirds of his closet and half his dresser to make room for Stella's clothes. He also kept the promise he'd made on their first date and never asked her to help with cooking. That evening he gathered various items from the pantry case into a pot. "I'll get out of your way so you can unpack," he said, and he did.

Stella felt as if the world around her weren't entirely real. Methodically she shook each dress out in the still, flat silence of the room. The street on the other side of the window was already fading, the October sun having set. As the room got progressively darker Stella looked around for a light switch, but couldn't find one. Ten years earlier she had never imagined electricity, and now she wasn't sure how to function without it.

Carmelo returned half an hour later. She sat in the wooden chair in the dark as he set a steaming pot down on the card table. He opened the dresser and brought out three small candles, which he set together on a saucer and lit with the cigar lighter he always carried. He was humming to himself, a melody she didn't recognize. In the light of the low candles, Stella saw the heat stains on the table between them. The pot contained *pasta e fagioli,* and it didn't smell bad.

Carmelo spooned soup into a bowl for Stella, then unwrapped a rind of very fine Parmigiano, sparkling with salt crystals, which he grated on top. She watched the shreds curl in the heat, a bounty of cheese from this man who wanted to show her now, again, how generous he was. Did they both already know it was too late? Or did only she?

They were tired from the train journey and the disrupted, emotional evening previous, so they didn't talk much. Carmelo told her what time he would leave in the morning, where to keep emergency change and valuables. When he ran out of things to advise on, he turned on the radio and tuned it to a station that played big band music. They finished eating, drank down glasses of red wine poured from a two-gallon jug. Then Carmelo took the dirty bowls and pot and left for the kitchen again.

Stella's stomach was a hard ball. She couldn't fight anymore, fight only to lose again. As the saxophones on the radio hawed and rumbled, she changed into her white nightgown, took off her girdle and underwear, and got into Carmelo's bed. Her mind was bright with the needling memory of what had happened in Montreal, of the warming marble pushing into her stomach as he thrust into her. As she waited for him to come back from the kitchen, she wondered if there was already the makings of a baby in her stomach, if it was already too late. She had to believe it was, that all hope was lost; otherwise, it would be unbearable every time she had to do it, to be thinking, *Is today the day he will put a baby inside me? Was I safe up until now?*

When Carmelo came back, he arranged the clean dishes on the cold radiator to dry. He blew out the candles, and in the streetlight from the uncurtained window Stella could see him remove his shirt, which he hung in the closet, then his belt and pants, which he draped over the chair, and finally his undershirt and briefs.

How did he seem so sure of himself in front of her? Had he been with so many women that undressing in front of one really didn't trouble him at all? Or did his lack of shyness mean he didn't care what she thought of him? Why should he, she supposed. He had no need to woo her anymore.

Today she saw what he looked like naked, surprisingly diminished without his neat clothes, even a little comic with his exaggerated laborer's tan, the unthreatening dough ball of penis and testicles swinging soft from a bird's nest of black pubic hair. Her stomach cramped, the physiological anticipation of what was coming. The fact that Carmelo didn't look so scary right now made her feel even weaker, more pathetic, for having given herself up to him yesterday.

Her husband came to the bed and pulled back the blanket, revealing the shape of her legs under the lacy nightgown. Kneeling on the bed to her left, he peeled the nightgown up her legs. If Carmelo was pleased to see she was not wearing any panties—that there would not be that kind of conflict, at least, tonight—he didn't give any sign. He shifted her buttocks away from the wall with one strong, decisive movement. Before her eyes in the half-dark, the shadowy shape of his penis began to change, bulging out from his darkened ball sack.

Here it was, it was going to happen again. Stella was outside and away from her body, just like that day in the pigsty when the invisible hand had closed around her own. She watched from that remove as Carmelo arranged her knees. Her husband—the man she would spend the rest of her life with—he actually didn't care how hurt and afraid she was; he would put her to use. A cold gush of air prickled up her hot, secret skin as he spat into the palm of his hand and reached down to rub himself. She could feel her heartbeat in her groin as his stomach came to rest for a moment against hers. Her dread and disgust gathered in her belly, a hard round stone. And then—there—it was inside her again.

Her female skin was tender and she shuddered as he first penetrated her. The soreness abated quickly, and for a while it was an absurd but otherwise unremarkable rhythmic activity she watched Carmelo engage in: push, and push, and push. His expression seemed distant as she watched his face above her. Periodically he cupped her breast through the nightgown, giving it a gentle squeeze.

After a few minutes of this, though, a different soreness took over as his plunging into her passage became drier and more abrasive. The discomfort increased steadily, and Carmelo seemed to feel it as well, because his thrusting sped up. Just as it was starting to become so painful Stella was wondering if she could ask him to stop, he made a noise in his throat and froze, his torso bucking backward, exactly as she had seen her father do over her mother. A few seconds passed, then Carmelo pulled himself away somewhat clumsily, his kneecap coming down on hers so that she gasped in pain and he apologized.

As Carmelo stepped into his briefs, Stella lay still, the draft emitted by the thrown-back cover slowly chilling the wetness that lay on the jelly-soft skin of her thigh. She would very much have liked to get rid of the wetness, but she was unwilling to touch it. The thought of feeling it on her fingers made her clench her hands together.

"Didn't you want to use the bathroom?" Carmelo said.

Stella shook her head, which was a silly thing to do in the dark, but she couldn't find her voice. He must have understood because he got back into the bed, pulled the covers halfway up his chest, and said, "Well. Good night." That was really it for him—all it took. After only a few loud, deep breaths, he was snoring.

Stella lay in the narrow bed with one hip against the cold plaster wall and one against her husband's hot thigh. There was nowhere to put her arms, so she folded her hands on top of her stomach. And in her exhaustion there was no more miserable thinking or terror or disgust or despair or confusion—somehow there was sleep.

This is what marriage turned out to be: shared life in a small space. Keeping on, but with a man whose personal habits she was unfamiliar with, instead of with the family from whom she had learned all her own personal habits.

Stella hated Carmelo's apartment building. They didn't have much, so it wasn't crowded. Their wedding gifts would stay at Bedford Street until they had a place of their own. But the shared bathroom was a daily humiliation. She had to walk down two flights of stairs and stand in line; everyone coming in through the front door could see who was waiting for the bathroom—a better setup for burglary or molestation Stella couldn't imagine. The toilet line was all men, and you could always count how many people were planning a number two because they came with a wad of toilet paper. Stella had spent her childhood shitting in the woods, but this—this was somehow worse. At least in the woods she had shat alone.

There was the oddness of all-encompassing intimacy with Carmelo, even aside from offering him her body for his use. There was, for example, the fact that if she needed to do things like tweeze hairs out of her underarm he was going to be there to watch her do it. Dressing in front of each other was awkward, although Carmelo seemed to take it in stride that his wife would see him do silly-looking things like tug his trousers and briefs down to his knees, then pull them back up for manly adjustments before buckling his belt each morning. This was married life, Stella realized. Doing private things in front of another person without any comment.

Stella was not truly suicidal, because she never wanted to die. She had fought death too hard for that. But, as the distinction goes, she often wished she did not have to be alive. Her current existence was a perverse realization of her greatest fear.

This was the period when the thought entered her head: *What is the point?* Of course there never is any point, but until you think that thought for the first time it doesn't matter that there isn't. And once Stella had the thought, it was stuck, soaked into her skin and tunneling along her arteries. Her fast, perfect fingers were dulled by it, her elbows harder to lift and her neck sore. Her days were gray and slid together. There were no bright spots, no memories she would take with her of this time, her early marriage.

Stella had never had a life goal before, a specific precious thing she badly wanted, the way her father had wanted to be American, or her mother had wanted a house, or Tina wanted a baby. But now Stella had something else, the pure, irrefutable knowledge that there was nothing she wanted at all. Not only did she have nothing left to lose, she had nothing left to win, either.

When I think of Stella's life during this time, I grieve for her. But my relationship with her misery is nuanced, because I am a product of it. As you have surely figured out by now, Stella Fortuna is my grandmother. And as you'll see if you stay with Stella even through this grimmest of passages in her story, my life is only one of many she spared by not ending her own.

Tony had bought the three-floor walk-up on Bedford Street with the notion that someday all three floors would be full of his progeny, a *palazzo* of Fortuna offshoot families. Now that those satellites were starting to come into being, however, Tony was having trouble getting rid of the tenants he'd rented to.

The family who had lived in the second floor had left peacefully as soon as they'd found somewhere else to go, and the Caramanicos had moved into that apartment just before Stella's wedding. But the lady on the top floor, Miss Catherine Miller, would not leave.

"It's my house," Tony told her, "so if I tell you to leave you have to leave."

"That's not how things work here," Miss Miller said, with the sanctimonious conviction of a retired schoolteacher. "I know my tenant rights. I can have my lawyer come down here and remind you of what they are."

Both parties enjoyed an enraged battle, and she might never have left if she hadn't had a stroke just before Christmas and been relocated to a care facility. In another circumstance Stella would have sympathized with Miss Miller; it came as no surprise to Stella that her father could make someone have a stroke. But she secretly resented Miss Miller for never sharing the secret of her independence. It was an irrational feeling of betrayal, because Stella had never gotten up the courage to speak to her except small talk about the milkman.

And Stella was acidly grateful to Miss Miller for her timing with her stroke, because now that she was pregnant and forced to visit it even more often, Carmelo's shared bathroom was intolerable. If I died, she had actually thought—had begun to say out loud to Carmelo—if I died right now at least I wouldn't have to use that toilet again.

"That's just a stupid thing to say, Stella," Carmelo would reply, but they moved into the third-floor apartment in the Bedford Street building the very same day that Catherine Miller's nephew told Tony his aunt wouldn't be coming back. Tony gave the nephew fifty dollars in cash for her larger furniture; Assunta and Tina packed her other belongings in boxes and stored them in the garage. Miss Miller would never come and retrieve them.

Stella could pee in privacy now, as often as she wanted, but now she had a toilet of her own she had to clean. She had a claw-foot bathtub now, but she never wanted to bathe. Her hair was short these days, but she still didn't feel like washing it. She was always hungry, but she hated to feed the monster inside of her. She would eat and she would hate herself afterward, rubbing and scratching the greasy feeling of guilt off her face and neck, leaving red welts on her skin.

She watched as her body went through the first changes of the pregnancy ruination she had dreaded her entire life. She had been vain, she had thought she was beautiful, and now she was being punished for her vanity as, one by one, the features she had been proudest of were taken away. Her flat belly thickened; it would never be anything but swollen or vacantly sagging for the rest of her life. Her once-smooth bronze skin broke out in various rashes. Her eyes were dull in the mirror, the whites turned reddish-yellow. The dark under-eye bags would merge seamlessly into the facial sagging of age, so there would never be a moment between pregnancies when her pretty face was restored. Everything beautiful about Stella Fortuna's life was over.

Worse than any of this physical humiliation was the fact that it did not make her husband stop desiring her body. He took her almost every night. Stella turned her face to the wall so she wouldn't have to watch him. There was no more damage Carmelo could do to her—the child had already quickened in her womb—and yet for some reason that knowledge didn't make her loathe and fear copulation any less. Staring at the wall, she fought off the smeared layers of associations—the nightmare, her father's leather belt on her naked breasts, the marble sink in the Montreal hotel. When she closed her eyes she remembered the wisdom of her mother—the best husbands were the ones who got the job done fast. Sometimes Carmelo was fast. Sometimes he was not.

She couldn't fight off her nightmare, so she learned to escape into it. The rapist was coming toward her with his big rough hands, and she would climb into the window frame, where she'd be safe from him. As Carmelo's penis bumped and scraped against her insides, she tried to build herself a vision of what was out that window, over the metal fence and beyond the shantytown. She pictured Ievoli, the glowing yellow-green of the citrus leaves in the April sun, the silver-blue of the September olive groves, the sunbaked July rows of bulging tomato stakes marching like soldiers along the terraced mountain.

Her world was a gray ache and she couldn't live inside it.

They made her go down to Sunday dinner at Tony and Assunta's, but she was ashamed to be seen by her family, knowing they looked at her and thought, *How nice and quiet she is now*, and *Someone gave her what she deserved*. She could hear their thoughts ringing around the dinner table in the undercurrent of their solicitous questions about her health. Joey was the only honest one, cackling about her fertility every time he saw her. Joey was honest, but he was still the worst.

Carmelo gave her money and told her to go buy dresses, but she didn't want to go outside. Her body hurt and disgusted her, and what was the point of buying a dress that wouldn't fit next week? He told her to use the money on whatever she wanted, whatever would make her happy, but nothing would make her happy.

At night, when she could find no respite in sleep between her trips to the bathroom, Stella sometimes closed her eyes and pictured the face of the first Stella, the wretched little ghost who had haunted her for a quarter of a century. "Are you jealous of me still?" she'd whisper into the dark. "Are you jealous of this?" Because jealousy was two-sided, and the second Stella did not feel lucky to be the living Stella anymore.

On Saturdays when there was no work to go to, Stella would play sick while Tina went to the wedding showers for their Italian Society friends. When she got home she would come up to Stella's dark room and try to cheer her up with smuggled cookies.

"Tina," Stella asked her sister one day, "do you believe there's really a God?"

"Stella! Of course there's a God. What are you saying?" Tina whispered, as if that would stop her omnipotent deity from overhearing.

"But why do you think so?" Stella asked. "Just because the priest says so? How do you know for sure, Tina?"

"Of course I know," Tina said.

"But how?"

Stella didn't expect an answer. Tina only had answers other people had given her, the answers other people had assured her it was correct to believe, and then she knew them beyond a shadow of a doubt.

But Tina had an answer this time, after a moment's hesitation. "I know there's a God, because if there isn't, what's the point of all of the bad things? There would be no point, so there must be a God."

After Tina left, Stella turned over this thought, so close an echo of her own. If her sister's answer had been any more sanguine, it would have been no help to Stella at all. But as it was, it was just enough to get her through.

Her mother had told her it would happen—that when it was her own child, she would understand, that there would be nothing she would love more. She had told her mother she was different. She had been wrong.

The connection happened on Ash Wednesday, 1948. Stella was sitting in the evening mass, hunger stirring in her bulging belly, and then the stirring wasn't hunger anymore, it was something else—something in addition to the hunger, a little sloshing wave of life. There was a baby inside her, asserting itself, and the baby was hungry, too. It seemed that, with this show of solidarity, the baby was telling her, *I'm your ally.*

It was not the most rational thought of her life—she recognized that even as she had it—but she was sitting on a hard church pew after a long day of factory work and she was tired and hungry and no one else cared. Well, the baby cared.

After that, she felt the baby every day. Now that she'd understood the proverbial spark of life inside of her, she couldn't forget it. Even when the baby wasn't moving, she knew it was there and thought about it. Stella could barely bring herself to talk to Carmelo, but she could talk to the baby, for many hours. She had never been able to sing very well, but now whatever songs she thought of came out just fine. Her voice bounced pleasantly off the apartment walls, and the echo she heard sounded happy.

Carmelo was stupid with joy at becoming a father. He rubbed his wife's belly and bragged about how big his son was getting to anyone who would listen. Let him brag. Stella had stopped caring about Carmelo. She still hated him, but the heat was gone. Her body was tired from the pregnancy and she needed to focus her energy.

Stella wondered about God's tricks in this matter of the baby. This had been the thing she had wanted least in her life, and God had changed her heart to make her want it more than anything. At least, that was her mother's explanation for Stella's attachment. Stella thought it was more like an infection in her mind; her thoughts were not her own anymore, no more than her body was hers. She remembered—vividly—that only months ago she had not wanted to live; now not only had that shadow fled her psyche but she was also desperately devoted to making something else live, as well. Her richness and her darkness had been filed down to one fist-size glowing globe she carried in her womb.

Tina smiled. Tina threw her a baby shower. Tina loved Stella and stroked her stomach. But Tina had an honest face and couldn't hide her envy even when she smiled.

Stella knew it was confusing to Tina—it was confusing to Stella, too. Tina had spent her whole life training to be a mother, wanted that life so much. Stella had not wanted it at all, had walked a dark road to motherhood, lived through days when she would rather have died. And here she was, swollen and beatific, the change accomplished within moments of the consummation of her marriage, while Tina tried and tried and nothing came. The doctor had run tests but hadn't found anything wrong with her.

Behind Tina's back—and sometimes not—the women would ask Stella whether it was Tina's fault or Rocco's. It was usually the woman's, everyone knew. Stella was tongue-tied by the question, although it was not an uncommon one. How could people be so stupid and cruel? Did they not see how much they hurt Tina? Did they want to hurt her, on some level? Make her pay for not making the sacrifices they had?

When Tina's face betrayed her—sad, confused envy—Stella would squeeze her sister's hand. "You are going to be the best aunt," she told her. Tina smiled harder, and Stella added, "It's too bad. My children are going to love you more than me. They'll say, oh, Mommy can't cook anything, we want to go to Auntie Tina's house instead."

Tina laughed and looked down at her skirt. "Well, Carmelo can cook for them."

"He better be planning on it," Stella said, snappishly to make Tina laugh again.

Stella loved Tina because those thoughts weren't her fault, and also because there was no room in Stella's heart now for any coldness or resentment.

Assunta saw Tina's envy, too. She made the unfascination on Stella's forehead at least once a day. She came up to the third-floor apartment to hang mint in the windows.

"First baby," she would say. "The most vulnerable time."

Carmelo wanted Stella to quit her job at Silex as soon as she knew she was expecting, but she loved to work. She managed to defer until May, by which time she was so large that the factory work had become unpleasant.

On Stella's last day, Tina brought a small portable party: a stacked-high plate of starchy S-shaped cookies and a tray of cold *ravioli*. The ladies of the assembly line picked the *ravioli* up out of the pan with their fingers, taking tiny bites and catching the sauce in their paper napkins. Everyone giggled like crazy. Stella had put together thousands of coffeepots with these women, but most of them she would never see again.

Stella went into labor on the morning of July 24. Down in her mother's kitchen, she walked in circles while they waited for the expected things to happen: the cramps accelerating, becoming more painful. Stella was cranky with hunger; Assunta wouldn't let her eat anything, on doctor's orders. It was an infuriating, endless day of bouts of intense pain and miserable summer heat, wet-hot with Connecticut humidity. She had just stepped into Assunta's bathtub to splash cool water on herself when her water broke, so at least she didn't make a mess.

This was when they called Carmelo. He rushed Stella to the hospital, where there was more painful, sweaty waiting. The hospital was as uncomfortable as Stella had anticipated it would be, as was being handled by an English-speaking male doctor.

Miserable, boring hours passed in repetitive agony. They laid her down on a paper-covered hospital bed and put her feet in stirrups. Stella had not been prepared for that. She was horrified to have herself on display, but the humiliation was completely over-written by the intensity of her pain. The thought of her mother giving birth like an animal on her minty bed in Ievoli flashed through Stella's mind. She didn't feel like an animal, she felt like a monster, a monster tearing her own self apart with her claws. At least there were only strangers around her and no one she loved could see her this way.

The time dragged on, and the contractions, and the pain. Stella had lost any sense of how long, how many, how much. Being trampled by the pigs—it hadn't been this bad, had it? It couldn't even hurt this much to die. The window on the far side of the paper curtain was dark. It was night, and night would never end.

"You need to push, Stella," the doctor said to her.

"I am push," she said, scrabbling for English words that wouldn't come out. "I doing push."

This is the end of what Stella remembered.

Later Stella and Carmelo's children would tell the story of what happened that night. The doctor left the surgery room to ask Carmelo whose life he wanted to save, his wife's or his son's.

"There is no choice," Carmelo had answered. "I want them both."

I remember hearing that story when I was a kid, about how Grandpa had to pick between Grandma and the baby, and he told the doctor no way, give me both. And I remember thinking, Wow, Grandpa, he's so tough and loyal, such a family man. A hero. No compromises.

Now I think about that story and I feel furious. He risked my grandmother's life for his stubbornness and pride; he valued a baby he knew nothing about over the woman he supposedly loved. And my heart breaks for Stella, who had to live in that marriage. How lucky I am that I can't imagine being married to a man who wouldn't immediately pick me.

Stella did not die that day, for the sixth time.

When she woke up, she burned in that way a body burns after surgery, every capillary straining to reconnect, to seal, to fight infection. The pain was familiar to her, but not its magnitude. Her body had been exhausted by the hours of pushing, by the removal of so much matter, by the loss of so much blood.

The hospital room was pink and her mind was as fuzzy as yarn. She saw her mother sleeping in a low chair with wooden arms. She turned her chin and saw the pink gown stretched over her own bosom. She struggled to figure out why she was in the hospital, and then when she reached her answer she began to panic, her mind sharpening, because she was not pregnant anymore. The feeling of the baby pulsing inside her was gone, a hole she now, abruptly, noticed. Gripping her deflated abdomen, she lurched up in her bed, or tried to, but was blinded by a wave of pain so intense she lost the hospital room for a flash—maybe for minutes, or hours, who could know.

She opened her eyes again, eventually, and tried to call out to her mother, but her mouth was dry. A tube ran into her arm; the skin around the needle prickled with bruise. She focused on that tiny discomfort, tried to build a wall between herself and the rest of her body. It was daylight; light came in pinkly through that damn paper curtain.

"Mamma," she said. Her voice was the sound of a piece of paper being crumpled in a fist. But Assunta was awake this time, and there was Tina, too, standing beside the bed. "Mamma. Where is my baby? My baby."

Tina helped Stella drink juice from a paper cup and Assunta sobbed, grasping Stella's hand so tightly both of their knuckles were creased with red and white.

"Mamma," Stella said again, but Assunta only had air for tears and for her circular prayer, *thank you God thank you Madonna thank you God thank you Madonna.*

Stella swallowed, and Tina helped her drink again. Her pelvis ached, an onion of ache. She tried her sister this time. "Tina," she said. Her voice, was that her voice? It sounded strange. "Tina. Where is my baby? Did they take away my baby?"

Tina looked at their mother, but Assunta was sobbing into Stella's hand. She was going to let Tina do this dirty work. Half of Stella's mind understood before Tina could say it; the other half couldn't understand it even after it had been said.

"Your baby's with God, Stella," Tina said. She had made it that far, and now she was no good anymore, because she had fallen to the linoleum floor to cry into her skirt.

Stella looked up at the ceiling. Her mother wept on her left and her sister on her right. She hoped a nurse would come along and take care of them because she couldn't speak to them anymore, or maybe ever again. She closed her eyes and dove into her pain.

Stella had carried to term a healthy baby boy whose corpse weighed ten pounds, four ounces. He had been in a breech position going into the labor, and the doctor, a rookie, had tried to make the baby turn. When the labor didn't proceed as expected, the doctor used forceps to reach up into Stella and try to pull him out. But the baby was just too big for the birth canal; his shoulders stuck. As the scene in the hospital had modulated into panic, the doctor performed a proctoepisiotomy, making a surgical incision that would marvel later generations—where, exactly, did he think the baby was? By the time they extracted the baby, he was dead, strangled with his own umbilical cord.

Agony, delirium, darkness, agony.

Had it been this bad when she was a child, being ripped apart? Was it just that there was more of her now, so she could feel more pain?

Stella had no control over whether she was asleep or awake. At the worst moments, sweat itching in her raw stitches, when the weight of loss on her chest was so heavy she battled to pull enough air into her lungs—in those moments, when she wanted nothing more than to leave herself, when sleep would have been the greatest reprieve, she had no access to it. She had to listen to the mourning and awkward bedside conversations of the terrible people who came to visit her. They were all terrible now.

Why did you let me live this time? she asked God, over and over. *What was the point?*

Sometimes she said it out loud, and if Assunta heard her she shushed her. That wasn't how God worked.

Tina wiped Stella's forehead with a cool, damp towel. She plumped Stella's pillow and dabbed water on her dry lips. "Good Stella, lucky Stella, lucky star," she crooned, making a song out of Stella's names. *Brava Stella, Stella Fortuna, stella fortunata.*

Stella waited until Assunta left the sickroom, then said, "You think I'm lucky?"

Tina was caught off guard by her sister's voice after so many hours of uninterrupted silence. "Lucky to be alive," she said, but it sounded like a question.

Stella felt the Eye on her. Her heartache compressed into a sickness she finally understood. "At least now neither of us has a baby," she said.

Tina blanched. "Stella. No."

"Admit it, get it off your chest so God can forgive you." Stella was so exhausted she couldn't put any fire into her words, but they didn't need any fire. "You were jealous of my baby and now, deep in your heart, you're happy that it's dead."

The expression on Tina's face made Stella's gut roil with hate—her big, stupid tears; Tina would try to cry her way out of this like she had every bad thing that had ever happened to her. Stella hated her sister more intensely than she had ever hated anyone before, even Carmelo, even her father. Even her father hadn't killed her baby.

"No, Stella, you're wrong." Tina wiped clear mucus from her chin. "I only wanted to love it. I wanted to love your baby and I am so sad for you."

"There's nothing you can say that would ever make me forgive you," Stella said. She had used up all her energy. She turned her face away and closed her eyes.

"Why are you crying, Tina?" Assunta asked when she came back.

"I'm not," Stella heard her sister say, then snuffling and nose-blowing.

Tina didn't sing anymore, but she didn't leave Stella's bed, either.

Mostly when Stella's eyes opened, there were Assunta and Tina, no matter what. But this time it was dark—the only light came from the hospital wing outside, and it was a man sitting next to her in the chair with the wooden arms.

"Carmelo?" she asked the darkness, because for a moment she wasn't sure.

"Stella." He was crying. She heard it in his voice—typical Carmelo, he made no effort to hide it from her. "My Stella, my star. My precious Stella. I'm so sorry. I'm so sorry." She realized he had been holding her hand when his grip tightened. "Please come back to me. Please don't leave me. Let me take care of you. Let me make it better."

Maybe Stella was the weakest she had ever been in her life, because she felt her heart turn. When she wondered how she would put all the bad things behind her, she realized that her mind did not even want to remember what they were, and the path was suddenly quite clear. She would bury the first year of her marriage with her baby boy. That was how she would save herself.

Stella Maglieri squeezed her husband's wet hand. "I'm here, Carmelo," she said. "I'm not going anywhere."

The hospital discharged her after four days, with the recommendation that she spend at least five weeks in bed. The doctor prescribed her a painkiller Stella took sporadically the first few days, but it made her so disoriented and ill at ease that she stopped. Anyway, the worst pain was in her mind and her heart, and the pills did nothing to divorce her from that.

Things that were difficult included sitting up or down, or any other action that put any pressure at all on her perineum. Going to the toilet was torture, reviving the agony of the not-yet-healed flesh the doctor had sliced to admit his forceps. The vagina is an organ of trauma, though, and as intense as this misery was, when it healed it did so completely.

During her days, Stella lay in bed, the skin on her arms browning in the late-morning light and her sore, hardened nipples leaking unused milk into the souring fabric of her nightgown, and unpacked and repacked her thoughts. Tina would come up before work with a plate of frittata or a muffin and a cup of coffee and put it on a chair by Stella's bed. Tina never said anything, and Stella usually pretended she was still asleep.

Carmelo made Stella dinner every night, hot food with meat so that she could rebuild her blood. But Stella often heard him talking to Tina in the kitchen, and she knew that many parts of the dinner her husband brought her were her sister's secret offerings. She recognized Tina's oven-fried chicken cutlets and knew the taste of her sister's tomato sauce, which was spicier and not as sweet as Carmelo's.

Assunta, whose legs had been inflamed with arthritis and who hadn't been able to work all year, sat with Stella and crocheted. Mostly they didn't talk, except the time Stella blurted out, "Mamma, what if it never gets better?"

Assunta's soft cheeks drooped sadly. She wrapped her hand around Stella's ankle under the blanket. "I know how you feel, my Stella. I lost my first baby, too." She was quiet for a moment. "But then God gave me you. My greatest gift." She gave Stella's ankle a gentle squeeze. "Maybe He has an even greater gift for you."

The funeral was Carmelo's idea. Antonio said it was a waste of money, buying a plot of land and a headstone for a baby who had never even taken a breath in this world, but Antonio didn't make decisions for Stella anymore.

They held the funeral two weeks after Stella came home from the hospital. She wasn't supposed to be out of bed, but it was only a few hours, a graveside service and the burial of the tiny casket with the embalmed body of baby Bob Maglieri.

"What kind of name is Bob?" her brother Joe had scoffed. "It's not a name at all. Why didn't you name him Robert, at least?"

Stella didn't owe anyone any explanations, and certainly not her good-for-nothing drunk of a brother. But she had named her dead baby Bob so that he would never have to share his name with any living child.

Stella wore a new black dress to the grave service. She walked between Tina and Assunta, each of them holding one of her arms, just like Assunta had walked to her own child's funeral on the arms of her own mother and sister thirty years earlier.

Stella threw dirt onto the lowered coffin—the bald, mustachioed funeral director had to explain to them what to do. Afterward the mourners would assemble at Bedford Street for a luncheon.

As their friends departed the graveside, Tina said, "Stella, can you forgive me?"

"Don't be ridiculous," Stella said. "Forgive you for what?" She looked at her sister sideways, wondering if Tina had to say more. She did.

"For . . . for being jealous." Tina's voice broke.

"Tina. You don't really believe any of that old-world bullshit." Stella threaded her arm through her sister's and pressed away the dread in her own heart. "The doctor made a mistake. No one else is to blame for anything. You can't listen to those stupid old cows who say things like that. They'll ruin your life."

As they walked back toward their waiting car, Za Pina said to Assunta, "What's the matter with Stella? She doesn't cry at her own son's funeral?"

"You don't know my Stella," Assunta said. "She has never cried in her life, not even when she was a little girl and she had her guts ripped open by pigs."

Carmelo slept on the couch until Stella had her stitches taken out. He moved back to their bed in September, when she was mobile enough to change the sheets with her mother's help. Carmelo would lie carefully on his side of the bed, afraid of accidentally hurting her during the night. He sometimes stroked her hair until he fell asleep.

Another month passed. Stella's healing flesh had closed all its gaps. The only pain she now carried was the metaphysical one.

Carmelo knew to wait long enough before asking. And when he did ask her, "Stella, can we try again?" one night in October, maybe because the ache she had to heal most desperately was the one in her heart, she said yes.

For the rest of her sexual life, which would last fifteen years, Stella gave her body to her husband without resistance or comment, even when she was so pregnant she thought her spine would snap or when she was so tired she fell asleep in the middle. As time passed, Stella learned complete separation of her mind and her interrupted body. She learned to crouch in the window of her mind, gazing out past the shantytown of her subconscious and far beyond, to the silvery blue of the Tyrrhenian marina and the mountain crowned by the Ievoli church *chiazza,* where the Most Blessed Madonna of the Sorrows stood, ever patient, ever beatified, her golden heart bleeding for her dead son.

In April 1949, Tina had been married to Rocco Caramanico for two and a half years. Stella was four months pregnant when her sister told her the definitive news.

"We will never have children. There's something wrong."

It shouldn't have been a surprise, after all this time trying, but somehow Stella was shaken. "I thought you said the tests . . ."

Tina brought over two cups of coffee to the kitchen table. Even though it was Stella's apartment, it was Tina who acted like the hostess. She set the cups down on either side of the jelly jar of violets Carmelo had picked for Stella yesterday.

"There's nothing wrong with me," Tina said, not without some satisfaction. "It's Rocco. When he was in New Guinea he got mumps, and it made his, you know."

"Sterile? It made him sterile?"

"Yes." Tina's face was red. "His thing, you know, it works fine." Stella had more observational evidence than she needed on that front already. "But what's inside hasn't got any . . . you know. No babies. He'll never be able to make babies."

The sisters sat through an uncomfortable moment of silence as the scatology dispelled and the finality of the situation settled in.

"But he must have known he had had mumps before you got married," Stella said. "He knew all this time."

Tina shrugged. She was staring at her coffee cup. Her eyes were round and bald-looking.

Could Rocco really have done that? Could he have married Tina, knowing how badly she wanted children, and then let her go on all this time with false hope? Even Rocco couldn't be that cruel and selfish—could he? But Stella couldn't ask her sister that right now; that would be a different kind of cruelty.

"Tina," Stella said finally. "I'm so sorry."

"We could get the marriage annulled if I wanted to," her sister said. "I could try again with someone else. The priest said there would be no problem in this case."

"Do you want an annulment?" Stella asked carefully, her heart lifting.

"No," Tina said quickly. "I said for better or for worse, didn't I?"

"But Tina, that's not fair, not if you didn't know—"

"We have a good marriage," Tina interrupted, her tone decisive. "We want to stay together even without children."

Stella's small hope that Rocco Caramanico might become part of her past vanished. But what did Tina even mean, a good marriage? Stella was speechless for a long moment as she tried to understand. What made a marriage good? Stella had never thought of marriage as anything but an arrangement to be endured in order to create children—an arrangement she had, for that very reason, done her best to avoid. How could Tina's marriage be good if it prevented the one thing she had wanted most in life, to be a mother? Stella swallowed the lump in her dry throat, a clot of confusion and sadness.

"You could adopt," she said, feeling futile.

Tina was already shaking her head. "We don't need another person's baby, with who knows what other person's problems. We decided no, we're happy the way we are. We don't have to pray about this anymore." She looked up and smiled. "It's going to be okay, Stella. I am going to have all of your babies to take care of. And who knows how many you'll have."

The answer was ten—ten who survived their childhood.

In June 1949, Louie graduated from Hartford High. Stella sat through the sweltering ceremony, fighting the urge to pee, and clapped loudly as her baby brother walked across the temporary stage under the basketball hoop to shake the hand of the principal. Tony had the diploma framed and hung it in the Fortuna living room.

Louie was spending the summer working for a friend of Zu Tony Cardamone's, a licensed electrician named Bill Johnson. Louie had to be at work in West Hartford by 6 a.m. on the dot—time is money, and an electrician's time is quite a lot of money. To get to and from work, Tony bought Louie a bicycle with shining black hubcaps. Carmelo took Louie aside and told him not to worry, he'd help him get a car.

Joey had a job, too, finally. Carmelo had introduced him to the hiring manager at the electric company. The manager, who liked Carmelo, had found Joey a position. Stella hoped her brother respected his job enough not to do anything stupid. She didn't want Carmelo to get in trouble for a bad referral.

On September 2, 1949, Stella gave birth to a baby boy, six pounds, six ounces. The birth was natural and uncomplicated, although—it must be said—not that much less painful than the time she had almost died in childbirth.

They named the baby Thomas, after his paternal grandfather, but with the American spelling. A healthy boy to carry on the family name. Of course Tina and Rocco stood up as the baby's godparents at the baptism.

*   *   *

This is where things started to speed up for Stella. It began with the hours mixing together so that the days lost any discretion. Mealtimes were meaningless; Stella ate when she was hungry, which was all the time, because the baby sucked her dry like an adorable cannibal. The only thing Stella let herself care about was him, Tommy, until she felt the next one coming alive inside her and then her caring was divided, and then there would be a third, and it was divided again, and so on and so on until she was so fractioned and diluted by her own caring that every other thing in the world receded into winking stars on a peripheral horizon. Fifteen years later, when the bearing was finally over, she would look at the forty-four-year-old woman in the mirror and struggle to itemize what had happened in the lost interim.

One thing that happened was Queenie. Cute as a button, she seemed, but in retrospect there were plenty of warning signs.

On a Tuesday evening in May 1950, Stella was sitting in her mother's kitchen, nursing baby Tommy, when Louie burst in, the screen door to the garden banging behind him. He ignored Tina, who was peeling carrots and whom he almost hit with the door, and Stella, who *tsk*ed him as she pulled a cloth over her bare breast and Tommy's pinched, concentrating little face.

Assunta was standing at the stove moving the pasta around with her wooden spoon so it wouldn't stick to the pot. "Mommy," he said to her back. "I want to get married."

Assunta turned around and looked at her son. "Okay, Louie," she said. "You going to find a girl?"

"I found one," he said. "And I asked her to marry me, but she said no."

Assunta and Tina both gasped and Stella hid a smile by turning her face into Tommy's blanket. "You proposed to a girl without bringing her here first?" Tina exclaimed as Assunta smacked him on the shoulder with the dripping spoon.

"What's the matter, you go so fast?" Assunta smacked him again, harder. "Are you in trouble?"

"No trouble," Louie said. "She's a good girl—very strict father." The drooping bags under his eyes—he'd had them since he was a little boy—gave him a canine effect that made him look particularly earnest. "I had to say something because I didn't want her to get away. I didn't want her thinking I wasn't serious."

"Sounds like you better tell us about this girl," Stella said. "And we better get our stories straight before Papa gets home."

Two weeks ago, Louie had accompanied Bill Johnson on a house call in West Hartford. It was the family's oldest daughter who let them in and explained the problem with the fuse box. She spoke perfect, fast English and Louie hadn't had any idea she was Italian until he noticed the wooden plaque over the door-frame—the pastel face of Jesus over the words DIO BENEDICA LA NOSTRA CASA. The pretty girl stayed and watched their work sharply. Louie was sweating with panic because he didn't want to jeopardize his job, but he couldn't leave without saying something.

In the end, the only thing he managed to ask her was her name. Pasqualina Lattanzi—a big name for a tiny person, as Louie described her, only *this* high and with a face like a doll's. Everyone, he would learn, called her Queenie instead.

He couldn't ask her on a date in front of Bill, so he memorized the address and as soon as his workday was over he biked back over. She was in the front yard, reading a book while she super-vised a gaggle of boys who were playing a war game around the crab apple tree.

"You have to get out of here," Queenie said to him. "My father will kill you."

"I'm not afraid of him," Louie said.

"Well, I am, and I don't want him to kill me, either." She stood up, put her book down on the chair, and crossed her arms.

"I'm just here to ask you out on a date," Louie said. "If your father wants I can ask his permission first."

"I don't date," she said, but Louie could tell she was checking him out.

Louie asked, "Why not? How old are you?"

"I'm eighteen. But my family's old-fashioned." Her broad American voice sounded anything but old-fashioned to him. "My father doesn't believe in dating. Only courtship, you know, like in Italy, with chaperones, and only when you're planning to get married."

"What if we wanted to get married, though?" Louie said, before he had thought out the words, and then quickly decided he might as well see it through. "Could we go on a date if we were getting married?"

"You don't know anything about me," she said.

"I'll learn," he said. "Do we have to get engaged before we can talk to each other? I can propose right now."

Queenie shook her head. "I'm in junior college. When I'm done and have a secretary job, I'll start thinking about settling down."

By now, one of her brothers had shaken loose from the group of boys. He came over and stood by Queenie's shoulder, which he just about came up to, and crossed his arms just like her. "You'd best be moving along, young man," he said, exactly like a very short version of John Wayne might have said.

"That's what I was telling him," said Queenie.

Louie moved along, but he stopped by the Lattanzi house on his bicycle every day on his way home from work.

"You've got to cut this out," Queenie would tell him. "You can't just keep coming by like this. You're going to get me in big, big trouble."

"I'll quit coming by if you agree to go out with me," Louie would reply. But she hadn't agreed yet.

When Louie told his mother and sisters about his predicament, Stella said to him, "You're as bad as Carmelo. Don't you know some women should just be left alone?"

"She wants to get married," Louie said. "If it weren't for her father she'd say yes and go out with me right now, I know it."

"You all know it, don't you," Stella said, but no one minded her. She looked down at little Tommy. "Are you going to be like that someday?" she asked him. "Just *knowing* you're the best thing ever and that you should always, always get what you want, as long as you're pushy enough?"

"You're one to talk, aren't you, Stella," Louie said.

"Your father will have to call her father and we'll invite them all over for dinner," Assunta said. "That's the proper way to do this."

"Yeah, bring her over here," Stella said. "Papa will make her get engaged to you whether she likes it or not."

Louie got engaged to Queenie Lattanzi in June 1950. They wouldn't get married until she'd graduated and found a job. "It's much harder for married ladies to find jobs," Queenie explained to Stella. "They think you're just going to quit to have a baby. So you have to look while you're still a Miss So-and-So."

Queenie's parents had been in America for a long time. Her old-fashioned father was a well-respected carpenter whose furniture was carried in all the best stores. He had finished his third-grade education in Italy—"The furthest you could go there, you know," Queenie would add defensively—and was a big proponent of schooling, which was why he was paying for Queenie's professional course.

Queenie herself had never been to Italy. She spoke perfectly fine Italian but made it clear that she looked down on people who made no effort to live in an American way. She had an Italian woman's wherewithal and an American girl's self-confidence. Now that she and Louie were engaged, she visited Bedford Street two or three times a week, bossily advising her future in-laws about how they could better their lives. They needed to install electric ceiling fans; this wasn't the village anymore. They needed to get a television for their living room; a person needed to keep up with the news. They had to clip coupons from the paper to save money at the store. They had to paint the walls of their house and hang art; no American lived in empty white rooms. And this—this was a much better recipe for blueberry muffins than the one Tina had been using.

The Fortunas all liked her, even if she was a little know-it-all. She was, Stella found, generally correct. She was correct, for example, about Tony, even if she was willing to say what no one else was.

It was Queenie who spotted something was wrong with baby Tommy, because even though she was young and unmarried she was the only one with context about what American babies were supposed to do.

"He's more than a year old," Queenie said. "He should be walking by now."

"Is that true, Ma?" Stella asked Assunta later.

Assunta looked down at Tommy, who was crawling awkwardly across her kitchen floor. Her mouth was pulled to one side; Stella could tell she felt bad for not knowing the answer. "It's true," she said finally, "you all were walking before one year old, I think. But maybe things are different here. Children aren't outside as much."

Now Stella was worried and made Carmelo drive them to the hospital. The doctor was unhappy with what he saw. Stella couldn't understand all the difficult medical language, but she could see there were terrible possibilities the doctor was not taking off the table. Tommy's poor little body—too little, the doctor said; it was not growing correctly—was subjected to measurements, tapping, stretching, and bending. For three sleepless weeks Stella wondered if God was going to take away another child from her.

The tests came back negative—little Tommy did not have cancer. He had a very rare condition that caused him to grow benign but growth-inhibiting tumors all over his body. He would always be small-boned; he would never make a sports team or hold his own if he got bullied. They had to be careful with this one—keep him close to home and out of trouble as long as possible.

As it turned out, "as long as possible" was "forever." Tommy would never move farther than across the street from his mother's house. He would be thirty-nine when Stella would have her incapacitating Accident. He might have gotten married, pursued his own dreams, but instead he would stay to take care of her.

On May 28, 1951, Stella gave birth to a second living son, Antonio "Nino" Maglieri, named for his maternal grandfather. Despite his namesake, he would turn out to be Stella's favorite, the last boy whose childhood she still had the mind and heart to enjoy before there were just too many babies spilling and spitting and crashing and crying. Louie and Queenie stood up as his godparents, even though they weren't married yet.

Nino would grow up to be a robust and jovial child with lots of friends and an easy manner for talking his way out of trouble. He was his older brother's protector and best friend; no one messed with Tommy in the schoolyard because no one messed with Nino anywhere. Without Tommy's medical woes to protect him from the draft, Nino would be called up in the ninth batch of the 1970 draft lottery. At least as Stella nursed her beautiful chocolate-eyed infant she had no way of imagining that when he would be just nineteen years old his perfect body would be blown apart by a landmine in a South Vietnamese forest.

When they got home from their honeymoon in April 1952, Mr. and Mrs. Louis Fortuna, as they were now, moved into the ground-floor apartment on Bedford Street, into the bedroom Stella and Tina had once shared. Queenie was not circumspect about her displeasure with the arrangement.

"There's just so little privacy here," she said to Stella and Tina. "We're *newlyweds*. It's not right to have people living right on top of us, opening the doors at any time."

"You know we all did it," Tina said. "Just until you save up some money."

"I'm not like you," Queenie said. "I grew up American, and in America we don't put up with what you did in the old country." She didn't say this meanly, but was she ever blunt.

"It's just for a while," Stella said to soothe, before Tina got upset. "Think of it as free rent."

"Hardly free." Queenie snorted. "Your father thinks because it's his house he can come right into my room anytime he wants. *Anytime*." Her meaning was plain, but she spelled it out anyway. "Stella, he comes in whenever he hears us in the middle of, you know."

"Of doing the job?" Tina asked, aghast. Stella was disgusted but not surprised. At least Tina didn't seem to know Tony used to spy on her and Rocco, too. How glad Stella was for the lockable doors and the flight of stairs between her married life and her father.

"And I've caught your mother going through my stuff," Queenie added.

"No," Stella said. "Mamma wouldn't do that." Queenie had had Stella's sympathy as long as she wanted to complain about Tony, but Stella was not going to let this little Kewpie doll spread malice about Assunta.

"No way," Tina chimed in.

"Wouldn't she," said Queenie.

"Maybe to help with your laundry, or something like that," Stella said. "But she would never snoop or take anything. If you think she would, you don't know her at all."

"Well," said Queenie. She sat back in her chair and didn't say anything else about that. Queenie might always be right, but she had also learned that when Stella took a position it was unbreachable.

Whose fault was what happened later, really? Well, it was Tony's fault—only Tony is to blame for what he did. But that doesn't mean other people weren't responsible, or complicit.

It was Assunta, for example, who brought Mickey into the family.

In July 1952, when Louie and Queenie had been back from their honeymoon for three months and, Stella surmised, the first-floor apartment was feeling a little crowded, Assunta made an announcement: it had been twelve years since she had seen her people in Ievoli, and she wanted to go back. She wanted to make a pilgrimage to the Madonna at Dipodi, to celebrate the festival of the Assumption, and to see her mother's grave.

In fact, Assunta had hatched a plan to make her straggler, Joey, grow up and start a family. He would never get a wife the way he was going, because he spent all his salary at the bar and with *puttane*. Assunta had tried crying and nagging, to no avail; now she'd decided maybe things had to happen in the opposite order: if he had the wife at home to support, he would have to settle himself down. She just had to trick him into getting married. Well, there wasn't much she could do here in Hartford, because she didn't understand girls like Queenie or how to impress them, and besides, she needed to get Joey away from his bad habits and from all the people who knew about those habits. In Ievoli, though, she'd be able to control the situation.

The pilgrimage scheme came together quickly. When she made her announcement to the family at Sunday dinner, she added that she would need a chaperone and begged Joey to come with her. It would just be for a couple of months.

"A couple of months? No way, Ma. I'd have to quit my job."

"No, you wouldn't," Assunta said, although of course he would. A good pensioned job that he'd only just nailed down. "Anyway, I already bought the tickets for us."

It was obvious to everyone what the plan was; Assunta was not skilled at subterfuge. Stella was only surprised that her father seemed to shrug the whole thing off.

"Women's business," he said. Tony had despaired of managing his son and maybe he figured Assunta's plot was worth a shot.

Joey and Assunta left on July 27. In the middle of September, Tony received a letter in Joey's badly spelled combination of English and Italian saying they were enjoying their visit, that they were going to stay in Ievoli for Christmas but then they would be bringing home his new wife, Michelina, whom he referred to as Mickey.

You did it, Ma, Stella thought. She was impressed. She wondered where Assunta had procured a willing female and what measures had been taken to force the two into holy wedlock. She hoped this Michelina was strong enough to make something of Stella's layabout brother. At mass Stella said a special prayer to the Virgin that her mother had picked well; after all, Assunta would only be able to pull this wife-assigning trick the once.

Joey and his new bride, Mickey, moved into the boys' old room on the ground floor of the Bedford Street house in January 1953. Mickey was already visibly pregnant, which said to Stella that this was a woman who got down to business.

Mickey, who had just turned eighteen, had grown up in Nicastro, although Assunta enumerated all her Ievoli connections—her mother was a first cousin of Za Violet from Pianopoli;

her older brother had married the Fortuna girls' school friend Marietta. Mickey was tall and had long smooth legs, which everyone knew because she walked around the house in little silk nightgowns. Stella wondered how things could have changed so completely in Calabria that it had produced this wanton creature. Mickey laughed loudly and flirted with any man around her—her brother- or father-in-law or anyone at all—touching their arms when she talked to them, sitting next to them on the couch and resting her head on their shoulders. Stella was darkly amused by how awkward Mickey made Carmelo, Louie, and Rocco, but Queenie was obviously not amused, and Queenie was the woman who had to put up with Mickey the most. Stella was looking forward to the day Mickey got some good manners smacked into her.

"I just can't do this," Queenie told Stella and Tina at least once a week. "I can't go on living with this woman. It was bad enough before, but now . . ."

Tina leaned in and lowered her voice. "What are you going to do?"

Queenie grunted. Stella, who was crocheting, darted a glance up to see Queenie's face. It was a sneer of fed-uppedness.

"Are you going to move out?" Tina asked.

"How could I?" Queenie said. "Your mother would never allow it."

Stella didn't have anything to say to console her. She was just glad she and Carmelo had a lock and door between them and all that.

In early May 1953, Mickey threw herself a baby shower, at the behest of her new friends from church, who came over and gobbled up pastries and brought all kinds of adorable miniature presents. It was chilly and rainy; Mickey directed them to Queenie and Louie's room to leave their wet coats on Queenie's bed.

This was the last straw, although Queenie must have been planning for a long time.

On the last Sunday in May, the Fortuna clan headed out together for eleven o'clock mass. Queenie wasn't feeling well, so she and Louie stayed home. Walking to church, Assunta and Tina speculated about whether there might be a baby on the way.

After mass, they stopped by Za Filomena and Zu Aldo's house for lunch. It was a beautiful day and the boys played in the front yard with Carolina's two-year-old daughter. Assunta headed back to Bedford Street first to start preparing her Sunday dinner; the rest of them followed half an hour later when Nino started to get fussy.

Stella could hear the shrieking before she set foot on the porch. At first she wondered if it was some trapped animal or the squealing of a malfunctioning pipe. But no. *Mamma.*

Stella thrust Nino into Carmelo's arms and waddle-rushed up the porch stairs—she was only four months along but carrying large this time. The unlocked door swung open on a dark and fetid hallway—the stench hit her immediately. When Stella pressed the light switch it took her a long moment to figure out what she was looking at.

There was her mother, hyperventilating on the floor of the front hallway, where she was kneeling beside a pool of vomit. Bloody bald patches of scalp showed through her wild hair; later Stella would find the clumps she tore out by the sink in the kitchen. There was something dark smudging one side of her face, which Stella would learn all too soon was diarrhea. There was fecal matter smeared on the walls, about waist-high, as if Assunta had crawled up and back down the hall on her hands and knees, trailing her soiled hands on the wallpaper. Above the shit were the scuffmarks where Queenie and Louie, in their haste, had betrayed their operation.

She did it, Stella thought, almost triumphantly, but that thought passed quickly.

Tina dropped to the floor by Assunta, saying, "Ma, what happened?"

As the sobbing started again Stella stepped over the vomit and made her way through the house, taking inventory. Queenie must have leapt out of bed the minute they all left for mass—playing sick, the little crook—and started loading up a moving truck; God knows where she'd found a moving company that was open on Sunday. In the four short hours the Fortunas had been away, Louie and Queenie had taken everything—every stick of furniture in the living room and dining room as well as out of the bedroom. They took the pots out of the kitchen cupboards and the soap out of the soap dish in the bathroom. The only sign they left of themselves was the faint sun stain around the spot on the living room wall where Louie's framed diploma had hung.

"*Malandrina,*" Antonio kept saying. No better than a high-way robber, that Queenie.

Maybe she wouldn't have stolen all your furniture, Stella thought, if you hadn't stolen a few free peep shows, you dirty old jerk.

But whatever sympathy Stella felt for Queenie was poisoned by Assunta's reaction to this calamity—over the top, certainly, but Stella didn't think it was a performance. Assunta actually thought she might not live through this: her favorite son taken away from her, her house ripped apart, her family in shambles.

There was no Sunday sauce that night; Queenie hadn't left a pot to cook in. "She took my *pasta strainer,*" Assunta kept saying, as if this were the most inhuman injustice of the entire day. "My *pasta strainer.* She could have at least left me something to strain my pasta."

Carmelo tried to herd them all out of the hollow apartment for dinner upstairs. But Assunta couldn't be left alone. Stella had bullied her into the shower, scrubbed the shit off her and gently rinsed her bloody scalp, then put her to bed. Assunta, drunk on her own grief, carried on with her hysterical weeping. Tina cried quietly in solidarity.

"Forget it, Carm," Stella told him. "It's hopeless."

In the end, Carmelo brought down a pot of pasta he cooked upstairs in the Maglieri kitchen. The ones who were fit to eat ate it sitting on the bare carpet in the living room. The boys ran in circles in all the empty space, and Nino knocked over the cheese.

Four days later, Queenie's speciously proper change of address card arrived in the mail, lettered in her secretarial hand. On Saturday, Stella left the children with Tina and made Carmelo drive her to the new house, which was on the West Hartford town line. The house was small, just one story, with redbrick siding and a square hedge. Louie and Queenie must have been saving assiduously for this, or maybe Queenie's parents had given her money.

Stella told Carmelo to wait in the car. "This won't take long," she said. She didn't want his sociability and compassion bogging her down.

Louie wasn't home, but it was just as well, because Stella's bone to pick was with her sister-in-law.

"Shame on you," she said when the pretty young woman answered the door. Queenie was wearing a flower-printed pink housedress that cinched at what Stella thought was an unrealistically narrow waist. "Shame on you for what you did to my mother. She's been nothing but kind to you."

"I don't have a problem with your mother. I think she's a nice woman, even if she is a little unbalanced." Queenie spoke quickly and forcefully, so Stella caught up with her meaning after it was too late to react effectively. "But your father's a pervert, your brother Joey is a loser, and his wife is a lazy tramp with no education. I'm not bringing children into that house."

Stella was bristling with anger, but there was nothing Queenie had said that, strictly speaking, Stella disagreed with.

"You didn't need to leave like that," she said finally. "It was cruel."

"I'm sorry you feel that way." Queenie's hard little face softened. "Your mother never would have let us go, Stella. And your brother Louie would never have the courage to fight with her."

Tony went down to see Mr. Greenburg, the Jew on Franklin Avenue, and bought furniture for the whole house again. Mr. Greenburg's prices were good and he gave credit. Pay what you want now, he always said, and then just give me a little more each week as you can.

"You could have made Queenie give you back all your furniture, Pa," Stella said.

Tony waved it off. "They're just kids. They don't have any money to spend. Anyway, your mother can enjoy picking out new furniture."

Stella wondered if he felt guilty but didn't think her father had that capacity. This was his version of a papal indulgence for his sins, only the pope was Assunta.

Mickey's baby was born in July, a little girl they named Betty. Tina and Rocco stood up as her godparents at the baptism. Stella was relieved Mickey hadn't asked her and Carmelo.

On the second Sunday of October, Mickey wasn't feeling well and stayed home from church. Joey stayed home with her to take care of the baby. When the rest of them got home, Stella was more disgusted than she was surprised to find the first-floor apartment had been emptied of all the furniture.

"Again?" Tina whispered to Stella.

"What a pig," Stella said, not bothering to whisper back. She was so pregnant she didn't have energy to do anything but lean against the picture-stripped wall. "Raised in a barn, like I always thought."

"I don't think she needed to make it all a surprise again," Tina said.

"Of course she didn't. She just wants everyone to talk about her like she's something special." From where she stood, Stella surveyed the damage, the empty room, the chip that had been taken out of the doorframe by undisciplined movers. "You know what, though? Serves them right. Now they'll have to pay their own goddamn rent and cook their own food and clean up after their own baby."

"Oh, the poor baby," Tina said, and before the waterworks could start, Stella chided her, "*Relax.* You'll see her plenty, just watch." How would they get by, though, she wondered? Joey had been unable to get back his job at the electric company and had spent the last six months sweeping clippings off the floor at a barbershop.

This time Assunta was angry, to Stella's great relief. "There was no need to fool us like that," she said.

"She's just a witch, Ma," Stella said. "A drama queen. She wants attention."

Assunta banged the cupboards one by one, ascertaining that the Joseph Fortunas had, indeed, taken her every last pot and even her new pasta strainer. "We would have given them whatever they wanted. We know how much Joey makes; we would have bought him his own house. He didn't need to steal ours."

"We wouldn't have bought him nothing," Tony interrupted. "This is the end for him. It's time for him to grow the hell up and be a man."

Now Assunta looked upset. "But Tonnon—"

"No," he said. "It's like the Americans say. They stole their bed, now they can lie in it."

In November 1953, Stella gave birth to a third living baby, a girl this time, whom they named Bernadette, after the saint in that movie Stella had seen during the war, the girl from France who

353

saw the Virgin on the hill. Carmelo's brother, Gio, and his wife stood up as the baby's godparents.

Bernie would be Stella's only daughter and would grow up unintimidated by the prospect of telling whole roomfuls of men what to do. She would turn up her nose at the various pitfalls of adolescence as she watched her brothers make every mistake in the book; she would eventually become the first person in her family to graduate from college, for which her proud father would insist on paying. Her no-nonsense personality perfectly suited her career as an accountant at a large Hartford insurance conglomerate, where she would eventually be made a VP. After years of insisting she never wanted to settle down—just like her mother—she would eventually change her mind, for which I am grateful, since she is my mother. She would marry an ethnically German computer programmer she met in a business development course at UConn—that's my dad, the blue-eyed, blond reason I barely pass for Italian.

My mom is a lone renegade branch on the Maglieri family tree, the only offshoot to move out of the Italian ghetto and into the suburbs, to read science fiction novels, and to refuse to baptize her children. But you would only have heard this story from a quasi-outsider, you know? A real Maglieri would never have written this down.

In May 1954, after months of planning and, most importantly, with Assunta's hard-won blessing, Stella and Carmelo Maglieri moved from Bedford Street to a house Carmelo had bought one town over, in Dorchester. Front Street was a crumbling wreck, and the Maglieris weren't the only ones heading out.

The new house was about twenty years old and cube shaped, like a bright blue birthday present waiting to be unwrapped. There were two bedrooms, two bathrooms, and a closed-off back porch that overlooked the marshy grass Carmelo would turn into his arbor and vegetable garden. There was a carpeted staircase Stella's boys would charge up and then go sliding down on their bellies for the next twenty years. Alder Street, the road was called, after a kind of tree, Stella would learn—*ontano* in Italian, a tree so common in Ievoli but which Stella had never once seen in America.

Eventually the second bedroom would be built out with two sets of bunk beds, a third set of bunk beds would be installed in the landing, and a fourth where the dining room table had been ousted—it wasn't like they ever used it; the boys usually ate standing up in the kitchen, and Sunday dinners were always at Tina's. Stella would convert her walk-in closet into a bedroom for Bernie, so that her daughter wouldn't have to share space with the hooligans. Still, the Maglieris would be perpetually one bed short, but there was always a shirtless teenage boy draped over the couch, stinky sock feet hanging off the end, or dozing on his belly on the carpet in front of the TV. Sometimes there were multiple empty beds, in fact, because some combination of boys hadn't come home all night, but with that many who can really keep track of them all. Certainly not Stella.

The house on Alder Street had a neighbor on its left, but to its right was an empty plot of land, which Rocco and Tina bought. Rocco didn't like the marshy quality of the ground and was paying good money to have it filled in with truckloads of soil. Then they would build a house exactly to their specifications.

They would always be right next door so Tina could help with the babies.

With the mortgage and the babies he had to buy new shoes for all the time, Carmelo got a second job, working barback at Charlie's Restaurant & Bar. He would work at the electric company from six until three, come home, fix some pasta, change out of his uniform, and head to Charlie's to open the bar at five. Eventually Carmelo would also take on a third job, working weekends for a landscaping company, mowing lawns and trimming hedges. But ends would always meet, if sometimes just barely.

In October 1954, Stella gave birth to her fourth living baby, her third son. Stella and Carmelo debated who to ask to be godparents. They weren't on speaking terms with Joey and Mickey yet. Instead, they asked Franceschina Perri, who was now Mrs. Carapellucci, and her husband, Frank.

Carmelo had picked out the name Gaetano, after a friend of his from the railroad who had died in the war. Gaetano— "Guy"—would grow up to be the wealthiest of Stella and Carmelo's sons, eventually running four successful restaurants, a bowling alley, and a vending machine supply company. Most of his brothers would work for him in some capacity, except for Tommy, who would always work at the electric company with his dad. Although he would never attend college himself, Guy would meet his future wife, Annabelle, a semi-professional tennis player and the daughter of a congressman, at a Wesleyan sorority party that his motorcycle-riding buddies decided to crash. Everyone liked her an awful lot, although she would break Carmelo's heart by turning his son into a Republican.

In December 1954, just before the first snowfall, Rocco and Tina moved into their new house. They had a spare bedroom for guests—an American luxury. Usually Tina would keep the door to this room locked so the boys wouldn't go tramping through and eating the cookie arrangements she had made for some *paesan*'s upcoming baby shower.

From the street, the two-story Maglieri house and the Caramanico ranch looked like they were the same height, since Rocco had had his house built on an artificial hill. For the next sixty years, whenever it rained hard, the Maglieri basement would flood, leaving a fetid stink it would take Carmelo days of airing to get rid of. The boys loved the flooding, because they would splash down the cement stairs and play water-war games in the seepage, although one time Johnny stepped on a screwdriver that was hidden under the dark water and ended up getting stitches in his foot.

Sometimes Stella would sit on her screened-in back porch and stare up the hill at her sister's clean white house and militaristically neat garden and wish she had a clean house and a dry basement and that all these muddy children were someone else's. But she didn't say anything to anyone about that, of course, because she was sure Tina sometimes sat next to Rocco in that lawn chair and looked down the hill at the puddle-filled grass of the Maglieri backyard and thought, I would trade this house and everything else I have for just one of those children.

Now the house on Bedford Street was empty, all of the grown Fortuna children moved out. Stella thought Tony would rent it again, but instead he put it on the market.

Stella remembered how the Fortunas had fought to buy that house, counting their nickels into that tin can. It had only lasted them one decade.

"Aren't you sad to be leaving, Ma?" she asked Assunta.

"It's too far from the grandchildren," her mother said. She meant Stella's children, not Joey's; Tony had not spoken to Joey since their exodus and Mickey was retaliating by not letting Assunta come visit the baby.

Looking at it another way, Stella realized, she and Carmelo had become the core of the family—everyone else had gathered around them, restructured their lives around the Maglieris'. Was that what they all owed her? They had put her where they wanted her, and now they made her their queen.

Louie and Queenie came over for the occasional Sunday dinner, but still had not started a family of their own. When Assunta had taken Queenie aside to ask her if there was a problem, Queenie had looked her in the eye and said, "Not that I know of, God willing. We're just waiting until we have more money."

"What does she mean, waiting?" Assunta had whispered to her daughters as they were washing dishes after Louie and Queenie had left.

Stella laughed, but her heart felt cold. She bounced baby Guy on her knee to make the chill pass. The thought flashed through her mind—Queenie had pulled off a trick Stella hadn't been able to. But the thought flickered away as if it had been someone else's memory of a distant past life.

"You know what I heard," Tina said. Her face was already red and Stella knew something wonderful or disgusting was coming. "If you don't want to get pregnant, you can have your husband put it . . ." She hesitated, excited for her revelation but scared to pick out the words. "In the *cul'*. He can do whatever he wants there and it won't make a baby. Or he can put it here," she said, making an evocatively thrusting gesture in the direction of her armpit. "Or he can put it in your mouth."

"Tina! Shh!" Rocco, Carmelo, and Tony were drinking *amaro* in the living room, not necessarily out of earshot, with the three older children corralled on the floor with their trucks and dolls. If there was ever something Stella didn't want Carmelo hearing, it was what Tina had just said. "Who did you hear that from, anyway?"

"The ladies at Silex," Tina said, secure in the authority of her American and Polish assembly-line friends.

"These are the same ladies who say you can tell the size of a man's thing by how long his nose is," Stella said, but Tina didn't hear her sarcasm.

"Yes, it's true." Tina sounded wistful.

"How would any of them ever know that, Tina? Unless they have seen more than one and can compare," Stella teased. "I think your Silex friends must be loose."

"No." Tina's face defensively flared even pinker. "They heard from *their* friends."

Assunta was still stuck on the predilections of her youngest son. "Tina, you mean Queenie lets Louie put it . . . put it in her *cul*'?" She eyed her daughter, concentrating on this new idea. "Or her mouth?"

"Ma!" Stella barked. The chatter from the living room had grown frighteningly quiet. "Ask her yourself the next time you see her."

Lying sleeplessly in bed that night, her breasts aching because Guy was already weaning himself, Stella turned the thought over and over. Would she let Carmelo put his thing in her mouth, if it meant she didn't have to get pregnant again? The thought made her want to throw up, and she couldn't make herself come to the answer *yes*.

Stella called garden men to plant a hedge at the front of her property to stop the children from running into the road when they were playing in the backyard. She enjoyed watching the men in their dirty close-fitting jeans dig holes and bend over pots. The whole job only took a few hours and boom, there was a lush green curtain separating Stella's private business from the rest of the world.

Carmelo was furious, claiming he could have installed the hedge himself and saved them a lot of money. Stella pooh-poohed his ire. "When would you have had time?"

Several months later, when she was feeling particularly fed up with Carmelo, Stella called painters and had them paint the house bright pink while he was at work. He would learn better than to make her mad.

Later, much later, after she went crazy, Stella would chop down the hedge herself with a pair of garden clippers. Her grown sons would marvel at the strength the destruction must have required.

Their first summer on Alder Street, 1955, Carmelo turned over the spongy dirt in the backyard, pumped out the water, and filled in the soil for a garden. He got up to weed in the earliest light of dawn before work. He planted zucchini, tomatoes, and peas. He planted two gooseberry bushes, unique Balkan varietals that had been smuggled past customs by an Albanian buddy from the electric company. He planted two grape trellises, one along the garden and one overhanging a picnic table.

Stella looked at the perfect leafy stakes and considered how Carmelo's garden looked like it could have been transplanted from a mountain terrace in Ievoli. They had come from distant villages, she and Carmelo, but in the United States their backgrounds looked almost the same.

The air here was too moist, and the winter too cold, but on a hot day in June if Stella lay on her back in the tick-infested grass by the garden and looked up through the bean leaves, translucent lime-green in the sun, she could imagine she was home again.

For the next fifty years, on afternoons as they worked in their respective gardens, Carmelo would call up the hill to Tina, or she would call down to him—do you have any extra rags so I can tie my beans? Did Freddy mow your lawn like I told him? Is your wife's vacuum cleaner still broken? Do you want to come have a glass of wine?

The gooseberries and the grape trellises would get chopped down, too, and the beautiful fifteen-foot fig tree, after Stella went crazy.

In August 1955, little knob-kneed Tommy started kindergarten. School was awful for Tommy. He was tiny and he couldn't run well or throw a ball—he had never learned that from his father, who didn't know anything about balls himself. The worst thing about the whole school situation was that he couldn't understand a word anyone said to him, because he'd never learned any English in the bosom of his Italian home. Tommy was a nonconversant runt, and that is a painful way to be forced to join society.

Tommy, as the oldest child of two immigrant parents, had it the worst. When Nino started kindergarten the next year, things were tough but not as tough, because at least he had Tommy. And then by the time Bernie went to school, two years after that, she was so used to hearing her older brothers speak English at home, and so used to the English-speaking television in their front room, that it was almost no trauma at all.

In October 1955, Stella gave birth to Federico. Carmela and her husband, Paolo, took the train down from Montreal to stand up as godparents.

Freddy would be the most handsome of Stella's sons, with his glossy black hair (before it all fell out) and his grandmother's down-turned chocolate eyes, the unusual Mascaro eye shape that had made Assunta the beauty of Ievoli, and which here in America got Freddy nicknamed "the Jap." He would inherit his father's musicality and eventually become the frontman in a local band.

Freddy, the fifth baby, would also be the breaking point for poor Stella's mind, which could no longer conceive of her children as individuals versus as a mass. Maybe four would have been all right, but five was just too many, and by the time the oldest were teenagers their name had become *TommyNinoGuyFreddy!* Bernie, obviously, was an exception, what with her being a princess instead of a hooligan.

Next up was Nicola, "Nicky," in August 1956, less than a year after Freddy. No one was really ready for Nicky. Stella hadn't even believed she could be pregnant until she was almost six months along; she'd become so inured to morning sickness over the last eight years that she hadn't managed to distinguish it from a hangover. Stella and Carmelo didn't know who to ask to be godparents on such short notice, so Tina and Rocco stood up again. The Maglieris had to wait to have the baptism until after the Caramanicos got back from their ten-year anniversary trip to Italy, which they had been planning for a lot longer than Stella had been planning on having Nicky. But at this point Stella and Carmelo were willing to cut a few corners, and they were sure God would understand.

Luckily Assunta now lived across the street. She was still working in the tobacco fields but could stay home on the worst days and help Stella with the two new infants. As much as Stella was annoyed by her father's proximity, she was grateful for her mother's.

Nicky, one of only two sons who would inherit Carmelo's famous blue eyes, would grow up to be the gentlest of the Maglieri boys. He loved animals, and Stella was always catching him slinking up the stairs with his jacket zipped around a suspiciously squirming bulge. Stella would have to go chasing him and banging on his door—"Nicky! What do you have in there!"— lest she find another squirrel he'd tried to save from a cat bleeding in his bedding, or another green garden snake coiled up in the bathtub. Nicky would be too gentle for the world, though, and would retreat into a cave life, spending his adulthood watching television in the bedroom he'd once shared with his brothers, stretching various disability checks to cover a medicating supply of weed and grape soda.

When you come from a large Italian family, not only do you simply have more relatives numerically than many American families do, but you also keep in closer touch with them. This means a socially obedient Italian American will have more special occasions than their non-Italian friends can conceive of. Funerals and baptisms, anniversary and graduation parties, babies' birthdays, but worst of all weddings, weddings, weddings, and the showers and fittings and shoe-dyeings that precede them.

Carmelo was a socially obedient Italian, and for better or for worse, Stella was married to him. This was why she spent what felt like every Saturday at a wedding. Carmelo made her go shopping for nice dresses, thinking that would make her feel better, but she hated being trussed up in sequins or silk when her breasts were leaking or her stomach swollen tight against the fabric. The music and small talk made her tired, as did picking out gifts from registries and smiling for people whose names she couldn't recall. She remembered how she used to love the September *fhesta* in Ievoli, the Italian Society dances during the war, but it was a different person who had been doing the dancing then than the one who was doing the remembering now.

Italians, in case you did not know, invite children to all occasions. This meant every week or so the hooligans had to be wrestled into their little suit pants, which were just the right material for sliding across newly waxed floors. The boys were the life of their own party, even if that meant dismantling the bride and groom's; no one knew whether to laugh at them because they were adorable in their tiny matching suits or to actually call the police. Nino, who had the practical mind of an engineer, was famous for coordinating drag races with empty serving carts stolen from venue kitchens. They never smashed a wedding cake, but they did once get a plate of marinara dumped on a bride's train.

It was around this time, 1958 or 1959, that Stella gave up and just let them do whatever they wanted. "Those are wild kids, Stella," people would say to her, in their reprimanding but unhelpful Italian style.

"What am I supposed to do?" she'd say back. "There's too many of them. I'm outnumbered." Let anyone who wanted to look down on her take the matter up with her Catholic husband. God had given her all these children; there must be a reason He had not given her the ability or desire to keep up with them.

Sometimes Stella couldn't bear the idea of another wedding. At first she would play sick, but then, increasingly, she would just not get ready and Carmelo would know he was on his own. He was no better at controlling the hooligans than Stella was, but Stella knew no chiding women came up to him to complain about his sons' behavior, which was only one of the reasons she felt no guilt. On these evenings, blessedly free, with only the littlest babies on her watch, she would bring a flask of wine up from the cellar and drink it alone on the porch, watching the sun drop behind the oaks in the marsh.

In January 1958 came Giovanni, named for his paternal uncle and godfather. On the heels of his too-soft brother Nicky, Johnny would grow up to be rambunctious enough for two. He would be the son who brought the most chaos into the Maglieri house, starting with the time he got kicked out of fourth grade for carrying a knife, but as an infant he was one of the easiest, from Stella's perspective. No goddamn colic.

Then, in fall of 1958, there was a miscarriage. Stella hadn't been very far along, less than four months, and this time she felt no grief, just a sense of hollow distaste as she flushed the globs of pink tissue down the toilet. Honestly, she didn't feel much of anything anymore; when she did, she drank until the feeling was gone.

Assunta and Tina came over to sit with Stella after work. The sisters would crochet while Assunta looked through Tina's anniversary trip photo album, which lived at Stella's house just for this purpose. Rocco had taken photos of Tina surrounded by pigeons in Piazza San Marco in Venice; Tina on the Spanish Steps in Rome, like Audrey Hepburn in the movie where she is a runaway princess; Tina in front of St. Peter's cathedral in the Vatican, so close to His Holiness the Pope. It was nice to think the beautiful things in the photos were their cultural legacy as Italians, even if Hartford had more in common with Ievoli than did the Venetian lagoon. Assunta turned the pages with so much wonder, it was hard to believe she had been doing the same thing every day for the last two years.

The evening quorum of Fortuna women lasted until Rocco or Tony came home from work and wanted dinner. Carmelo, of course, would not be home from his shift at the bar until eleven at the earliest. So Stella had the evenings to herself—herself and her seven children—and to fill this unsupervised time she usually brought a bottle of Carmelo's wine up from the basement.

When Domenico was born in February 1960, he was everyone's favorite, maybe because for a while people thought he would be the last. As an adult he would be everyone's least favorite Maglieri boy, because he would destroy his good marriage with alcoholism and waste the rest of his short life as a drug addict. But he sure was an adorable baby, with a round face and a full head of fluffy black hair. They called him Mingo, or just Ming, after Carmelo's uncle.

Joey and Mickey stood up as his godparents. Carmelo thought asking them would heal the family rift. Life hadn't been easy on the Joseph Fortunas. They were living in the same apartment they had run away to in 1953. Mickey still dressed like a tramp, but motherhood had mellowed her out; Stella could tolerate her through a Sunday dinner.

Joey and Mickey had two little girls, and Mickey was cooking up a third. Stella wasn't sure whether Mickey's daughters were normal, since Stella lived in a world of small boys, but the Fortuna girls seemed savage to her, wild eyed and undergroomed. No wonder, Stella thought, since their mother was just a large child herself. The girls would dismantle Bernie's toys while

Bernie looked on with condescension. Stella had to explain to her daughter that her grubby cousins didn't have toys at home. She had to teach Bernie to hide the good dolls in her pillowcase so the poor little Fortuna girls wouldn't ruin or steal them.

In July 1961, Stella gave birth to her ninth living baby, Enrico "Richie" Maglieri. He was eight pounds and popped right out after only forty-five minutes of labor, God bless him. Queenie and Louie would stand up as his godparents.

Richie would grow up to be a perpetual bachelor. He would never find a way to reconcile his sexual orientation with his macho Catholic family's values, and so never told anyone—never had any kind of partner at all. Maybe I should look at the bright side here; maybe his reticence saved his life, vis-à-vis the AIDS crisis that took two dear friends from his community theater group. Meanwhile, his brothers act like Richie just never got his act together to woo a lady. Even now they'll say, "Poor Richie, he never found the right girl. Who knows, maybe he still will." If anyone suggests anything about the closet the family will jump down your throat defending him. But that's just it, isn't it? If gayness is a slander to be defended against, there's not a lot of room for a man like Richie, who wouldn't wish to cause anyone any hurt and who doesn't admire boat-rockers, to say anything at all.

Assunta came over one Saturday morning in April 1963 to find a box of dried pasta spilled across the kitchen linoleum. Baby Richie, who had learned to stand, was holding himself up by the garbage can, his fingers gripping the slimy liner bag, and Mingo was prising open a second box of pasta, which Assunta took away from him, leaving him mopey. Where the other boys were was anyone's guess.

Stella was on her knees in front of the downstairs toilet. Her hair bun was sleep-styled to reveal just how much white had come in.

"I'm forty-three years old, Ma," Stella said. She felt like a cabbage you find in the bottom of your vegetable crisper two months after you forgot it there. "How can I still be getting pregnant?"

Assunta rubbed her daughter's back and helped her stand so she could flush away her nausea. "Women in my family are strong," Assunta told Stella, pinching her hip. She added in English she had learned from the television, "Built to last."

On January 4, 1964, Stella gave birth to a final baby boy, whom they named Arturo. Artie was the second son to inherit Carmelo's blue eyes. He was such a liar you couldn't believe a word he ever said, but a lovable scamp nonetheless. When he was only twelve, he would save up his lawn-mowing money to buy a beat-up shell of a Mustang for two hundred dollars, then restore the whole thing all by himself—a crooked little genius with an engine, that one. He would marry his high school sweetheart, Nancy, who was mixed Sicilian and Cherokee. They would have four daughters, half of whom grew up to be scrupulously honest and the other half of whom took after their father.

Artie was an enormous baby, almost eleven pounds, Stella's biggest. He came out naturally after two exhausting hours of pushing. It was not a pleasant experience. It was a week before Stella's forty-fourth birthday and she had had just about enough of this goddamned nonsense.

When her husband came in to see her in the hospital room after the delivery, Stella said to him, "I'm done, Carmelo. You can sleep with whoever you want, but it's not going to be me anymore."

DEATH 7
Choking (Change of Life)

On the morning of Friday, July 24, 1970, the day she almost died for the seventh time, Stella Maglieri woke up in a wet pile of sheets, drenched in her own sweat, her head pounding with a medium-grade hangover. The day would be hot, as hot as the day before had been, and to make the sweating worse Stella was going through her change of life.

The clock on her dresser read eight ten. The bed next to her was empty. Since Artie was born Carmelo had slept in the armchair downstairs in front of the television. He would have left for work three hours earlier in any case.

Stella put her feet on the floor, feeling blood pooling in the soles. Lately her feet were tender in the morning. She didn't wonder too much what the soreness meant. Her body was a ruined mess, covered in scars: the burns on one arm, the surgery seam on the other; the crescent in her now-silver hairline; the sutures across her abdomen from the pig trampling; suckle-heavy breasts and torso thickened by eleven term pregnancies; stretch marks on her loose-skinned upper arms she didn't even understand (why would *that* skin have stretched?); bunions so extreme her big toe turned toward the other four like it was addressing a panel of judges. Her ankles were as thick as her calves, like the tree-trunk ankles of the old mountain-climbing village ladies she and Tina had smirked about in their youth. Stella had used herself up, and now it was her time of life to sweat out her passage into cronedom. Sweat and sweat.

Stella did not look at the old-looking woman in the mirror as she tied a handkerchief over her hair. She tightened the knot in the back so the cloth squeezed at her tannin-throbbing temples. Somehow, this gave her some relief from the hangover—a trick she had learned in the last two years. She pulled on a pair of ankle-high nylons and stuck her feet into the powder-blue slippers she would wear until she had to leave for her night shift.

The door to the boys' bedroom was still closed. The teenagers would sleep all day unless someone woke them up, but someone wouldn't be Stella. She liked to enjoy this peaceful morning time before all the activity kicked up, even if enjoying mornings meant sitting through instead of sleeping off her wine headaches. She shuffled down the blue pile carpeting of the stairs—carefully; the stairs were narrow and the carpeting too thick for perfect safety—and fixed herself breakfast in the kitchen: two pieces of chewy bread and a cup of wine. She didn't toast the bread, just pulled out the soft interior with her fingers, then sucked on the crust, grinding it against the empty sockets in her gums, using the bread to scratch an ancient itch.

Meanwhile, upstairs in the house's only full bathroom, Stella's daughter, Bernie, was buttoning up the striped shirt of her work uniform. Bernie had just finished her junior year in high school and had a part-time job as a cashier at Gardener's Market. She was supposed to be at work at eight thirty and had only just woken up, but since she didn't wear makeup or blow-dry her hair or anything like that, she didn't need much time in the mornings.

Her last chore before she ran out the door was to leave food in Penny's dog dish. None of her brothers would remember, except Nicky, but he was thirteen and could easily sleep until 4 p.m. and then poor Penny would starve all day. Bernie ran down the stairs and through the living room, paused to give her mother, who was sitting at the kitchen table, a kiss on the forehead, and snatched two slices of bread from the plastic bag. Mouth full, Bernie continued out onto the covered porch, where they kept the dog food and Penny's bowl. The bowl was full.

Chewing the bread, Bernie considered what she was seeing. Why hadn't Penny eaten her food? Normally she was clamoring for her breakfast, yipping and snuggling Bernie's knees as she tried to scoop. But Penny wasn't even here. Was this her food from yesterday? But wait—Bernie had slept over at her friend Patty's the night before, so she hadn't fed the dog since Wednesday morning. In fact, she hadn't seen the dog in days. But someone must have. There were eleven full-time people living in this house, and plenty of passers-through.

"Mommy, have you seen Penny?" Bernadette asked the unlit kitchen before she realized her mother wasn't there anymore. Bernie went stomping up the stairs—not with any particular emotion; her work shoes were just bottom-heavy—and ventured into the den of the snoring and farting. The den, where the older teenagers slept, was definitely the worst place in the house. She knocked hard first—she did not want to have to see anything unpleasant her brothers might be doing in their teenage sleep—and then opened the door to let the room air a little bit before she stuck her head in.

"Ey!" she said. There was no sign of life, but she knew the drill. "*Ey.* Quit faking. Have any of you seen Penny?" No movement from either set of bunk beds. Bernie smacked a bare calf protruding from the top bunk closest to the door, just about at eye level. It belonged to Freddy, who kicked out blindly but meaning it. Bernie stepped back in time. "Freddy. Have you seen Penny?"

"No. Go away."

"Guy?" She reached into the lower bunk and shook her brother's shoulder. Guy didn't respond at all. He would pretend he was asleep even if the house was on fire, just to make his point.

She tried Nicky. "Nicky," she said as he rolled over sleepily. "Nicky, Penny's missing. Have you seen her?"

"Penny's missing?" he said, his voice sharp and upset, but his eyes were still closed. He might or might not remember any of this conversation after Bernie left.

She was going to be late for work, but the more she thought about Penny, the worse she felt. Unless Bernie saw the dog with her own two eyes, there was no way she would be able to believe Penny was anywhere but in a ditch on the side of Farms Boulevard; the traffic that whizzed right by had claimed countless Maglieri family pets over the years. But Penny was special. Everyone loved that dog; she was the sweetest thing, with her coppery little face.

From her mother's bedroom, Bernie dialed next door. Auntie Tina and Uncle Rocco were at work, of course, so no one answered. She tried the number for her grandfather's house across the street, but no one answered there, either. They had probably unplugged their phone. She would have to go in person.

Swallowing the last of her dry bread breakfast, Bernie crossed Alder Street and knocked on the door of number 4, then let herself in. Sure enough, everyone was home, although the house was almost silent. Auntie Mickey and her daughter Betty, seventeen, were sitting on the couch, watching the television at a very low volume. The other girls must have been asleep, or maybe out in the backyard.

"Hi, Auntie Mickey," Bernadette said. "Hi, Betty. Have you guys seen Penny?"

"Hi, honey," Mickey said in her nasal, accented English. "We saw your penny?"

"Penny, our dog." On the television, Captain Kangaroo was singing. "Did our dog come over here?"

"No, honey, I haven't seen no dog," Mickey said. "Not over here."

Betty regarded Bernie with no expression. They should have been friends—they were almost the same age—but Bernie had never seen her cousin exhibit any personality. For example, here she was with nothing to do but watch television on a Friday morning. Betty was supposedly training to be a hairdresser, but she had some nervous problems and no one seriously thought she would ever hold down a job.

Well, Bernie might as well be thorough and ask her grandfather. Grandpa Tony was never nice about the family pets, seemed to find it amusing that the children became so attached to animals—to teach them a lesson last summer, he had killed Stella's white pet goat and roasted her in the backyard, cackling as he ate her. That was such a shocking story; Bernie had gotten a lot of mileage out of it with her girlfriends. But the fact that Grandpa Tony didn't love family pets didn't mean he hadn't seen Penny. In fact, it might mean he knew exactly where Penny was. Bernie felt a tickle of suspicion. "Where's Grandpa Tony?"

"In his room, honey." Mickey's eyes were fixed on Captain Kangaroo.

Nursing her bad feeling, Bernie walked down the yellow-papered hall and to the last room on the left. Doing her best not to picture her grandfather in any of his states of dishabille, she knocked on the door and called through it, "Ey. Have you seen Penny?"

There was a long moment of silence before Tony's voice came through the door: "Forget the little beech. She shoo' run into the road. We don' need no more puppies around here."

Typical. *Mean old man.* But Bernie was going to be late for work. She would have to worry about the dog later. She let herself out the back door so she wouldn't have to say good-bye to her aunt or cousin.

Later, standing behind her register and waiting for the occasional customer to come through with their produce, Bernie would turn over what her grandfather had said to her, and she'd realize he hadn't told her he hadn't seen the dog.

The reason Mickey and Joey were living in 4 Alder was because their apartment in Hartford had burned down in the summer of 1967. Not only had they lost all of their worldly possessions, insurance was refusing to honor the claim, because Joey had purchased the coverage too recently, or something like that.

The truth was, the insurance company had told Joey they would commission an investigation if he requested one, but that if they did so he needed to be prepared for whatever their inspector might find. In other words, if the inspector found certain kinds of evidence, Joey should be prepared to go to jail for arson and insurance fraud.

"What are you afraid of, Joe?" Stella had asked her brother. "If you didn't burn down your own house then there's no evidence they could hold against you."

Joey waved her off. "They're all a bunch of crooks. They'll fix it all up so they don't have to pay, even if that means I go to jail for no reason."

"Crooks," Stella repeated, disgusted. Her brother pretended not to catch her sarcasm.

Meanwhile, the Joseph Fortunas were homeless. The late 1960s, when the John Lennon was the most popular hairstyle, weren't a heyday for barbershops, and Joey barely brought home enough money to feed his kids. By the time of the fire, in 1967, Joey and Mickey had five girls: Betty, then fourteen; Mary, eleven; Janet, nine; Barbie, five; and Pamela, three. Joey didn't see any reason his parents shouldn't help him out in this time of need.

"You've got that whole house, Pop," Joey had argued. "Two extra bedrooms you aren't doing nothing with. We'd just stay with you for a little while, till we get the money together to buy a new place." Joey and Tony both knew there never would be a new place, that Joey and Mickey would never get the money together. But Assunta didn't know that, or chose not to know it, and cried and begged and fretted until Tony said yes. Tony didn't have the stamina that he used to for arguing with his wife.

So Joey and Mickey and their five daughters moved into Tony's house at 4 Alder Street, across the road from the Maglieris and the Caramanicos. So many boy cousins on one side of the street, so many girls on the other. Joey and Mickey took the small bedroom, and in the style of the Maglieri boys they stacked two sets of bunk beds in the larger room for their daughters.

Now three years had gone by. It didn't seem like Joey and Mickey were any closer to moving out—more like their new plan was to wait until they inherited the house they were already living in.

Stella tried not to go over there unless she couldn't help it.

Across the street at number 3, Stella had finished pulling the laundry out of the washing machine and pinning it on the pulley line that ran between the Maglieris' and the Caramanicos' houses. She left her basket on the porch and went back inside; maybe she would watch some television. But first she opened the refrigerator to survey. She could use something to settle the acid in her stomach.

There was one bowl of cold pasta with sauce, leftover from supper the night before. She pulled the bowl out and put it on the table, then, before sitting down with her fork, poured herself her second glass of wine for the morning. By the time she finished the pasta, she had also finished her third. She could feel her brain shrinking away from her skull, could hear her heart pounding in the back of her throat, against the cavern of her consciousness, but the hangover had started to recede into the softer, more forgiving feeling of drunk.

She remembered that first time she'd learned what wine could do to her, that day in the cold winter of 1940, that first year in Hartford, the day Tony hadn't come home. She remembered how she'd sat with her mother and sister and they'd poured one another tall glasses of wine until they were too drunk to play cards.

Stella gazed across her kitchen at the framed photo taken in 1918, her mother and father standing on either side of the dead baby Mariastella—the photo hung by Stella's refrigerator now. Assunta was so young in that picture, only nineteen, so beautiful, Stella had realized as an adult—beautiful in her ordinariness, in her unflattering directness, in her strength. These were things you didn't see about your mother when you were a child.

Thinking of Assunta now, she poured herself a fourth.

A year and a half earlier, in December 1968, was when she went.

Tony and Assunta had been sitting at the kitchen table eating supper while Tina washed dishes at the sink. There was a thunk and Tina turned around to look and there was Papa but not Mamma. Assunta had slid right under the table, hitting her head on the radiator on the way down. Tina rode with her in the ambulance all the way to the hospital, but the doctor said she was already dead.

They gave it a fancy English name no one could remember. In short, there had been something wrong with her heart—perhaps the same thing that had killed her father so young.

When the paramedics opened Assunta's dress to try to perform emergency resuscitation, a bundle of mint, bound together with a bread bag tie, fell out of her brassiere.

Stella had not been with her mother in her last minutes, and Tina had—there was something Stella could never have back.

Tina had gotten laid off from Silex that summer; the company was being bought out and many of the assembly-line workers lost their jobs. She was forty-eight, and it was a strange age to not have a job; it took her almost a year to find another factory job she could do without passing a literacy test. In the meantime, she stayed at home with Tony and Assunta. Tony still took some odd construction jobs in the summer, but he had diabetes trouble, and keeping up with his diet was too much for Assunta, especially with all those granddaughters in the house. Mickey was hardly a help. She was more the type to be cooked for than to cook for others.

Meanwhile, Stella had decided to go back to work when Artie started kindergarten. She got a job on a corporate cleaning crew in the Families First insurance building. Carmelo told her over and over she didn't need to work—she suspected it was a blow to his pride to have his wife working as a cleaning lady. But Stella loved being productive again, loved having a place besides her house to go to and belong, and a cleaning crew was as good as anything else she could get, at her age and without having held a job in twenty years. The shift went from 3 to 8 p.m. so that they wouldn't get too much in the way of the nine-to-five insurance agents. Some of the crew were Jamaicans, who made Stella remember the ladies she'd met at the tobacco farm all those years ago, from whom she'd learned her earliest English. But most of Stella's fellow cleaners were Puerto Ricans, who spoke fast, energetic-sounding Spanish to one another and who would giggle with surprise when Stella chimed into their conversation—she usually had no idea what they were saying, but other times the words they used meant almost the same thing in Calabrese.

The day Assunta collapsed, no one at Alder Street knew how to reach Stella. The cleaning ladies moved from office to office; there was no way to locate them until the shift was over. Bernadette called the cleaning company's central dispatch, but they told her they had no way of passing on the message.

Bernadette was waiting for Stella when she got home.

"It's Grandma," she said. She was already crying. "Grandma's dead."

Bernie was not a liar or a joker; Bernie did not make mistakes. But Stella thought she must have been lying or joking or mistaken. It took Bernie half an hour to make her mother understand—a hamster wheel of a conversation so excruciating she was almost laughing by the end of it. Stella had marveled at her daughter's wrongheaded persistence. Papa was the one who was sick, not Mamma. Mamma was only sixty-nine years old. Assunta wouldn't drop dead behind Stella's back like this, giving her no chance at all to prepare.

Then it clicked. The world was swallowed.

The wake was an awful thing. Assunta had been loved too much by too many people who were too surprised by her loss. Even the hooligans were subdued in their scuffed-elbowed jackets and mediocrely knotted ties. Little Artie, the wicked imp, cried through all four hours of hand-shaking and registry-signing, just as his late grandmother would have—tears rolling silently down his round cheeks and blotting the silk of his tie.

Stella did not go to her mother's wake. She was not fit for a receiving line. She barely was able to go to the funeral. She had not shed a tear in forty-five years. She had not shed a tear when her own baby died. Now it was beyond her control—Stella who could control the world with her will could not even control herself. She sobbed like a hysterical child, her chest heaving until her ribs were sore, her throat so raw she tasted blood. She cried so hard, she wondered through her delirium if she was haunted by Assunta's ghost already—Assunta the emoter, whose weeping could wash away even the worst things. This was the worst thing, and Assunta wasn't here to wash it away.

Stella shuttered the venetian blinds in her bedroom and drew the blankets up over her head. She didn't eat or drink any water or go to the toilet—there was nothing to pass because she was so dehydrated. The bedroom became dank with the smell of her unsloughed skin and tears and unwashed hair.

In her darkness, she remembered how Assunta had collapsed when Louie and Queenie left—how she had torn out her hair and vomited and smeared her feces in animal desperation. Stella had been disturbed by her mother's behavior, had thought that manifestation of grief barbaric—inhuman. Now she understood. She wished she could shit out her own grief, pull it out by its roots. But she couldn't—she wasn't Assunta. All her life Stella had thought she was so strong, but now she learned that it was Assunta who had been the strong one—Assunta who had been truly in control of herself. Stella, meanwhile, had no means to excise her own demons.

The wound was unhealable. Stella could never say good-bye. There was no chance for redemption. There was only "never again," the beginning to so many sentences now. Never again would she see her mother's mischievous smile, hear her girlish laugh. Never again would she sit with Assunta on the back porch and tell stories. Never again would she taste her mother's *raù*. Never again would she feel her mother's cool hand on her forehead as she chanted the unfascination, or her warm hand on her shoulder blade to steady her when she was rattled by the rush of the world around her.

Bernadette had never seen her mother like this. No one had.

She tried to get Stella to drink some water or soup. Bernadette was crying herself; she had loved her grandmother. Stella realized, with the dissociation afforded by her grief, that she was not being a good mother right now. She didn't care.

"Mommy," Bernadette sobbed. "You're scaring me."

The world is a scary place, Stella thought. She stared out the window at the street, on the other side of which was the house her mother no longer lived in. The world is a scary place, and you're all alone in it, and you might as well learn that now.

Now Stella drank whenever she wanted.

She had lost Bob—that had been a terrible thing. She hadn't known if she would live through that. And then she had lost

Assunta. She hadn't known there was a place so dark as the one she tumbled into after she had lost her mother.

Of course, she didn't know yet in the summer of 1970 that there would be another layer of darkness coming. In half a year's time she would lose her Nino somewhere in the jungles of far-off Vietnam. She didn't know now that she had already seen him for the last time, before he shipped out this past spring when his draft number was called.

So Assunta was gone; Tony was a cranky goat-slaughtering diabetic. Stella was descending willfully into alcoholism. Alder Street was overrun with Joey and Mickey's shabby girl progeny, and with Carmelo's obnoxious teenage sons with their motor-bikes and thunk-engine used cars.

Stella still went to church with Carmelo on Sundays to receive Communion, but she didn't pray anymore. Praying made her feel as foolish as getting caught talking to herself in the grocery store.

At Gardener's, Bernie's hands shook with nervous energy as she counted out customers' change. She had become fixated on the fate of the dog. If Penny was dead, there was nothing Bernie would be able to do about it, but she needed to know one way or another. She needed to go home and to challenge her grandfa-ther—she was convinced now that he knew what had happened.

When she couldn't bear it even one more minute, she made one of the produce boys cover her register so she could seek out the manager, who was back in the deli. "I have to go home, Mr. Fastiggi. I don't feel well." As long as there was some truth to it, and there was, she could look him in the eye when she said it.

He looked her up and down. "You look okay to me."

"I'm sick to my stomach," Bernie said. Again, not a lie—her stomach did feel funny with the nerves.

The manager sighed. The two deli boys exchanged looks; they thought the girls always got off easy. But so what? "Can you make it until twelve thirty? Then Janice can cover for you when she gets in."

Bernie's watch said twelve fifteen. Fifteen minutes wouldn't make any difference in whether the dog was alive or dead, would it? "All right," she said. Then, remembering to seem a little desperate, she added, "I'll try."

The clock on the mantel above the television chimed twelve thirty and Stella lurched awake. She had fallen asleep sitting up on the couch, but it couldn't have been for long, because her head buzzed softly, still happy with the morning wine. Her crocheting had fallen to the floor and the needle had come out. She picked it up and thought about what she would eat for lunch.

As she rose, her gaze fixed on the empty driveway of 4 Alder. Mickey must have gone out; Stella wondered whether she'd taken the little girls. Sometimes Mickey left them with their grandfather for hours as if she genuinely thought he was babysitting. Tony wouldn't even remember to give them anything to eat; he could hardly feed himself.

Stella didn't like going over there but decided she was going to be a good aunt today. She could make the girls sandwiches while she made one for herself. She didn't have anything else to do.

Sliding through the last of her morning drunk, Stella looked both ways perhaps overzealously before crossing the street. The grassy lawns, electric green from the week's rare summer rain, shimmered for her in the midday heat. There was no breeze, but at least outside the sun dried away her layers of sweat.

Stella let herself in the back door without knocking. There was no one in the kitchen. She followed the sound of the television to the living room, but no one was there, either. Apparently Mickey had taken all the girls with her this time. Having crossed through the whole house, Stella opened the front door to let herself out that way, but happened to see little Pammy sitting on the floor of the hallway, her bare legs crossed Indian-style, making an old Chatty Cathy doll walk up and down the floor-boards in front of her. Had Mickey left her here by herself?

"Allo, Pam," Stella said.

Pam looked at her silently. None of Joey's girls were big talkers, Stella figured because their mother didn't give them a chance to say anything.

"You hungry, Pammy?" she said in English. "You want me to make you *sanguicci*?"

Pam shook her head.

Stella tried not to be annoyed. "You want to say, 'No, thank you, Auntie Stella'?"

"No, thank you, Auntie Stella," Pam repeated obediently.

"All right," said Stella, but that was when her mother-instinct kicked in, through the soft fuzzy pulsing of the wine. Something was funny here. Pammy was only six—why had her mother left her alone? Why was she sitting in the hallway? What a strange place for her to play with her doll. "Pammy, you here by yourself?"

"No," her niece answered. "There's Barbie and Grandpa, but they're playing."

"Where are they?" Stella asked. She hadn't seen anyone in the backyard.

Pammy used the doll's arm to point silently to the closed door behind her. Tony's bedroom.

Stella felt her heart speed up before her mind did. "What are they playing with the door closed?" she was asking Pam out loud, even as she was already thinking, That can't be why she's not wearing any pants. How had she not registered that it was strange for Pam to be sitting on the bare floor in only her underwear?

"They're playing the game," Pam said. "I have to wait for my turn."

He wouldn't, Stella thought, but she knew he would—the pieces snuggled together in her mind, like a plug fitting into a socket. She had always known he would.

She bent down and swooped Pam up in her arms, sitting the little girl on her left hip in the clamp of her elbow. She tried the doorknob, which was of course locked. Her skin roiled with the memory of her recurring nightmare, her father running his large hard hands over her body. Without thinking through whether it was the right thing to do, whether she might hurt the little girl, Stella threw herself against the door. She was lucky because the frame was made of cheap pine, and it splintered and gave. Pammy made a grunting noise in her ear and gripped Stella's neck. Stella heaved herself a second time, and the door flew open.

The curtains were drawn. Before Stella could think through whether she wanted to see what was happening in this dank bedroom she swatted the light switch. She already knew, she already knew, there was no surprise. Her eight-year-old niece Barbie crouched on the bed, her face bent over her grandfather's crotch and her tiny bare bum pointing toward the door so that Stella had a clear view of where her father was putting his fingers.

"No!" Stella shrieked. Her voice sounded inhuman to her, like the dying shrill of a pig being drained. It came again, the shriek: *"No!"* Hooking her naked little niece around the waist with her elbow, Stella snatched Barbie off the bed as Tony sheepishly pushed himself to a sitting position, pulling the blanket over his groin.

"You." Stella's chest heaved with fury. "Monster."

"Stella," he was saying, waving his hand, waving it away. "It's no big deal. I didn't ruin them."

"Monster!" She was fighting her way through a blur of emotions and impulses, to scream, to be sick, to tear him with her fingernails, but the little girls were there in her arms and the wine-blood beating against her temples made her slow and confused. Her own hatred and disgust for her father, the crusted dome encasing Stella's life, built up layer by layer over fifty years of encounters and nightmares and grief, descended on her.

The little girls. She had to get them out. "I'm coming back for you," she spat at him, and she turned and rushed down the hallway, almost tripping into the clear glass front door in her flight across the street.

Thank God none of the boys were in the living room when she got home to number 3—she hadn't thought that through, what if they had been? She bundled Pammy and Barbie up the stairs, slipping on the too-thick pile carpeting and sliding backward a jarring single step, almost taking all three of them down to the bottom. Naked Barbie was silent and stiff, awkward against Stella's side. Pammy was crying snottily into Stella's blouse.

She sat the girls on the bed, wrapping Barbie in a crocheted sham. "What's wrong with you?" she shouted at them. "What were you thinking, letting him do that to you?"

The girls were silent. Pammy had abruptly stopped crying, and they were staring at her with identical brown, sullen eyes—cow eyes, Stella thought, as she had thought many times of Tina at her most frustratingly obtuse.

What was *wrong* with them? How stupid were they?

"Well?"

She wanted to shake them, but then—*No, Stella. What's wrong with* you? They were just little girls. Little girls at the mercy of a monster with a heart as cold as a rock.

"Girls, you *never* let someone close you up in their bedroom. *Never.* You understand me?"

They nodded, and Barbie's eyes slid to the door. Maybe it was the wine that made Stella stumble over that thought—was it confusing that she had just closed them up in her bedroom? But they must already understand there were differences between women and men.

"Your body," she tried again. "It's the only thing you have. You never let anyone touch it. *Never.*"

"I'm sorry, Auntie Stella," Barbie said, and Pammy echoed her, "I'm sorry, Auntie Stella." Pammy's voice was snuffly;

Barbie's was clear. Stella wondered at the girl's hard little soul, how long she had been playing her grandfather's "game."

"Don't apologize to me," she snapped, and heard how she sounded. *What are you doing, Stella?* She put a hand on each of their heads. "You don't apologize, you hear me?" It still sounded harsh, like she was asking them to apologize for apologizing. "I love you," she made herself say. It wasn't easy, because she wasn't a great liar, but she couldn't think of what other thing to say to comfort them. "I just want you to protect yourselves when no one else is there to protect you. The world is full of bad people. Your grandfather is a bad, bad person, and you need to protect yourself from him."

The girls stared at her with their sister-matching faces.

"Okay?" she said.

They nodded.

Her head was pounding now. What should she do? Clothes. She dug through her drawers for something little girls could wear, finally thought to take short pants and T-shirts from Richie and Artie's drawer in the hallway. They were about the right sizes for Barbie; everything was too big for Pam but would have to do.

What now?

Oh, if Mamma were here—but she wasn't.

Stella led the girls downstairs, sat them at the kitchen table. Mickey's car still wasn't back. Stella made the girls sandwiches, mayonnaise and slices of American cheese. She made one for herself, too, and they ate in silence. Stella's mouth was so dry, she struggled to swallow. She wanted to pour herself a glass of wine but not before she figured out what to do about her father.

"I have to go back across the street now, just for a minute," she told the two little girls. "You stay here at my house, okay?" They nodded. "You can watch television, or you can play in the back-yard"—*play*—she shuddered—"or whatever you want, but you *stay* at my house. All right?"

They nodded again.

Not sure if she was doing the right thing—leaving the girls all alone, or letting her father escape his bad deed, they both seemed equally wrong—Stella stormed back across Alder Street to number 4. Waves of guilt washed through her, so distracting they folded the world around her into an unknowable haze. Stella could have left Pammy in the hallway, she didn't have to bring the poor little thing with her into Tony's bedroom when she went barreling in—could have spared her that much at least. She hadn't had to turn on the light, seal Barbie and Pammy both in the burn of that image. How bad was Stella, running them across the street with bare bottoms for all the world to see. They were tiny, but they had feelings and shame. Her mind began to tick through the long list of shames she had never been able to shake off in her fifty years, and suddenly, for the first time in a long time, she had an urge to pray to God, pray that she hadn't given them a shame they would never shake off.

Stella banged her way through the house, slamming doors open and closed again, barging into the bathroom. Her father was nowhere; there was no one there at all. The television buzzed in the living room, the sickly fake cheerful thing in this miserable house. There was no one in the basement, or the backyard or even the shed. Where had he gone, the ugly bastard? It wasn't like he could drive away.

Stella went back to her house to sit nervously with the little Fortuna girls. They watched television and Stella stared out the window at the house across the street, waiting for either Mickey or Tony to come home.

Janice was ten minutes late for her shift. As soon as she had punched in, Bernie ran for the parking lot. Gardener's was only a few blocks away from Alder Street, but she had a car—Nino's old Chevy, which he'd given to her to use until he was back from Vietnam—and when you're sixteen and you have a car you drive it everywhere. She raced home, to the extent that one can race without disrespecting any traffic regulations, and pulled the car directly into her grandfather's driveway.

She found him sitting on the weird cement back porch he'd poured that year he was going through his cement phase. His legs dangled off the side like a kid about to jump into a swimming pool.

"Where is my dog?" Bernie put her hands on her hips. "You tell me right now."

"How shoo' I know?" The set of the old man's mouth was defensive through his pepper-gray three-day stubble.

"Where. Is. My dog."

He made a heavy-handed flapping gesture. Her concern was misplaced, inconsequential.

"*Where.*"

"I take care of her," Antonio said.

A stone formed in Bernie's stomach. "What do you mean, you took care of her?"

"You don't have to worry about her no more."

"*What did you do.*"

The heavy wave again. His face was unhappy, though. "I take her far away, leave her where she can't come back. Maybe someone else find her."

Bernie was so angry she shouted. "Where?"

"Far away. Too far you find."

She took a step toward him and, almost of its own accord, her hand shot out and pinched at a flap of flesh on the side of his neck, under his ear. She felt his thyroid contract under her thumb as he groaned in surprise. "You're going to show me," she said. As he reached out with his big hands to overpower her, she pinched harder and he gasped in pain. "Now. You get in my car right now."

Bernie had no idea why he listened to her—she was strong for a sixteen-year-old girl, but her Grandpa Tony was an ox of a man, even into his seventies, and could have made her regret her attempt at coercion. But he stood and walked obediently to the driveway, pressed himself into the passenger seat.

The drive was more than an hour of highway and then winding streets toward the southeast Connecticut shore. They drove in silence punctuated only by Bernadette's hatred and her grandfather's blustery driving directions. The old man had never learned to drive a car, but he never forgot a street. They turned off the hedged lanes of hilly beachside neighborhoods, Bernie slowing to a crawl in the small-town traffic of summer tourists heading toward the beach or home for lunch. In the end, Tony pulled them off onto a dirt path running through the wetland reeds toward Long Island Sound.

"Here?" Bernie said.

"Around here."

"Why the *heck* would you leave her here?" For Bernie, "heck" was swearing.

He'd been out this way with his friend Sandro, who owned a construction company and sometimes had Antonio do day jobs. Sandro had picked Tony up on Tuesday morning—it must have been just after Bernadette left for work—and in a fit of inspiration Antonio had grabbed that damn dog and brought her on the ride to the construction site. Sandro had pulled over here, in this marsh, and Antonio had left the dog on the side of the road.

"What were you *thinking*," Bernie said.

"I don't want no more puppies." He shrugged. "She have more puppies, more puppies every six month."

"They're not even *your puppies* to worry about," Bernadette said, her eyes smarting with furious tears.

Penny had been out here three, almost four days, if she hadn't starved or drowned, if she hadn't been eaten by a fox or a hawk—she was just a little thing.

"We're not going home until we find her," Bernadette said.

"She gone," Antonio shouted. His verve was returning. "You never find her."

"Well, then it's your fault if we're here all night," Bernie said, and she started off down the path toward the Sound, calling, "Penny! Penny! Here, girl!"

Stella was sober by the time Joey's Oldsmobile pulled into the driveway and Mickey emerged from the driver's side, one brown platform shoe at a time—how did she walk in those things, and why would she at her age? The car also emitted the three older girls, listless Betty, Janet, still so runty for eleven years old, and bony, mean Mary, who was fourteen, all sternum and scowls. The Fortuna females congregated around the trunk for a long minute, then paraded up the driveway with whatever parcel they had bought during whatever shopping trip they had just taken using whatever money they did not spend on the rent they should have been paying to live in their own house.

Stella watched from the armchair by the window, only realizing how cronishly she was craning forward and squinting when her neck started to ache. Her heart was already pounding with anticipation of her confrontation with Mickey. How could she have left her babies alone? Didn't she have any common sense? Stella wanted to take the woman and shake until her little brain rattled in her skull.

For the last two hours, Barbie and Pam had stayed in the Maglieris' living room, watching whatever came on the television next. Richie, Mingo, and Artie had trickled in during the early afternoon, exhausted by their morning war games in the woods, and now the five cousins were all sitting on the red couch or the blue carpet, watching *The Guiding Light*. Stella had always let her children run around as they chose with little supervision, as long as they didn't burn anything down, but now, thinking about what had happened to these girls made her feel guilty for leaving them. Nevertheless, she did. Mickey was their mother and it was the mother's job to control this situation. As she crossed the street for the fifth time that day, Stella fought her way through the same ring of thoughts that had tormented her since she had broken down her father's door: Was it only Mickey's children, the ratty, uncivilized little scamps? Or had he preyed on others? Had he ever, ever been left alone with Bernie? The thought—again—made Stella want to vomit. Not her Bernie, it was impossible. Her heart rejected the idea before she could test it further. What about the boys? Were they safe? And, or—were they dangerous? Did these monstrous tendencies bleed down into yet another generation? Stella remembered hints her mother had dropped about the Fortunas in Tracci, how Assunta had described their one-bed house as a pigsty of disease and animal behavior. Finally Stella understood what she must have meant by animal behavior. Was the whole family poisoned?

Mickey was putting away groceries when Stella let herself in through the back door. Janet was sitting at the kitchen table and eating directly from a bag of Ruffles. Stella studied the skinny little girl, who didn't acknowledge her aunt's scrutiny. It was impossible to tell by looking, Stella thought.

"Is Papa here?" Stella asked.

"I haven't seen him, honey," Mickey said. Even when she spoke Calabrese to Stella, she still said "honey" in English. "Maybe he took Pam and Barbie for a walk."

"Pam and Barbie are over at my house," Stella said. She was not going to make a scene in front of another unhappy little girl today. In English, she said, "Janet, I gotta talk with your mother. Go sit in the living room, okay?"

Janet made no verbal acknowledgment she'd heard Stella, but after a moment she slid out of her seat and disappeared down the hallway, leaving the open bag of potato chips. For all Stella knew she hadn't been being obedient, had just whimsically lost interest. An enigma, that one, like her older sister Betty.

"What is it, Stella?" Mickey said. "Is something wrong?"

"Yes," Stella said. "Yes, Michelina." Now that the time had come, after all her preparation, it was too hard to say. "You have to move away from here," she said finally.

"Oh, Stella, you know we can't do that." Mickey had taken an English muffin out of a new bag and was breaking it open with a fork. "We haven't got the money right now. You know how business is for Joey. We can barely feed the girls."

Stella wanted to argue with that, to remind the nincompoop of the department store bags she had seen her lift out of the trunk of her car just moments earlier. She fought down her impulses and brought the conversation back to the most important point. "Michelina, you have to move out of this house. I don't care what you have to do, you have to figure out a way." She cringed against the words, lowered her voice in case the girls in the living room were listening. "Your daughters aren't safe here. Do you understand me?"

Mickey looked up from the butter dish and the crumbs on the counter. Her dark eyes were sharp on Stella's. "What do you mean?"

"They're not . . . they're not safe with my father." *Just say it, Stella.* "Mickey, I came over here today and I found him . . . I found him touching them."

Mickey returned her attention to the English muffin. "Oh, it's nothing. He just likes to play with them."

Stella had often wanted to do this woman violence but never more than in this moment. "Mickey," she said. She was struggling so hard to restrain herself that perhaps her urgency wasn't coming through clearly. "Mickey, he's not *playing* with them. He's . . . he's *touching* them. He's . . . using them like *puttane*."

Mickey was quiet. She was spreading the butter, soft from being left on the summer-warm counter, thickly in the muffin's spongy interior. Stella waited. Finally, Mickey said, "Well, it's not like he's raping them, is he?"

"You knew." For a passage of time, Stella was blinded by shock. She had been ready for denial, for stupidity, for whining or for hysterics. She had not been ready for this. "You knew," she said again. "You knew and you let him do it anyway?"

Mickey shrugged sadly. "What can I do, though, Stella? It's his house."

"You *knew* what he was doing to your daughters and you *let* him?" Rage was a patina over her vision, obscuring the kitchen and this witch of a mother. "You *left* them here with him? What, to make it easier? So you wouldn't have to watch?"

Mickey didn't say anything now. Her wheels were turning, Stella knew, trying to find a way to make this conversation stop, to make Stella go away.

"You're a terrible person," Stella said, "but your children are innocent. You better do something about this or I'll do something myself, and you won't like it."

"What do you want me to do, Stella?" Mickey said. She had opted for crying, her showy openmouth style. "I can't make a fuss or he'll kick us out. We don't have any money to live somewhere else."

Stella stepped toward her sister-in-law, forcing her up against the wall, and she grabbed Mickey's face in her right hand. Mickey was too surprised to squeal.

"This isn't about money, you stupid bitch." Stella pinched harder—she would be only too satisfied to see purple circles like clown rouge on Mickey's face tomorrow—and then released her. "You get your act together and find somewhere to live or I will call the cops and report you all."

"For what?" Mickey said between her sobs.

"I'll think of something." Stella stepped away from her sister-in-law. "You go get your little girls at my house now. They need their mother, even if she is a stupid bitch."

That was all the invitation Mickey needed to flee the kitchen. Stella heard her let herself out the front door. She turned to gaze out the window at the vivid green lawn of the backyard, where there was no sign of the monster, her father.

Now what?

Instinctively, Stella felt her work wasn't quite done. She took a carving knife out of the drawer by the sink and let herself out onto the back porch to wait for her father.

More than two hours and no sign of Penny. Bernadette was hoarse but stubborn. She couldn't call out anymore, so she clapped as she walked up and down the wetland paths. The heat had receded, leaving the damp air feeling falsely cool, and the diagonal light of the yellow-orange sun splattered among the knee-high reeds where the marsh water pooled.

Bernie cried silently as she walked and clapped. It was too much time. If Penny had been here she would have come by now. She'd walked every footpath between the highway and the ocean for a stretch of two miles. She'd whistled and poked unwillingly with a stick among clumps of bushes, hoping she did not find a carcass. Not knowing would be better than knowing at that point, she thought. She could not know that Penny had been adopted by a loving beach family just as easily as she could not know that Penny had been dismantled by raccoons.

She wiped the salty snot from her chin with the inside of her striped Gardener's uniform sleeve and blinked away her tears. No mourning in front of her grandfather; only rage. She watched him from this distance as he stood twenty feet from the car, clapping halfheartedly every so often. Bernie had locked him out of the car so there was no way he could avoid the task she'd set him. The old goat was going to stick it out till it was over.

Well. It was over. There was nothing more she could do here.

The bastard. Bernadette wished, earnestly, that he would die.

She was heading back to the car—more than halfway there, how close she came to missing—when she heard the rustling and stopped. Yes, rustling in the grasses, the length of a football field away, but she heard it.

"Penny," she croaked, embarrassed at her own hopefulness. She cleared her throat. "Penny!"

The dog ran toward her, reeds parting as she barreled through, her coppery fur ratted and her little legs covered in mud.

"Penny!" She knelt, and the dog leapt into her arms. Her legs were so weak and shaky that she missed and hit her chin on Bernie's knee. Bernie scooped her up like an infant, cradling her and cupping her face and crying helplessly. It was too good to be true—Bernadette felt that God, whose existence she had been questioning all summer, had given her a miracle. The sweet little dog should have been dead—three days in this hostile wilderness with nothing to eat. But here she was.

On the drive home, Bernadette blasted the radio and sang along euphorically to the Rolling Stones. She rode with Penny in her lap, stroking the dog's heaving ribs whenever she didn't have her hand on the stick shift. Grandpa Tony was quiet in the passenger seat. Bernie hoped he was swimming in shame.

As the highway approached Hartford and she got ready to take their exit, Bernadette turned the radio all the way down. "Old man," she said to him. "You ever touch this dog again— you ever touch any of our animals—I will kill you myself. Okay?" When she said it, she meant it. She was not a violent person, but rationally, if an act of violence was for the good of society, she could do it, she thought. And this would be a service. "I will kill you myself, with my own two hands."

He snorted, but he didn't say anything. They pulled into the driveway at number 3 Alder Street and Bernadette leapt out of the car with Penny clutched to her chest, slamming the door behind her and leaving her grandfather to walk himself home.

Stella was sitting on the back porch of 4 Alder Street at 5:15 p.m. when Tina came over to check on her father after work.

"Aren't you supposed to be at your job?" Tina asked. "What are you doing here?"

"Waiting for the old man to get home," Stella said. She showed Tina the carving knife she was hiding behind her leg. "I had to take today off work so I can tell him I'm going to kill him. He needs a little fear in his life."

"Stella!" Tina was alarmed.

"Come here, Tina." Stella patted the porch beside her. "I want to tell you why I want to kill him, but I have to whisper."

Tina listened to the whole story with wide eyes. "But what can you do, Stella?" she said at last.

"I can tell him I'm going to kill him if he does it again."

"You can't do that." Tina was scandalized.

"Why not?"

"You can't say that to your father!"

"Can't I?" Stella snapped.

"You have to show him respect in his house."

"What has that man ever done to deserve any respect?" The pall of her loathing for her father expanded to engulf her sister. How could she be such a worshipful cow, even after all that had happened? "These are innocent little children, Tina—Mickey's children, and mine! We must do anything we have to do to protect them."

"But you *can't* kill Papa." Tina's voice was full of fear. "Not your own father."

Stella sneered at her sister in disgust. "After what he's done to those babies, the old man can go straight to hell, and I don't care if he's my father." A dark thought prickled in the back of Stella's mind—Tina was over here at number 4 all the time. Could it have been possible she knew, too? Or had an inkling? Stella was so upset by this thought that she dismissed it quickly, but some suppressed resentment inside her bubbled up and before she could stop herself she said, "If you were a mother yourself, you'd understand. You owe your life to your children, not to your father."

Tina's eyes fell to her lap as she tried to digest this—probably tried to pick through whether Stella was right or just being mean. The sting of childlessness hadn't lessened in twenty years of knowing, in twenty years of pouring her heart and attentions into Stella's children to make up for not having any of her own. Stella had no business attacking her. Tina wasn't the enemy here. But she was an easy target, and in that moment Stella hated her for mouthing back the same platitudes that had allowed Tony to carry on his monstrosities for the last five decades.

What was said was said, and Stella was done talking. They sat in silence on the porch, Stella gripping the knife, until Tina finally stood and brushed off her lap. "Well, Stella, you be careful," she said sourly. Tina was probably thinking, Well, she'll get whatever she has coming this time. Stella didn't say anything as her sister walked away.

You're waiting to hear the story of how Stella almost choked to death that July day in 1970, I know. We're almost there now.

Assunta used to say that sitting flat on granite or concrete was what caused hemorrhoids. Stella didn't know if a doctor had told her mother that or if it was received folk wisdom, but she'd repeated it often. Stella kept hearing her mother's voice as the house's shadow stretched over the porch and the concrete under Stella's bum grew cold.

It was perhaps six o'clock when Antonio trudged up the cement sidewalk he had laid along the driveway. Stella pulled herself awkwardly to her feet so that she could intercept the old man at the back door. Her legs balked and then rejoiced at restored blood flow. She realized she was still wearing the powder-blue slippers.

As she moved, the carving knife she'd had hidden in her skirt was exposed and must have flashed in the sun. Antonio's eye was caught by the glint. "What's that, Stella?" He seemed weary as he trudged up the stairs.

She was shaking—why was she shaking? There was nothing she wanted more in her life than to have this man no longer be part of it.

Stella raised the knife so that he could look it in the eye. "You want to know what this is?" she said. "I will show you everything you need to know about it in a minute."

His laugh sounded tired. There he was, so old but still so big, looking grimy in his grease-stained Red Sox cap.

"Are you gonna kill me, too, Stella?"

She didn't know what he meant by "too," but she didn't want him thinking she was arbitrarily dramatic. "If you don't stay away from those girls," she said. The vision came back, the skinny bare legs. She fought off the nausea. "Yes. Yes, I will kill you myself if you don't stay away from them."

He was coming toward her. Her heart sped up, pounding—what if he attacked her? Would she actually be able to use the knife on her own father?

"You don't know what you're talking about, Stella." He was stepping around her and pushing open the door. "It's none of your business."

How could it be she had no power over this man? He was old and broken, but he still walked past her like she wasn't even there. Her heart was already defeated, had retreated into itself as if he had made all the decisions for her, again. She wanted to go home and lick her wounds—had to remind herself that the confrontation wasn't over, she hadn't lost yet.

She didn't have the passion for it, or the energy, but in the end it's only about the action itself, not what's behind it. She made her hand move forward and pressed until she felt the tip of the knife bury in the crotch of his pants. She had no way of knowing if the sharp tip met with scrotum or was halted by the prophylactic thickly stitched seam.

"Whoa!" her father shouted.

"Go ahead," Stella said. "Give me an excuse to cut off your balls." She pushed a little harder and he yelped just like their little dog Penny. "Any excuse, old man. You can't learn to mind your own balls, I don't know that you need them. That would solve your problem and mine, wouldn't it?"

"You crazy bitch!" Antonio swung at her and tried to move away, but the doorframe stopped him. "Mother Mary, save me from this crazy bitch!"

His voice cracked, and Stella took a step back, suddenly paralyzed by misgiving. He was her father, after all. Her awful, filthy father. An animal who wasn't fit for a barn, who had stolen from her, piece by piece, her home, her country, her dignity, her teeth, her mother, her freedom, who had made her into this wretched rag of a middle-aged woman.

She couldn't do it.

"Never again," Stella said. Her weakness sat like a stone in the bottom of her heart. "You hear me? Never again."

"Go to hell," he told her, ducking into his kitchen and shutting the door. She watched him through the glass as he watched her back, wary. Then he shuffled off in the direction of his room.

Her chest aching, Stella headed back across Alder Street, toward the pink-orange sun that was settling into the treetops behind her house.

The television was on, but all the other lights in the house were off. No one was home but the little dog, Penny, who leapt off the doormat, where she was curled, and wagged maniacally, licking at Stella's calves as she tried to enter the house. The boys' dirty dinner bowls were piled in and around the sink. They never could learn to rinse out their own bowl. How many hours would that one little thing have saved her over her life?

None of her sons—or her daughter, for that matter—were anywhere to be found. A Friday evening, suppertime—where could they be? Bernie was most likely at her friend Patty's. The little boys, Artie, Richie, and Mingo, were surely at Tina's. Mingo was Tina's favorite and he practically lived over there; he often didn't even come home to sleep. The teenagers were probably racing their buddies' dirt bikes in the empty strip of road behind the high school.

Stella poured a short glass of wine, downed it, and poured a second. She had spent the whole day sober, missed her work shift for that nasty old man. She needed something to eat; she'd had nothing since the cheese sandwiches. There was nothing in the refrigerator; whatever Carmelo had made for dinner had been polished off—a casualty of having so many teenage boys in the house, their friends cycling through like the place was Union Station, or Hartford county jail.

In the drawer at the bottom of the refrigerator was a supermarket packet of chicken parts: legs and thighs chopped so their blunted bones stood out against the plastic wrapping. Yes, Stella thought, this much I can do. Even Rocco Caramanico had been able to cook chicken. She put the package on the counter, found a pasta pot beneath the sink, filled it with water, and put it on the stove, turning the burner under it on high. One by one, she dropped the chicken parts into the pot of water. The peach-colored flesh was slimy between her fingers, and the water quickly clouded.

Stella looked at her creation, this food that she was cooking. She was making herself chicken. She was fifty years old, and she didn't need anyone—she didn't need her father, whose balls she had held a knife to; she didn't need her husband, who had fed her the last twenty years. She was no one to the world—she wasn't pretty, she was old, she wasn't such a good mother—but she was everything *she* needed. She could work, and she could fight. She had survived all of everything. She had survived.

She sat at the kitchen table and waited for the food to cook. She was hungry now. The bad feelings of the past had set in.

She drank a third glass of wine, watching the shadows of the faucet and the sun-catcher in the window stretch across the stove. She had begun to live the old nightmare again, end to end. There was her father pinning her in the corner, his hands sliding over her buttocks, her ribs, her breasts. She fought her nausea with a fourth glass of wine. She waited for the vision to abate.

As the broth was coming to a boil, she thought to add salt and pepper. Was there something else you put in chicken? She didn't know. She drank a fifth glass of wine, the comfort of fuzzy detachment sliding over the discomfort of her vivid memories. On the stove, the water in the pot bubbled, issuing a delightful steam that made her shy back when she held her face over the roiling liquid.

In the dark kitchen, she removed four pieces of chicken from the pot with Carmelo's cooking tongs, put them in a bowl, and watched them steam into the heavy July air. As she waited, she drank another glass of wine. The steam rising from the chicken in this moment reminded her of the dew evaporating from the leaves of the ilex in Ievoli all those years ago. Everything was different, but this thing—this evaporated water rising into the air—this was the same.

She was grasping.

She had lost herself.

When the chicken was cool enough to eat, she picked up a piece with her bare hands and wolfed it down. The chicken was not delicious—it was gummy, almost stomach turning—but she was ravenous. She selected a second piece of meat from the bowl and began to chew and suck. Suddenly there was the stretch in her throat, the esophagus pulling taut around the aspirated bone. She was coughing but there was no air, so she wasn't coughing. She was sputtering, and then she was clawing. Her airway was blocked, and she couldn't get it out.

Could it be? It wasn't this serious. Was it?

It was. There was no air, only a suggestion of air, a suggestion she couldn't accept. The dog was barking, but the barking sounded far away.

Her vision of her dark kitchen sparkled around her. This was wrong—this was not the way she would die. Not after everything she had already survived—not a chicken bone. She would not die eating her own cooking.

Drool ran down her chin and splattered on her hands, on the counter. She tried to cough, fought for air. Nothing. Darkness, settling. Stella dropped to her knees, bracing herself against the floor and pounding her fist against her chest. She felt the bone move in her throat, but there was no mercy.

Stella thought of her mother, who had died young at sixty-nine—realized that she, Stella, would die even younger. Her mind fixed on the image of the dead baby, her sister Mariastella. This was the last haunting, she thought. That damn ghost was finally going to get her. In those last moments it wasn't her husband or her children Stella thought of; it wasn't her monstrous father, who'd ruined her life and now was ruining the lives of others. It was the haunting hollow eyes of the dead baby that filled her mind. Even through the seizing pain in her constricted throat, the fireworks of the bursting blood vessels, Stella was thinking, after all this time, after all your better efforts, I can't believe this is how you're going to make me die.

She couldn't hear because of the crashing of deoxygenated blood in her ears. But as Stella knelt on the cold tiles of her kitchen floor, Tina was calling her. Tina had looked out across the lawn between their houses and seen that number 3 was completely dark; it had not seemed right. She still smarted from Stella's comment about motherhood and thought about letting the malice stew all night so they could have a good picking-apart tomorrow. Stella's three youngest sons, tuckered out from a hard summer's afternoon, had fallen asleep on Tina's carpet in front of the nightly news. Tina could have arranged some throw blankets over them, turned out the light, and spent the rest of this quiet Friday with Rocco in the kitchen, where he was playing solitaire. But instead she was overcome by a nagging desire to go next door, to see it through with Stella tonight.

There was no answer when Tina called out for Stella at the front door. She caught the sound of Stella's pounding over the murmur of the news and hastened to the dark kitchen. Tina didn't know the Heimlich maneuver, but she did know how to whack with her fist and she had the strength of an ox, like her father. For once, she didn't think twice or worry that she didn't know what to do. She whacked. She whacked and whacked and the chicken wing slid free.

Stella leaned against the sink cabinet, gasping. Her teeth were purple from grape sediment.

"Tina," she said finally. "Tina. I almost died."

"I know," Tina said. "It's been a while."

Obviously this next part of the story I'm about to suggest to you is just fiction, because I don't believe in ghosts, I don't think, and I certainly wouldn't ask you to believe in them. But bear with me for a moment. Imagine that maybe it could be a possibility—that a little girl whose life was cut short might leave a residue of herself, literal or imaginary, that might haunt the loving mother from whom she'd been parted. Imagine that residue—let's go ahead and call her a ghost—imagine that ghost stood by to watch her mother's grief, suffered invisibly at her side, yearned for her soft touch and warm comforting bosom. Imagine how the ghost's ectenic little heart might have broken to watch her mother replace her with another baby with the very same name, watch her pin her maternal hopes on this beautiful, perfect new daughter. Imagine what it must have felt like to have your life snatched away from you unrealized, and then to see all traces that you did live gradually erased by a more robust, more lovable, generally superior new version of yourself.

I'm not asking you to believe in spirits or a soul that might be shut out of heaven by its own grief or envy; I wouldn't ask you to believe anything I didn't believe myself, and I don't believe in anything. But what if we said that the power of human faith is in making things real even when they are not—that by giving imaginary entities our credence we allow them to assume power over us—to step into being? Because what is faith but a willingness to believe?

And now the little ghost followed in lockstep as this girl, her replacement, blossomed into the life the ghost might have had if she had not been severed. Imagine she watched her replacement become beautiful, clever, beloved, wooed. Imagine the ghost's hatred, her resentment, her implacable yearning for these things that her living sister took for granted or rejected outright. It might come to seem that she, the replacement, was the enemy. Imagine how the first Stella might have lashed out—imagine her violent impulses to teach that second Stella a lesson, teach her how precious and precarious life is, make her ask herself whether she deserved all the gifts she'd been given by fate. Imagine how it might have been those attacks themselves that shaped the living Stella's personality, made her so stubborn, so self-protective, so shut off from the romance and companionship the little ghost craved. Imagine that now, after half a century of vengeance and diminishment, after one last good-faith effort to do her worst, finally, finally, she had her revelation.

I understand why to the first Stella the second Stella might have looked like the enemy. I understand the jealousy and the loathing and the exquisite sorrow of watching your replacement take everything you were denied. But the Stellas should never have been enemies; they should have been the most faithful of allies against the monster they had in common, the man who had taken away each of their lives in different ways, who had never considered regretting what he had destroyed, who had tortured their sweet shared mother, the woman each of the Stellas had loved more than they'd loved the rest of the world. Half a century after he'd ended the first Stella's life, bringing home his war flu and callously refusing to call the doctor; a quarter century after he'd taken away the second Stella's life, beating her resistance away and forcing her to do the one thing she feared more than death itself; still, here and now, Antonio Fortuna was ruining the lives of other little girls.

Why did the first Stella keep trying to kill the second? It was their father she should have killed.

So now imagine this: the little ghost watches her sister—this collapsed, aching woman—choke to death, pounding her fist on the clammy white tiles of her kitchen floor, and she has a change of heart. As the littlest sister, Tina, comes running to the rescue one more time—how lucky that she is always, always there—the ghost thinks about how the second Stella brandished that knife, how in that moment, if only they'd had the courage, together they might have cut off his right to ruin any more lives. She feels a swell of energy, an excited beating where her heart would have been. As Tina puts their mutual sister to bed, the first Stella separates herself from her constant companion and drifts across the street, bonelessly traverses the aluminum siding—since, after all, she doesn't exist—and slides into the old man's bedroom, where he is wheezing in his dirty dreams. Even on a night like tonight, she thinks, he loses no sleep.

The first Stella sits there on his dresser, next to the gold-plated watch he puts on for card games with the boys, in front of the framed Fortuna family photo taken Christmas of 1940, which has stood on its felt feet in this very spot since Mamma put it there fifteen years earlier, and the first Stella watches him sleep, her anger and hatred inside her cramping together into a shining ball, collecting all her bad feelings in her gut, just like the second Stella would have—for the first Stella would have been just like the second Stella in many ways if she had been allowed to grow up. All night she sits and watches him, her fury coalescing, until the old-world miasma of her settles on his skin and clogs his nostrils and even he can't sleep through this anymore—he wakes nervously, discomfited, he tugs at his blankets and cowers under his pillow but he knows something is very wrong, she can feel his diseased old heart hiccupping in his chest. She presses down on him—she's not quite ready yet, she hasn't decided what she is going to do, but she isn't cowed by him the way her sister is. He has never been her master.

As the first twilight of dawn glints in the swampy dew of his backyard, Antonio Fortuna hears the soft *thufft* of his back door closing against its rubber jamb. It is his daughter Tina, come over to fix him breakfast before she leaves for work. Crazed by insomnia, his chest seizes with anxiety. The first Stella feels the skipping slap of his heart against his rib cage and she presses down just a little harder. He attempts to shove her off, but he can't see her, doesn't know what she is. He forces himself up, puts his feet on the floor, his yellowed undershirt and underwear milky and rank with sweat, and the little ghost cringes away. As Tony pulls on his burgundy bathrobe, the first Stella swallows her disgust and leaps onto his back, clamping her invisible little arms around his neck. She feels him shudder under her oppression. Yes, she will have witnesses for this. A ghost must be witnessed whenever she can.

As he opens his bedroom door, Tony rolls his shoulders. He doesn't understand the first Stella but he suffers her weight—he tries to shrug her off. "Tina," he says as he rounds the corner into his kitchen. "Tina, help me. I don't feel right."

Tina has set a pot of rolled oats in water on the range and is turning on the burner. "What's wrong, Papa? Sit down. I'll make you coffee."

"Tina," Tony says again. His voice is a goat's bleat, a goat like the beautiful white pet goat he killed. "Tina." And finally Tina looks away from her cooking and at him, alarmed. "It's your sister Mariastella," he gasps. "She's going to kill me."

At those strange last words, the little ghost takes her cue and she squeezes her arms around his neck with all of her shining hatred and fury.

And just like that, she chokes the life out of him.

Obviously, this notion of a ghost is all fabrication and fantasy, and has no place in an otherwise meticulously researched family history. Tony most likely woke up from a nightmare about his second daughter Stella, who had threatened him at knifepoint only hours earlier; that was surely what his last words to terrified Tina meant.

At the hospital, where Tony Fortuna was pronounced DOA, they said it was a massive heart attack that had killed him. It's not uncommon for heart attack victims to feel like they are choking, which explains why Tony had spent his last moments clawing at his throat. He died with his own skin under his fingernails and red gashes in his neck.

Part IV

 # OLD AGE

A vecchiaja è na carogna.
Old age is a bitch.
—CALABRESE PROVERB

Cerebral Hemorrhage (Dementia)

This is the last time Stella Fortuna almost died. This is the Accident.

It was December 8, 1988, but December 9 was coming. Stella, sitting in her spot on the couch, happened to notice the time at 11:52 p.m., and after that she couldn't take her eyes off the clock above the television. She watched the minute hand tick up, and up, up, up. At midnight it would be the twenty-year anniversary of her mother's death. Assunta had been sixty-nine years old; tonight, Stella was just shy of sixty-nine herself.

There was nothing that marked midnight, the passing of an ordinary day into an oppressive milestone. The CBS news broadcast paused for a liquid detergent commercial. Stella tried to make herself feel any different than she had before. "Mamma?" she said into the open air of her living room, and then she felt foolish because her mother wasn't there. Stella poured herself a glass of wine from the bottle she kept between her feet. Her hands were shaking, but that was because she had made herself jittery, so much wine and only some cold pasta for dinner a few hours ago.

You pray to God for the dead, for the souls in purgatory, so that God will show them mercy through your faith. Assunta had taught Stella that when Stella was just a tiny girl, from the first time she had taken her to the cemetery to clean her dead sister's grave. Assunta would have wanted Stella to say prayers for her soul. "Hail Mary full of grace," Stella said guiltily into the flashing dark of the television-lit living room, but in this moment she couldn't remember the words. She hadn't prayed in years. It was so hard to focus her mind or heart on God these days—hard not to feel silly talking into the dark.

Twelve twenty-three. Stella poured herself another glass of wine, then replaced the bottle, which listed slightly in the cushioning of blue carpet. The carpet was lumpy with age, the plush matted into pills, dark on top from years of shoe grime the vacuum couldn't remove. Stella had been treading this carpet now for thirty-five years, as had her nine wild sons and her one straitlaced daughter and their hordes of friends and opportunistic acquaintances. Now the house was empty; even her baby, Artie, had married and moved away.

Thirty-five years—it was more than half her life. She was more this person, this wife and mother, than she had ever had the chance to be any other person.

How Assunta had loved this house—how proud she had been of her son-in-law Carmelo for buying it. How many hours she had spent sitting on this couch and dandling one grandchild or the next, singing old songs and shelling beans and laughing with her daughters. But Stella had spent many more hours there without her mother. Twenty empty years of hours.

Assunta had suffered so many hardships—famine and illness and loss, an overbearing and neglectful husband, physical toil and pain and heartbreak. And yet she had loved her life so much. Here was Stella, now, the unwilling replacement matriarch, her body so broken and yet unbreakable, with none of her mother's joy or effortless affection. She took a few swallows of wine, and also swallowed back her sheepishness and shame. "Mamma," she said into the air, trying to sound like she thought she was talking to someone. She closed her hand around the bone *cornetto* Assunta had given her half a century ago. "Mamma, are you happy with me? Did I do it right? Did I do what you wanted?"

There was no answer, of course. But it wasn't a question Stella wanted to know the answer to anyway.

It was twelve forty, and the cold had crept in. Her arms in particular felt chilled to their bones, and Stella wrapped her shaking hands in the skirt of her cotton housedress. With age, her arms were becoming doughy and bloated, and the scars from her burns had rippled, obscured in loose liver-spotted wrinkles. Sometimes Stella ran her fingers over this textured surface that was now part of her body, thinking of the sandbar at Rocky Neck when the tide had just gone out.

Stella embraced the warm thought of the beach. Assunta had loved the beach when the children were small. She wouldn't go in the water or wear a bathing suit, but she packed her three-gallon yellow Tupperware bowl with cold pasta, another with an oil-drenched salad, and she made the kids eat all day long whenever they came in from the water—*the ocean makes you hungry,* she'd say. Pasta at the beach—everyone will think we're guidos, the boys would tease, but they'd eat it, sandy or not.

It had been at least ten years since Stella had been to the beach. Bernadette had invited her to come stay with her girls in a summer cabin for a week on the Cape last August. Stella had declined, but maybe next year she should say yes. What was she worried about missing here?

Pouring herself another quivering glass, Stella focused on the cold, trying to let it seep into her chest and wrap around her heart. They said you felt cold in the presence of a ghost, but surely there must also be some other signs. It was December in Connecticut, after all, twenty-something degrees outside in the buffeting wind. She would need other evidence if she wanted to persuade herself she was haunted.

"Mamma," she said again into the dark, but this time it was just to hear the sound of her own voice.

Now it was one thirty, and the local access programming had come on. The newly grainy sound and picture brought Stella back to herself. She was drunk and blurred and didn't know what had happened to the last hour, but at the same time the core of her mind was lucid, a bell-clear fugue of mourning. She had never gotten a grip of herself, but a milestone was no time to get a grip.

The wine bottle was empty. A sign that she should go upstairs and let herself fall back asleep. But she didn't want to. She wanted to be haunted, and if she couldn't reach her mother's spirit, she would just have to haunt herself.

Stella lurched out of the soft cave of the couch, sobered momentarily by the jingle of pain in her stiff knees. She left the bottle and the glass on the floor in front of the television—later, they would be forensic evidence for her children—and stumbled into the kitchen.

It took her all the distance to the cellar door to get her bearings. Her heart was pounding, all that settled blood circulating once again. Her head spun as she braced herself against the doorframe. But the swirl ended quickly—she was not as drunk as she'd thought. What did it mean, this light-headedness? Was her heart about to give out, as her mother's had, and her mother's father before her? Sixty-eight was not a bad age to die.

Nevertheless. She crossed the kitchen and drank two short glasses of tap water out of the glass that had been upended in the dish drainer. Should she eat something? She felt the water sloshing against the wine-pickled lining of her stomach. But if she ate, that would keep her up even later. Should she just go to bed?

No. A piece of bread, a slice of American cheese from the frosted plastic deli bag. She collected her crumbs in a cupped hand and dropped them in the sink. That was better. Her head felt soft and liquid, but the spinning sensation was gone. Now she would go get her next bottle.

The uneven cement steps to the basement were narrow, like all the stairs in the house, not long enough to support the whole of

Stella's short, wide foot. It was not the first time Stella had wished for a light fixture at the top of the stairs, instead of the lone bare bulb whose chain she could only pull when she got to the bottom.

The stumble happened when she was already two-thirds of the way to the bottom. This time there was no invisible ghostly hand trying to shove her toward her fate; this time, there was no one to blame for the Accident but Stella herself, grief-drunk, alcoholic, pathetic old Stella. She put her foot down poorly, too far forward, so that the front half of her bunion curled unsupported over the edge. She should have been able to reclaim her balance—there was the rail, the walls—but her hands flew out in vain, and she was careening down the stairs. Her head made first contact, her forehead smashing open against the corner of the wooden shelf at the bottom of the stairs, blinding her with pain stars. Staggering once, she fell again, backward this time. Too stunned to manage her own limbs, she hit the ground, her cranium bouncing once against the cement floor. Her ear registered the sound of the crack even as inside her head a roar of pain was swelling, deafening.

She had made this journey ten thousand times—what had gone wrong this time? Her last splatter of consciousness was to turn her head to see who had pushed her. But there was no one there on the steps, only the dim blue flicker of the television reflected on the gray wall.

Stella's eyes opened to darkness. Her head was pulsing with a wave like a very loud sound, but without any sound at all. She knew where she was—she was in the basement, she had tripped on the stairs, or something like that—something had happened and she . . .

She tried to stand, pressing her palm on the cold wet cement of the floor, pushing herself up. The world rolled over her in a swirl of pain and simultaneous nausea. But now here she was, she was standing, she was supporting herself on the wooden shelving, she was pulling on the beaded aluminum cord of the light. The sharp brightness of the bulb provoked another roll of disorientation.

Her head cramped as she looked down at the floor. The blood was everywhere—a flat, dark puddle that spread across the slanting floor and toward the drain. What a mess she had to clean, and with this awful pain. She took a roll of paper towels from the shelf of cleaning supplies right in front of her—at least she didn't have to go back upstairs in this condition—and then she took a second roll, because she was afraid to get back down to her knees. But she did. She got back down. The sickness was worse than any nausea she had ever felt, worse than the boat over the Atlantic, worse than the morning sickness of any of her pregnancies.

The end of the paper towel roll eluded her, and she struggled for too long, who knows how long, to unwrap it. She found it finally and tugged the first sheet free of its gentle adhesive, then ripped off a sheet and put it to the puddle on the floor. The paper towel was instantly a cardinal red square, redder and brighter than the shadowy blood around it. It will never be enough, Stella thought. She unwound the roll, one loop and then again, and balled up what she had removed. She pressed it into the blood puddle and it was instantly soaked through.

Bad, it was bad. She would never get it all. She pulled more paper towel free, as much as she could, but her arms were heavy and tired. She was hyperventilating—why? She was acting like an idiot. But the paper towels, they were no good, they did nothing. A second wad, and then a third, and still they just turned red, and her hands were covered in blood, bright red like she was wearing a pair of gloves made of fine red leather. A fourth wad, and it was still no good, and then the final wave came over her and she was falling forward into the floor, her cheek coming down on a wet pile of paper towel.

It was cold now, much colder than before. Her skin crawled with tremors. Even the sticky blood was cooling under her fingers. She couldn't call out, because there was no one to hear her this time.

When Carmelo came home from his closing shift at Charlie's in half an hour, he would sit in the brown armchair in the front room, pull the wooden bar to raise the footrest, and fall asleep there with his shoes on. It wouldn't occur to him that Stella would be anywhere but upstairs in her bed.

Tommy Maglieri worked the 4 a.m. to noon shift at the electric company. At 3:15 a.m. on Friday, December 9, he came over to his parents' house, as he often did before work, to do a walk-through to make sure everything was as it should be. Who does that kind of thing? Well, Tommy does. He is the reason Stella was rushed to the hospital, why she did not die for the last time on the basement floor.

You know this part of the story already. Stella's brain was hemor-rhaging inside her cracked skull; they needed to find a way to relieve pressure. The doctors had one idea—an experimental procedure, which the patient had a slender chance of surviving—they would cut damaged tissue away from the frontal lobe to make space. The lead surgeon was eager to attempt the proce-dure for academic reasons, although he did not misrepresent it to the Maglieri children who were keeping vigil in the visitors' lounge. Even if the surgery were a success, their mother would be a vegetable for the rest of her shortened life.

Insurance would not cover the unapproved procedure. It would be $100,000 out of pocket. But who is going to be the one to say, *No, we didn't do everything we could?*

"That's eleven grand each," Tommy said. "For Mommy. You got eleven grand for your mother, don't you?"

Tommy, Bernie, Guy, Freddy, and Richie could come up with eleven grand each. Mingo had his share—this was before the heroin problems. Artie and his new wife had four grand between them; Artie borrowed the rest against wages from his brother Guy, who was also his boss. Nicky had nothing but his disability checks, but Tommy had always known he was going to cover Nicky, like he always did. Johnny didn't show up for the family meeting. Tommy covered Johnny's share and pretended he thought Johnny would pay him back someday. Well, maybe that was how it was meant to work out; it wasn't like Tommy needed that money to support a family of his own.

As you already know, the doctors were wrong about Stella's prognosis. Maybe their science was better than they thought. Maybe they had never met a patient like Stella, with her stubborn immortality.

This is the beginning of the longest thirty years.

When they cut out your frontal lobe to stop your brain from crushing itself, they cut out forever parts of who you are. They cut out your inhibitions, although they do not cut out your fear. They cut out the part that lets you access your facial muscles, so afterward you smile all the time, even when you are angry. They cut out your empathy, although not your affection.

They cut out some parts of your memory, but they also root up other parts that you'd buried or denied, and they leave those pieces sitting right on the top, like potatoes that have just been pulled out of the ground by their vines and are lying in their garden rows, waiting for you to come shake the dirt off.

These are the things that filled Stella's mind during her coma, when her remembered world was whittled down.

So fresh, the memory—tumbling down the basement stairs.

Sixty years earlier—the ghostly arms pushing against the door of the Ievoli schoolhouse—her little sister's foot tripping her as she fell out of the way of the swinging wood.

That sticky summer morning of 1941, waking up from her nightmare on the floor of the Front Street bedroom with Tina's hands wrapped around her throbbing arm.

Her mother's kitchen on Bedford Street, Tony bashing her head into Assunta's altar to the dead baby when Tina revealed Stella's secret stash.

The rain-wet lane on via Fontana, January 1926—the invisible hand clutched around her own as the pigs tipped her over into the icy mud—little Cettina's wide eyes silently staring.

The cold tiled floor of her dark Alder Street kitchen as she choked on a chicken bone—Tina, kneeling behind her.

Tina sobbing on Stella's arm—*Can you ever forgive me? For being jealous?*—at the funeral of baby Bob. *You don't really believe any of that old-world bullshit,* Stella had said.

All her life, Stella had believed she was haunted by the ghost of her dead sister. Now, finally, she saw the truth—she was haunted by her living one.

At first, she can't say anything. She wakes up in that hospital room—her second time—and she cannot move, she has to lie there and watch her sister's sweaty pink crying face hang over her, let her sister dab her with sponges and grip her fingers. It takes a long time—maybe days—before Stella is in charge of herself enough to say, *Get out.*

Her children are there, different combinations of them, always Tommy and Artie and Bernie and sometimes Freddy and Guy and Richie, the boys' wives, her sister-in-law Queenie, they hold her hand and pat her leg. They are so happy to hear her speak that they don't listen to what she says. Stella says again, *Get out.*

Then she has to make them understand her—make them believe. *Get out.*

She reclaims use of her arm, lifts it to point at Tina. *You. Get out.*

The children tell her, *You don't mean that, Mommy. She took care of you the whole time. She slept on the hospital floor. She loves you more than anyone else in the world.*

Get out.

Tina is agonized; she sobs, she shouts, *She doesn't know what she means!* But Stella sees guilt in her sister's eyes. Tina knows what she did. That is why Tina slept on the hospital floor, sponged Stella's unconscious body. That is why Tina fed Stella's children and poured wine for Stella's husband. Because for sixty-seven years Tina has tried to stifle her jealousy—has tried to hide it under good deeds. But she is poisonous, she is dangerous, and she knows it.

Get out, Stella says. *You know what you did.*

For the rest of her life, no one believes Stella, that Tina knows what she did. Her addled brain is wrong, and cruel. But Stella's conviction has replaced all her other convictions. All her life, Tina has wanted Stella's life. When they were girls, Stella's pretty face and cleverness and charisma. When they were young women, Stella's admirers. Stella's kind, handsome husband; Stella's multitude of children. Every selfless thing Tina has ever done for Stella has been a resentful attempt to stuff down her own jealousy.

To point a finger at a sinner is to have known the sin yourself, Nonna Maria had taught Stella. But the surgery has removed this ingrained life lesson. In the murk of her mind, Stella no longer can see the finger of accusation turning on herself.

They let her go home on New Year's Day, 1989.

There is a birthday party.

Look at this woman here. Look at this beautiful woman.

Everyone is cheering and clapping.

You know what the doctors said? They said she would never walk or talk again.

He's trying not to cry, her son. Like his sentimental father. And there's Bernadette, crying openly, just like her grandmother would have.

Stella smiles and raises her hand at them. She sees her fingernails are painted red.

Well, they were wrong, weren't they?

Clapping again. All these roaring people in her living room, all her children, their now grown-up childhood friends who used to eat olive loaf sandwiches in her kitchen.

Stand up, Ma! Show them how wrong they were!

That place in the back of her head pulses with that low-grade heat. She grasps Tommy's hand and stands like he says. They are whooping and clapping, all these tall dark-haired children towering over her, with their white-blond children looking up with their wide light-colored eyes from where they're playing on the floor. How funny that her own children's children have nothing left in them of her, just one generation removed.

But the whooping has turned into the tarantella, and the clapping has broken into a rhythm. *DUH-duh DUH-duh DUHN . . .*

Stella waves her arms. She won't do the whole dance today. She smiles.

What a woman! It's the tallest one shouting—Freddy. *What a woman you've got yourself, Dad!* And they change tune, her sons bellowing in Calabrese, which not all of them speak very well. *Ai jai jai chi mugliere mi capitai!*

There is Carmelo, crying of course. He kisses Stella very gently on her cheekbone, just below the bandage. *What a woman I married,* he says.

Some things get better, some things don't.

*   *   *

She stands, she walks, she dances.

Her language comes back to her. Not always the right language.

She crochets—fast. She can make anything—spreads, hats, scarves. They don't always look very nice. She combines colors like Christmas Blend with Valentine Pink.

The grandchildren watch TV with her while she crochets. She loves them. None of them are old enough to remember what she was like before. The Maglieri grandchildren will grow up thinking it is standard to have an unintelligible crocheting grandmother engaged in a blood feud with her sister, and who might at any time stop strangers in the street and hand them Mardi Gras beads or miniature sticks of deodorant she hides in her red purse. The Maglieri youth will be so conditioned by the Accident that even as adults, when they are old enough to be used to the world, they will marvel at their friends' alternate grandmother experiences.

At mass, Stella tries to pray, but all the words are gone. She tries to think of God and the Virgin, but she can't concentrate.

She doesn't speak of her mother. Maybe Assunta was one of the parts they cut out of her mind with their surgical knives.

She doesn't drink anymore, either. The doctors say not to let her, but it doesn't matter, because she doesn't want to drink anymore, or maybe she does, but she doesn't correctly identify what wanting to drink feels like.

Can Auntie Tina come over for Christmas dinner, at least? Stella's children beg her.

They don't understand. They don't understand the danger.

"She's jealous," Stella tells them, over and over. She killed my baby, she wants to say, she almost killed me seven times because of the evil in her heart. But when she tries to explain why, she can't find the words.

She can't remember the *mal'oicch'* unfascination spell, because she never believed in it enough to learn it back then and now she believes and it's too late. Instead she makes the sign to ward off the *invidia* when she sees her sister, a fist with index finger and pinky sticking out, two horns to pierce the Evil Eye.

"Stop that, Ma," her children say. "That's rude."

These children, who have never had to fight for their lives, who have never struggled for anything, are worried about rudeness.

They start having two different Mother's Day parties, one pink and white cake at 3 Alder Street for Stella, then a second at 5 Alder Street for Tina. They have pasta at the first party, coffee at the second. Tina makes the pasta for the first party, which she isn't allowed to attend. Stella pretends she doesn't know about the pasta's provenance.

Stella has eleven grandchildren now. Tina has none.

Mario and Carolina Perri come to visit from Las Vegas, where they moved when Mario retired. They can only visit one of the Fortuna sisters at a time, because of the rules.

She's still angry, five years later? Carolina asks. She was Stella's maid of honor forty-five years ago.

You can't take her seriously, Tommy tells her. *She's not right in her head.*

She always was very stubborn, Carolina says, reaching over to pat Stella's knee.

Stella smiles and pinches Carolina's arm so hard, Carolina shrieks and pulls away.

Stella's son Tommy takes her to the seven thirty mass every day. He walks her to the altar to take Communion, and she lets the priest put the wafer in her mouth. She doesn't remember what it felt like when she used to believe it became the body of Christ on her tongue. She has not felt absolved of her sins for many years.

She crochets fast to distract herself from the memories that they didn't cut away, and buried memories that are lying there like potatoes now. Baby Bob, the hotel in Montreal, Nino.

She makes so many blankets, she can't give them all away. Tommy leaves them in the Goodwill bin.

You gonna make me go broke, Ma, he says. *Buying all this yarn.* But he takes her to Jo-Ann Fabrics three times a week for more.

When crocheting fails to distract her, she repeats her stories. She can no longer emote, so to her audience they are only words. Maybe to her they are also only words; maybe the doctors cut away her pain and left only her obsession. We'll never know.

"My husband raped me on my honeymoon," Stella says to a young man and woman eating breakfast together at Franklin Diner. They smile at her. She doesn't realize she spoke in Calabrese.

"Shhh, Mommy, that's not true," her son Freddy says as he guides her away. "You don't go around saying things like that to people."

In August 1996 the Maglieris throw Auntie Tina and Uncle Rocco a surprise fiftieth-anniversary party. They rent out DiMarco's banquet hall on Franklin Avenue and lure Tina by telling her it's a baby shower for Franceschina Carapellucci's granddaughter Angie. The family will joke for years about how Tina brought six trays of angel wing cookies to her own surprise party. Sweet little Mikey Perri brings an extra suit jacket for Rocco, who arrives thinking he's only dropping off Tina. Tina and Rocco are so stunned, they both cry.

Almost eight years have passed since Stella and Tina have been in the same room. Carmelo and his children trick Stella into attending by pretending the party is for her. They guide her up to the high table, where, half a century after the event, the entire bridal party has been reassembled for a photo (except, of course, Fiorella Mulino, who died so young, *benedic'*). Carmelo sits between Stella and Tina, gesticulating jovially to block his crazy wife's line of sight.

Stella realizes the truth, but she lets them all think she's been duped. She doesn't want to miss the party. She dances to "Pepino Suricillu" and the Chicken Dance. She claps her hands and waves her arms and chews her chicken parmigiano with the new dentures Tommy got her.

She is careful not to turn her head in her sister's direction so she can't see her or her pervert husband, Rocco. Fifty years have passed, but she can only remember his selfish lies and his wandering eye. Happy Anniversary to them.

"They will rot together in hell," she tells her son Richie when he brings her a Diet Coke.

"Sh, Ma," Richie says. "Be nice for one day, will you?"

They have a fiftieth-anniversary party for Stella and Carmelo the next year, but it's much smaller, just dinner at a restaurant.

Stella gets very angry in the springtime, when she becomes stuck in the memory of baby Bob kicking in her belly that gray spring of 1948 when the world was crushing her and he was her only ally. She channels her anger into physical activity. When Carmelo is out helping at his son Guy's restaurant, Stella finds a pair of hefty garden shears and uses them to fell Carmelo's grape trellises, the gooseberry bushes, and the young peach tree. *God only knows how she hacked through that trunk,* her children will say. *Who knew Mommy was that strong.*

Why would she do such a terrible thing? they ask each other, and reply, *She's not right in the head. What can you do.*

Later, Stella cuts down Carmelo's two beautiful fifteen-foot fig trees. No one's ever seen figs like that before or since, *purtroppo*.

In the fall Stella gets angry again when the crisp weather reminds her of Montreal, and she carries the feeling of cold marble against the pit of her stomach. She burns all the photos in the kitchen sink. Carmelo comes home from the bar to a house reeking of carbonized plastic. Smears of black and gray smoke have ruined the apple-patterned kitchen wallpaper, which Carmelo will have replaced.

Stella's son Tommy sits in front of her, a folding chair drawn up to her armchair, his knees touching her knees. He moves his mouth like he's talking. Stella can't tell if she's going deaf or if he's teasing her.

Stella's oldest granddaughter graduates from high school. She will go to one of the best universities in the country. Stella won't recognize its name, and no one will ever successfully explain the big-city job the granddaughter eventually gets. But Stella will proudly attend all her graduation parties, and happily pose for pictures wearing the granddaughter's flat tasseled cap.

Her other grandchildren will become mechanics, hairdressers, nurses, bankers, auditors, graphic designers, restaurateurs. One will become the principle of an elementary school. One will own a country club, another a funeral home, another a car wash. One will go to Hollywood and act in movies produced by J. J. Abrams, Jodie Foster, and the Coen brothers. Stella won't recognize those names, either, but she'll enjoy watching her granddaughter's face, thirty feet tall, on the screen at the movie theater.

*   *   *

Carmelo is crossing the parking lot at the post office when he is hit by a car—an eighty-nine-year-old driver who presses on the gas instead of the brake.

He survives. After he is released from the hospital with three broken ribs, his children wait for his postconcussion confusion to clear up. It never does, and eventually they realize he has also suffered a massive stroke.

Her daughter, Bernadette, takes Stella in her blue car to Lyman Orchards. Stella used to take her children there in the summer. You pick whatever is in season—strawberries, apples, pumpkins—then pay by the pound. Today they pick blueberries.

Stella picks and picks. She is so fast—she was always faster than Tina when they were younger, picking chestnuts, harvesting olives, selecting tobacco leaves. Well, Tina's not here; Bernie didn't invite her. Something else for Tina to be jealous of.

Stella has a straw hat, lavender, with a flopping brim that covers her face. The sun doesn't bother Stella; she is tough. She picks till her plastic barrel is full to the top. When she stands to look for Bernie she sees her many rows of bushes away. Stella waves; she has to wait for her daughter to come over, because the barrel is too heavy for Stella to lift.

Oh, Ma! What did you do? Bernie laughs. She can barely carry the barrel down the hill to the farmhouse, where they tip the berries into plastic bags and weigh them. Bernadette is rubbing her forehead. *I had no idea she would pick so much,* she says to the girl at the cash register. *Can't I write you a check?* The girl has an orange bandanna tied over her head, knotted at her neck, the way Assunta used to wear a cloth to cover her bald patches. *I'm so embarrassed. No ATM?*

In the car on the way home Bernie stops at a drive-through, hands Stella a lemon ice in a paper cup.

Tommy takes Tina and Rocco on a trip to Italy and France to see the old relatives who are still left alive.

Mingo is staying with Stella and Carmelo while Tommy's away. His wife has left him and he has been released from rehab, supposedly clean. All Mingo has to do is keep an eye on Stella, make sure she gets her medicine and doesn't try to harm her husband.

But it makes her so mad to see Carmelo sitting there in his chair, stupidly watching television. Now when she sees him so weak, like a baby, the fifty-seven years of their marriage evaporate and she can only think about the time he overpowered her— as fresh in her brain as if it had happened this morning, she can still feel the stockings pulling taut against the soft flesh of her thighs, even though her thighs are now fluffy with age, and she hasn't worn nylons in twenty years. It makes her so angry she wants to hurt him, and now she can.

What are you doing lying on the floor, Dad? Mingo asks when he gets home from wherever he was—my guess would be the bar. But Carmelo is incoherent. He has a large bruise on the back of his head.

Stella is sitting in her chair crocheting.

Mommy, what happened to Daddy? Mingo asks.

He did a bad thing is all Stella has it in her to say to her son.

Stella doesn't finish the blankets she crochets anymore. She makes half a blanket but then loses interest and starts a new one. While she crochets Tommy sits next to her and unravels the neglected blanket, rerolling the yarn for her to use again next time she loses interest.

Rocco Caramanico has a stroke and dies. The dying part takes him three days. He is intubated and can't talk, but he's not ready to go. He flaps his arms and tries to communicate with all the nieces and nephews who come see him.

You're our second father, they tell him, crying. Many of Assunta's grandchildren got her crying gene. They sit vigil with Tina at the hospital bed until he finally goes. Then there is the two-day funeral.

Tommy brings Stella to the wake, which makes everyone nervous. She stands in the receiving line—the deceased's beloved sister-in-law—accepting condolences. She lets this go on for three hours before she starts telling people, *He wanted to marry me, not her,* pressing mourner's hands, *and she is going to rot in hell for her jealousy,* at which point Richie bundles her into the car and drives her home.

Louie's kidneys give out. Queenie is inconsolable. She loses sixty pounds.

It wasn't a perfect marriage, she tells her nieces and nephews. *We had our ups and downs like any couple. But I really think he was the best of them.*

Stella doesn't cry at Louie's funeral. But that's only because Stella doesn't cry.

When Carmelo dies, more than six hundred people sign the logbook at the wake.

It is anyone's guess how Stella feels at the funeral. She registers no emotion. They had been married sixty-three years, twenty of which passed after she had her mind cut out. They had raised ten children together. They had attacked each other—they had broken each other in different ways. They had buried their hatchets and found peace, only to have their peace medically disrupted. They had stuck it out.

Everyone besides Stella cries like hell. I cry like hell. I loved Carmelo. I'm crying now thinking about him.

But no one else had to forgive him for the things Stella had to forgive him for.

Now it's only the women left. How it started, how it will end.

Tommy now owns the house at 4 Alder that used to belong to his grandfather. Tony left the house to Tommy in a surprise bequest that fractured the Fortuna family forever. People-pleasing Tommy tried to make it right, invited Joey and Mickey to stay in the house they thought they'd inherit, offered them money, which they took. But Joey died the next summer while the blood was still bad; thirty years have passed, but the cousins don't speak.

Tommy moves Stella across the street when Carmelo dies. It will be easier to take care of her there, since number 4 is only one story. And walking through number 4 none of the Maglieri children have to picture their absent father, who should have been sitting there reading a paper and sipping a Michelob Light.

Ninety-five is very old, and the days are soft and run together. Stella can't always hold on to the number ninety-five. Sometimes she tells people she is one hundred, or one hundred twenty. It doesn't seem unrealistic.

Whenever someone comes to visit, she takes them to her bedroom and points at the studio photo of her ten children, taken when Artie was three. *Those are my twenty children,* she says. The photo is positioned in front of a wall mirror, so in fact there are twenty children there, sort of. No one is sure if she really thinks she had twenty children or if she is pulling their leg.

An old woman comes to visit. Stella knows her from somewhere, but can't quite place her—maybe from church? The church is where most of the old women are. Her hair is white and wispy on top and underneath is charcoal-gray.

"What are you making today?" the old woman says. She talks loud enough that Stella can hear her, so Stella smiles.

"It's a blanket for my daughter, Bernadette," Stella says. The old woman's face tightens. Is she jealous? "You know my daughter, Bernadette?" Stella asks cagily. The *invidia* is evil; she will test this old woman. "She's very smart. She has a beautiful house on top of a hill. Her husband built it for her."

"He didn't build it, Ma," the old woman says. "But I'm glad you like it."

Stella spends her days crocheting in her armchair in front of the bay window. She can see straight across Alder Street into the bay window of her jealous sister, Tina, who has put new pruned shrubbery in front of her house, thinking wasting money on landscaping will make people like her more.

Tina is sitting in her own armchair, staring wistfully right back.

Now I have told you what I know about my grandmother, Stella Fortuna, everything I've been able to dig out of public and private records. It is your turn to decide what you believe. Maybe you, as an outsider, can see something that we who are too close cannot.

I have come to understand Stella as a woman of incredible will and strength, of charisma, of innate intelligence. She was not a woman of her time, and she was made to pay a high price for her unwillingness to conform. If only Stella had been allowed to live her life on her own terms, how might things have been different? I wouldn't exist, it's true—would I write myself out of this if it would spare her the suffering? No, I wouldn't, selfish girl. So I've written myself into it, instead.

One hundred years after she died, I went in search of the first Mariastella Fortuna. I went to Ievoli, at the summit of the little mountain overlooking the olive valley and the two seas. The village is all but empty; there isn't even a mailbox in it, because the post doesn't come here anymore.

Ievoli is a ghost town, but I could not find Mariastella's ghost. If it clings unhappily to this earth, I don't know if it could haunt anyone. I know little of the occult, but it seems to me that a ghost must be remembered to do any haunting. No one remembers the first Stella anymore. The only photo of her must have been destroyed; no one has seen it in years. When I started writing this account, I knew what the first Stella looked like. Now I can't really remember much of her face, only the round black eyes. After me, maybe no one will remember anything.

I went to the Ievoli cemetery, to see if I could find her. I said a prayer, even though I don't believe in a god. I walked through the uniform mausoleums and I touched their cool marble walls, pressed my face to the protective glass façades of the burial vaults, peered through petals of real and silk flowers to try to make out names that might be hers. But of course she isn't there. She has no loving survivors, no one to light her candles or pick away the clover sprouts that found purchase in the cracks of her tomb. That is, if she even has a tomb; who can say that her bones haven't been moved and the space recycled during the hundred years that have passed with no one to look out for her.

There are no Fortunas left in Ievoli—or maybe anywhere else; I haven't been able to find any. They are gone, eradicated, the monstrous men driven away to the farthest parts of the globe, California, Argentina, Australia, where they have been absorbed one way or another, the women quietly married out into new families and new names. Mariastella Fortuna, if she still lurks somewhere among the living, is the last of her kind, a little ghost with a bad name.

Epilogue: *Hic Jacet*

It is the Saturday before Christmas and I have a cooking date with Auntie Tina. I park my car strategically in Stella's driveway and visit with her first so she won't give me the silent treatment. She is watching Turner Classic Movies in bed; I lie down on the white duvet next to her and she holds my wrist between her silky fingers. For forty-five minutes we watch *The Bad Seed* together—for some reason it's always on when I visit. Stella is not feeling talkative today; from the way she keeps wriggling her jaw I can tell she's not wearing her teeth. But periodically she turns to give me her squashed close-lipped smile and stroke my arm. I'm not sure she knows who I am, but she loves me anyway.

I kiss her good-bye when I notice her eyes are spending more time closed than open. As I cross the street I can still feel the spongy pads of her fingertips pressing gently on my arm. I think of how much love she has to give and feel that familiar tiny heartbreak that even now, in their dying years, she cannot give any of it to her sister.

Auntie Tina is in the basement kitchen when I arrive. She is already kitted out in her once-yellow apron and her hair kerchief—I assume she has been cooking since dawn, judging by the hundreds of hockey-puck-esque *totò* cookies lined up on the three prep tables. She is clammy with sweat when I kiss her cheek. Last year she went to a new doctor for her general physical and he was so alarmed by how much she sweats that he made her do a whole battery of lymphoma tests. No ninety-seven-year-old woman should sweat like that, he said. Yeah, well. Joke was on him.

"You go see you grandma?" is the first thing Auntie Tina asks me.

"Yup."

"You no wanna make her mad," she warns.

"I sat with her for almost an hour." I know she already knows this—I am sure she has been checking for my car.

"Maybe you go see her again when we finish?" she suggests. "She lonely all day."

"All right," I say sadly. "Come on, let's get cooking."

I'm here to "study" Auntie Tina's recipes, which is tricky. I've been over to "study" cooking many times before, have endured hours of chastisement and sabotage, and the unspoken truth of the matter is that although Auntie Tina doesn't want her recipes to die with her, she doesn't really want anybody else to be able to replicate them, either. O! the inner turmoil of cooking with your niece! The terrorizing balance of instruction and mysticism you must strike to keep her from getting uppity! No wonder Auntie Tina is so sweaty.

The *totò* are already baked and cooled, so next we have the frosting. You have to frost the cookies all around to seal in their moisture. Naturally I am not to be trusted with this sacred task; Tina will handle the cookie-dipping and delegates to me the less critical application of sprinkles. I am only a few cookies in before I reveal my insurmountable inadequacies and Tina snatches away my sprinkle shaker. She finishes the job alone, dipping the cookies with her left hand and sprinkling with her right.

I just want to say, I make my own *totò* at home and they come out perfectly fine. Not that I'd ever be able to hold my head up with them around here. But my non-Italian friends like them.

I exile myself to the sink, where I wash the morning's accumulated dishes, including Auntie Tina's Tupperware batter bowl. It is the biggest individual piece of Tupperware I've ever seen, a mealy weatherbeaten sea-green color. It has cracked along the bottom and been repaired with duct tape. About ten years ago my mother, who has characterized the Tupperware bowl as "disgusting," bought Auntie Tina a new one as a replacement; Tina promptly regifted it.

When the cookies are frosted and drying, we troop upstairs for a lunch break. Auntie Tina pops nervously up out of her chair every few minutes and rummages through the fridge again to see if she's forgotten anything she might be able to put out for me. She offers to make me some *pastina* and I decline four times. There are seven dishes already on the table—*lupini*, homemade *suppressata*, pickled mushrooms, chicken cutlets, *pizzelle*, someone's leftover sausage and peppers from a couple nights ago, *mustazzoli* that my Aunt Queenie made. "Not so good," Auntie Tina confides as she unwraps the plate. I dutifully break off a piece, chew, and pronounce that Auntie Tina's are better.

It is after lunch, as we are rolling little meatballs for little meatball soup, that I broach the subject of my project. "It's almost done," I tell her. "Thanks to you, and all your help."

"You finish you story about you grandma?" Tina puts down a grape-size meatball on the full tray of perfectly uniform grape-size meatballs. "What you say about me?"

"You want to read it?" I tease.

But Tina doesn't laugh. She hesitates, then says, "Maybe you can write that it's no her fault, that she no right in the head."

"What's not her fault?"

But she doesn't tell me what she means. Instead, she says, "Maybe you can write that it's no true that I was jealous for her."

"Oh, Auntie Tina." The jealousy, again—of all the things that shouldn't matter anymore. And yet neither Stella nor Tina will ever recover from their own remorse—they will suffer for the rest of their lives for the way the world came between them, each blaming the other for her weakness, each secretly blaming herself for her own. But there is nothing for me to say that will make that better.

I see she is crying, voicelessly, like Assunta would have cried, her tears tipping off her ancient cheeks and adding their umbrae to the already mottled apron. "You can write that I love her and I only want to take care of her."

"Auntie Tina." I feel a prickle of my own tears, but that would not be helpful. Tina cannot heal the rift with Stella, and now she is putting all her hopes in me, as if I can somehow save the story, find the happy ending. "Everyone knows you love her," I say, as I always do. "Everyone knows how hard you try."

"I love her," she says again, swiping her runny nose with a paper towel. "I always love her. Maybe you can write that."

"Yes. I will write that." I grab her hand across the table and squeeze to cement my promise. My fingers are covered in gummy raw beef; hers are as clean as if she hasn't just rolled two hundred meatballs.

"You was using too much water, makes the meat sticky," she chides me, shaking off my hand. Her nostrils are pink but her tears are gone.

She pushes herself up out of her seat and comes around to my side of the table, where my tray of little meatballs is only halfway full. "Too big," she says, picking up an offender and rerolling it between her fingers. "Oh no, this one too small."

"Here, let me—" I try. But it is no good. In her most subtle way, which is to say not very subtly, she slides the tray out of my reach so I can't interfere and rerolls each of my meatballs, one by one.

"Oh well," I say, getting up to wash my hands. "Guess that's the end of that."

Auntie Tina, who is already setting up her frying pan, pauses to give me a rueful smile. "You no worry," she consoles me. "When they in the soup, nobody gonna know which meatballs you make."

Author's Note

The Seven or Eight Deaths of Stella Fortuna is a work of fiction, but for those interested in its historical inspirations, I will name just a few nonfiction resources and encourage the curious to seek them out: Ann Cornelisen's work, particularly *Women of the Shadows*, is a useful outsider's perspective on Mezzogiorno daily life in the mid-twentieth century. Jerre Mangione and Ben Moreale's *La Storia: Five Centuries of the Italian American Experience* is a starting point for any inquiry into Italian-American immigration and the emigrant identity. For those who would like to read more about Calabrian history, I recommend Gay Talese's *Unto the Sons*, which also contains a rare detailed account of an Italian soldier's Great War experience. Another illuminating book on the Great War in Italy is Mark Thompson's *The White War: Life and Death on the Italian Front, 1915–1919*. I was fascinated (in a mostly unmagical sense) by a 1970 collection of essays about the Evil Eye edited by Clarence Maloney and published by Columbia University Press under the title *The Evil Eye*. A more complete reading list would go on for quite some time, so I'll limit myself to naming just one more personal inspiration, Toni Morrison's novel *A Mercy*, which elegantly frames the conversation about what people have been willing and forced to do in order to be American.

My inspirations were not only textual, and Stella Fortuna would not exist without the larger-than-life characters among my Italian-American relatives, especially John Cusano; Connie Rucci; the late Filomena Rotundo, who passed away just before I was able to show her this book; and above all my great aunt and

435

precious friend Connie Sanelli. From the non-Italian side of my family, I owe sincere thanks to my paternal grandmother, Patricia Grames, for instilling in me the value of preserving family and local histories.

My most profound thanks to the entire village of Ievoli, which welcomed me with open arms during my research. Luigi Mascaro, the retired *postino*, and his wife, Caterina Gallo, took me into their home sight unseen, drove me all over Calabria, and educated me in the delights of the Calabrese proverb. Rina Scalise, the owner of Ievoli's bar, was kindly forbearing as I spent long hours drinking her coffee and frowning at my notebook. Feroleto Antico *municipio* officer Francesca Mascaro and historian Franco Falvo were invaluable sources of *comune* history. I am grateful to many other Ievolitani and Sepinesi for sharing their lives and stories with me, including Nicola and Anna Mascaro; Marisa Mancuso; Angelina Fazio; Federico Gaetano; the Cusano-Maglieri clan, Mariangelo, Teresa, Walter, Mariteresa, and Martina; and my sweet friend the late Saverina Gallo. Thank you to Chiara Scaglioni for bringing Stella back home to Italy, and to Gioacchino Criaco for showing me new ways to think about Calabria. Finally, to Francesca Fragale, whose friendship I was lucky to bumble into early in my research and whose advice on the subjects of Calabrese dialects, folk music, recipes, and local traditions cannot be overvalued.

I am deeply grateful for my "day" job coworkers at Soho Press. They are, without exaggeration, a second family, and have been great champions of this novel since its inception. For what they have taught me, consciously and unconsciously, about writing, storytelling, and life, I would like to thank all the authors I have had the good fortune to work with as an editor, but particularly Andromeda Romano-Lax, Francine Mathews, Lene Kaaberbøl, Stuart Neville, James Benn, Cara Black, Peter Lovesey, Mick Herron, and Irene Levine.

I have had the great privilege of being published by the

extraordinary institution Hodder & Stoughton, and have been overwhelmed by the care the entire team there has taken with Stella. First and foremost, my most heartfelt gratitude to Editorial Director Melissa Cox, who has been both a passionate advocate and a visionary. No author has ever been more grateful to have had their manuscript come to an editor's attention. I also must extend my very warmest thanks to Lily Cooper, who has guided Stella through the editorial process with grace and exactitude; Louise Swannell, who is the publicity director every other author wishes they had; Alice Morley, Carolyn Mays, Al Oliver, Barbara Roby and Lydia Seleska. I am especially lucky that the Hachette sales force included Mariafrancesca Ierace, my first Calabrese reader, who happened to be born only a few miles away from Ievoli and who gave me terrific dialect advice. At home in New York, I am forever grateful to the Ecco/HarperCollins team, most especially Editorial Director Megan Lynch.

Warmest thanks to the agents who have taken Stella all over the world, but especially Kate McLennan at Abner Stein and Rebecca Gardner, foreign rights director at The Gernert Company. Most of all, thank you to my inestimable agent, Sarah Burnes, for loving Stella, for being so smart and tireless, for changing my life.

For their thoughtful critical feedback, I humbly thank my marvelous early readers, Casey Donnelly and Karen McMurdo. Thanks to my once and future writing groups, but especially to the TTC, Karissa Chen, Erika Swyler, and Jennifer Ambrose, who has been Stella's spiritual third sister through all the many drafts.

While writing this story about sisters, I was ever grateful for my own sister, Katherine, and her twin, Jeffrey. My deepest thanks of all are for my parents: Michael, who made me a book person; and Linda, my first and most important reader, who indoctrinated me with storytelling. My most unpayable debt is to my grandmother Antonette Cusano, who would not have read these words even if she had lived to see them, and who never knew how much she gave me.

And finally, my husband, Paul Oliver, my partner in all things and the reason I believe, emphatically, in love stories. Thank you for being there every step of the way, for reading and listening, for understanding my prickly brain and overheated heart. How lucky I am to have you to dedicate this last line to.